00036310

823·914 EVA

D0530473

THE CAVES
OF ALIENATION

PARTHIAN

LIBRARY OF WALES

Coleg Sir Gâr
Canolfan Ddysgu
Llanelli
Learning Centre

Stuart Evans was born in Swansea in 1934 and brought up at Ystalyfera in Glamorgan. He read English at Jesus College, Oxford. After service in the Royal Navy, he taught at Brunel College of Advanced Technology and, from the mid 1960s, worked for BBC Radio in London as a producer in the Schools Broadcasting Department. It was as a novelist that he established his reputation, with eight long, technically complex novels which are more inclined to the philosophical than is usual in English fiction. They include *Meritocrats* (1974), *The Gardens of the Casino* (1976), *The Caves of Alienation* (1977), and a quintet known as *The Windmill Hill Sequence*. He also published two volumes of verse, *Imaginary Gardens with Real Toads* (1972) and *The Function of the Fool* (1977). He died in 1994.

THE CAVES
OF ALIENATION

STUART EVANS

PARTHIAN
LIBRARY OF WALES

Parthian
The Old Surgery
Napier Street
Cardigan
SA43 1ED
www.parthianbooks.co.uk

The Library of Wales is a Welsh Assembly Government
initiative which highlights and celebrates Wales' literary
heritage in the English language.

Published with the financial support of
the Welsh Books Council.

The Library of Wales publishing project is based at
Trinity College, Carmarthen, SA31 3EP.
www.libraryofwales.org

Series Editor: Dai Smith

First published in 1977
Library of Wales edition 2009
Foreword © Duncan Bush 2009
All Rights Reserved

ISBN 978-1-905762-95-8

Cover design: www.theundercard.co.uk
Cover image: *Coast of Pembroke* by John Piper
© Estate of John Piper with kind permission
of the National Museum of Wales

Printed and bound by Gwasg Gomer, Llandysul, Wales
Typeset by Lucy Llewellyn

British Library Cataloguing in Publication Data

A cataloguing record for this book is available from the British Library.

This book is sold subject to the condition that it shall not by way
of trade or otherwise be circulated without the publisher's prior
consent in any form of binding or cover other than that in which
it is published.

LIBRARY of WALES

That was my choice which now is my rejection:
The caves of alienation, and the chant
Of phantom dancers, the anger and the fury.
And still between rifts of smoke in the acrid darkness,
For a gleaming moment, still the bright daggers besieging
This fiery lump which passes for a heart.
There is one sort of daybreak, a death renewed;
Here is another, a life that glimmers and wakes.

Henry Reed: *Philoctetes*

Thou art a little soul bearing about a corpse.

Epictetus

FOREWORD

One of the defining moments of modernism in art takes place in 1907, in Paris, with Picasso's painting *Les demoiselles d'Avignon*. It signifies a crucial rupture with the figurative style of his 'blue' and 'pink' periods, and the brutal starkness of this portrait of five prostitutes – two of whom seem to be wearing primitive masks or to have the faces of baboons (and none of which has anything to do with Avignon) – astonishes and shocks even friends and fellow-artists such as Braque, Matisse and Apollinaire. Given their hostility, Picasso himself seems uncertain about the picture; the canvas is rolled up and put away. It prefigures a great many other portraits of women Picasso makes, but it's not until 1909, and his two representations of Fernande, the woman then current in his life, that the decisive moment arrives. One of these works is a portrait painting in oils and the other a bronze bust; but there would be no point supposing either a prior 'study' for the other, since they avail themselves of the same claim to visual multi-dimensionality. This is the moment of *Cubisme*, a development which, whatever its initial strangeness, is based on the straight-forward perceptual principle of the fragmentation of a form into multiple facets to reveal as many of its aspects as possible, and from as many angles.

This is a period when the new, self-styled science of psycho-analysis is revealing the human personality itself as an amalgam of manifold aspects, some of which are hidden from public view and even from private introspection, and manifested only through dreams, archetypes or pathological behaviour. The influence on artistic practice of this new view of consciousness and of personal identity itself is profound, and the break-up of Renaissance laws of perspective which Cubism represents in the visual arts is matched by the death of the omniscient narrator in the novel.

Some writers will resist this – it's the death of the father and of God the Father; but others embrace the narrative possibilities liberated by the loss of univocal authority.

From 1914 to 1922 James Joyce labours on *Ulysses*, a huge work which recounts the course of a single, otherwise unremarkable day through several loosely-interlocking subjective narratives of a detailed personal intimacy unprecedented in the novel. Joyce goes on to write (it will occupy him from 1922 to 1939) *Finnegans Wake*, in which the dream-memory of a single character goes back into the multiplicity of a phylogenetic unconscious – 'the uncreated conscience of my race' already predicted by an earlier work – which, given Joyce's tastes and linguistic flair, sometimes seems little less than a kaleidoscopic pun-sum of the Indo-European languages. Meanwhile, William Faulkner is writing briefer, more vernacular masterpieces in *The Sound and the Fury* (1929) and *As I Lay Dying* (1930), in both of which a banal enough family story is seen and told unforgettably in different voices – including that of a congenital idiot – from a variety of confused or contradictory points of view.

This is not so much the literary background as the imaginative bedrock out of which is hewn and carried piecemeal to the surface Stuart Evans' novel *The Caves of Alienation*, published in 1977. Its structural premise can be stated simply: the unknowableness or irreducibility (whether through intimate acquaintance, psycho-analytic theory, literary analysis, anecdote or gossip) of the human individual.

The central character of the novel is Michael Julian Caradock, himself a novelist famous enough and controversial enough to have biographers contending over his life and work, and who is seen posthumously through a miscellany of further views, opinions and reminiscences by those who knew him, and through extracts from his own writings.

Caradock, it seems, was a writer who also considered himself an intellectual, and there is a good deal of discussion of various major European writers and philosophers – Joyce, Proust, Camus, Nietzsche, Sartre – who are cited as active and ongoing influences on Caradock's thought and published work. In the extracts from his own books and in the evidence supplied by his surviving acquaintances, there's also a considerable amount of private confessionalism and/or public speculation about his relationships with a number of different women during the course of an erotically active life (these women function in some sense as 'Muses', though the relationships seem primarily sexual and Caradock is described as an 'emotional pragmatist'). A number of these women add their own views of their former lover, though one declines to be interviewed about him.

Another key theme in the book is Caradock's social background, which might represent an almost too-classic trajectory in his progress from 'Cwmfelyn', a mining village in South Wales, to his life as a student, then teacher, at Oxford. Evans makes it clear however, that Caradock is from a wealthy family, while his views on Wales and the working class of his own village are uncomplimentary.

Oxford, in fact, seems to be the only place where Michael Caradock, at least for a brief period, feels at home; but, after success as an author, and a period in London, it is to South Wales he returns – to 'Glanmor', and an isolated house on an estuary. Here he lives alone in what appears to be a state of intense self-questioning: a remorseful, retrospective psychological crisis – and finally begins a new and disastrous love affair with a neighbour's wife.

In one sense, *The Caves of Alienation* is a murder story. And all of what we learn of Michael Caradock is assembled retrospectively, as a sort of dossier – witness-statements almost, the often conflicting testimony of those who knew him, from his teachers at the local Grammar School to friends from Oxford or London and critics or biographers who have written on his adult life and work. Some of the details obviously echo the outward facts of Stuart Evans' own life and career, but opinions on Caradock are so plainly at variance, so coloured by admiration or animus, that it's not clear how much of this novel is (or is intended to be seen as) 'an essay in auto-biographical fiction' – as some of Caradock's own work is described. Yet, despite an often unflattering depiction of Caradock, a lingering sense of authorial wish-fulfilment emerges from this composite portrait of an intense and arrogant man whom a succession of handsome women, and a number of extremely intelligent men, find brilliant and irresistible.

Stuart Evans was born in Swansea in 1934 and brought up in the village of Ystalyfera in the Swansea Valley – at the time a mining community perhaps not dissimilar to the Cwmfelyn of the novel. Like Michael Caradock, Evans went up to Oxford, and afterwards worked in London as a teacher and then for the BBC. He published several other novels, the most widely-noticed of which were *Meritocrats* (1974) and *The Gardens of the Casino* (1976). He also published a five-novel series known as *The Windmill Hill Sequence*, and several volumes of poetry appeared from small-press publishers. All of his work, however, both prose and poetry, is currently out of print apart from two poems which appeared in Meic Stephens' compendious *Poetry 1900-2000* (The Library of Wales, 2007). This ambitious and indeed difficult-to-place writer is one of the forgotten figures of Welsh fiction.

Stuart Evans' other novels also show frequent evidence of an unfashionable philosophical bent and an individualistic voice. But *The Caves of Alienation* remains an approachable work, although one that may, in the last analysis, be more singular in conception than completely satisfying in execution: perhaps the disparate material is too fragmentary, too inconclusive, to create a sufficiently vital sense of Michael Caradock's own personality; and to some readers this central character may not seem as fascinating, or as clever, as he was to many of those assembled on the page to discuss him. Novels about writers can sometimes beg a specific, often awkward question: how *good* a writer was Michael Caradock? With Gustav von Aschenbach in *Death in Venice*, say, or Stephen Dedalus in *A Portrait of the Artist as a Young Man*, the reader has no difficulty in presuming the fictional author the equal in sensibility of Thomas Mann or James Joyce. In *The Caves of Alienation*, though, one sometimes feels Evans to be a better writer than his putatively more celebrated fictional creation – one less prone to bogus-sounding classical titles, second-hand philosophising or allegorical novels peopled by characters with Ruritanian-sounding surnames. Yet circumspection may be advisable. Was this deliberate? Some of the criticism voiced in the novel of these aspects of Caradock's work is itself scathing in its accuracy. Did Evans intend to create an overweening novelist *manqué* and a minor monster of vanity and self-regard? Or is the warped face in the mirror of fiction sometimes his own? Is this subtle irony or self-laceration? 'Michael Caradock – the Enigma... the prejudices and passions, the angers and delights of this extraordinary man, possibly a genius...' Or possibly not. Perhaps this is the decisive question. And there are sufficient extracts in this work for the reader to make a judgement.

The Caves of Alienation is, then, a complex and equivocal work; and one that consciously distances itself from most of the English-language fiction written in Wales in the twentieth century, not only in its multivocal style and experimentalism but also in its class standpoint and sense of what are often referred to as 'roots'. Thus, despite his upbringing in a mining valley, Caradock has the good fortune to have inherited independent wealth even prior to his novelistic success (it's made clear that his family owned coal mines rather than laboured in them), and at times he articulates a hatred of the place he was born and contempt for its working-class inhabitants. These attitudes are, it's true, condemned by others, but even those character witnesses who considered Caradock misanthropic, unpatriotic and a life-long snob are invariably part of a well-educated middle class; and this too sets the tone of the work against the grain of much prose fiction written in Wales, with its emphasis on proletarian life – an imaginative variant, one sometimes feels, of what the French term *ouvriérisme*.

This is an unusual and striking novel which in structure, scope of outlook and preoccupation with key trends in European culture declares itself radically different from most British novels of its period and, in looking so determinedly and stubbornly elsewhere, sets the measure for its own boldness and originality.

Duncan Bush

THE CAVES OF
ALIENATION

1

Dawn through dirty clouds. Curious liquid shafts of light probing through the billowed sludge and the water gleaming as the tide turns. Catching now the wings of a skimming V of a skein of whitefronts making with stretched necks for the areas of the dawn. A shot. The cry of seabirds and waders. The endless scream of gulls. Morning, soon the waters will cut the island off and it will be another solitary bitter daybreak. An empty bottle, a throbbing weary despair without fear, without grace, without the hint of spiritual elegance that is all there is left to aspire to. The twenty-ninth or the ninetieth. Drink or bottle? What does it matter?

Savage trudging across the spit of land, compact, double-barrelled, before the sea cuts him off from his breakfast. Glances up to the blind windows, without pausing, and knows I am here in the gloom and fuddled in some restless *dream perhaps asleep. Hunches into himself more as the pale rays edge through the pewterish static scowl of the sky and trudges on.*

The White House stands out above the ness with the small wood. She lies there innocently, innocent in sleep, her black hair long, tousled about her pale, fine-boned face; lies there relaxed and open and opulent. But in sleep innocent.... He snores resentfully in the other room. Poor, doomed fool. Fashioned to be her dupe.

Creeping waters. Without seeming to move the sullen, darkening clouds seep inward on the indifference of light, so that now there is a pentafid thrust of sun's rays a long way out to sea, spotlighting the broken grey in a wavering line of silver. And beyond that more cloud.

More alcohol. Pretence is useless. Solitude no longer a luxury, away from the bullying alleyways of the city, the chain-reacting resentments of a social day and snaps of sexual excitement, soon casually past, a pair of pretty legs and unrestrained bosom, curry smells out of basements, smell of fruit off a stall, oddly fresh in the fumes, voices, hips in swirling skirt, buses, madmen gabbling about their private wounds hidden in city rags, sweat dampening the evening paper in the hand, nylon thighs rustling against one another, squalid little pubs with plastic rococo, savoury breaths of frying sausages, a cobbler in a plate-glass window like a friendly advert for the past in a throwaway culture, a big boy hits a small boy out of sight, overnight kebab houses and publishers, stretched and spreadeagled stockinged girls on sex magazines, tired faces, laughter on a discord, shuffle of people homeward, nowhere, trying not to touch on the formicine

2

tracks and carrying pointless burdens. There it was possible after the ninth drink or the nineteenth to be lost and truly luxuriant in the drift of stragglers through no-man's-land at eighteen-thirty. Possible to pretend that each waking hour was for breaking down images received, reshaping forms and rearranging components upon meaningful palimpsests. And sipping the acrid spirit possible to pretend that the juices would foment and refoment inside the secretive ducts of consciousness to distil one day something subtle and pure. Nonsense, of course. Sense and intellect are seldom properly alive together.

Possible to pretend a form of hatred there. Here there is only reality. The pervasive reality of hawk, harrier, owl. The secure stalk and arrogance of the grey heron through the shallows. The pike in the fresh, deep stream. The kingfisher upon his shitten nest, unperturbed.

Now the water is up beyond the spit. Grey seepage across the flats. Lemnos is intact again. Clouds merge into an undulant fawnish spread, tached with dirty shades of grey: without even a hiss the thin even slow-acting rain falls on the little wood, over the white house above it, where she stirs in her sleep, smiling at some dreamed cruelty, rippling at the prospect and memory, over the huddling village, in the cleft above the harbour. The corrosive Welsh rain dissolving poisons in the clean country air. As the anabatic waters push on without ever remitting. And the island is itself once more.

The cry of seabirds; the confused blob of memory as the watercolours of the vast and intricate picture run together and nothing is clear; dream voices in the receding seabirds; sweaty, drugged sleep – not Asclepian; the weary throb of

3

an acquired taint.... The waters running the colours together in over-flat no-man's-land, cries of pain, betrayal in bird voices and the sweating sky...

Well, certainly he was always very promising. I took him only in the sixth form, but we obviously knew in those days of relatively small numbers who was good at what. By that time he had become rather an affected fellow – partly, perhaps, because of home influence. The Caradocks were more than comfortably off – coal-owners and what-have-you. He was very independent. A bit supercilious to the staff. I remember he used to speak in a sort of English accent before he ever left this part of the world. And, of course, as soon as he went to Oxford, he cultivated English mannerisms, which didn't sit easily on him at first. When you met him, say, during a vacation, he'd pretend to be very reticent and aloof. But, of course, the mask often slipped. And, for the first few years, so did the accent. I don't think many of his teachers took to him a great deal. This is an industrial area and most of us come from working-class homes. We were used to a very straightforward type of boy, hard-working and unpretentious. Caradock wasn't like that: apart from giving himself airs, he had very little perseverance. If he couldn't do something easily, he gave up. Having said that, in *my* subject he was outstanding. But he knew it and that did not make him a sympathetic pupil. He was a very sensitive lad, I suppose; but he was also unusually arrogant. In fact, I'd say he was about the most arrogant boy I ever taught.

T. P. Leyshon (aged 72). Formerly English master at Cwmfelyn County School. Extract from the unedited

4

transcript of material for the BBC radio programme about Caradock, 'The Bow of Heracles'.

I think that most of the evidence from people who knew him as a boy in Wales supports the idea that he thought of himself as 'different'. He was brought up in what seems to have been an over-genteel atmosphere and pretty sheltered before he went to school. It seems to have been a rough and traumatic experience. Most of the other kids knocked about from an early age and so stood up to the routine rough and tumble of the playground much better than Caradock did. I suppose I spoke to a score of people who remember him at that time, as well as to friends in later life who say that his account of his schooldays was either savage or scathingly farcical. But I think this separateness had other sources which were external. Children hear what their parents say and often copy adult attitudes. The Caradocks were an unpopular Tory family in a pre-dominantly working-class area and so the children who went to school with Caradock, and he was a timid child, took out on him some of their parents' feelings about the class of people he came from. They did not want him – although this, of course, did not apply uniformly – in their games. And if he did join them, invariably he seems to have ended the day running home in tears. It must also be said that his foster-mother was very anxious, as Spender puts it in the poem, to keep him from children who were rough. I think this mattered more when he was a small boy and much less when he was at the County School, where there was an intellectual parity. But even there he was a complete rabbit at games. And he was tolerated rather than accepted.

David Hayward. Professional historian. Appointed by Caradock's estate to write an official biography. In the same radio programme, 'The Bow of Heracles'.

Oh, he seems to have had a frightful time. Although one could never be sure with Michael, especially after he'd taken a drink or two. In fact, his childish experiences seem to have been perfectly usual and the scale of bullying about which he tended to complain was absolutely nothing compared to what most of his contemporaries who had been to public school had gone through. It's my belief that all children are pretty vicious because they have an opportunity to be, while adults, either from fear of retribution, retaliation or because of some veneer of civilisation, are invariably frustrated. Michael had a very bitter memory of some occasion when a group of children had threatened to stuff him into a drain. Well, this is absolutely nothing to some of the things I remember at my school, where there was no respite at the end of the day. And, what I think is quite important, there was never any question of sexual coercion of the sort that most boarders know of. Michael did not like or understand homosexuals and was rather horrified by stories about other people's school experiences. It left him with a distaste for any kind of physical bullying. But, in other ways, intellectually, and sometimes emotionally, he could be something of a thug.

James Faber. Fellow of Blackfriars College, Oxford. Contemporary and friend of Caradock during his post-

graduate work at the University. In the same radio programme.

Two ravens, huge against the washed blue and white sky, swept on still wings past the big window; then disappeared below the cliff edge at the end of the big sloping meadow. The raven uses the future tense. What does that matter when crass tomorrow is already with us and yesterday's tortures are revisited in the prospect? Domitian is in Rome and the brutish age amasses in the brooding climates. No man can be a lover of the true or the good unless he abhors the multitude.

Watchful, superstitious, the guardian of the Ozolian spring breathed heavily, leaning backward into his heaped pillows, gasping, exulting in the sense of suffering. He was eager for all the distant, multifarious altars which he had seen through screens of trees or suddenly in some clearing where, with graceful deliberate ritual, alien and barbarian people sought the solace of gods. But the candlepower of his own reason had melted the hydra-blood frozen into the fibres of his garments. Now he was a torn beast himself, desiring with loathsome nails to tear the adhesive soaking fire out of his spent flesh. Feeling capable, now, of pain and nothing else but pain, he exaggerated his pale inhalations of tepid air in the stuffy sickroom. He felt some sort of smile tighten across his face and it stayed there, slowly fading, as the mind drifted far away from the flicker of association that had caused the smile.

He had a distant memory of being very happy. Able to strangle griefs as they occurred and then... years of stoic work. His blasphemies had been indiscriminate and loud, in the sight of sacred authors, hurling darts at totems and fetishes, detecting the scheming politician behind the tears of the despairing witness.

Somewhere, far away, beyond the wood to the west he heard the sound of many dogs barking in excitement.... And there was sparse December call of birds.

From nowhere came the memory, but surely of no event that he had ever lived through, of an extraordinary silent garden party with marquees and many elegantly dressed men and women. He was, there, as a child, feeling confident and trusting. He could hear blackbirds in the summer trees. Songbirds. There were clouds tinted as delicately with pink as cream rose petals. It was all a formalised arrangement on the ancient pressed lawns as ritualised, he could see from his present vantage point out of time, as those ceremonies in front of altars at which he had spied mockingly. The women in long silken dresses and wide-brimmed hats made consciously beautiful gestures: the men, who were all tall, bowed and inclined their heads. Without warning, though there must have been some gathering of clouds, some darkening of the sky, some fearful stillness, there was an unusually terrifying storm. First, a great gust of wind that bent stout trees, hurled over tables, off which glasses smashed; then drenching rain with flash after flash of trident lightning and the loudest thunder he had ever heard. Soundless children wept and opened their mouths in screams – but the elegant adults rushed for cover with set, turned-in faces, bulging eyes and slack, sagging mouths. As they stamped to shelter, they knocked aside the frightened children. He could not put a name to the event, to the day, to the occasion. His drugged, drawn-out memory was doubtless overplaying the scene: but there was the clear image of a little girl dressed in a white dress trampled on muddied grass. His own hot tears. The noiseless stampede. The thunder.

He opened his eyes. One of the ravens soared into view above the cliff edge, the heavy flight all at once graceful.

> And by myne eie the Crow his clawe dooth wright
> Delight is layd abedde, and pleasure past,
> No sonne now shines, cloudes han all ouercast.

All will be well. Cras. Cras. After Domitian, the Antonines. And after Marcus Aurelius, Commodus. Weary, burdened man whose unfulfilled desire was to relinquish duty succeeded by an evil son.

> And after Winter commeth timely death.

On a wave of pain again, he heard the baying dogs, remembering distantly a boar hunt somewhere in the Black Forest.... The deep-throated ululations of bloodlust and fear from the dogs, a sight of the small-eyed, red-eyed solitary beast, whose tusked fury might rip a man from crutch to breastbone in one thrusting rush. The harsh gutturals of the men, fancifully clothed, beating the recluse out of cover. Hallali. Archaic horns heard in the depth of silo-sheltering woods. And above the trees against a cloudless December sky the towers of Sir

Bercilak de Hautdesert. An outcast, a solitary torn by the pack.

Galen limped into the room with the four-o'-clock pills and a drink. Smiling, trying not to react with any show of pity.

'Do you hear it?' Landgrave asked.

'The dogs?'

'Yes...'

Galen gave him the capsules and the weak whisky drink.

'I'd try to sleep,' he said. 'Do you want another drink beside you?'

Landgrave moved his head slowly from side to side. The light began to fade. Galen looked towards the curtains but did not move to draw them across. Landgrave did not see him leave the room.

Behind the pale flame steadily wavering across the ancient page seeped the spreading brown waste. First a single precious volume. And then the blaze of the library against the darkening sky. The expedient, chewing Goth grinned as he unlocked the floodgate which flushed foul waters through the sacred cellarage. From it stole up the odour of disease, commonplace, stale. Among the trash of spent condoms, plastic vessels, floating sewage, a still yellow froth, were the Ghirlandaio *Adoration of the Shepherds*, the Botticelli *Primavera*, the Titian *Venus*.

Night had come. The birds were silent. In California, from a jeep, drinking from flasks, they pursued the imported boar with jocular howling, grinning like hounds. And the forest was dark. The trailing, thorned arms grasped and wound at him as he was a child again and ran from the maddened beast that would eviscerate him. Ran howling from the unsignalled firestorm and was held by the sharp, gladiate thorns.

The fire raged and the hissing water foully mounted in swathes around the straining of his limbs. The window-square dimmed. The boar drowned in blood from the spear thrust in his throat, as the hounds attacked for the last time.

And then there was again a comet moving faintly against the clear northern sky....

Closing passage from the final episode of Laocoön, *posthumous novel of Michael Caradock, provisionally titled by Hazel & Sims after consultation with Caradock's literary executors. The novel is thought to have been finished but may not have been revised.*

Before proceeding, it will obviously be necessary to describe the pathology of this disease 'mythopoeia'.

Even those critics most sympathetic to Caradock's work, such as Stephen Lewis, admit that he is often deliberately – consciously – obscure; and from the evidence of his friends – or, at least, those who claim to be his friends, for it is doubtful that Caradock held many people in such close esteem – we are able to deduce that he enjoyed posing as a mandarin. There is no doubt that he was an elitist in matters of art and education and that he was even prepared to boast of it. But part of my thesis – and an important part – is that his right-wing attitudes were much more pervasive: in *Promethead* we have an almost naked admiration for the Nietzschean hero, Waldeck, resistant to torture even when it is self-inflicted, but soothing himself with paternalist fantasies even at the height of his misanthropy. All the novels which lead up to this massive exercise in self-deception show signs of this same Olympian contempt – either in the central character's resentment, or dandyism, or plain cynical mockery of others. The short, conceited *Coriolan Overture* that followed it might even be interpreted as a deliberate attempt to foster a public myth. And the posthumous novel, *Laocoön*, with all its idiosyncratic and highly arbitrary allusions, suggests to many critics that Caradock's hatred of the time in which he lived and of people had become a clinical condition.

His obsessive interest in certain myths – those of Philoctetes, Heracles, Prometheus, Laocoön, Parsifal and his devotion to Nietzsche, selected bits of Hegel and what he took to be the Stoic ethic – stems from his need to dignify his own shortcomings by relating these myths to his personal experiences.

Richard Snow: The View from Lemnos, *a study of the use of myth in the novels of Michael Caradock. Medusa Books, 1972.*

Michael wasn't political at all. Not in any practical sense, that is. He *loathed*, really *loathed*, what he thought of as left-wing trendiness. Which I think we were all accused of at one time or another, but most of his own ideas were impossibly vague. He really wasn't interested in making things work, which is I suppose what politicians are for.... I think a lot too much is being made, nowadays, about his dandyism. It simply isn't true. What Michael wanted more than anything was to be unobtrusively a

12

part of a particular set – to which I belonged and Leighton belonged. I was married at the time to Leighton Rees. And my brother... and it really was very amusing. But he could be quite urbane. Always very charming, if he took one out to dinner or something. You knew that you wouldn't have to fight him all over the taxi. He tried terribly hard to be 'cool', if you know what I mean....

I can't honestly say that I was very much aware of him as a sexual presence. In fact, for a while, I half-suspected he was comme ci comme ça. But David Hayward seems to think he had innumerable affairs, as well as the big one with Brenda and the horrid business just before his death. Nobody was very much aware of them. I think Michael was probably very devious with and about women. He liked being enigmatic about more or less everything, which was usually amusing: but he really did keep that aspect of his life truly secret.

Angela Petrov, former friend of Caradock, in BBC radio programme.

From *The Low Key of Hope* on to the unfinished *Laocoön*, Michael Caradock's central characters have certain things in common: most of them are rock-ribbed puritans who have at some time or other fallen from grace, most of them have developed to a critical point an early sense of resentment, most of them are ambitious for some special-ised status and coldly ruthless in establishing a reputation for high personal integrity.

Baldwin, the newspaper reporter, in *The Low Key of Hope* is a genuine snob, worried about his accent and

13

working-class origin, deeply insecure in the London quasi-bohemian society that he has chosen to move in. Fleming in *Carcases of Tall Ships* goes out of his way to be a misfit, when it would have been so easy for him to be an acceptable officer. Both of them are sexually circumspect: Baldwin is determined to make love only to women he really loves and feels enormous disgust with himself for, as he sees it, taking advantage of Natasha's frustration; Fleming is cold to the point of rudeness in side-stepping the evident invitation of Roberta Calloway, although up to that point he has been perfectly happy to receive her confidences and confessions. Laertes Jones in *Broods of Folly*, Caradock's only attempt at sustained comic writing, is a caricature of these earlier characters: the pure fool, unashamed of his naïveté or anything else, who is nevertheless scandalised by the monstrous world in which he is trying to find, and from which he is trying to save, his sister. But in *Promethead* and *Laocoön*, Caradock uses these same puritan and resentful traits of character, alongside an intense ambition and ruthless integrity, to create in Waldeck and Landgrave two honestly tragic figures for our time; men of severe personal honour, desiring to serve a world in which they have no longer any place, whose prophecies of doom are ignored and derided. One of the epigraphs to the *Promethead*, from Nietzsche, is revealing: *To take upon oneself not punishment, but guilt – that alone would be Godlike.* This is evidently Waldeck's ambition: and he fails to achieve it. Two aphorisms from the same author occur in the *Laocoön*: *The soul must have its chosen sewers to carry away its ordure...* and: *The*

14

philosopher has to be the bad conscience of his age. Coriolan Overture is much more a work of fiction than autobiography in its manipulation of factual events in Caradock's life but differs significantly from the 'pure' fiction in two respects: Marcus Conrad is not plagued by a puritan conscience and is remarkably insouciant, moving easily and confidently through his early life – but finding the Volscians no more attractive or appreciative than the Romans.

It is the purpose of this study to examine not so much the character of Michael Julian Caradock but the ideas which he set out in his novels and essays about the problems of man in the mid-twentieth century. And also to deal with his misanthropic despair in the context of his books, rather than by rehashing once more the appalling events which brought about his death.

An examination of his loneliness and the nature of his hatreds – they were much more than resentments – through his published work is more likely to reveal the true character of the author than hearsay and gossip. To borrow another remark from Nietzsche: *When we talk in company we lose our unique tone of voice and this leads us to make statements which in no way correspond to our real thoughts.*

Stephen Lewis: The Novels of Michael Caradock. *Molyneux, 1971.*

With a curious tingle of satisfaction, Baldwin decided upon a strategy of silence. After all, he told himself, what was good enough for the old artificer, is good enough for Sid Baldwin.

He chuckled to himself and sipped the raw Algerian wine as though it was something choice. That's it, he thought, silence, exile and cunning. He had fulfilled the second requirement by getting out of Shotover and more or less cutting himself off from his family, now was the time to practise the first discipline and acquire the third attribute. He thought much faster on his feet than most people and was able to work a couple of moves ahead, but he had made the mistake of talking too much: to Smolenski, to Gladwin, to Cummings – even to June. Baldwin's trouble was that he trusted people too easily, he confided too readily. It was possible that they'd been laughing at him all the time.

Baldwin had always been a quick learner and here was the end of the lesson. He drank the rest of the wine without noticing the taste. Then he heard June Farquar's laughter and the flush of anger swept upward over his face again. She was with Instone who, at that moment, glanced across at him, smiling mirthlessly. Baldwin tried to fight down the conviction that they were talking about him. For a daft moment he thought he would go over and ask them; ask them what was so funny. Instead, he went to the bedroom and scrabbled about among a pile of coats for his mack.

'Hey oop, old lad,' said Cummings' voice from the door. 'Th'art not boogering off 'ome so early, are yeh?'

Cummings waved a bottle of wine at him, grinning, leaning against the door frame, fair haired and foxy eyed but a hundred per cent friendly. Baldwin thought of his strategy and smiled without parting his lips. It occurred to him – on the spur of the moment – that this would make him look enigmatic. And, anyway, he did not feel like smiling.

'I said I'd only look in,' he said. 'I've got to make another call.'

He shrugged into his mack and shifted the knot of his tie carefully, looking at himself in the dressing-table mirror. His own quiet voice, with its flatness and the slight northern inflections, sounded pretty confident to him. Perhaps a bit suggestive.

Cummings dropped the fake accent and came into the room, pouring wine into his own glass and slopping some onto the pale gold carpet.

'Really?' he said. 'Do I detect a hint of Valmontian decadence in that honest Lancashire yeoman's jib?'

Baldwin smiled his tight-lipped smile to specification. Cummings studied him vinously, from close quarters, leering.

'You old hound dog,' he said, pointing at Baldwin in mock accusation. 'The Mutterer's here all alone. It's Natasha, isn't it....'

Still smiling, Baldwin put a gentle hand on Cummings' chest and pushed him out of the way without saying any more.

'You old bastard!' said Cummings, to his retreating back.

There were couples sitting on the first two flights of stairs as Baldwin went down: one pair quarrelling in urgent whispers; the second snogging vigorously, the man's hand flickering undecidedly over the girl's sternum; the third sat in silence – the girl sulky, cold, smoking, the man gazing at her with deep-set pathos in homicidally unhappy, dark eyes.

It was wet in the square, and the plane trees had lost most of their leaves which made it slippery underfoot. He walked towards Kensington High Street station on the Circle Line, playing with the idea of going the other way towards Victoria and actually calling on Natasha. She was unhappy and neglected enough to... in fact she had virtually suggested it. Baldwin shook his head vigorously. It would be wrong. He did not love her, although he would have liked to take her to bed. It would be using her loneliness and unhappiness. That would be inexcusable.

Anyway Cummings would believe what he wanted to believe, and the news room, those who cared, would believe Cummings. Most of them couldn't give a damn.

The tube was fairly empty at that time of the evening. Baldwin read the card advertisements and thought of ways in which he might make use of June's humiliation of him. That was the knack: to make every experience count, however painful it had been at the time. But then some chance association on one of the adverts as he got out of the train at Edgware Road conjured up an erotic picture of her half dressed and the idea of it all happening for someone else, as it surely must, made Baldwin feel physically sick with a sense of self-pity and deprivation.

By the time he'd walked along the dim, damp street back to his digs, he'd fought the image out of his mind. He concentrated on his new oath of silence and wondered how he might go about taking lessons in elocution, without it being obtrusive.

From The Low Key of Hope. *Alvin & Brandt, 1954.*

I can't say that I knew him well, because I'm not sure that anyone did. In those days he was known as Julian Caradock and I suppose that aged about sixteen or seventeen we were what you would have called friends. Then he went to Oxford and I went to Edinburgh and the relationship lapsed gradually.

18

As an adolescent he was a terrific talker about himself: what he was going to do and how. Or else brooding and questioning. And usually in love with someone who didn't want anything to do with him. Ironically enough, at that time he got on very badly with girls, when most of us were stretching our wings. And that made him very scornful.

Dr Geraint Bevan, consultant physician and former schoolmate (aged 44), in BBC radio programme.

His attitude was almost prudish, which is not particularly normal in boys of that age. In fact he was one of the few I ever taught who got anything out of *The Rape of the Lock* other than an acute sense of disappointment. Lawrence wasn't on the curriculum in those days, but I used to discuss modern writers with one or two pupils who were going to take English at university. Caradock had always read whoever it was. And even at that age he was capable of really hating a book. He detested Lawrence: but he liked Eliot and Baudelaire and then Joyce. Anything to do with disgust...

T. P. Leyshon, former English master, in BBC radio programme.

The comfort experienced in remembering an unsolicited, unexpected act of gentleness from a woman, as generous and unselfish as any sexually motivated gesture can be, is perhaps foolish and almost certainly illusory. But there is that brief reliving of a few moments when shades of the adolescent prison-house of self-absorption snap open and there is a sudden bright, fresh day full of sunlit innocence: the first hint of spring.

19

Those few moments are all too brief. Nietzsche says that 'the most vulnerable and at the same time the most unconquerable thing is human self-love; indeed, it is through being wounded that its power grows and can, in the end, become tremendous'.

Perhaps some of us contrive wounds, sensing the doubtful power of self-reliance. What follows is an inevitable dis-illusion, a feeling of betrayal: even when the betrayal itself has been deliberately, even elaborately arranged, a studied disenchantment of the heart. The bitterness, the amertume, that follows next is a sentimental luxury. But for those of us afflicted with the self-love that Nietzsche describes, it is a period in which we build up certain emotional reserves, only to expend them profligately in other similar bursts of careless spiritual energy.

Self-inflicted wounds do not make supermen and instead of tremendous power we experience powerful self-contempt. After a while, we are weary of being wounded: we become ingenious at protecting ourselves while still in the habit of living dangerously. The ultimate recourse is retreat: and retreat inevitably means defeat. So that, on this beautiful afternoon, remembering a casual meeting almost twenty years ago, the initial sense of warmth and comfort became a perception of failure.

From one of the lyrical essays 'An Idea of Remembered Love' in the collection The Philosopher's Stone. *Hazel & Sims, 1965.*

It was a lovely day, even for that gehennical tract of earth. Marcus lit an oval Turkish cigarette and contemplated the lumpy mountain across the valley, in a golden afternoon haze that hid its pocks and warted black tips. Marcus breathed in deeply, and coughed.

He liked to think that he shared with eighteenth-century rationalists a truly profound indifference to Nature – someone had driven through the Lake District admirably with the blinds of his carriage lowered. Marcus was accordingly surprised to find himself, not only thinking that a scene he was accustomed to despise was pleasing, but also disposed to climb – or partly climb – the mountain.

Any attempt at elegance was regarded in the village as swank, but Marcus was becoming inured to the covert grins, or much more open amusement, of people he passed in the street. His college blazer was vermilion in colour, with which he affected a matching bow tie and narrow, tapering trousers. He also carried a walking stick. No doubt some of the mockery was contemptuous, born of resentment and envy; much of it was without malice – a reflex to someone who was making an effort to be an individual. He was indifferent. He went around with his head slightly tilted, looking through his rimless glasses at some exquisite cerebral irony in the middle distance, smiling a little.

It was in this state of pleasing inviolability and apparent abstraction that he walked along the drab main street of the village, before turning past the diffident church into a twisting road which led past detached bourgeois houses with pocket lawns and names of inspired banality: the homes of teachers, clerks, successful grocers and drapers, the village dentist, solicitor and pharmacist, to the river. At the top end of the valley it was little more than a wide stream, which could be crossed on stepping stones. Marcus was making for a few fields used for pasture, away from the industrial sector, under the gentlest slope of the mountain. He tapped his light, tan shoes doubtfully with his stick, wondering if it was possible to walk elegantly through agricultural land, however verdant; then swung it in a debonair arc as he saw a slender, rather attractive girl approaching. Less slender as she approached but perhaps more precisely attractive, he recognised Virginia Roope, wife of the red-haired pharmacist. She had pleasantly full breasts and very evident, enticing hips. Now, dressed in a flowery summer dress with rather a flowing effect, her charms were not as obvious as they had been a few evenings ago at the minute branch of the county library, where high-heeled shoes, a rather tight fawn skirt and a close-fitting blouse had shown off her excellent legs and aphrodisian figure to greater advantage. Her image had remained quite vividly with Marcus and he had taken due note of that. She would be about twenty-seven or eight, certainly less than ten years older than he was.

At the branch of the county library where they had re-established an acquaintance that had always been slight, they had joked a little about the books available.

She stopped at the gate of her house, Aldergrove, in a pose of studied elegance that was more or less successful. He raised his stick gracefully. Each of them smiled.

'Hullo,' she said. 'Isn't it a beautiful afternoon.'

'Enough to make me feel recklessly energetic,' Marcus said. 'I was even determined to climb the mountain.'

She laughed within a pleasantly contralto range. Her

accent wasn't specially noticeable.

'I'm sure you deserve a rest,' she said. 'Isn't Mods supposed to be the most gruelling examination in the world?'

'The modern world, at least,' said Marcus. 'But mercifully it is still two terms away. I was extremely stupid the other evening when we met at the – er – library....'

Virginia Roope laughed in the right place at the hesitation.

'You were looking for Gibbon,' he said, 'and, of course, I have a copy which I'd be delighted to lend you.'

'How very kind of you,' she said. And blushed prettily. Marcus felt himself wantonly stirring as he looked at her, fresh but fully favoured in the floral dress. In spite of the fact that she was older than he, she seemed at that moment touchingly young: he felt happily amused and protective.

He made a gracefully disparaging gesture.

'A pleasure, Mrs Roope.'

'Oh, please, do call me Virginia.'

He inclined his head with an appreciative smile.

'I've become very interested in Julian the Apostate,' Virginia said. 'He'd be in Gibbon, wouldn't he?'

'Very much so. What interests you?'

'Well, his apostasy, I suppose.'

'Quite. The last major attempt to hold out for pagan dignity in a decadescent world. But for all that, curiously puritan. He took a vow of chastity quite early on in life.'

'Really? He'd have gone down well in this place.'

They both laughed and Marcus thought he saw a hint of lasciviousness flicker (demurely enough) in her eyes.

'Oh God,' she said, smiling still, 'it's such a change to

23

have an intelligent conversation. I'm not being disloyal. Don't think that. But my husband's interests are exclusively scientific and I'm not allowed to work. Still, I mustn't keep you from your exercise. What is it? *Mens sana...*'

'*In corpore exiguo*,' said Marcus.

They laughed again.

'I'll hand the book in at your husband's shop,' he said.

'It really is very kind of you. Are you sure you won't be using it?'

'Quite.'

'I'll tell you what: why don't you come to tea and bring it with you. I'd love to have a longer talk.'

'Thank you. I'd like to. Are you specially interested in the later Roman Empire?'

'Oh yes. Very much.'

'I thought I might bring one or two other books.'

'I'll look forward to it. Not tomorrow. How about Friday?'

'Marvellous. Thank you, Mrs... Virginia.'

She smiled, blushing once more, and went into her just-so garden. Marcus went on towards the mountain, tapping his walking stick rhythmically on the rough road. He wondered in a vague way what she might be doing the next day – but remembered that Thursday was early-closing day in the village and no doubt she and her husband would be taking a drive somewhere.

From A Coriolan Overture, *Caradock's 'essay in auto-biographical fiction'. Hazel & Sims, 1969.*

I suppose I should explain we were fairly young men together with a taste for wine and inclined to somewhat maudlin confessionals late at night. The Virginia woman is unhappily married and sexually sophisticated: this is typical of Michael's ability to make something much more dramatic than it was. The real woman, who gave him his first sexual opportunities, was in fact the Classics teacher at his school. And I rather suspect the whole affair – if that's what it was – was clumsy and accidental. But it obviously mattered a great deal to him. Michael had read modern languages in the sixth form, but he had a pretty fair grasp of Latin already. Then he came up, and found that he had absolutely no Greek. So he decided – again this was quite typical of him – to learn what he could during vacations. He approached this particular girl, whose name was Helen, something I'm quite sure that Michael had taken account of, and she agreed to help. She was a few years older than he was and lived a dozen miles away. So that was that. I'm not sure on whose initiative, because Michael was ostentatiously delicate about that sort of thing, but it happened abruptly one evening over the Nicomachean Ethics or whathaveyou....

James Faber, Oxford don. Recorded in course of BBC radio programme.

You know I am genuinely puzzled that very few people seem to see the intentionally funny, self-mocking aspects of the *Coriolan Overture*. Apart from the lyrical prose in the two books of essays, it's the only remotely happy thing that he wrote. I mean, you would perhaps expect Snow to miss the point, but so does Stephen Lewis. And when you consider that it occurred between the

Promethead and the last novel, it is singularly lacking in despair or hatred or worry.

David Hayward, biographer. In the same radio programme.

All some kind of torment. The emaciated frame with shrivelled testicles and pectoral flap unfastened, the skull already grinning as with one finger upraised it spells out the lesson of carnal anguish. Those who live by the flesh shall die by the flesh and this great rotting certainty hangs on the rafters of feverish painting consciousness. Ach.

It wasn't always so.

There she lies, in that White House, across which the grey gauzes of rain swirl, the harlot madonna; lies as she dusts his pitiful books, catching sight of herself in a mirror, full lip curled, black soft-falling hair and grey secret eyes, pale face. She smiles at herself, knowing that she lies. Looking out across the deep strand of water to this tumulus past which the grey rain sweeps. It could not be so...

Oh God. That sudden realisation across a dim, stuffy room that it was no accident that she was sitting in that way, that her stillness was deliberate before one slow sensual movement. Fear and ecstasy bucking up into the gorge, choking the word.... Her eyes rising slowly from the page, her face burning, the long staring moment, long long long, until her thighs opened a little more and closed and I felt her go rigid and relax, all across the room. And I did not know what to do. Oh Helen. First tremulous memories of these shaking fingers on her clothes and... Helen.... Tense and smiling, then softly enveloping...

Vortices of webbed, clouded memory, eddies of sensation

clutching at nerve strands like miasmal claws of mist around naked branches. An overpowering nausea. Vertigo. After all this time.

What is it? Eight. Eight-thirty. It can't be more. The tide is up to the wooden jetty of the Red Lodge. Light smudging across the dun-grey south towards the east. The staggering mind somehow once again crossing a dangerous room. Rain, dull rain, on a garden with overblown roses, shiny black earth and scatters of petal. My silly frightened hand on her tense shoulder...

Colours of hell are pale pink and grey, the colours of blood. Fiends move corpuscular against the soul. Dust hath closed... Ha! What else, what else, what else?

121. Ext. Glanmor. Day. Aerial view of Glanmor estuary, with Caradock's house on islet, right of frame, cut off by rising tide; and Glanwydden headland on left of frame. Pale sunlight on still sea. Hold. Until	MUSIC: Richard Strauss: *Tod und Verklärung* (7b.) (Hold under Lloyd)
Slow panning shot inland to village	(V/O) *Lloyd*: Once, twice, each day the small island is cut off from the village by the fast, often treacherous tide...
122. Ext. Glanmor village. Day. View of islet from top of main street, as though some way out to sea, angle foreshortened to conceal	

relative narrowness of estuary
channel. Hold

(V/O) *Lloyd*: and while the
small community of
countrymen went about their
work, unaware of his brooding
presence, Michael Caradock
stared out, whatever the
weather, whatever the season,
upon his own monochromatic
despair.

Track along street, slowly.

The painter, Leighton Rees,
comments

123. Ext. Glanmor. Day. Cut
and zoom in on Rees, at
vantage point above harbour
looking out on islet. Rees turns
to camera. Hold

Fade down Strauss. And out.
FX. Seabirds, wind, etc.

Rees: (Sync.) Frankly I had no
patience with him, from quite
an early stage in our
acquaintance. At that time
what has been dignified as
bleak despair seemed to be
sullen gloominess. It's quite
true that Caradock was always
a misfit, but he worked at it.

C.U. Rees. (head and
shoulders)

Medium shot Rees to take in
gesture then

If you take all this beauty the
falseness becomes apparent

124. Ext. Glanmor. Day. Mix
to long panning shot from left
to right, beginning at tip of
Glanwydden, slowly coming
around to White House,
pausing over the jetty, in
around the harbour with Rees
in shot, down over the village
and out onto islet...

(V/O) *Rees*: It is inconceivable
to me, perhaps because I am a
painter, that anyone in this
place with its wildness, its
quality of light, its infinite
variety of mood and
composition in sky and
landscape should have
cultivated so assiduously
morose and destructive
humours in the way that
Michael Caradock did.

dwelling on water and play of
light upon the water...

picking up flights of ducks low
over flats towards islet...

dwelling on reeds and round
to trees and Caradock's house
where hold on blank,
curtainless windows

(V/O) *Rees*: Those windows
were put into the house by a
painter and for me it is sad that
the eyes which looked through
them could see no more in this
landscape than they were able
to see in the industrial valley to
the east where Caradock's
hatreds were incubated.

125. Ext. Caradock house.
Day. Zoom in on the blind,
staring windows

*Sequence from television programme on Michael Caradock,
'Landscape of a Prophet', with narration by poet Trevelyan
Lloyd.*

Garnett looked at the neat little boxes with their scraps of grass, the gentle curving roads, the well-made flower beds, the young slim trees. He shook his head and his face tipped over into an ironic grin. An old man with a white moustache sat on a green bench, placed there by a grateful council in memory of Alderman Taliesin Price, smoking peacefully. Garnett went and sat alongside him.

'How are you,' said the old man.

'Morning,' said Garnett. 'Beautiful day.'

'Pretty fair.'

'Whatever happened to Paradise Terrace?' Garnett said.

'Oh.' The old man shook his head and smiled. 'The new development,' he said, waving his pipe at the estate. 'Knocked it down, the old terrace.'

'Did they?' Garnett said.

'Bungalows. Very nice, mind you.'

The old man blew out thick blue smoke.

'You from these parts, then?' he asked.

'I've been away for a long time,' Garnett said. 'I used to live here.'

'I thought you must, remembering the old terrace.'

'Yes,' said Garnett.

He leaned back and imagined the long crescent of red-chimneyed houses, the curiously ugly huddle of ancient tips over to the left, grass-grown and tufted, then the humble park with its slide, its long seesawing swings and high conical roundabout, and a balding patch of ground which did as a football pitch. Then the curious no-man's-land of flat scarred earth where some Victorian works had been abandoned into rust and rubble and weedy ruin. The stream was still there which they had dammed to make reservoirs, which they bombed with rocks, watching the flood sweep into their crazy network of canals.

Robert Garnett; Will Rees and his little brother Thomas; a tall kind boy with a red face and a blue cap straight on his head, wearing short trousers still (although he must have been thirteen), called Stanley. And a much more usual ruffian called Doug who had started the bombing. Robert Garnett's parents didn't allow him to play outside the grounds often, but on this particular day he had been invited to spend a whole day's holiday with Will Rees at his granny's. Will Rees' granny, who lived in Paradise Terrace, had been a servant with the Garnett family many years before. Her name was Rosie and she was now old, but everyone still called her Rosie. She had asked specially if Robert could come and play with Will and Thomas and his parents had known he would be safe with Rosie. Garnett laughed. It had been a remarkable day. Since then he had spent remarkable days in dozens of different cities all over the world. And yet that day had been something special: special enough to bring him miles out of his way just to have another look at Paradise Terrace.

'What's your name, if you don't mind me asking?' said the old man.

'Garnett,' he said. 'Robert Garnett.'

He turned to study the old man's reaction. He did not expect much enthusiasm. A family that had made a lot of its money during the late nineteenth century out of coal and ore and various industrial speculation could not be expected to be popular. And furthermore a family that kept itself aloof.

31

'Garnett!' The old man took his pipe out of his mouth and his blue eyes opened wide. 'Not one of the old family that used to be here. Dan Garnett the Works.'

Garnett nodded.

'Good God!' the old man said. 'Fancy that! Well, well. You'd be Cyril's boy. Dear me. They're all gone, now. All the old people.'

The old fellow began a long and ramified story, with detailed reference to this or that relative, complicated liaisons by marriage, intricate reminiscence about circumstances and events that linked him to this chance stranger sharing Alderman Price's memorial bench. Garnett remembered that bright sunny morning crossing the patch below Paradise Terrace, looking at a rabbit in a hutch, watching chickens jerking about at the end of a garden, as Rosie's daughter, Mrs Parsons, took them to the extraordinary treat of that sunlit holiday among the ruined landscape that Robert Garnett's family had no doubt had a hand in creating....

From 'Paradise Terrace', one of the stories included in Caradock's first book, Metaphors of Twenty Years. *Vortex Press, 1950.*

The absence of childhood *imagines* upon whom the sensitive poet's conscience might base subsequent psychodynamic patterns is evident. At the same time the degree of social control exercised by an overly puritanical tradition, beneath which flowed a hidden river of older paganism and sexokinetic vitality, seems to have had a lasting effect on Caradock's life and work.

The elaborate constructs engineered by the tortured

writer in the last five years of his life to achieve an autotelic system of libido-damming, which was obviously volitional, argues a desire on Caradock's part to regain the syntonic security which he felt when young and rejected.

This standard conflict of pleasure and reality principles is commonplace in Welsh life, where religious revivalist movements in the nineteenth century swept the country, preaching a harshly retributive divine intervention, but (in this author's judgement) it is a race phenomenon going way back beyond the nineteenth century to pagan rituals and ceremonies. It is surely no accident that the admittedly ersatz rites of modern druids in the annual festivals of literature and arts (Eisteddfodau), which were invented by a nineteenth-century literary hoaxer and poet, have been so eagerly amalgamated with rigidly puritan religious doctrines such as Calvinism. And the conflict between sensuality on the one hand and a repressive religious mores on the other has been a rich source of psychofictional investigations by Welsh artists.

Caradock was a devout member of the Anglican (Episcopalian) Church during the pubertal period of high emotional receptivity, as befitted his social class; but although the Nonconformist denominations are agreed to be more restringent, the Anglican Church is also emphatic in its association of sin with the guiding pleasure principle. His later rejection of religion in all its forms led to a condition of theopsychoid guilt along with hyperactive sexual energy. From this condition there developed the melancholia of his later years, which prompted the volitional withdrawal from normal contact. This may be seen as an isolation mechanism to give Caradock time in which to re-establish the moral reassurance which he associated with his Welsh upbringing and to which he was returning.

This writer's extensive researches into the psychomorphography of the area, in relation to Michael Caradock's mental content as evidenced in his literary output, form the basis of this study.

From Irving Haller: The Centaur and the Druids: *an analysis of the psychosocial background to the novels of Michael Caradock. Heseltine, 1972.*

A question of time... the inexorable tide still rising. And suppose the breakwaters give. Burst through of the still noisome swirl of the muddy sea and oblivion. The give in the capillary wall, the haemorrhage, the flux of blood, bringing a red tide of oblivion. Blood-dimmed indeed.

And inevitably the barbarian hand, the Cyclops with the one blaring eye of malice, seizing the boulder to smash... what? Anything. I fear the stupid, I have always feared the stupid, because of the evident delight they take in cruelty.

In children it is undisguised, not disguisable. There is always the malign dull-eyed, prognathous presence who smashes with harsh slurred syllables into the games of the timid and the innocent.

The waters rise. The blood pounds.

The rain ceasing, a watery hope of sun behind the dirty whitewash of cloud and a flight of birds, shelduck or mallard, headlong in purpose, suddenly making for the shore.

Through the red haze of burning shut eyelids... sluicing of water, splashes, throaty stupid laughter.

I'm pretty sure that he loathed most of us, most of the time. Michael actually *needed* to dislike people.

Angela Petrov, former friend, in BBC radio programme.

Let's face it, if Caradock hadn't come to a violent end, there'd be none of this fuss. What have we had? Five or six books in the last couple of years and now this programme and I daresay they're cooking up some mess of potage for television. He was *not* a very original or remarkable writer, although he was a pretty accomplished literary con man. And if it hadn't been for that murder and all the scandal around it, he would have been a good deal less noticed than has happened. I'm quite prepared to declare an interest: I thought he was odious from the very first time I met him at Oxford and off and on over the years, though we didn't cultivate each other. He was a real bloody popinjay – once he'd found his feet. I can't think of a better word....

George Shelley, Sunday journalist and former acquaintance, in BBC radio programme.

The true iconoclast sweeps through the grandest seraglios with a cool and impartial vandalism, flinging open doors, chasing out the eunuch attendants, arrogantly sure that what *he* is doing is right and will one day be of some significance.

Here, in this daydreaming city, the most hawk-faced burners of totems and scorners of idols go all the same to the tipsters and the touts for advice which they pass on in trembling tones. Shamans mumble in the Kemp or the Cadena; witch doctors tell the bones in the Tackley; thaumaturges quiver their delicate noses over the steaming entrails in the Lantern or the Stowaway; and necromancers brood over tacky brews in draughty cells deep into the mild misty relaxing night of the Thames valley.

Into this mysterious and arcane fug comes the stranger exorcist. He is among them but not of them. He understands their language but cannot speak it. He recognises their right to lay waste and steals scraps and relics for his own private collection. He knows who the powerful new spirits are: but they have no power over him. Because they are the old spirits in new shapes or using new techniques of domination. The new artist is for himself, for change on his own terms. He is not clubbable. He is not interested in popularity. He does not want awe or adulation: but respect. He will take no one else's word for anything. He knows his own mind.

And yet he is, at first sight, a mildly comical figure – trying out this or that pose, this or that uniform, finding himself out as he exposes others. You will see him shambling through the rainy grey streets, on his own, sulking and confident, knowing that his only lasting friend is Time. The saboteur curator, the lubricious virgin, the moved mover in his corduroy trousers and utility shirt who reserves his most sincere laughter for himself.

From 'Portrait of the Artist as a Young Turk', one of a group of sketches in the miscellany Metaphors of Twenty Years. Vortex Press, 1950.

Axel Waldeck became subject to bouts of insanity from August 15th, 19—. From this date onward, his normally cogent appreciation of human needs and political expedience, within the confines of a grander vision for his fellow countrymen and indeed for the wider community which he was determined to serve, was sometimes paralysed by moods of desolation. Encompassed by an entirely normal, even productive, way of life, these spells of impotent rage became more frequent in the course of ten years in which Axel Waldeck was ignored by the people he wished to serve. The ensuing waste of his massive talents, strategic and tactical, in the economic, diplomatic and military manipulation of his country's affairs, induced a brooding self-concern about his own past misdemeanours and mistakes, as well as a much wider, almost vengeful nihilism, based upon his interpretation of a nothing universe in which there was no possibility of meaning, order or spirit. The climax of these fits of raging futility was usually some privately expressed outburst of fury, some mad gesture of defiance in which the intense frustration densely coalescent in Waldeck's mind and personality shrieked for destruction at the indifferent lightning. In the abatement of this wrath and despair, Waldeck's pride reasserted itself, his fiery wish to serve, to contribute by the example of his will and the determination of his vision to the general good, surged again inside him. He would work as though there were no despair.

Since Axel Waldeck had always been a comparatively rich man, he was able to maintain in his state of self-exile the small but loyal staff who had served him during the necessary wars and the difficult years of subjugation or actual exile. He organised them under a Chief of Staff, held daily conferences – as long as the madness was not upon him – and with them drew up detailed plans for every normal contingency affecting the just and beneficent rule of his country and the alliance to which it belonged and would one day lead. Into the closely knit and jealously secret congeries of thwarted talent and ambition Piers Ganuret was admitted by accident: his apparently dead body had been found by two of Waldeck's staff, while out riding, in an abandoned car. When it was noticed by one of them that he was still breathing faintly, Ganuret was taken into the Waldeck hermitage and over some weeks nursed back to health.

His early convalescence coincided with one of the spells of Waldeck's despair. Ganuret was walking along a colonnade of artificially shaped conifers, leaning heavily on a stick, when he saw the stocky, obsessed figure approaching with automatic step. He had never heard of Axel Waldeck.

Waldeck's eyes were on the ground, but as he drew level with Ganuret, who was gratefully anxious to be pleasant to any member of the household that had saved his life, he raised his gaze. Ganuret was fixed with a blank but intense stare.

'What have you to say to me?' said Waldeck.

'Nothing, sir. Except to pass the time the day.'

'What do you wish to know?'

The young man was bewildered and shook his head in an embarrassed silence.

'I shall tell you what you wish to know,' Waldeck had said. 'You wish to know how to live without faith? The question is fatuous. I shall pose all the real questions which amount to perhaps only one in my own time. And I have no need of this persistent prompting.'

'I'm sorry...' said Ganuret.

'Do not be sorry, young fool,' Waldeck answered. 'You

are naked and defenceless. You have nothing and owe nothing. Unaccommodated man. I shall explain – I should explain, if there were occasion – the dilemma of the noble illusion in a blandly irreligious, concupiscent world being sucked through space into nothingness.'

'I'd be very happy to learn, sir,' Ganuret had said.

Axel Waldeck approached the young man closely. Ganuret saw the vividly blue, staring eyes and the tiny blood lines traced on the eyeballs and smelt a sourish breath. Although the man before him seemed robust, even vigorous, he had an impression of intense sickness working in that thick, deep-chested frame.

'Imbecile,' Waldeck snarled.

He stamped away, his eyes once again fixed ahead of him on the gravel. Ganuret still did not know who he had been talking to and, on returning, found those who had taken care of him evasive. Even the affable Major Ganz, who appeared to be responsible for his well-being, parried any questions about the troubled man in the colonnade.

That night he awoke to the sound of disturbance somewhere in the grounds of the manor. He got out of bed painfully and went to a window from which he looked out onto an astonishing scene. A wheat field in the dip below the domestic gardens was blazing. In the unreal red glow of the flames, Ganuret saw a howling figure running with a torch from one bale to the next, pursued by many other men, who were fanning out to cut off the veering, weaving paths taken by the single runner. Eventually, they caught and overpowered him. Ganuret felt exhausted; he collapsed into a chair and sat back, panting, waiting for his heart to stop pounding. By the time he was strong enough to get up again, the glow in the field was dying down but he could see the silhouettes of many men moving systematically about, dousing the fires and setting things in order.

He stumbled back to his bed and lay there in an exhausted state between sleep and waking, listening to strange harsh noises, motors starting, occasional crashes. Urgent voices as a door was briefly opened and slammed. Sick and feverish impressions: so that when he was properly awake he did not know if he had dreamed them or if they had happened. Then he slept deeply.

The doctor, the same patiently unsmiling man, was beside his bed when he awoke and the uniformed Major Ganz stood a pace or two away. The doctor was holding Ganuret's pulse gravely.

'Did you have a disturbed night?' he asked in his cool, watery voice. 'Your pulse is racing.'

He did not wait for a reply.

'He is far from well,' he said. 'He cannot think of moving yet. Do not worry, young man. I shall give you something to relax you.'

Introduction and prologue from Promethead, *novel. Hazel & Sims, 1967.*

Readers may wonder why the task of a literary biography has fallen to a professional historian.

In the first place I disclaim any literary pretensions. While I knew Michael Caradock reasonably well, I was not an intimate friend. There were few of these privileged people. Nor did I participate a great deal in the literary world to which he belonged while living in Oxford and London. I do not seek, accordingly, to pass any kind of critical judgement on his work, simply to relate it to the events of his life.

This life came to a violent end in dramatic circumstances, heightened by the inevitable attention of press and broadcasting. Certain aspects of Caradock's life have been overemphasised and, under commission from his literary administrators, I have taken it as my duty to set the record straight, as impartially as I am able.

I trust that in this my training as a historian qualifies me to accept the commission. I am confident that purely literary aspects of Caradock's work will be admirably dealt with in other quarters. But whether or not a biographer, however diligent and meticulous, may ever claim to have presented the entire truth rather than a version of what may have been true, and thus perhaps another fiction, is a question of which any reader must take adequate warning.

David Hayward: introductory note to The Life of Michael Caradock. *Hazel & Sims, 1974.*

2

The few remaining blue-black scars on the mountains around the small valley town of Cwmfelyn have all but healed; now and again the sun will strike the ruin of a brick arch, to make an industrial relic as mellow as the fragment of an ancient abbey; there are still in the lower valley tracts of land on which nothing will grow. But elsewhere the patient rehabilitation of Nature goes on: on a spring morning the green land, made lumpy by the ravages of the industrial revolution, seems to be stirring, there is the pleasantly harsh reassurance of rooks, the blackbirds sing prodigally, the little river runs fast and clear over a stony bed, a profusion of broadleaf trees is coming to terms with the new season; where there were once coal tips, disciplined conifers possess the hillside.

So Nature is reclaiming the land to which Griffith

Caradock, master mason, came in the early years of the nineteenth century and which in the next decades he was to see transformed from a rural demi-paradise into an industrial inferno. Griffith did not mind. He was always massively industrious, a clever craftsman willing to turn his hand to many trades; he was thrifty, if not mean; prudent in his way of life though not spectacularly religious. At about the time he was establishing himself in a small way as a builder, he married Gwen Pritchard, daughter of a miller of already comfortable means.

They lived, it seems, a peaceable, quietly devoted life, establishing the bourgeois traditions of several generations to follow them. Griffith worked hard and prospered – without attaining or aspiring to the wealth and position of the iron-masters and coal-owners who profited from the industrial exploitation of the area. His children maintained Griffith's steady increase in fortune and observed the same habits of caution, moderate puritanism and economy. However determined one may be to deal only with the evidence to hand, it is impossible not to speculate about what Griffith Caradock would have thought of his great-great-grandson.

Two of the seven children born to Griffith and Gwen died in infancy. Two others lived only into their early twenties. Of the remaining three, Ann, the only surviving daughter, married a revivalist preacher, who seems to have been a man of fierce scorn for material things, and who viewed with some disfavour the entrepreneurial energy of his wife's family. The eldest of the three, Evan, appears to have been most like his father in temperament and drive.

He took an early interest in the business concerns of Griffith Caradock and broadened their base, by investing in other industries outside building – tinplate, brickworks and steel. The younger of the sons, Isaiah, while showing little aptitude for industry, persuaded his father to go into trade. He began modestly in his own grocer's shop, but in due course was able to open two more and to diversify into hardware and outfitting.

Griffith and Gwen Caradock both spoke Welsh as their mother tongue, so that their children also had it as their first language: but the family was Anglican and, during the torrid revivals of the late nineteenth century, when real misery was put into perspective by the breath of hellfire around the corner, maintained a stolid indifference in the face of Nonconformist encroachment. Besides, while lacking in pretension, the family status was improving – and the gentlefolk went to church, not to chapel. Griffith, a stern old man in the extant photograph, with a direct eye and little hint of humour about his features, would probably not have cared. Evan and Isaiah were quick to take account of the advantages of influence and respectability. Furthermore, Evan married a clergyman's daughter: Rachel Daniel, a remarkably pretty girl in the affecting sepia portraits of family archives, who spoke English only and who had been brought up according to principles of English gentility.

Evan found the Welsh language useful in dealing with his men, with whom he seemed to have an effortlessly rough-and-ready relationship; but none of his six children was encouraged to speak it. Isaiah, a gentler version of his elder brother, married, in his early forties, Rebecca Lloyd, the daughter of another tradesman. She was wholesome in appearance, Welsh speaking and fifteen years his junior. Two years after their marriage she and her child died as she gave birth. Isaiah did not remarry: he became an accepted adjunct of his brother's household, although he insisted on maintaining a place of his own. When the sons inherited their father's estate jointly, no provision having been made for Ann, the daughter, Isaiah seems to have been content to let Evan administer everything outside his own area of expertise. Both prospered.

Of Rachel's children, the three daughters – no doubt with her encouragement – married professional men. There is some evidence that she, a former schoolmistress, held her husband's industrial success in mild contempt, while in no sense despising the income it derived; the daughters, too, were quick to succeed to directorships in family companies when the appropriate moment occurred. There were three sons. The youngest, Paul, was sent to Oxford, became a minor canon in the Welsh marches and seems to have lived a happy, unworldly life well away from the rest of his family. The middle son, Samuel, was put to work with his uncle Isaiah, managing his shops and learning the techniques of local trade. Griffith, named after his grandfather, was intended from the first to take over from Evan Caradock the main direction of the family affairs. Both sons had spent a few years in London – Samuel to work in a bank, Griffith in some minor capacity in the City – and it seems clear that Evan Caradock's determination that his older sons were to carry on the family enterprises must have overruled any more genteel ambitions that their mother might have cherished for them. Three well-married daughters (one to a physician, one to a parson and one to a solicitor) plus one clergyman were as far as Evan was prepared to go.

But the Caradock energy and business acumen were, all the same, tempered by the refinement of Rachel. There is ample historical evidence that small family-based industries declined in South Wales at that time for a variety of reasons, but there is little evidence in family documents that either Griffith or Samuel relished their inheritance. Soon the family's industrial interests had all been sold out, but substantial sums of money were invested in property and stock. They maintained the shops that Isaiah had started, though without conspicuous success. They both aspired to be gentlemen.

Samuel did not marry. Griffith, from the evidence of family papers, fell and remained deeply in love with Jane Rhydderch, daughter of an old friend of his father's, the local GP, in the gruffest heart-of-gold tradition. For many years the doctor and Evan Caradock had taken long Sunday walks together, they went to the same church and occasionally entertained one another according to the convention they shared, which was to meet for a chat and a drink rather than for a formal dinner party. Jane was sent to a ladies' college in England. When she returned to Cwmfelyn, Dr Rhydderch, from whose jottings and letters most of our information comes, was amused by the extent of Griffith's infatuation. It must have been a very justifiable passion. Rachel, Griffith's mother, had been pretty: Jane Rhydderch was beautiful – she wore big hats, close-fitting bodices that emphasised an enticing bosom and a tiny waist, and swirling skirts. In her photographs there is a hint of irrepressible merriment, a light in the eyes, which contrasts strangely with the unsmiling, heavily moustached Griffith. She appears to have acceded readily enough to a marriage that must have pleased both sets of parents. From all accounts she was strong willed and possibly was instrumental in the selling of industrial interests after Evan Caradock's death. The letters she wrote to Griffith, on the few occasions when they were apart, are elegantly phrased, sincere, affectionate. They had two sons – Howell and Edmund.

Both boys were sent to a minor Welsh public school, which they seemed to enjoy. Howell was good at games but in no sense ambitious. Edmund, four years his junior, was cleverer and, from childhood, more mercurial. Upon his brother Samuel's death, the entire Caradock fortune – not vast but considerable enough – passed to Griffith. In 1917 Howell volunteered for army service, which was a source of pride to both of his parents. He saw some action towards the end of the war, incurring a slight wound. Soon after the Armistice, Griffith Caradock himself died and left his entire estate to Jane.

Her younger son, perhaps because he was like her in temperament and taste, was her favourite. He missed the war and went up to Lincoln College, Oxford, where he received a generous allowance. His mother did not care about his academic success, as long as he met the right sort of people. He was an easy-going, attractive character and enjoyed three years reading History, working well enough to achieve a moderate second which qualified him for an appointment at a boarding school in Sussex. His years at the University were relaxed but in no sense riotous and most of his contemporaries remember him as a good-tempered, high-spirited young man much interested in the early cinema. While at Lincoln he met the daughter of a Classics don at another college, Vanessa Rabone: they were married in 1925. Vanessa, a year or so older than her husband, had herself taken a good degree but had given up thoughts of a career in publishing to look after her widower father. This posed no problems: Edmund Caradock liked Oxford and it would not have been difficult for him to find a similar teaching post. But J. L. Rabone had other ideas. He took rooms in his college and encouraged the young people, with undoubted wisdom, to make their own life together, away from Oxford. J. L. Rabone is widely remembered as a gentle scholar, of modest ambitions but felicitous style, by his colleagues and pupils. He was to outlive his daughter and son-in-law by seventeen years.

Vanessa's sister, Mrs Belinda Lagravette, describes her marriage with Edmund as wildly happy. Edmund's mother was generous, Vanessa had a small income of her own – so they were able to supplement his schoolmaster's salary to enjoy various small luxuries. In August 1930, when their only son Michael Julian was two years old and in the care of his grandmother in Wales, Edmund and Vanessa Caradock were killed while driving in their sports car between Zürich and Basle.

Understandably the grief and shock suffered by both families was terrible, but Jane Caradock's firm good sense and J. L. Rabone's balanced compassion made the agreement on the future of the surviving baby a relatively simple matter.

Belinda was about to emigrate to Canada with her husband. She would have taken the child, but wanted a family of her own. Besides, such a course of action would have deprived Jane Caradock and J. L. Rabone of their grandson. And Howell Caradock, invalided out of his career in the regular army some years before, after a serious accident, was very anxious to adopt his brother's son. His own wife, Phyllis, had been told that she could not have children. She was desperate to have the boy. It was a satisfactory solution which, in their wretchedness, they were all relieved to accept.

Michael Julian Caradock might have spent his childhood in the soft and peaceable countryside of southern England with young, intelligent and lively parents; or he might have gone to Canada and become part of a thriving vigorous family in Vancouver. Instead he was brought up by a reserved and nervous couple in a rainy industrial valley whose despoliation was at least in part the fault of his family. They lived in a house built by Evan Caradock in about an acre of ground, masked by trees, set somewhat apart from the rest of the village.

Passage from the opening chapter of the official biography of Michael Caradock by David Hayward.

He was in his usual place: sitting on the battered ledge looking over the steep edge of the mountain down the valley towards the sea that everyone knew was there, a few miles away, but which no one ever saw. Smoke seemed to be belching from

49

every stack in the three works directly in view. What might have been a diffusely benign, promising, red sunset filtered angrily through it. There was a nip in the October air. Tudor was reluctant to approach him that night; very still, the grim, self-mocking, half-smile chiselled onto his mouth, eyes fixed and unblinking as though focused on some bitter joke inside, that only he knew about. He showed no sign of knowing that Tudor was there, looking triumphantly at the drab murk of the green landscape dabbed and smeared with black, thinking that tomorrow he would be away and promising himself that after a year or so he would never be back.

'All right,' the old man said suddenly, without looking round, 'don't just stand there like bloody Pyrrhus grieving at joy. I didn't think I'd be seeing you.'

'I hoped you'd be here,' Tudor said. 'I wanted to say goodbye.'

The old man grunted.

'It's meant a lot to me, Mr Jones. The talks we've had. Up here.' Tudor was not sure that he wasn't making a fool of himself. 'They've helped me see things in a sort of perspective.' He waffled on. 'If that's possible at my age...'

I bloody nearly didn't come myself if only you knew it, young Tudor. See you trying to hide the hope in your face and pretend a thousand things you don't feel, boy. Trying to hide the pity for poor old Jones who never got out of it and stayed buried in the fine falling dust that piled up over the years. But I don't envy you tonight, boy. I don't envy you your gold and green and grey corner of Arcadia in the pastel English weather, or your big career, or your first sight of Manhattan, or your year off the Boulevard St Michel, or your awe under Mount Olympus; or your cabarets, concerts, lectures, love affairs; your boardrooms, brothels, first nights, publishers' parties, late-night sittings, moonlights and thunderstorms. Whatever they are, Tudor, I don't envy your triumphs and disappointments; the intensity that you'll live your life with, the grief, the wonder. Wishing you nothing, because I don't envy you, I'll say something like: Well, get on with it, then. Don't hang about like a bloody mooncalf. Go on. Get out there and start living, will you? And you will go, my boy, a bit puzzled that there was no token of goodwill, only a kind of anger; and think: Poor old Jones. He's envious and I don't blame him. Stumbling down the tussocks of the mountain with your long thin stride and your serious face. Poor old Jones. Well, boy, he's thought that often enough in the past himself. But tonight that weight of nothing that is what time has become for him, that weight of unfulfilment, that load of emptiness lies very lightly. The grimy old field with its clinkers and slag, the grey dirty grass, the scrub and rushes, corner bog and poisoned tree, is full of folk – Llew and Gwydion, Mabon and Myrddin, Gwyn and Peredur and Taliesin; but the others as well – the other less beautiful ones over the years whom no one can put names to. The ordinary ones who have toiled and suffered and struggled with the rain and the wind, the sourness of the seasons, the smoke and the dust, the tyranny of existence, in all its forms. And have rejoiced: sung, sometimes danced, told their stories and made their myths, fleshed out with the fictions that different mortals need in different times. And there are still badgers over the hill there, and more birds than *you* can put a name to, somehow the streams and rivers have stayed clean. And it is *my* place, young Tudor, and these are *my* people. Whatever they are to you. I hope I have done something for you. Poor old Jones. Jones the Failure. Embittered old rhetorician on a barren hill staring at the sky, complaining about what he never might have been. But late as it is in the day, you've given me something too. At least tonight. A sense of belonging somewhere. So you go without envy.

The sky, instead of softening with the dusk, brightened like the last of a fire that is allowed to die. Tudor and the old man stood in silence together watching it flaring behind the smoke and for a long time after, as the angry red faded into deep vermilion and stars began to appear and the lights flicked on in the valley, dim strings, markers of a labyrinth. Occasionally there was a fiery whoosh of red light from a furnace in one of the works.

When the time came to speak, Tudor did not know what to say. He looked helplessly at the old man. Mr Jones leaned heavily on his stick.

'Well,' he said, 'go home and pack. Get on with your life.'

The boy nodded and turned away. He walked quickly from the sad, resentful old man. Then he heard Jones' voice say quietly but clearly:

'Good luck.'

He started to run along the rough track towards the street lights.

Closing passages from Angry Sunset. *Vortex Press, 1952.*

24. Ext. Cwmfelyn. Day. Travelling shot of street in Cwmfelyn: terraced houses, occasional shops, many now empty, pubs, chapels. Turning off past council estate, semi-detached, then detached houses. Square white house in its own grounds, set apart from rest of village	MUSIC: Male Voice Choir singing in Welsh (*Gwenyth Gwyn*) (3c.) (Hold under Lloyd) (V/O) *Lloyd*: Cwmfelyn is now almost a ghost town, but more gentle as a phantom than in its life and vigour. When Caradock walked along these streets, there was still a lot of local industry....
25. Ext. Cwmfelyn from air. Day. Cut to aerial view of village, from mountain: showing dilapidated mine, resown tips, empty ground with village sweeping up opposite hill	Three pits, now all closed down, were then working; further along, other industries. And down the valley two steelworks. But for all that, the community knows these days a prosperity then undreamed of. And it is a greener and a brighter spot...
26. Still of Cwmfelyn in 1930s	than the place which Michael Caradock hated, or affected to hate, so much as a young man.
27. Still of Cwmfelyn under pall of smoke... (circa 1936) 28. Still of valley seen from mountain (1941)	He was a willing, almost a conscientious, misfit in the cultural and social life of his village. Cut off, as he liked to think, by his background and family from all real contact

29. Still of village carnival in 1930s

with other people, and yet prevented by his foster mother's anxieties from escaping to a private school.
(Lift music briefly and lose.)

30. Still of village from air with Caradock house noticeable. Zoom in on house and hold:

The young man in *A Coriolan Overture* enjoys his sense of otherness....

31. Ext. Cwmfelyn scene. Day. Dramatisation of novel. 'Marcus' (played by James Maple) in blazer and cavalry-twill trousers leaves Caradock house, swinging walking stick... medium shot

MUSIC: Richard Strauss: *Ein Heldenleben*. (1.D.)

Medium shot 'Marcus' walks down the hill from house towards the village. Into distance and around corner

Close shot 'Marcus' pausing and lighting black cigarette. Three 'miners', still begrimed from pit (these were days before pithead baths) approach from opposite direction. Two of the men smile slowly....

54

c.u. 'Marcus' inhaling his
black cigarette

'Miners'. Two older ones with
broadening smiles. The third,
younger man, spits
deliberately and violently into
a hedge. Medium shot

'Marcus' reacts. Then shrugs
and walks on jauntily enough

*Sequence from television programme, 'Landscape of a
Prophet', with narration by Trevelyan Lloyd.*

Howell Caradock evidently enjoyed the army and after the
incident at Jericho in 1925, during the Mandate, when he
was badly hurt, was at a loss for an alternative career. He
returned to his mother's house at Cwmfelyn and retained
his army rank. He spent some months in plaster and is
supposed to have suffered considerable pain throughout
the rest of his life, although he complained of it to very
few people. He had very few friends. Jane Caradock's
affairs were in the hands of a solicitor who practised in a
town some distance away.

This solicitor, F. Cecil Jenkyn, had never had any
connection with industry. His immediate ancestors had
been farmers first, then businessmen, investing in legal and
medical careers for their sons and in good marriages
(among the gentry) for their daughters. F. Cecil Jenkyn had
joined an established firm, helped develop its practice,
accepted a partnership and, in due course, senior direction.

No solicitor turns business away – but Jenkyn enjoyed the confidence of relatively rich clients drawn from a fifteen-mile radius. He was quick tempered, hard working, openly contemptuous to people whom he considered his inferiors: but this earned him the grudging respect of the very people he bullied. His wife was a former governess who remained in awe of the family she had served. They had one daughter: a frail, fair-haired, spoiled girl, adored by and adoring her father. She came to depend on him a great deal and he was in the habit of indulging her. F. Cecil Jenkyn was a man of volatile energy, which his daughter Phyllis did not inherit, but he bequeathed her a great deal of money and his determination. Consistent ill health and over-anxious parents had contributed to her expectation of always being granted her own way. Shortly after his return to Cwmfelyn, Phyllis Jenkyn and Howell Caradock met and within eighteen months married. Jane Caradock was relieved that her amiable but unassertive son would have someone to look after him. (She had no worries about the younger Edmund, with his enthusiasms and his intelligent, lively wife.) F. Cecil Jenkyn was satisfied that his daughter had found a husband who would give her no trouble, whose financial status was more than pleasing. They were married in October 1926. In February 1928 Phyllis suffered a miscarriage; she was told she would not be able to bear children and this came to her as a severe shock.

The GP at the time, Dr Ivor Alexander, now a hale eighty-seven and living on the coast about twenty miles away, remembers the young woman's grief and Howell's gentle if uncomprehending approach to her. Jane Caradock was, naturally, sympathetic; but many different witnesses suggest that she worked very hard to conceal extreme impatience with her daughter-in-law. After the death of Edmund and Vanessa, she became more resigned to things as they were. The Rev. Cledwyn Rogers, then curate in the village of Cwmfelyn, also recalls the extent of Phyllis Caradock's despair as he heard it from his vicar and is inclined to think that she perhaps deserved a deeper sympathy than she was accorded. Certainly, Dr Alexander is sure that, in trying to bring the couple to a more resilient point of view, he was insensitive to Phyllis' own psychological problems.

Phyllis Caradock nursed her sorrow. Howell Caradock did nothing very much. He read the financial pages, he transacted business on his own and his mother's behalf, he played a little golf. Of his very few friends, two – Leslie Chambers and J. Rudmose Bowen – say that he sometimes talked of taking up this or that work. Chambers, who in due course became a partner in the Jenkyn legal practice, describes Howell as lamenting, wryly, the decline of the family's industrial interests; on the assumption that an ex-officer was *de facto* suited for management. Bowen, a golfing acquaintance, remembers that Howell Caradock contemplated leaving Cwmfelyn. While Jane Caradock offered no objection and would probably have welcomed her son's finding something positive to do with his life, Phyllis became immediately ill at the threat of being moved away from her parents. The symptoms that she developed were convincing. Dr Alexander, who treated her, makes two relevant comments: that less was known in those days about psychosomatic disorders; and that a neurotic condition is still an illness. In retrospect, he is disposed to admire Howell Caradock's reserves of patience.

Then Phyllis' problems were eclipsed by the deaths of Edmund and Vanessa, who seemed to have been blithely unaware of anything but their own young and lyrical marriage. This is probably an exaggeration: but both Jane Caradock and J. L. Rabone were undemanding parents and there is no reason to suppose that the relationship between Edmund and Howell was ever close. Shortly before his death, the Rev. Taliesin Poole, then in retirement in Herefordshire, but once vicar at Cwmfelyn, spoke of Phyllis' near hysteria when she heard of Michael Julian Caradock's birth. He spent several hours trying to comfort her.

So the child was in the care of a sensitive but sometimes hysterical woman who, having herself been delicate, was determined to watch over him with the same kind of doting anxiety. She fussed over him, perhaps with the subconscious intention of making him as dependent on her as she was on her own father. Jane Caradock might have made some impact upon her grandson's upbringing: so might J. L. Rabone – but when Jane died suddenly in 1934, J. L. Rabone saw his grandson rarely in the subsequent years, returning easily into the celibate comfort of an Oxford college which, in those years at least, made old griefs more bearable. He died in 1947, a few months before his grandson went up to his university.

Howell Caradock was always keen that Michael Julian should go to a good public school and was certainly prepared to spend as much on the boy's education as was needed. If not Rugby, or Clifton, or Repton, or Blundells, at least the school to which *he* had been sent. Phyllis resisted. The child was too delicate. War had come and there was such danger... Jane Caradock was not there to put forward a point of view. F. Cecil Jenkyn was. For a variety of reasons, Howell Caradock usually gave in to the wishes of his wife. When he did not, he was no match for his father-in-law.

So Michael Caradock was the victim of paradox in that the very woman who encouraged him to identify with a class feeling that had very little to do with Cwmfelyn, or the valley in which it lay, was instrumental in sending him to local schools, where he was forced to be a part of its daily life. Small children, if they are allowed to, try to adapt. The boy picked up phrases, locutions, words that made Phyllis wince. He was sometimes bullied: having been overprotected, he did not know how to deal with the situation. In the evenings he was comforted.

If the Caradocks had been Tories since the days of Evan, because they woke up and found that they were, the Jenkyns were ideological. Howell Caradock more or less believed that the working classes were thriftless, feckless, lacking initiative and susceptible to agitators who were motivated by envy. Phyllis was absolutely certain of it.

D. J. Herbert was headmaster of the elementary school at Cwmfelyn and happened to know Howell Caradock through a connection with his maternal grandfather, old Dr Rhydderch. He told the foster-parents that they must either 'stop coddling the boy into a nervous wreck, or put him in a bloody prep school'.

But Michael Julian Caradock went to school among

children from homes where the Caradock family was loathed with a virulence that matched its own deep-rooted contempt.

Extract from David Hayward's official biography.

By the time that boy was sixteen or seventeen he'd read Baudelaire, Verlaine, Rimbaud, a lot of Valéry, Gide, Thomas Mann, some Joyce, not to mention Goethe, Dostoyevsky, Melville, Stendhal; and the stuff you'd expect – Eliot, early Auden and the others. The one he couldn't get on with was Proust. Funny. Anyway the point I'm making is that he couldn't wait to spread his own wings. He realised there was a lot more than the valley and if he resented anything it was the constricted way of life. And it *is* constricted. And also the claustrophobia of his home. From what I hear, Phyllis Caradock was a silly affected woman, but the boy wasn't interested in social or political stances. He wanted to be part of a bigger, if you like a more permissive, world. A world that tolerated eccentricity and elegance. He was an innocent.

John Morris, retired clerk in chemical engineering company in neighbouring town, resident in Cwmfelyn. Thought by some critics to be the original of Jones in Angry Sunset.

Michael Caradock – the Enigma. Donnish exile; fastidious bon viveur; part-time bohemian; passionate puritan; Axel in his castle; Faust in his study; *Prometheus* pinned to his rock; surly recluse bent upon his own destruction.

The Man may be drawn in bold outline, with confident strokes; the Writer emerges from a subtle complexity of shape and colour like the central idea of a cubist conception.

60

But the Enigma is a vague sketch: miasmal, wraithlike, shadowplay of cloud and sunlight in a strange and ancient woodland.

In pursuing the Man and assessing the Writer, it is my purpose to capture the Enigma: to define and describe the prejudices and passions, the angers and delights of this extraordinary man, possibly a genius; to put under a spectroscope the love-hatred he bore towards his native land – the love-hatred which took him away and which drew him back, which was the spur to his fame and the impulse towards his death.

We begin with the small boy, already something of a dreamer in the gardens of his big house, where he played for the most part alone: and the rude shock that came to him when he was thrown into the robust rough and tumble of the local junior school playground. The grazes on hands, knees and elbows healed: those on the mind festered.

Derek Parnell: In His Own Country, *critical biography of Michael Caradock, published within six months of his death. Guildenstern, 1970.*

Sweet sleep. Say rather the cloying sweetness of putrefaction. A sticky, gummy respite for a few minutes from the million cuts of memorised self-pity. Reach for the bottle. Empty. Send the manuscript over the water, over the dull rain-threatened estuary to the smug village and the white house, over the seas – bearing a message of despair, tainted by the fingers reddened by plague.

A master of destruction wounds himself and it is that very wound that forces him to live, though sick and mad, in some high frosty tower from which the morning looks clear and the pearl mist rises off the shining lake. More and more mountains come into view and suddenly the huge and terrifying peak that jolts the recuperating, dawning conscience back into insanity. The fierce brow contracts and knots in tears and despair springing acid to the eyes. Implosion of grief and fear and self-pity. A small boy set upon by the ganged-up mysteries he will no longer attempt to struggle with.

Perhaps. Wandering alone through empty rooms, always with mirrors, gazing, wondering, peering into cupboards stuffed with junk, old music, meaningless, valueless objects never thrown out. Gazing at the rain over the dank valley sweeping up from the hidden sea, running into smoke and ochre fumes darkening the dun and barren mountain to grey. Always the sudden ambush, the unexplained hostility, the laughter behind a curtain and one's own name woven into the mocking noise. Pin-pricks, what are cudgel blows? The buffoonish smile of the weakling with brains greeted by the snarl of the emboldened lackey. The Fool and the Kapo. Sycophants around the infant führer, who has grown into an accounts clerk or a hag-ridden navvy. It is only that there the brutality was nearer the surface, more obvious; listen to the savagery in the acacias, the hiss between the teeth of the tamarisks. Grey playgrounds and the ritual of threat and conciliation. One does not hate as long as one despises: but early one learns to despise the clownish attempt to win the favour of the strong and stupid. Self-hatred comes only with age.

Morning moving up there beyond the even silverfish

62

lacquering of cloud. Somewhere the sun as on those sharp-edged peaks where the mad and lost Nietzsche corrugated with pain knew what warmth there was of the heights, above that cloud, somewhere the sun blazes pitilessly down on our accident.

Do not think of her now as she moves. The power supple in those resiliently submissive limbs. The intricate and new sense of triumph in fibre and nerve and muscle; her smile and the laugh, corpuscles and cells, lymph and hormone and plasma, strictly perishable. Making her some instrument of destiny and cruelty and misery. What she would not: that she does.

Trees are empty. And no birds sing. Purposeful flight and the routine calling to a purpose. But no song.

She lies and smiles. Smiles easily. The rest of us lay bare the grimace which tells the truth. The waters rise and rise. She is in danger perhaps. A disturbance in the cloud. A faint straight thrust of light onto the stirring water, until then sullen.

The qualities shared by Caradock's central characters have very little to do with any kind of warmth or compassion. Baldwin, Fleming, Waldeck and Landgrave are self-regarding to a degree: they are all clever, well read, reflective men – concerned with Man and more or less indifferent to men. Each of them, significantly, is at pains to render himself invulnerable to assault and disappointment, suspicious of those around him, even the most dedicated, beyond all reason. Their only feasible relationships are with certain women and even then these relationships are nervous and selfish. Among men they are all, however powerful and intellectually commanding, defensive, wary, almost paranoid.

The lighter characters – Marcus Conrad in *A Coriolan Overture* and Laertes Jones – are also remarkably cold: their main concern is to develop a carapace strong enough to protect them from small hurts, and antennae sensitive enough to avoid major dangers. Each of them is an impure fool, profiting from gullibility with well-simulated surprise – in other words, a hypocrite. Hypocrisy was something Caradock claimed to recognise and despise in himself.

It is, however, to the early novel, *Angry Sunset*, that we must turn for the first signs of this contrived independence which to many people, who know and love valleys like the one in which Caradock spent his youth, seems to be a wilfully distorted portrait.

With little interest or concern for literature in his home background, the young man was befriended by an accounts clerk, John Morris, whose family circumstances before and after marriage had frustrated what might have been an excellent academic career. Morris was a voracious and disciplined reader, a ready talker and a great encourager. Furthermore he was apolitical. He was about forty when he became interested in Michael Caradock's eager and receptive mind, but many people have chosen to take him as the model for the disappointed and embittered old man, Jones, in *Angry Sunset*. Like Jones, John Morris had been forced to abandon his early academic aspirations because of family poverty upon the death from silicosis of his father; like Jones, he married a woman whose health deteriorated almost immediately; like Jones, he was a fluent and erudite man, given to fanciful philosophising. But it is worth noting in the first two respects that Howell Caradock also resembled the fictional character: his career had been thwarted by circumstances outside his control and he had married an ailing woman. We have little to go on as to whether this reserved and obscure man sometimes gave vent to outbursts of bitterness, but there is absolutely no evidence to suppose that John Morris was ever disposed to complain.

Jones seems to me to be rather an amalgam of Morris' wide-ranging literary and historical imagination, Howell Caradock's somewhat pitiful stasis and perhaps a dozen other frustrations observed by the quick eye of an ambitious young man who was terrified of being trapped in that village, in that particular house, or by *any* woman whose demands were going to prevent him achieving what he had set out to do.

Nevertheless, the stark and brutal picture of the valley, remarkably different from the gentle setting for the lyrical stories in his first published volume, bears little resemblance to the truth. The young man is determined at all costs to get away and *find* himself somewhere – anywhere – else.

Stephen Lewis: The Novels of Michael Caradock. *Molyneux, 1971.*

There's been far too much made of the man's dislike of this place. His bitter memories of a glowering adolescence and so on. He was unhappy as a kid, yes. But so are most kids – if not in school, then at home. The main thing in his life was to do something big in literature. And to do that he thought, quite rightly, that he had to get away from Cwmfelyn. All this garbage about his hatred is the result of legends built up in books and in the press after his death.

I think that Caradock's problems were as much a reaction against his life at Dan-y-graig, with Howell and Phyllis Caradock, and the family as a reaction against this community.

And, by the way, that's as much a guess as anything else. He was a reticent lad and he said nothing to me about Cwmfelyn because it would hurt my feelings, and nothing about his foster parents, except very obliquely, because it would have been indiscreet.

John Morris, early mentor, in BBC radio programme.

The paradoxes of Nietzsche are (for me, at least) endlessly interesting. I believe that man is a master of destruction, in particular of self-destruction, but I cannot see that it is the wounds that he inflicts upon himself that force him to live. Perhaps I am obtuse and Nietzsche does not mean 'to go on living', for unlike Nietzsche I am not able to see that 'the thought of suicide is a great consolation'. Suicide is not acceptable because it is the ultimate act of defeat. It is no consolation, even as a thought, because it is unthinkable. Especially unthinkable to one who esteems the wound as a literal *raison d'être*. My rejection of suicide as a possibility (please notice that I do not use alternative) is not based on arguments, moving as they are, to be found in *The Myth of Sisyphus*. They are based on the much more despairing thesis that suffering in some form is inevitable and must be borne: not because it is better to live than to die, but because it is not possible to admit defeat as part of a rational process. If we become too weak because of hunger or torture, we shall die; if we become mad so that we hazard our bodies or neglect them, we shall die; if our judgement is deranged, we may obey an impulse to kill ourselves which is irredeemable. But we cannot rationally sit down and plan our defeat. We are defeated when we are defeated. Or we are not. Not defeated. The wound, especially the self-inflicted wound, is a foolish exercise in living to test how much we can bear. The accidental wound, when we are physically or psychologically or morally or emotionally hurt, however agonising, is something that we accept as part of learning how we are, not how to be. The self-inflicted wound can be accidental: occasioned by birth, environment, circumstance; the accidental wound can be self-inflicted: the result of carelessness, selfishness, malice.

Committed to hospital, recently, for minor surgery, I became aware that I was submitting to a necessary but not an essential wound. I was, as so many others must have been who are not in urgent need of treatment, as interested as I was frightened. How would I, inconspicuously brave, to say the least, bear the pain and inconvenience? How would I behave, before, during and after the disposal of my well-being into the hands of a totally dispassionate professional? I diagnosed, accordingly, on my own behalf, a chronic spiritual hypochondria. The notion of a physical wounding came as a diversion, a relief – in the antiseptic and comfortable conditions of a good teaching hospital.

This may seem a frivolous train of thought, especially in the context of our long, shared history of war and inhumanity: but the Wound, self-inflicted, accidental, or mystic, is of considerable interest in the mythologies of the ancient world (for example, Philoctetes) and in medieval legend, where the implications of the Wound which will not heal as suffered by a sinning, guilty chieftain (for example, Amfortas), cause suffering on a much wider scale in that the land is waste and visited by disease.

Philoctetes, however he came by his wound – accidentally in some stories, as a result of human or divine malice in others, through his own perfidy in a third version – must be restored in order to win a particular battle: that is, to put an end to a state of waste, in this case the Trojan War. Amfortas, physically and morally wounded, must be restored to health so that famine and pestilence be banished from his lands. In each case, there are elaborate formulae of questions and answers that must be worked through before the restoration is possible. In each case, a relatively pure protagonist is necessary in the personae of Diomedes on the one hand, and Parsifal on the other.

Both essential myths are susceptible to the sophistications of their respective periods, disparate, equally interesting and fascinating in their points of correspondence. And it is hardly necessary to refer to the numerous poems and plays about Philoctetes, and certainly not to the complex development of the central imagery of the Grail legend, as developed by T. S. Eliot and many others.

I may be entirely wrong, because my scholarship is unquestionably lacking, but I don't think that anyone has connected the Wound with certain hypotheses put forward by Nietzsche. And so, I am inclined to put forward a theory of my own: that we all suffer from an elemental wound that we become aware of only in early middle age. This wound is real, whether it was dealt by circumstance or imagined circumstance: it is the wound of rancour, disappointment, frustration and despair. In its noisome foetor we suffer a delirium in which we are full of hatred for what has gone, what is and what is likely to be. Self-pitying, we list justly all the occasions when we have been badly used, mocked, beaten, assaulted. And depending upon our psychological condition, we give ourselves up totally, partly or briefly to this hatred. After which comes guilt. We are prepared to take on to ourselves the consequences of the black hatred in a huge guilt: our hatred is our guilt. Punishment would be an expiation for the hatred and for the evil that bred hatred. But we take upon ourselves a guilt which cannot be expiated by punishment because it is something we begin to enjoy. And we despise ourselves for this. Once again it is Nietzsche who comments that 'he who despises himself esteems himself all the same as self-despised'.

What is the real guilt? There is a war that we have to join to stop; a land that may be saved by our purgation. And we do not care.

Extract from 'An Elemental Wound', title essay of a collection. Hazel & Sims, 1963.

I think he really longed to get away. I couldn't blame him, I must say, because I found it a very constricting place. I came from Cardiff which is a port, as you know, and a really pleasant cosmopolitan town. And because I'm a Jew I was used to the pleasures and perils of mixing with other people, and also a fairly liberal outlook on politics and the arts and so on. So the narrowness of Cwmfelyn at that time surprised me and depressed me. I taught Michael Caradock Maths and he was absolutely no good at it but then in the sixth form he joined a literary society that I'd started and I got to know him. There was something there, I thought. And of course it's been proved. The other boys were good, harder working, intelligent, but Caradock had an extra curiosity. There were some very good girls, but he had very little success with them, and as a consequence pretended to be aloof and supercilious. I talked to him quite a lot about books and, I like to think, helped him along a little. He knew French and English literature pretty well, but I introduced him to people like Freud and Jung and various philosophers. In fact – it makes me laugh now, but it was serious enough at the time – I had a flaming row with Leyshon (I think he was called), the English master, because I'd put Caradock onto Nietzsche. I don't know whether you've talked to him, but he didn't like the boy. In fact, very few of the staff did. There was a Classics mistress, whose name escapes me, a very pretty girl. They got on very well. Perhaps that did something for his confidence.

... Yes, I think, on the whole, he hated the school and the other pupils quite a lot. Not to mention the village. It really was dismal, you know. Not so bad for me because I could go home at weekends to Cardiff and I was thinking of marrying. But for a young and ambitious boy. Awful. Another thing: I find the valley Welsh, even in the South, about as unresponsive to new ideas as it's possible to be. They don't trust people and yet they make a great show of warmth. As soon as Caradock showed signs of wanting out, so to speak, he was as much a stranger in his own

70

village as I was or as you would be. I knew nothing of his family except that they were Tories and kept themselves as much apart as possible from the rest of the village. My landlady rather liked them, as I remember. She was C of E and had some vague connection with the family....

H. (Howard) Paul, formerly Maths master at Cwmfelyn County School, now Headmaster, Brook Vale Comprehensive School, London, NW.

He not only hated the place, he hated the people, he hated the working class and he really... he was the most misanthropic individual I ever met. I was astounded to hear him go on, at Oxford – all very brilliant, very mordant, you know. And what he could not see was that the bloody Wykehamists and Etonians were laughing *at* him not *with* him. I can't think of anything more sickening. So he was thumped in the schoolyard, but I'll bet the teachers never laid a finger on him, as they did me, and as they did all the other poor sods who were in Caradock's school whose daddies weren't majors. And a lot of those kids came to school, if I know anything about it, with ragged arses and hollow stomachs. And of course they resented him. They had everything to resent.

George Shelley, journalist, in BBC radio programme.

Oh, all children are vicious when they've nothing better to do.

James Faber in BBC radio programme.

Behind the walls of Dan-y-graig, Phyllis Caradock was able for the first three years of her care of the child to live in a fantasy of English middle-class gentleness. She read Beatrix Potter and A. A. Milne and the little boy lived in a world of nannies, nurseries and talking toys quite foreign to the realities of life in Cwmfelyn. Howell Caradock was content to watch in a somewhat bemused way, no doubt enormously pleased and relieved that his wife had something to devour her interest. She was unquestionably happy....

The awakening from the gentle world of children's books came when Michael Julian went to school. He went at first without any fuss, but within a few weeks had to be taken by George Parker, who worked in the Caradocks' garden several days a week. It was a school of all sorts and conditions. There were the sons and daughters of doctors, teachers and other professional people; there were the children of the proud, chapel-going working class, as immaculately dressed, as meticulously cared for, already carrying the latent hope of their parents. But there were also the children of the defeated and embittered workers, some of whose fathers were out of work, some of whom came from overcrowded and violent homes and who knew far too well what it was like to be thrashed for nothing on a bad Saturday night, to see their mothers abused, to be clouted by older brothers or sisters out of sheer bloody-minded temper. Left to fend for themselves from a very early age, they were prematurely wise about sex from the evidence of their eyes, giggling behind shrubs on the mountainside; or of their ears, awake in small, cramped houses.

In later life Michael Caradock claimed to have an unerring talent for knowing how and when the 'rat-pack', as he called them, would move; and he kept himself well apart from any clique, or identifiable group. It appears that from the moment he left Wales for Oxford, he was always anxious to keep aloof: in fact people who knew him during his naval service and his many acquaintances in London remark that he was always careful to keep apart from the interests and attitudes of those among whom he might find himself pigeon holed. He wanted to be an outsider.

D. J. Herbert was headmaster of the elementary school during those few years so bitterly remembered; and a fairly cordial acquaintance, if not a friend, of Howell Caradock. He does not think that Michael Julian adapted too badly to his school. He points out that in those days there was less theory, less money available, resources were incomparably poorer and that there was less equality in village life. Furthermore, at least fifty per cent of his pupils came to school because they had to. He remembers, with some amusement, the attendance officer (known as the 'whipper-in') who rode the streets on a small motor-cycle wearing a well-cared-for brown trilby bellowing the draggling children into school. These children had no interest in being educated and received no encouragement from parents who were as anxious as anything in those hard times for them to be out at work bringing in a few badly needed shillings. The fact that Caradock was a very bright child did not endear him to these others. It is doubtful whether Caradock was ever teacher's pet: most of the teachers probably disliked his already arrogant confidence in his quickness of mind, and had neither liking nor respect for his background: but the teachers treated him circumspectly where they were often severe to other boys, and when his work was good he was, of course, praised.

Mr Herbert, now seventy-eight, is inclined to see Caradock in the perspective of these others. There was not, he insists, much bullying at the school: isolated examples, normal childish badness. He thinks that what Caradock must have experienced was largely accidental, at the hands of slightly older children. 'You know the kind of thing. Weakness brings out the worst in some, doesn't it? And I think the boy became nervous and seemed to be more cowardly than he was. He was, at best, only tolerated in gangs. So he was easy prey for the kind of lone wolf – not much good at anything, not much liked by his mates, probably a bit mean by nature, who was looking for someone to take his general sense of grievance out on. And who may have heard his father say of the Caradocks, "bloody Tory trash", or something of the sort.'

Almost certainly Mr Herbert is right. In the twenties and thirties the 'haves' were resented by the 'have-nots', especially when they seemed to do very little for what they had. Phyllis Caradock had inherited an outlook from her father, F. Cecil Jenkyn, that the unemployed were largely shiftless and work-shy people, without initiative or any sense of responsibility. While Cwmfelyn and its valley were not hit as severely by unemployment in the thirties as other parts of Wales, or indeed other parts of Britain, there were substantial numbers of men out of work, and on certain days of the week they would be seen in the main part of the village near the Labour Exchange, collecting their dole, and stopping, if the weather was good, to chat. Caradock, in response to my questioning, once described large numbers of them squatting on their hunkers, in the way of miners, or standing in groups, apparently for long periods, talking. He could not recall much mirth or jollity in these gatherings. But no doubt the men concerned felt that they had little to feel jolly about. Caradock admitted that these groups of idle men made him feel uneasy, even as a small boy.

Extract from David Hayward's official biography.

'Late on the Saturday afternoon, the first trucks began to arrive from the South. It was a beautiful summer and the trucks were loaded with men in shirtsleeves and light clothing, all excited, some no doubt drunk, pale arms and faces – faces split in enormous gash grins, laughing, occasionally thrusting up their right arms with the fist clenched....

'I watched from my study window. I had rented a house in a southern suburb of the city, believing at the time that my exile from power would be only a temporary matter. It was a new and entirely disagreeable sensation – to feel so entirely impotent, knowing that I could have prevented the crisis, convinced that I could speak to the men and make them understand, certain that they would still trust me.

'I had travelled in the South at the end of the war and they had welcomed me, even though the feeling between the Communists and ourselves was bitter. There was no question that the Communists were, with allied parties, in control: the entire area was industrial, the people were poor in spite of the war boom and the extraordinary chance that they had missed the worst of the bombing of industrial plant; their memories were long and bleak. Traditions, economics and language cut them off from the North with its Royalist allegiances, its rich agricultural heritage, its peasant self-sufficiency, avarice and independence. Yet they had welcomed me. I was a popular hero, then. I rode, standing up, in the back of a small open car which was pocked with bullet marks where I had come under fire. They knew the story, of course: we had been ambushed by a pocket of the collaborationist militia on our way to the capital for a Victory march and we had stopped to fight. Claudian was with me even then, very young, working as a propagandist. It was too good an opportunity to miss and Claudian made the most of it. My closest aides were worried and wanted me to travel in a closed armoured car – not to expose myself to a possible assassination attempt. Claudian argued against it. I was a popular hero: heroes were not afraid: I was to stand up in an open car, confident that the mob would tear to pieces anyone who dared raise a hand against me. I have never been troubled by physical fear, but I knew exactly what risk I was taking.

'Some years before, when I was still a junior colonel, I had been sent with troops to the area during a period of unrest. My orders were to put down the earliest tokens of revolution. And I should have done so. Conditions were very bad, at that time, before the great war. I drove through the area, first, to gather whatever impressions I could on the widest scale – Laix, Karlsberg, Köningsbad, Vallibre. In the towns and villages there were men in the squares and streets, standing in groups on the kerbs, arguing on corners. Unsmiling, grey-faced men with dulled eyes and hunched shoulders in shabby clothes – the harvest of despair ripe for the opportunist scythe; ragged children, with pinched faces, barefoot and alive to all the excitement. No one had enough to eat. There was no hope. In a village outside Vallibre they stoned my car.

'That night I returned to Laix, dressed in old civilian clothes, and went out into the working-class quarters in the east of the town. Seen close, their eyes were not dull: there was in all too many the feverish yellow glow of deep resentment, the light of undernourishment, of humiliation, of the hideous desperation that comes to a man who sees his wife wasting and his children sick from want. I mingled with them, saying little, listening. I wanted more than anything to help these men. I spoke their language. They were my people. I wanted to serve them and deliver them from this misery. And I knew even then that I could do it; that it was my destiny to serve.

'A few days later in the same town we received word that crowds were drifting in the direction of the Town Square. There was no reason – no specific reason for a demonstration – no festival, no anniversary, no visiting dignitary, not even a municipal meeting. They were not marching. No processions with banners and slogans. Just a movement of men, for the most part silent, diffuse but gathering in mass and momentum as it approached the Town Hall. I climbed to the highest point in the building and watched them approaching, it seemed in independent groups, through the streets, watched the crowd growing and swelling, watched them quicken pace. I ordered my troops to line up, armed, in front of the Town Hall. When the square was full, there was only a low savage murmur, a guttural, choked sound of powerless rage. No shouting, no sign of riot even though the protest seemed to be spontaneous and under no overall discipline. If they had attacked, I should have ordered my men to fire – at first over their heads and then into the crowd. I became bitterly ashamed. It must not happen. I left the building and walked down the steps of the Town Hall into the crowd. I did not speak to anyone; I did not try to argue, much less threaten or cajole; but I stopped every now and then and looked at a man, who seemed to me to be strong and resolute, looked at him in the face, seriously. Without speaking. Eventually, on an impulse, to one such man, I offered my hand. He grasped it. Then another, then another.

'It was the most colossal luck. It needed only one of them to aim a blow at me, to fell me, it needed only the first demonstration of hostility for a bloody and evil riot to break out. If it had been an organised demonstration, or if the Communists had been able to improvise rapidly enough on the extempore expression of frustration and discontent, it might have been the beginning of a bush fire that would have engulfed the whole industrial South of our country within a few days. It would have meant civil war.

'I claim no credit for what I did. It was an impulsive and a foolish gesture, but I do not regret having made it. When my superiors in the capital heard of it, I was quickly relieved of that command. The right-wing government and the Chiefs of Staff thought I was too dangerous a radical to be entrusted with the work. I was removed to a routine appointment in an African territory, from which I returned only after the outbreak of the war. I was, I remind you, an insignificant junior colonel. Very few people, no more than a dozen or so, knew my name. But, naturally, when I returned to the South after the liberation, my political enemies had bruited it everywhere as belonging to the erstwhile commander of a company of troops who had been sent there during the depressed years to quell any signs of rebellion.

'Yet they welcomed me. I knew, I was sure, that I could unite us. That I could serve *all* our people. I could hear the echo of my sense of mission in their voices, in the shouts along the way. Within three months, because I submitted to election when I could have taken power, I had been outmanoeuvred politically, deserted by my allies in other countries who saw fit to work against me, and rejected by my people.'

Axel Waldeck's head, leonine as a stone emperor, thrust back so that his jaw jutted forward and the lamplight caught the deep, grim lines around the wide, tight-lipped mouth, as he paused: but his eyes remained impassive under the thick brows. He shifted them to Ganuret, breathed in heavily through his nose and pushed the decanter of brandy at him. Ganuret did not move.

'You can imagine,' Waldeck went on in the same even voice, 'with what bitterness I watched those trucks arriving in the capital, bent upon imposing their angry will on the nation, organised and drilled to achieve chaos. You can imagine my rage at opportunities lost. The trucks went on arriving from the South all through the next day, a Sunday. Dissidents in the capital itself began to mobilise and demonstrate. The riot companies were deployed. Then, came the news that other opposed units, loyal to the King, were coming in from the North. A mob went along one of the most fashionable streets, where the bourgeois liked to sit on Sundays in summer on the café terraces, overturning tables, smashing windows – but they were dispersed quickly enough by the gendarmerie without need of riot companies or the army. The detachments from the South, ferried in, were camping in rough conditions in the three woodland parks to the south-west of the capital. What worried me and my staff (Ganz and Claudian were with me) was their discipline. They were working to orders and to a strategy.

'In the afternoon I made my way on foot to the Cathedral of St Ursula in the Place Royale. There were a lot of people on the streets, which surprised me because, erroneously, I expected the populace generally to share my own foreboding about the danger imminent. Of course, I was not recognised. A demonstration was called, for 1500 hours, in the Place. Once again I climbed, as I had done in the town of Laix, to a point of vantage dominating the square and the streets which fed it: but this time, in the tower of the cathedral, I was able to go much higher and to see much further afield.

'I was frightened. Not for my own body which has always meant little to me. But deeply frightened for all that I realised, however imprecisely and foggily, I believed in: civilised order, unselfish service, freedom of ideas and art, voluntary brotherhood. There were unruly crowds here and there – bawling and milling about, watched by the riot companies; there were sporadic incidents on a minor scale.

But then came the two disciplined, tramping columns from the western parklands, growing as they were joined by sympathisers. I watched the streets emptying before them, the shopkeepers scurrying to shutter their windows, the sudden emptiness of fear. I don't suppose you, Ganuret, have ever experienced the hollow silence of a curfew. It was something of that sort. The march on the Place Royale was brilliantly organised. As they approached the two columns became four, eight, twelve – until all the streets leading to the square were full of marching men and they were shouting. Not imbecile slogans: ululations of indecipherable words, comprehensible only as awakened wrath.

'Eventually the square beneath was full of them, full of an unbelievable din. I was thankful that there was no sign of an opposing band of demonstrators, in spite of the rumours that had reached us; and that the army and the police were keeping calm and playing for time. To what purpose I could not tell: it seemed that the evil moment of extreme civil violence would only at best be delayed. The roar rose in volume to an immense crescendo and then seemed to falter. It is an experience that I cannot adequately communicate: a great rage of sound, as all-devouring as a great wind, suddenly at the height of its violence seeming to quaver, to miss a beat; from being a huge concerted cyclonic force, to break up into disparate, separate eddies of noise, failing to reassert itself, never again regaining its original impetus. And where there had been an apparently solid mass of people, there were now spaces in the square and small whorls of activity spinning off so that what had been a huge concerted density of impacted energy seemed visibly to be breaking up, dribbling into the streets around, scattering in power. By what miracle, I did not know.

'Then I saw that it was no miracle. The Royal Standard which had been flying above the Palace had been lowered. A uniformed officer, escorted by four armed soldiers, was marching across the forecourt with a notice. He affixed it in a special display case outside the gates, usually for bulletins about royal events.

'I realised what had happened. Suddenly all the latent fury was dissipated, the demonstrators were confused and their organisers could not get around fast enough to resurrect that rapturous anger that is necessary to sustain a mob. The King had abdicated and, for the moment at least, there was no focus for their rage and it was almost already spent....'

Extract from Promethead. *Hazel & Sims, 1967.*

Waldeck, more than any other character in the fictive sequence, reflects the contra-active forces at work in Caradock as determined by his psychosocial experience at the post-infantile stage of development, when he must have been relating nascent pregenital sexuality to external sense data and to psychosensory conceptualisations, as yet unformulated, based upon apperception.

A significant passage in the book describes two riots, witnessed by Waldeck, neither of which burgeons. In both there is the same climactic progression towards a fulfilment which is never reached: in the first case, the impulsive drive is generalised, uncertain of itself, unfocused in its purpose; in the second the *antrieb* is precise and disciplined. But nothing happens. In both instances the excitement subsides short of the promised orgasmic climax, though there is an important difference in that Waldeck in the first minor disturbance quells the uprush by his own courageous, forthright action; while in the second he is an impotent voyeur, so to speak, and the hyper-significant climax is prevented by a force outside his control – the *abdication* of the King, an unexpected and complete acceptance of a state of impotence.

Once again both these situations relate to the psychodramatic foundations of Caradock's work, which are firmly based in the ethological protocols of Welsh valley life. Caradock was able to recognise in the dissatisfaction of the unemployed masses, during his early childhood, the resentment on an incremental scale of socially inherited totemism of an imposed sexual repression and contrived to equate this sense of sin, the need to avoid the climax of libertarian self-assertion, with his own libido-damming, no doubt in recollection of his own post-masturbatory guilt feelings during adolescence when the physico-social influence was still strong. The stronger and more controlled, more dangerous, outbreak of feeling described in the second incident, observed significantly from the *spire* of a *cathedral*, is an expression of Caradock's recognition of his own ego-gnostic tolerance of his sexo-neutral character adjustments, directly related to his deliberate rejection of his homeland, its Puritan chapelism, while recognising (in relation to his emotional discommitment) an intrinsic failure to achieve a consummatory orgasmic response.

Irving Haller: The Centaur and the Druids. *Heseltine, 1972.*

Absolute cock! The whole thing. I don't think that Caradock had any sympathy with working people. He had a facile gift for using anything that came his way and the unemployed in the thirties when he was a kid were nothing more than that. I mean, this fear of latent forces and all that rubbish. Ridiculous! There's a totally daft passage in that long and tedious book, *Promethead*, where the proto-fascist central character goes into a crowd to shake hands with them. Absolute fantasy! Caradock wouldn't have known an angry crowd if he'd met it in Radcliffe Square or the University Parks and he had no more idea about what would cause anger in ordinary people than he had about proper professional philosophy. I remember him very well as an undergraduate, as I've said. I belonged to a small group who met every day in the same pub and we were hard drinkers and hard thinkers and we had no time at all for that kind of affected, immature posturing. I remember saying at the time that he'd probably grow out of it. The pity of it is, I suppose, that he didn't.

George Shelley in BBC radio programme.

41. Studio interview with Fay Mackail (Trevelyan Lloyd off camera)

Mackail: Well, sympathy is a loaded word, isn't it? I don't know. I think he understood himself pretty well, you know? And I think that he didn't much like what he saw. He was not in the least unscrupulous, but he was ruthless. And ruthless with himself. I knew him *quite* well over a number of years,

	but it all went so far and no further. I think at the point where he left London, he'd given up. He was profoundly bored with himself.
Medium shot Fay Mackail to take in elegant posture and dress	*Lloyd* (o/s): You were close to him, weren't you?
Close up Fay Mackail	*Mackail*: I don't think so. He was close to me, if you like. I told him the truth. Michael made up fictions in which he had a good part. Not necessarily the lead, but Kent or Horatio or, if an attendant lord, a fairly lively one. You know?
Profile Fay Mackail, smoking	*Lloyd* (o/s): Can I get back to this matter of sympathy? Do you think too much has been made of his – what shall we say – hostility to his native valley?
As opening shot	*Mackail*: Too much has been made of almost everything. If he'd died in hospital of some disease, there would have been far less fuss. In fact, I doubt whether you'd be making this film…

85

c.u. Mackail profile	... Michael was always much more upset by floods in Florence destroying pictures than floods in Asia destroying people. And I really think he was ashamed of this. You know? I think he started to brood...
Fay Mackail (as opening shot)	... and so he went back to Wales to find out what was wrong. Why he was bored with himself. Why he didn't give a damn for anyone. There were other contributory factors, but I think he had a conscience about his really deep indifference to suffering....
Medium shot	Lloyd (o/s): He was searching for himself?
Fay Mackail laughing	*Mackail*: No! No, no, no, no... He was facing up to the excuses he'd made to himself for being the man he was. D'you know what I mean?

Fay Mackail interviewed in television programme, 'Landscape of a Prophet' *by Trevelyan Lloyd.*

Well, in these islands after all, you have to be English to take yourself for granted. Welsh, Irish, Scots, Australian – you name them, you'll find some little niggle of guilt at work. And as for Jews like myself, we're the champions at feeling guilty. Whether it was real or imagined I think that Michael Caradock had to contend with a sense of guilt. He probably never admitted it: but he had renounced his native country and he treated his foster-parents quite unkindly, from what I understand, because he had let certain childhood humiliations ulcerate into a rather melodramatic hatred. You can't do that and remain sane. Which is why he had to go back. It was nothing to do with politics, because Michael Caradock wasn't interested in politics....

Honestly, I had heard nothing of an affair. Certainly not when he was still at school. The idea is ridiculous in a Welsh valley at that time. That way round at least. I've heard of young male teachers taking out girls who were still pupils, but not the other way about. But I do remember, as I think I've already mentioned, that this particular young woman was kind to him. He liked Latin and I think she gave him a bit of extra tuition during his free periods when he was trying to get into Oxford. So she got to know him pretty well, I suppose. It may have developed after he'd left; I wouldn't know. I'd gone by then.

H. Paul in BBC radio programme.

So long ago. The excitement of realisation. Your face flushed, your breathing quick and your breasts rising and falling. Reaching out nervously to touch...

The first passionate clumsy embrace, the touching comedy

of inelegance. Better not to think of it. Better to drink again. Drink until oblivion comes without drunkenness, until whatever happens, happens.

Someone must come. But not now. The island is cut off and the tide is running high. Nacreous sky with the pale gold hidden sun. The rising cry of the gulls. Cold light. Have I not set my lands in order? The waters now at grey peace letting the filtered light play across them in tentative movements.

Why is she so much with me today?

How could anything have been different?

In that place. The snickering and prurient obscenities on street corners if we had walked past together. The dull stares and malice. The scandalised chapel-stalkers. I read in these peasant faces the same kind of subtle, malign cant.

I swore never to conciliate again. Waiting for the blow, the kick after the wheedling of an auspicious moment. All mixed up in Helen's gentle liberation.

I do not know whether you loved me or whether you were merely helping me to discover something....

But I did love you....

Pigeons circle around the cote above the White House in a flock. Gunshots from the dingle wood...

Richard liked the old quarry. He liked the rough red faces on the straight sides of rock and the deep blue pools. He liked the bent and wizened trees on the long ridge above the rock face, all leaning towards the east, and beyond the trees and through them were the crosses and angels and broken columns of the village cemetery.

He liked it too because, in the quarry, it was possible to believe that you were in the heart of the country, away from the coal mines and the works, the grime and black dust that seemed ingrained everywhere else. There were birds and animals you would not expect to see in an industrial valley, although of course they are to be found in all such places in the quiet hills or woods that have not been despoiled.

Grandfather Watkins knew all about birds and animals and quite a bit about flowers (though Richard pretended not to be interested in flowers, which were cissy). He could name every tree, including some which sounded extremely rare, and there was always something interesting that he could point out. He walked slowly because of his back, leaning heavily on his stick every now and again, with a long measured stride. When Richard was impatient he would run wildly on through the ferns across the thick quick turf with the wind scouring his face and the breath pounding at his heart. Then he would wait, panting, for Grandfather Watkins to catch him up.

'Look, Dick, over there. Above the cliff. That's a hawk. D'you see him just fluttering the tips of his wings to keep still in the air? Isn't that marvellous how he can do that? Now in a minute you'll see him swoop down – phwoosh – on his prey. There! A mouse or a rat or something like that. You run about so fast, you miss things.'

Richard wondered what it felt like to be the mouse, doing nothing very much, going quite happily through the grass and – phwoosh! It was cruel but Grandfather Watkins always said that Nature was cruel. They passed two men with a greyhound padding beside them. The men greeted Grandfather Watkins in Welsh. He lifted his stick and replied – something about the weather.

'Who were they, Grandfather?'

'Poachers after rabbits,' said Grandfather Watkins in a whisper, with a rather sly grin.

Of course they were no such thing. The land was common ground, so the men could not possibly have been poachers. But Grandfather Watkins thought it much more exciting if they were made out to be cunning gipsies of the sort who had camped in the village often when he himself had been Richard's age. In spite of himself, Richard found himself thinking about the long lean jaw of the greyhound with its savage teeth and the small terrified rabbit being run down before it could reach safety. He could imagine what it felt like to be chased and to know that, step by step, the pursuer was overtaking, with relentless eyes and snarling, grinning jaws.

Extract from 'The Quarry', story in Metaphors of Twenty Years. *Vortex Press, 1950.*

'I'm sorry, Peter,' Alison said, 'I think all the Biggles books are out. You've read *Biggles Sweeps the Desert*, have you?'

'Yes,' Peter said.

'That's just come back. It's the only one I've got. Let's see what's on the shelves.'

Alison went over to the shelves labelled 'Boys' Adventure' with him. They looked at the titles of the books, but Peter was not reading any of them. She was standing close to him and he could smell a nice, fresh, soapy smell. When she reached across, the silk sleeve of her blouse touched his hand and for a second or so she leaned against him. He hoped that she would not notice he was trembling. She didn't. She hardly seemed to be aware that he was there, concentrating on the books. Peter looked at her with adoration. Alison smiled brightly at him with her lovely greyish eyes.

'Here you are. They tell me this is very good. *Dave Dawson on Convoy Patrol.*'

Peter took the book and their fingers touched as she gave it to him. The bell on the door pinged behind them. It couldn't last. Peter knew quite well who it would be. Alison turned, her eyes lively and interested to see who was there. It would be two or three of the loutish boys from the County School sixth form, who came and made stupid jokes and flirted with her. Her skirt swirled a little as she turned and Peter had a strange hollow feeling in his stomach as he noticed how round and lovely her body was.

'Hullo,' she said. And she was blushing. 'Are you on leave? When did you come home?'

It was far worse than the loutish boys from the County School sixth form. It was Gareth Buckstone in the uniform of a corporal of the RAF, with a mouth full of white teeth and merry brown eyes.

'Hullo, love,' he said. 'How you keeping? You're prettier than ever, aren't you?'

Peter noticed Alison, still blushing, making sure her blouse was properly tucked into her skirt and quickly touching her pretty, curly hair, with a feeling of helpless, hopeless chagrin. Here was he terribly in love with her and here was she, evidently, he could not deny it, terribly in love with Gareth Buckstone, who was – for all that he was a jolly, handsome, young man – a far cry from Biggles or Ginger or even Dave Dawson.

'And you're just as cheeky,' Alison said. 'How are you?'

'Going to Africa,' he said. 'To Kenya. This is embarkation leave.'

'Oh...' she said.

And Peter thought there was something odd in her voice, as though she was excited and happy and at the same time very troubled.

'Well, since you're here, you can make yourself useful,' she said. 'Help me carry these books into the back room.'

'OK.'

Minutes passed. Peter opened *Dave Dawson on Convoy Patrol* and gazed miserably at a blur of print. There was no sound from the back room and they hadn't come back even though there were two more heaps of books to be carried in. Peter wished that Alison had asked him to help: he would have been more than delighted to. As it was, he tiptoed across the room and peered through a chink in the curtain that screened off the little storeroom. He already knew what he would see: Gareth Buckstone kissing Alison. But she had her arms fast around the airman's neck, so that the blouse was stretched tight around her body and she was pressing herself against him most earnestly. Peter at last understood what the word 'passionately' was supposed to mean.

He thought of knocking on the counter to ask to book

out *Dave Dawson on Convoy Patrol*, but instead – not because he was feeling polite or generous, but because he was afraid she would be angry with him – he took it back to the shelf, and as quietly as possible let himself out.

That evening he tried to read *Treasure Island*, as his father had always wanted him to, but he did not enjoy it. And two days later, in spite of the vow he had made to himself, he went back again to the Lending Library. Alison was wearing a very pretty dress. She smiled at him. He saw that she was using powder and lipstick. It made her look even more beautiful.

'Good morning, Peter. Haven't you got anything to bring back?'

'No. You were busy. Moving books with Gareth Buckstone, the other day.'

Alison laughed, but she did not blush as he expected her to.

'Yes. I was. Are you going to choose something?'

'Alison, can I have a murder book?'

'What – a detective story?'

'Yes.'

'I don't know. How old are you, Peter?'

'Nearly eleven.'

'Oh, that's quite big. I'll find you something good.'

'How old are you, Alison?'

'You shouldn't ask a lady her age, Peter. But since it's you, I'll tell you a secret. I'm nineteen.'

'Alison, if you need help here – I mean when Gareth Buckstone goes to Africa – I can come and move books.'

Alison smiled. She reached out her hand, which was

very soft with long pointed nails, and touched him gently on the face, smiling into his eyes.

'That's very kind of you, Peter. Very nice. When will you start?'

'Now, if you like.'

But the door pinged and there was laughing Gareth Buckstone, all debonair and teeth, with a box of chocolates in his hand.

'Hullo,' he said. 'Who's this, then? My rival?'

'This is Peter,' Alison said. 'And he's a very nice boy. He's going to help me in the library.'

'I'm not so sure I like that,' said Gareth Buckstone. 'Here you are, lad. Get yourself a wafer in Lambertini's.'

Peter's face was aflame. There were tears flooding up into his eyes and he didn't think he could keep them back. He snatched the sixpence from Gareth Buckstone and tried to say something but choked. He ran out of the shop, feeling shame and humiliation, hearing Gareth Buckstone laugh as he shut the door. It was, no doubt, a kind enough laugh – but Peter did not care....

Extract from 'Lending Library', story in Metaphors of Twenty Years. *Vortex Press, 1950.*

Metaphors of Twenty Years was published while Caradock was still at Oxford. The Vortex Press was a small, one-man publishing house, run by Reginald Webber, which was dedicated to the encouragement of new authors. Webber was a volatile man of very definite opinions who kept the Press going, first of all by sinking into it every penny of a substantial legacy, and subsequently by a capacity for improvisation that amounted to genius.

Introduced to Webber by Jeremy Philbrick (now a Conservative backbench MP), Caradock found that his first mentor was a romantic socialist with a taste for lyricism. The miscellany of stories, prose poems, essays, sketches and epiphanies collected together in *Metaphors* is an accurate reflection of Webber's editorial preferences. Caradock was a prolific writer while at University and these were the selection made from a much more voluminous batch of stories and reflections. Correspondence between the irascible Webber and the young Caradock reveals that it was only with great reluctance that the publisher agreed to include the three essays – 'The Foundling Generation', 'Subtopia' and 'Hubris Revisited', and the three sketches – 'Portrait of the Artist as a Young Turk', 'The Cloister and the Cadena' and 'Mastermen Unready'. Webber writes to the young Caradock: 'I do not think that they are anything like as good as your prose poems or the stories where you exploit your natural lyrical gifts and where you show some real feeling for your characters and their lives. In the essays and things you've got very self-consciously dandiacal and I think much too precious. I'd rather have three more stories and more prose poems. You're an ambitious lad, but the kind of thing you've been trying in the essays and sketches needs a touch more experience of life and more control in the writing.' Caradock, throughout the correspondence, is obviously eager to be published and not to offend Webber, but he shows himself to be as strong-minded – and obviously got his way: 'I'm sorry that you don't like my more astringent pieces, but would respectfully suggest to you that they are necessary for the balance of the book. I *am* ambitious and I don't want to be thought of as a lyrical writer only (though I'm obviously delighted at what you say). In fact, I think the stories and prose poems alone would not only make a rather cloying book, but would misrepresent the sort of person I am and the sort of writer I hope to be. I really am nothing like the gentle, nice character who seems to have written those particular pieces. I hope you will agree and that this will not affect your interest in publishing the book.'

Critics have generally found more to agree with in Webber's point of view than in Caradock's, though in the perspective of his complete works, the essays and sketches are of the greatest interest. The book is a very ambitious project for a young man of twenty, but the quality of the writing is uneven. The six stories *are* gentle, lyrical, and seem to describe a much more pastoral landscape than that of Cwmfelyn. But in four of them there is a bitter flavouring which hints at the melancholy which was at the root of Caradock's alleged misanthropy. In 'The Quarry' there is the misunderstanding, apparently trivial but in truth profoundly significant, between the grandfather and the child, after they have witnessed the killing of the hare by the two dogs. The old man is amused by the chase, the boy is appalled (as he is throughout by the cruelty of Nature) but afraid to explain his reasons for no longer going on walks with his grandfather in case he will be ridiculed. The discovery of the murdered girl by the four boys, on their idyllic afternoon blackberrying, is a genuinely chilling moment – and once again suggests the almost sinister insistence in Caradock's work, from the very beginning, of a cruel and violent nightmare which is close to the surface of even the most happy and pleasant circumstance. Any feeling of euphoria is short-lived, vulnerable to sudden and savage disappointment. 'Kingfisher' is perhaps the most distressing of the stories, culminating as it does in the helpless tearful rage of Rhys; a marked contrast to the froideur of Garnett in 'Paradise Terrace', who seems to accept the destruction of the lovable street with a shrug that is more contemptuous than stoical.

Caradock's celebrated asperity is more noticeable in the essays and sketches, and significantly the focus of all of these is outside Wales and Cwmfelyn. In view of the over-dramatic emphasis on Caradock's hatred for his native town and its people, it is necessary to point out that, in the earliest book, the satirical vituperation was turned upon the world outside. If we ignore the unsuccessful and artificial 'Subtopia', there are two acute essays and three amusing, self-mocking sketches, in which the dandiacal posturing is excusable because it is seen as absurd. But in these the pitiless eye of the author is coldly and curiously directed at the new circles of acquaintance that the young man was making. The stories and the self-revealing prose-poems show little evidence of any anger, although there is plentiful indication of a profoundly melancholic uncertainty. Whereas the Oxford literati (in 'The Cloister and the Cadena'), the confident young politicians and executives (in 'Masterman Unready') and Caradock himself in his 'Portrait', come in for merciless treatment, the characters in the stories are all observed with sympathy. In particular, the two stories which involve women – 'Lending Library' and 'The Flower Clock' – offer almost idealised portraits of kindness and feminine generosity. The reader is reminded that these observations must be taken in the wide context of Caradock's later and more important writing: but they go some way to challenging the more sensational accounts of a corrosively embittered elitist.

Douglas Rome: Michael Caradock *in Writers of Today series, 1969.*

Caradock met Idris Lewis on the train bound for Oxford. Lewis was going up to Jesus, a less fashionable college, but the two men liked each other and remained in frequent contact. At his own college, Caradock shared rooms with Michael Beauchamp-Beck, an old Etonian of vastly different background. They became firm friends and in due course, gathering confidence and enthusiasm, the three young men established a camaraderie that was to include a number of their contemporaries from many different colleges. To this friendship Beauchamp-Beck brought an assurance and a range of acquaintance that was matched by Idris Lewis' alert and academically brilliant mind in enhancing the experience of both men. Caradock's contribution was more obscure. Neither Lewis nor Beauchamp-Beck (both senior civil servants) disguises the opinion that Caradock was less intelligent: but both admit to an early conviction in his artistic ability. Both use the same word 'intensity' to describe his moods; both hint that they were soon aware of an objectivity that was entirely different in quality from their own acquired intellectual detachment. Beauchamp-Beck says: 'Michael was an object to himself, just a little more interesting than all the other objects around him.'

Of course, these two men were invited to read all Caradock's early writing. Beauchamp-Beck was seldom a confidant: 'Well, I used to get a bit bored with all the agonising about some virtually invisible moral crisis and I'd tell him to piss off. In the gentlest possible way. Idris used to listen very patiently....'

Now with the Department of the Environment, Idris Lewis states: 'I spent a lot of time chatting with Michael. I was quite fond of my home, although I fully intended to make my career elsewhere. He did not like Cwmfelyn (which is a much less attractive place than my own native village), but for a while, when we first were in residence at Oxford, he saw it with an affection that I believe and that other people who knew him well (such as Michael Beauchamp-Beck) believe was absolutely genuine. There were two reasons for this: Michael always had to be *against* something. Throughout his life, as many of his friends had to witness. At Oxford, of course, when we were freshmen, it was tradition, rigmarole, that passed for tradition, public schoolboys, hearty idiots who still existed in profusion, ex-servicemen – I don't suppose many people today realise how bloody stupid they could be while pretending to be ancient and wise – and the poseurs. Whatever his faults, Michael unerringly spotted what was fake or unreal, especially when it was a matter of art. I loved Oxford and I liked my home. Michael Beauchamp-Beck was at home everywhere and a very serene man even aged twenty-one. Michael Caradock was nervous and resentful at first, but he learned quickly. So. The point is that those early stories were written when he felt unhappy about Oxford and everything at Cwmfelyn became good and even beautiful.'

Extract from David Hayward's official biography.

The railway station at Shotover stood on a long bleak ridge above the town where it caught the worst of the weather. When the trains for the South pulled out they followed a long loop of track which took them in a semicircle around the town, sprawled in a shallow bowl of flattish hills.

Baldwin gazed without emotion out of the compartment window at the ugly, draggling streets, the sooty stacks and rows of uniform terraces, the back-to-back houses immediately below the railway line, the hopeless washing under a grey-brown pall of murk and smoke. He had expected to feel elation mixed with relief: at last he was getting away from the drab and ugly streets, the self-satisfied plain bluntness of the people, who described themselves as ordinary folk, from the throng who had known him since he was so-high and knew too much about him, the people who called him Sid or Siderney (mocking) and who could and would catalogue his miserable, pusillanimous childhood and adolescence. He had not expected to feel the slightest pang of regret: from now on he was Baldwin in his own head and Hugh to the very few people whom he would allow to become intimate. He felt nothing at all.

As the train lumbered around the loop slowly, he picked out landmarks that had been part of his twenty-one years in the place – St Mark's Church, the civic buildings, the Grammar School, the steelworks. He found the patch of scruffy trees that marked the municipal gardens and in his mind followed the street which ran away from them down to the bus depot where his father's grocer's shop stood.

In a distant way he was sorry, but he was determined not to feel guilt. He imagined his father opening the shop, no doubt with what he would call a heavy heart. Perhaps not: perhaps for once the business would take second place and he would stay home to comfort Baldwin's mother. She had been upset. He saw, a little too vividly for his comfort, her weeping face gaping wide in an impossible grief, impossible because it was uncontrolled and out of all proportion.

'Come and see us often, won't you, Sidney? You're all we've got.'

'You'll do as your mammy says, won't you, son?'

No. Baldwin was not going to feel the slightest guilt. As far as he was concerned it was going to be a clean break with them, with Shotover, with ordinary folk, with Graham Biggs, Len Fairchild, the Reverend Geoffrey Holloway, Les Parker and the lot of them with their mediocre minds and their narrow ambitions which meant that they sneered automatically at anyone who was reaching for something extraordinary, something fine and unusual. As far as his parents were concerned, they had only themselves to blame – that he, a clever, sensitive boy, should have been destined to take over the business. He could smell the place as he thought of it; and his father's much-obliged smiling, as he wrapped little items with putty-white fingers, most deftly, turned him up. He should have been sent to university, to Oxford or to Cambridge, or allowed to fend for himself abroad. From the age of about sixteen he had looked forward to National Service as a means of release – but he had been cheated by a perforated eardrum. Their selfish and myopic desires for him had brought about this moment, this bitter rejection. He was sorry but he knew quite well that they would both quickly find an appropriate cliché to help them live without him. His father had wanted him for the business: his mother had wanted him where she could fuss at him, interfere with his leisure, sanction his pursuits and pastimes. He would feel no guilt. He remembered the bitter scenes when he had got himself a job on the local paper.

'We've given you a good education, Sidney, and now you owe us something.'

'For Christ's sake, I get three distinctions in my Higher School Certificate and you want me to be a grocer.'

'Don't use such language to your mother. You're too big for your boots, my lad. The business has been in the family for two generations now and what was good enough for your grandad and me will be good enough for you. We've a respected name in this town for fair dealing and decent living.'

'I'm going to work on the *Messenger*. You can't stop me.'

'We'll see about that.'

No. Baldwin had nothing to reproach himself for. His luck had at last turned with a job in Fleet Street, and he was willing to work himself down to the elbows to prove what he could do. He thought of Joyce setting out for Paris, determined to follow his high ambition – away from the stifling air of his home and family; of the quarrels between Baudelaire and his family; between Rimbaud and his parents; even the disciplined Eliot had had differences with his father about settling in England where he would work best. Baldwin smiled at himself, but he felt an inner warmth of satisfaction that he was in such a distinguished tradition.

Fleetingly the image of Ruth Duncan at the library occurred like an unwanted ghost in a brand-new building where the ground had not been exorcised. She had been kind. She had let him kiss her and caress her – only so far and in what ugly circumstances: in dark bus shelters, miserable little alleys, behind the church hall. He was grateful to her – she was an attractive woman, quite a bit older, and she could have taken her pick of quite a few interested men. But she had seen something in him that the other moronic girls of his own age had missed and he must have given her something. They had parted on the best possible terms, of course, but she had been a little sad. Baldwin thought kindly of her – but there would be other Ruth Duncans, just as attractive and with better minds. After all, what was she doing trapped in a place like Shotover, working in the library, if she did not lack some vital spark of energy and imagination?

Baldwin did not like himself very much. He did not think he was a very nice man. But then it was not necessary for an artist, especially a very serious artist, as he intended to be, to be a nice man. Most of the really great had proved themselves to be difficult: selfish, opportunist, egomaniac in one way or another. Baldwin was not dismayed.

The train gathered speed. The clank and creak of the wheels after the long curving run acquired a new and assertive rhythm. Baldwin opened Volume One of *À la recherche du temps perdu.*

Extract from The Low Key of Hope. *Alvin & Brandt, 1954.*

3

53. Ext. Cwmfelyn. Day. Aerial view of Cwmfelyn, spinning into the Grammar School, perched on the side of the hill to the north of the valley

MUSIC: Wagner: *Siegfried Idyll* (8b) Hold under...

54. Ext. School. Day. Cut to tracking shot, slow, in through school gates, empty yard...

FX. under music Footsteps...

55. Ext. School. Day. Cut to small boy's view of main school building...

Gymnasium...

New block, steep angle...

56. Int. School. Day. Empty classroom... hold	Cut FX. Begin to fade music Cross fade: *children's voices* declining Latin noun
Cut to empty school hall	Cross fade: *children's voices* (Latin noun) and end of hymn sung in Welsh (R'wyn gweld o bell y dydd yn dod). After *Amen*: single *male voice* speaking in Welsh. (Prayer)
Pan on School Honours Board – with glare of sunlight through windows on black and gold surface	
Pan quickly around hall – pictures of wise old men, plaques, windows, lights, doors, to	Single *voice* continues with prayer
Open window and mountain on opposite side of the valley. Hold	*Voice* begins to fade and Cross fade *Siegfried Idyll* (8 n. NB) to climax
57. Ext. Cwmfelyn. Day. Mountainside, plentifully scarred but in sunlight. Camera tracks in on lower slopes	(V/O) *Lloyd*: However innocently the childish voice had joined in the traditional hymns and prayers, the adolescent's mind wandered, especially in summer,
Sweeping shot up to height of *Careg Hywel* (highest crag	through the open windows onto the mountainside.

overlooking village) and…	Finding no freedom. Looking for escape
58. Ext. Cwmfelyn. Day. Panoramic view of valley as of now	from the claustrophobic school and finding only the dour, spoiled, daunting mountains…
59. Mix to Still of valley in thirties, with full industrial activity…	Peak music.

Sequence from television programme, 'Landscape of a Prophet'.

Phyllis Caradock's influence naturally diminished as the boy grew up, though there were the ritual visits to 'Grandpapa Jenkyn' and resolute attempts on her part to keep him firmly dependent upon her. Gradually, however, he spent more time with Howell, whose days were long and empty. Howell took and read *The Times* and the *Financial Times*, but (his golf-club friends suggest) more out of a sense of decorum than any lively interest in money, markets or politics. He pottered in his garden, often to the chagrin of George Parker who was employed for a few days each week. The injury to his back made it difficult for him to perform anything strenuous and he was not much inclined to literature or music.

Most of his reading was confined to military history. When he began to take Michael Julian with him on his long plodding walks around the hills, above Cwmfelyn and neighbouring villages, they talked about soldiers, the fine life and dedication of an officer in a good regiment, the honour of service. Idris Lewis says that Howell Caradock told the small boy that there was nothing he wanted more than to see him in the army; at the same time asking him, man to man, not to reveal this to his foster-mother, because she would be badly upset. Soon after Michael Julian entered the County School, the Second World War began....

The County School offered Michael Julian more freedom than he had dreamed possible. Homework and study became a refuge which he was quick to exploit. An early talent for languages and a ready appreciation of English Literature, suitably encouraged, set him off on a long and fascinated quest. Phyllis Caradock was proud of the boy's endeavour; Howell Caradock was touched that Edmund's son was so like Edmund, always with his nose in a book. J. L. Rabone, the boy's scholarly grandfather, was sent regular reports about his progress.

Without knowing it, Michael Caradock had already inherited a comfortable sum of money. Held in trust for him, until the age of twenty-one, was the legacy of Jane Caradock, whose will appears to have set out to thwart the likely domination of Phyllis and the Jenkyn family. Since the will must have been drawn up for her by F. Cecil Jenkyn, it probably gave the alert and sardonic lady no little pleasure to make her designs secure in law. Michael Caradock had no idea of his inheritance. Years later, two legacies – from J. L. Rabone (modest) and Jane Caradock (considerable) – were to enable Michael Caradock to live comfortably while he established himself as a novelist. For the time being, Howell and Phyllis Caradock kept the boy in ignorance of the money.

At school, the headmaster, J. H. Temple Morgan, admits that he did not like the boy. He was, the former head states, always aware of an indoctrinated sense of superiority which made him a poor mixer. 'But, beyond that, there was an almost inbred sneer. (You will understand that I say this with the benefit of hindsight.) But this became even more apparent as he grew older and became more aware of his undoubted talents within certain prescribed areas. Notably, English Literature. He was quite a good linguist and interested in the Classics. But there were two things which I held, and hold, against the boy – of course, they made no difference to my attitude to him as a pupil. The one was his laziness: born, I suggest, of a mistaken and inculcated belief that what did not come easily wasn't worth having. The other was his total indifference to his national and local heritage. Being a Welshman meant nothing to him. And even in the sixth form any attempt that I, or other members of staff, would make to interest him in our literature and our culture would be met with a scowl of apathy.'

Mr J. Idwal Price, inevitably known to generations of schoolboys as 'Jip', takes modest pleasure (in his seventy-sixth year) in a reputation for affable irascibility. He taught History and Latin at the Cwmfelyn County School to junior and middle forms, but is as well remembered for his enthusiastic coaching of rugby football teams – stripped down to serge waistcoat and trousers, immaculately bicycle clipped, with enormous galoshes, 'thundering amidst the early, untutored rabble of tomorrow's Triple Crown'. The phrase is his own and characteristic of the man. About Caradock he is neutral: 'Funny boy. Useless at any sports. But not bad. Not bad. I remember a terrible row between Paul, the Jewish Maths teacher, and Tecwyn Leyshon: because Paul who was a very cosmopolitan fellow – as you might expect, brought up in Cardiff with his particular background – had tried genuinely to interest a likely pupil in various European ideas. So he'd recommended Nietzsche to this lad.... Ssshh! If he did! Tecwyn Leyshon into the staff-room: "Listen! Don't you interfere with my bloody sixth form with Fascist shit!" To a Jew, mind you. Paul was very sallow. But you could see the change in his face. "I beg your pardon?" "Don't you beg my bloody pardon. It's bloody subversive. You are telling my boys to read shit, Paul. And I won't have it." Terrible row. Paul was a quiet and clever man. He asked questions, in a civil voice. Tecwyn Leyshon had to answer. Because we were all there and none of us fools. And, of course, it transpired that the terrible crime was that Paul had told Julian Caradock about Nietzsche. Well, several of us laughed out loud. Now the point of my story is that this receptive boy, arrogant and unappealing as he was, had to contend with Paul on the one hand and Leyshon on the other. That isn't exactly right. But Paul was a young man. And he was lame because of some congenital problem – so he wasn't in the army. And, you must see this, Europe and European culture (in spite of the Nazis) were absolutely *vital* to Paul. *We*, the British, had to win. And if we didn't have freedom of thought, what chance was there? Of course, Paul had read Nietzsche and I would say Leyshon hadn't. I daresay he'll tell you! Whether or not it was a good idea, at that time, to suggest such an author to Caradock, I don't know. I had no real contact with him. I taught him Latin in the junior forms and a year of history – the Stuarts and Early Hanoverians. Then he moved on. Helen Westlake taught Latin to the senior pupils, at that time. She was a nice girl. Very young and very bright. I think she came from Hereford. But the only affection I remember (not that my memory is what it was) Caradock showing to any members of staff was to her and to Paul. It was a difficult situation from his point of view: the Jenkyns and the Caradocks and having to adapt.'

J. H. Temple Morgan is adamant that any kind of liaison between a teacher at his school and a pupil was impossible. 'We were a small, closely knit and essentially respectable community. Such a relationship would not have remained secret and would not have been countenanced. Of course, I knew that Caradock was taking lessons in Greek with Miss Westlake after he had left school. But there was never any suggestion of gossip. Miss Westlake lodged with Mrs Eynon Walters who was a member of my own chapel. It is unthinkable.'

Some of Caradock's own remarks about his development at school are perhaps best remembered by John Morris whom he used to meet at the Welfare Library and Institute. Morris says that he does not know if any passion in Michael Caradock could have possibly been more important than his desire to escape. Mr Morris remembers too that his dislike of his teachers was prompted by his impatience at their insistence on narrow curricula and very limited attainment: 'Leyshon couldn't see beyond early Yeats, and Temple Morgan thought that a State Scholarship was a dove descending from heaven.'

Caradock's later progress at the County School passed Howell and Phyllis Caradock by: they were pleased when he did well and probably relieved that he was less unhappy than he had been at the elementary school. Leslie Chambers thinks, however, that Howell Caradock, who seldom opened up his private thoughts, was disappointed when the boy began to take more and more interest in philosophy and the arts. Their few years of intimacy were over and the simple, decent soldier with his accounts of General Montgomery's strategy and the situation on the Russian Front could no longer compete with the new and exciting ideas that his foster-son was discovering.

Extract from David Hayward's official biography.

Helen Westlake was young and attractive. Not exactly beautiful, but good looking and a lovely figure and so on. You know the way that young boys are and the way they talk. Obviously a good many had fantasies about her. I remember when she took us for Latin in Form Five, we spent most of the time waiting for her to cross her legs: and we were pretty terrible at Virgil, I can tell you. Julian Caradock would have none of that. If anyone said anything coarse about her, in a perfectly normal way, he would blush and walk off. But he shared the same attitude. There were two or three other women teachers who came in for this, as I say, entirely healthy and normal treatment. But where most of us were fumbling our way towards sexual maturity with girls of our own age, I don't think that Julian had much but these fantasies. And he spent a fair bit of time with her. I think she gave him extra coaching in Latin for his Oxford entrance.

Dr Geraint Bevan in BBC radio programme.

You see, from my point of view as a conscientious teacher, I wanted him to grasp the fundamental masters of English Literature. Shakespeare. Chaucer. Milton. Wordsworth. Keats. Browning. After that, by all means, stretch his wings. But none of this fanciful skating around after Rimbaud and James Joyce and continental philosophers. Now, Paul came from – obviously, he came from a European background and he had this Jewish thing of being a bee from his own hive and gathering honey from all the different flowers. I'm not anti-Semitic, by the way, as I'm sure you'll understand. It's almost, if I can put it this way, an historical observation about the acclimatised Jew in Western European society. Be that as it may – Paul (no doubt from the best motives) was young, overenthusiastic and the wrong sort of influence on a boy like Caradock. As I've already told you, I was from a working home and I always regarded myself as a radical. But Paul was, you see, a Marxist. But wild with it. And as we have seen in the last decade that sort of thing is out-and-out dangerous with unformed minds. The Latin teacher was a different matter: a woman called Westlake – young, not bad looking. And, as some of these girls are, very conscious of it. Like Paul, the Maths man, she encouraged what I'd call the egregious side of Caradock. For example, if they were studying as set books Livy or Virgil or Sallust or

Horace, they would also be reading in a more cursory way five or six other authors. You could put money on Caradock taking up Juvenal or Martial or Suetonius. And this young lady, Westlake, did nothing to hold him back. Now, in a steady pupil, this might have been quite good teaching: but with a fellow like Caradock, full of affectation and notions of superiority, it was a disaster. Of course, I'm not talking in terms of results, but in terms of character. Results, after all, are relatively unimportant.

T. P. Leyshon in BBC radio programme.

Life at the County School and in the village was constricting but not unpleasant. Now, given that Michael Caradock had no great faith in human nature to start with, which I think was true, there was then something that hit him very hard and which he talked to me about a great deal because I am a Jew and it must have hit me even harder: that was the evidence from the concentration camps at the end of the war of the ultimate wickedness of men to one another. He was about fifteen and a deeply sensitive boy with a very powerful imagination, and he was more than ordinarily appalled by the photographs and accounts of Belsen and Buchenwald and so on. At the same time – and this he told me – his foster-father, whose name I have forgotten, had for years been telling him about the first war. Michael Caradock had since been reading Graves and Owen and all the others and he had seen pictures of what the trenches were like. These two horrors were coalescing in his mind and intensifying enormously the routinely juvenile revulsion with man that

114

quite a lot of adolescents pass through. And I think that at this time, he was not aware that he had been adopted. So that he thought he was the son of a man the best years of whose life seemed to have been in a situation of carnage.

Well what can you do? It's no good directing a boy in that frame of mind to the contemplation of perfect objects: I introduced him to the more dramatic European philosophers – moral philosophers – in a rather vague hope that the more ideas he took in, the more he would realise certain generalities about the nature of Evil – what is it Sartre says: about it not being a question of the temporary and remediable isolation of an idea? He was reading a lot of poetry himself and at the same time, as far as I remember, Miss Westlake had introduced him to the Greeks in translation – not the philosophers so much as the great dramatists. My conversations with him were all on an intellectual plane, but I think that with her he was more relaxed. Quite natural, of course. So that I think you have a sketch, if you like, for the big picture of his life. The abiding pessimism and despair at the inevitable triumph of evil and chaos, a sense of isolation and rejection which was made more intense when he was told about his parents' death and so on, and the idea of solace and comfort from the love and affection, whether idealised (as I'm quite sure it was at the time) or realised (as perhaps it became), of a gentle and slightly more mature woman.

H. Paul in BBC radio programme.

Who is that? Savage, perhaps, walking on the cliff above the headland, always with a gun. Steady tramp through the damp, plashy ground. The chill air seeping through even a countryman's impermeable skin and the complaint of the seabirds. Inland the hoarse harsh fecklessness of the rooks.

Poor old man. I think of him now always as old. I suppose he passed from youth to late middle age in a matter of months. Strolling wherever there were trees and grass banks to obscure the drab and dirty valley. A slow, ponderous step because of the injured spine, the calm rather vacuous expression of his military face, thinking of what might have been – the honour of retreat and defeat with stoical acceptance, the triumph of victory with decency. A strange tale about the sunrise on a ridge in the heart of the mud waste through a watery, misty sky transforming the jagged tree stumps and churned ground with its craters of filthy water and tangles of wire, its corruption and tatters of waste metal: and the light catching a flight of birds in the distance rising: silence and stillness. His sense of uplift and tears. And out of the wall of an escarpment a putrefied hand held out, as though in supplication. Without the words to express the sorrow that seemed to rise and to be drowning in him. A lull in the desperately even conflict of his dim understanding of himself.

Stumping the green sparseness looking for brightly coloured birds – bullfinches, goldfinches, woodpeckers, kingfishers, linnets, waiting for the sun to strike a flat calm surface of water, hoping for the dart of trout in the quick-running upland river that purged itself of grime. Poor, slow-thinking, unfocused man. With a puny child whose mind was too full of fantasy to comprehend anything real.

The slow walks and blurts of conversation. The loneliness. Before there was any rationalised catalogue of resentments and reasons and excuses. No love: just a generalised sadness.

There was not enough, there never has been enough, love.... Whose fault is that?

The man walking on the cliff out of sight. Pale grey cloud above the wood, the White House, the village. Out to sea a darkening bank of approaching rain cloud. The wind dropping. Lap of water. Continuum of sea-noise bird-cry. Rattle of glass and bottle. Two – only two – maudlin tears dribbling down a stiff, pumice face.

Alcedo atthis ispida. The bright bird swept down over the dark and muddy water of the canal. Blue and chestnut-red. Long plunging beak into the fetid water, the thick soupy surface. Rearing up again: green lights on the turquoise back: the blue-red blur of the twisting bird against fresh green of May trees. The overhung bank above the still dank water.

Beyond the trees, heaped sleepers, lined trucks of the Railway Waggons Repairs, shale underfoot – a half-inch of grime and dust. Around rusted old machines, wheels, axles, shafts, twisted sections of line, battered, useless drams... helpless on their sides like wounded animals.

There was an overhang of springtime trees above the dark water for two or three hundred yards. And there... there... was the brilliant bird. Its colour, splendour, its assurance. Out of the green darkness flashing into light and along the dull reaches of water. *Alcedo atthis ispida.* Kingfisher! He would have waited hours longer for the sight. The beautiful creature swooped down in a flurry of colour and he lost it. Well, he would have waited longer. And in another age he would have been closer to the birds and animals, the trees and open fields – before all the works had ravaged his valley. He leaned back against an old tree and saw falcons killing on the wing, buzzards like religious totems on wayside poles, the keen red fox playing with cubs, lithe stoats writhing through long grass, the slow strong purpose of ravens.... He was dizzy with his images of what the land once was – and himself a farmboy in sweet-smelling summer with the gnats playing above clear water and a hint of autumn already in the air. A soft girl perhaps beside him in the dusk, laughing and silly....

The bird arose again steeply out of the water. He heard raucous noise of children, who shrilled around a corner over the old stone bridge. One of them had a catapult. He watched, in a stupor of amazement, as the evil child took aim and shot at the lovely rising bird. Inevitably the shot struck home and the kingfisher dropped into the rushes along the canal bank. The children shrieked in delight and triumph, and pummelled the boy with the catapult in their pleasure.

Before he was aware of the hot tears on his face, he heard the shrieking, wheezing groan of rage rising in the back of his throat, so that, involuntarily, snot fell from his nostrils as he sobbed with immediate despair. In a reddish fog of fury, he began to run at the shouting vandal children....

Extract from 'Kingfisher', story in Metaphors of Twenty Years. *Vortex Press, 1950.*

The six stories in the early miscellany all share this basic sympathy for people who are emphatically *not* sophisticated or intellectual or rarefied: the grandfather in 'The Quarry'; the four small boys in 'Blackberries'; the young woman and her RAF lover in 'Lending Library'; the returning, disillusioned Garnett reacting to fact and memory in 'Paradise Terrace'; the young man and the mature woman in 'Flower Clock'; and not least the miner in 'Kingfisher', whose hardness and resilience in many other respects is carefully established. All these stories suggest that the young Caradock felt kindly to people and particularly to the people of his native valley. Whatever the harsher judgements offered in the same collection by the prose poems and some of the essays, the fiction is firmly rooted in the lives of decent, uncomplicated people and truly innocent children. Ironies are circumstantial: communication easily breaks down. And the rest is a sort of hurt silence.

The only note of optimism – in the stories, at least – occurs in the last: 'Flower Clock'. Here the resilience and disappointment of unambitious people is made to flower into something lasting and pleasing. In the simplest and most innocent terms the boy and the woman – the one miserable, the other discontented – comfort one another for a few hours during a grubby sunset and a long, quieting dusk over the bay. And they leave one another a little restored.

At the same time, some critics have reasonably pointed out that Caradock's early stories, whatever their quality, were tentative experiments owing more to traditional Welsh sentiment than their author would have later allowed. Hostile critics have suggested that the stories were an almost cynical front for the minor savageries of the essays and sketches. What they ignore is the evident care that the young Caradock put into the writing of these pieces and, in their determination to index his discontent with his origins, they ignore his disillusion about human nature.

The clue to Caradock's own feelings as a young man, at a fashionable Oxford college with a splendid academic reputation, writing furiously and sometimes well, is in the prose poems. Again it must be noted that most of these fragments are full of sympathy for the Cwmfelyn valley, the neighbouring towns and (above all) for the people. Where 'Evening Walk' and 'Palais-de-danse' describe an urgent impatience to get away from the place, and the Paris and Oxford sketches convey the intoxicated sense of freedom, 'Night Passage', 'Frost' and 'View of the Bay' are gentle, lyrical and very nearly loving.

Stephen Lewis: The Novels of Michael Caradock. *Molyneux, 1971.*

Bloody stupid contraption, Henry thought. The great orange finger of the minute hand cranked up a space to twenty-three minutes past. There was an audible clunk somewhere underneath the red and white and green of the flowers, which Henry realised he had been registering for the last hour. Clunk. A Flower Clock. Who ever heard of anything so stupid? Where else in the world would the municipal authorities think of anything quite as banal? Clunk.

And she wasn't going to turn up....

Henry felt like weeping. But that wouldn't do. He thought it would be much better to be savage and bitter, to learn effectively to despise women, like Alfred de Vigny. All the time, however, he was overcome by numbness, a creeping numbness as though he was about to have flu: his body feverishly sore, his head confused. He remembered how pretty she had looked when he had at last managed to ask her to meet him – long, gold, fair hair; innocent blue eyes – but rather pale and cold; the fragile face like a figurine in porcelain. She was so unlike all the other girls, who were earthy and carnal like the women in Juvenal's Sixth Satire.

And she was not going to turn up. She had never intended to. She had perhaps been laughing at him all the time. She might, even now, be with someone like Horace Pugh or Glyn Leyshon, who would brag about touching skin second night.

The sun had gone down over the hill. Henry wondered if he would ever be as miserable again. If it would seem like misery after he had freed himself from the whole desperate place and girls like her: trite little mind in a pretty, wicked body. He became aware of a woman sitting on the next bench who seemed to be watching him.

She was over thirty, well built, and she was smiling. Henry had an idea that she had been watching him for some time. It was that sort of smile. He looked rudely at her. The woman was wearing a white dress with blue spots, a summer dress. Her legs were crossed and she was showing both knees, which were round. She went on smiling: not directly *at* Henry, but he was quite sure she was smiling about him. It was probably obvious to a mature woman that he was a miserable little boy whose girlfriend hadn't turned up. Henry got up. There was nothing left but to go home. He touched the two pound notes in his pocket. He hadn't expected to spend both: but they'd been there. He had to pass the smiling woman on his way out of the gardens. The bloody clock went Clunk.

He looked very severe and abstracted as Rimbaud might have looked in a similar mood, though Henry thought he fell far short of the sort of sophistication that must have come easily to Rimbaud. As he passed the woman, she said: 'Didn't she turn up? Don't worry. It's not important.'

'I beg your pardon, madam,' said Henry, with presence of mind.

'I'm sorry, love,' she said. 'I shouldn't have spoken, but you looked so miserable. I'm sorry.'

'Not a bit,' said Henry suavely. 'Don't mention it.'

The woman laughed. It was a nice, deep, contralto noise and made Henry more aware of the full, ripe body out of which that earthy chuckle came: the big breasts and the plush hips, the wonderful femaleness of her. Most unfragile.

'Sit down for a minute and tell me about it,' she said. 'It'll help a bit. D'you smoke?'

She took a packet of Players out of her handbag. Henry took one and sat down. Perhaps she is a prostitute, he thought. But he felt reassured because he had only two pounds and a few loose coins and he did not think that was enough. Nervous though he was, there was something kind and pleasant about the woman.

'What's your name?' she said.

'Henry.'

'Mine's Beryl. You don't look like a "Henry" to me. More like a "Harry". Can I call you "Harry"?'

122

'If you want to.'

'You call me Beryl.'

'Yes.'

'What happened, Harry? Is she very pretty?'

'Very. She said she'd meet me by the Flower Clock here. And I thought...'

'And she hasn't turned up. And she's with some bastard.... Sorry, Harry. But that's what he is, mark my words. Don't be unhappy. It honestly isn't important. Tell me about yourself.'

'There isn't much to tell,' said Henry.

But he talked. And she smiled. And she listened. Henry was aware all the time, especially when she moved a little, of her body, of the sexual rapport that seemed to exist between them: but it was more important that she was listening, she was taking him seriously. Smiling most of the time: yes. But her face – which had lines around the eyes and the lips and was in a serene way very beautiful – was interested and the smile was not condescending. He told her about the girl but he did not mention her name. And a bit about himself, his ambitions. He spoke incidentally about Alfred de Vigny and Baudelaire and Catullus and W. H. Auden. She was certainly not a prostitute.

After a while she said: 'I'm getting tired of this clock. It makes such a noise all the time. Let's go and walk along the front.'

'Into the sunset,' said Henry.

'Why not?' she said, laughing.

So they left the gardens and crossed the road onto the short incline that led to the promenade above the bay. They did not speak and they walked a good yard apart, but they were very definitely together. No doubt people who passed them thought that they were brother and sister or even mother and son: but *they* knew they weren't and they knew that their intimacy was something that no one else could guess at, let alone share or spoil or trespass upon.

There were a few streaks of red and gold after the sun and a slow, soft grey twilight. Henry was walking closer to her and he suddenly, without thinking, took her hand. This she accepted and walked nearer yet to him. He was taller and felt protective, although he knew quite well that she was stronger as well as older.

'I haven't asked you about yourself,' he said.

'There's nothing much to tell,' she said, teasing.

'There must be.'

'All right. I'm married. I've got three children. I'm thirty-seven. Last night I quarrelled with my husband and he's taken them all to see their granny. I wouldn't go.'

They sat down on a bench facing the west watching the light fading. Greatly daring, Henry put his arm around her shoulders, expecting to be repulsed. She snuggled against him. But in an odd way: she wanted him and his male presence and his comfort, but not in any direct sexual way. He was fairly sure that if he had tried to kiss her, or to touch her breasts, she would not have stopped him: but he didn't try. It was not appropriate. She went on talking quietly. Her hair was soft against his face and there was a strong perfume that she wore which pleased him and her dress was soft and smooth under his arm and her arm and body beneath the dress was pliant and exciting.

'We quarrel a lot, I suppose,' she said. 'So just for once I thought: "All right, I'll be young again. Bugger them all." And I made up as I used to when I was eighteen. I put on a pretty dress. I gave myself a day out. I didn't know what I was going to do and I certainly didn't intend to be doing this.'

'Why were you in the gardens?'

'I was happy there. Then I saw you looking so miserable.... It honestly doesn't matter.'

She turned her face towards him, pale in the darkness, and she kissed him slowly but gently. Henry held her tightly.

'I must go home now,' she said. 'Will you take me to the bus?'

'I don't even know where you live.'

'Not anywhere near you. My bus goes from the Central Garage.'

Henry was almost ashamed to feel relieved, but it was too good to last. He gave her his arm and she took it. They walked away from the sea, the lovers, the stars becoming brilliant, towards the town and the Central Garage. Once more they said very little. Occasionally she leaned against him or pressed his arm and he thought that she might have been thinking what he was thinking. It took them twenty minutes to reach the bus station and Henry had never felt more secure or happier.

He had almost forgotten what she looked like by the time they reached the light of the garage. He turned to her with eager curiosity, so that she laughed. He was seized with a sudden, adult lust, which she perhaps recognised

125

because she stopped laughing – or let the laugh trail into nothing.

'When you go back,' Henry said, 'will you sleep with... with your husband?'

'We share the same bed,' she said. She paused. 'Yes,' she said. 'If that's the way it turns out.'

Henry nodded as sagely as he knew how to.

'Thank you, Harry,' she said. 'I mean that. Thank you.'

He watched her walk across the oily floor of the garage towards her bus and read the names of the villages and towns it passed through. She got into the bus and sat on her own near the front. A moment later the driver and conductor appeared. The bus started noisily and lurched out of the garage.

He did not think that she had looked around for him. He could not imagine what she was thinking or feeling. As the bus disappeared around the corner, Harry stepped out of the shadows and he too muttered, 'Thank you'.

Extract from 'Flower Clock', story in Metaphors of Twenty Years. *Vortex Press, 1950.*

Apart from a busy childhood as the youngest member of a lively and eclectic family in London and several happy years at Eton, Michael Beauchamp-Beck, Caradock's Oxford room-mate, had already completed National Service as a subaltern in the Royal Horse Artillery, thereby widening even further the gap between their relative experience. Beauchamp-Beck had served for a few months in post-war Germany, where he suggests any lacunae in a young man's worldly wisdom were quickly filled in. He had many acquaintances at Oxford, from school and from the army, and regarded Michael Caradock and his Jesus friend Idris Lewis, also fresh from school, as amiably comic companions for a joke at teatime, but much too green and impressionable to be taken seriously. Caradock was wary of the Etonian, his smart friends, his unself-conscious elegance: but profited from watching him and learning various useful social formulae.

Both young men got on well but kept their distance during the first Michaelmas term. Beauchamp-Beck was reading for Honour Moderations in Latin and Greek, so had more in common with Idris than with Caradock, who was reading English. He was impressed by Lewis' grasp of the Classics and by the breadth of his reading, which compensated for his innocence in other respects. With his usual good nature, he comments: 'Young men are notoriously patronising of innocence and I must confess that I regarded Michael and Idris as first and second gravedigger when I first met them: strictly comic relief. As you will remember, National Service made an enormous difference to people and those who had already done two years of it before going up thought of themselves as men and the ones who hadn't as schoolboys. The contrast between them was simple: Michael wanted to be different, Idris didn't care. As it happens, Michael and I got to know each other and like each other well after our first term – but even if we had not, I'm quite sure we should never have quarrelled. Anything that I knew that he didn't, he wanted to learn. He used to ask about wine and food and all kinds of things that I took more or less for granted. In fact, I never thought that I knew much about any of them. Then, quite suddenly, Michael matured.

'The change came during the first Christmas vacation and I assume it was because of Helen Westlake. Idris Lewis and I both talked from time to time about Greek authors, and Michael, who knew Latin pretty well, always hated the fact that he couldn't read Greek when we could. So that's why he decided to take lessons. I don't know what happened between Helen and Michael because he would not talk about her. Once when I was drunk, I teased him – probably a bit coarsely – and he was furious. I'm quite sure that he was in love with her and that she must have given him, one way or another, a lot of confidence and encouragement. The point was that Michael went down at the end of the Michaelmas term as a rather shy, nervous, defensive boy and he came back in the Hilary term still a boy – but quite sure of himself and ready to come to terms with the rest of the world. I can't tell you much more. I think she left the village about a year later and to the best of my knowledge he never saw her again.'

Extract from David Hayward's official biography.

It was wet and cold and the streets were dismal and muddy in the dim electric lamplight. Three or four days before Christmas so that the few modest little shops had tried to dress themselves up festively. In the parlours of the low terraced houses off the main street, there were paper chains, coloured bells and the occasional Christmas tree with little coloured lights. For the first time, the village did not seem to him drab and impoverished and he began to think with kindness about the unpretentious people looking forward to their modest festival and the children with their presents and carols.

He laughed at himself aloud. The change was too sudden, too drastic. Perhaps. But he thought – although he was not sure – that it was necessary to be really happy in order to imagine the feelings of others and in order to wish happiness for them. Pretty trite.

As he walked, lengthening his stride, down the steep slope, he thought back over the afternoon and heard again in a great harmonious blur the music of the *Christmas Oratorio*. He saw her vividly – sitting in an upright chair at the table in a dark green skirt and a white jumper with a high polo neck, her knees pressed close together, her hands folded on her thighs, perfectly still, her face composed and serene, her eyes smiling deep inside as she listened to the music. And from time to time she had turned to look at him, not speaking, not smiling any more obviously, but looked at him long and seriously – yet with that hint of a smile that was beyond ordinary laughter, as though lost and yet not lost in the music. Two or three times she had looked at him in this way and he had been able to accept what she was saying without asking questions, without any gauche attempt to make it all explicit.

When the music stopped she got up and took the record off the machine – then she walked over to him and held out both hands. She guided him up onto his feet and stood for a moment looking up at him, still happy and serious, holding his hands. That was all. He thanked her and went away.

He would not see her for another fourteen days at least – but for the first time in his life he felt completely happy. He

thought that that day he had learned, at last, to love someone unselfishly; that trust was more important than desire,
that gentleness mattered more than eloquence, that what
was shared was more important than what was possessed.

He tried to remember any part of the music, but he
couldn't. So he sang 'Hark the Herald Angels Sing'.

*Extract from Section III of 'Diary of a Fortunate Young
Man', from* Metaphors of Twenty Years. *Vortex Press, 1950.*

*The idea that pain ennobles is absurd. Who said that? The
question is why suffer bravely. Gemissez, pleurez, priez.
The stoics were fools like Elizabethan lazars using ratsbane
and spearwort and crowfoot to fester small wounds into
ugly and noisome sores the better to receive the alms of
admiration. Do not suffer reticently. Howl, howl, howl...*

*There is no dignity and all the works of this universe are
a mockery of the idea of dignity and decency. Death is not
an insult: the wanton childish gods cannot conceive that we
are intelligent life and that therefore even when we proclaim
the meaninglessness of existence, we should nevertheless
say that Death is an insult. How can it be? Death can only
be a relief. The inexorable logic of becoming or the blind
illogical accident? What matter? Oedipus is blind, Lear
mad. The brightness in the Western sky is the red light of
burning civilisations yet unborn. Howl: because if you do
not howl, the soul grows in upon itself and festers more
corrosively than ratsbane applied to a scratch on the fleshed
areas of the body. The wanton immortal gods understand
nothing of our feeble notion that we have souls....*

If Helen had not gone away and we had somehow made

it possible.... A green boy of twenty, knowing nothing, understanding nothing – and an innocent woman ten years older. A great joke, justicers: not to be missed.

All that meaningless reticence: the metaphors, the dishonesty of the metaphors. The stoical fictions perpetuating a dishonest perspective: an idea of dignity. Do you know Johannes Vermeer's View of Delft*? I have never seen Delft... never that view. We have Art that we may not perish from Truth. Tell it like it is....*

My hand tentatively reaching and her own arms limply at the sides of the upright chair and then pushed back over the back of the chair so that her breasts jutted forward.... Touching her.... Then moving to kiss her as she sat quite still with her arms down the side of the upright chair.... And somehow lying on top of her on the floor of her cosy little room in Mrs... what was she called?... Don't remember. Her skirt up over her stockings and her eyes closed, her mouth slightly open... thinking that she was sobbing.... Oh my God. Even now!

What a good joke to live with? Purge the memory of all self-pity. There is no view of Delft, only one of Bosch's gardens of delight.

64. Studio interview with Fay Mackail

Mackail: Oh yes, there was certainly someone. (*Pause*) Quite definitely. And she had a truly profound and lasting influence upon him for the rest of his life. And for the good. Because he was very easily depressed and with her – as a very young man – he had been extremely happy. D'you know what I mean?

131

Close in on Fay Mackail, smiling and silent.... Close up Fay Mackail

Lloyd (o/s): Did you know any more about her?

Mackail: Obviously. But I don't think this is the place to talk about it. She was quite a lot older and for various reasons it was all impossible. But she gave him confidence. You know? Perhaps you don't. The kind of thing an older woman can do for a rather neurotic young man...

Profile Fay Mackail

... Quite honestly, I think that's all anyone needs to know. It doesn't matter what her name was or is. (*Pause*)

Lloyd (o/s): But their relationship was obviously very intense. A sexual relationship...

Close up Fay Mackail, smiling ironically

Mackail: Of course! What else? And, in my opinion, he spent the rest of his life looking for her. Or, at least, for a substitute...

Fay Mackail interviewed in television programme: 'Landscape of a Prophet' by Trevelyan Lloyd.

Marcus looked down at her in some amazement. Everything had happened so quickly. And the careful labyrinth of his private self had been so effortlessly explored by this passionate Ariadne before he had known what was going on. He had arrived with Gibbon, Burckhardt and Glover, expecting tea, cucumber sandwiches, and the sort of refined sexual saraband of suggestion, counter-suggestion, hint and ambiguity that they had already rehearsed on their two previous meetings. It would leave both of them slightly flushed, mildly excited, a little stimulated: but quite intact. And now here he was, unashamedly and unselfconsciously naked, poised above her, while Mrs Roope herself lay more openly abandoned than Danaë to the stars. It had been extraordinarily simple as an initiation. Thoroughly delightful. The admirable Virginia Roope had managed all with the most facile skill, to the rather startling extent of being entirely prepared for the momentous event.

She is quite shameless, he thought. Thank God! Who would have guessed. So straightforward! She lay on the Roope marriage-bed, on a hideous pink quilted eiderdown, with her eyes shut and a little smile on her lips, superbly unconcerned. Marcus found it absurd that he should have registered indelibly the pattern of the pastel-floral wallpaper, the form and graining of the wardrobe and dressing table in light walnut, unimportant details about the room et cetera: and that he should already have forgotten what making love (making love?) to her had been like. What precisely it had felt like to ease himself gently into her body and to feel her thighs tightening around his thighs and her hips spreading as she helped him penetrate higher... deeper...

133

My God, he thought. Realising that he was once again, so soon after, tautly erect.

She opened her lazy, rather hot, eyes and looked up at him. There was no suggestion of a smile. Recognising something in his face, she looked down, along the bed.... Immediately she hooked a soft, insistent arm around his neck and pulled him down onto her, beginning immediately to move and manoeuvre her body. Oh my God! he thought again, remembering – as he pressed his tongue into her avid mouth, struggling the while to keep an assiduous hand on one breast – that Roope's Pharmacy did not close until six o'clock.

When it was all over for the second time she was less magnificently languorous. He saw her glance quickly at the dainty watch on the bedside table.

'Pow!' she said. 'What a lovely surprise you turned out to be.'

Marcus thought that he might perhaps have been a shade too precipitate. He had been quite appallingly aroused and very much lacking in experience.... He was not quite sure how to find out. Most of his information came from novels and rather elementary handbooks that had circulated at school, of which he had affected to be disdainful. He refused to believe that Lawrence could possibly be accurate. Joyce, perhaps: in the Molly Bloom soliloquy. Nothing that he had read had much to do with what had happened between them on that afternoon. He watched her putting stockings on. She did not seem displeased.

'Hey!' she said, looking up, fixing the suspender. 'You'd

better get dressed. What! Not again! You *are* an excitable young man, aren't you.'

Wearing only pants, a suspender belt and stockings, she stood up and came close to him. She kissed him once.

'Very, very nice, though,' she said. 'Very gentle when it matters and not gentle at all when it counts. That wasn't your first time, was it?'

She made her voice casually inquisitive, as though she were asking if it had been the first time he had tasted oysters or Pernod. There was no point in lying.

'Yes,' he said sheepishly.

'Pow!' she said, again, softly, smiling up at him, whispering the plosive sound through sensuous lips. 'We'll have to go through Julian the Apostate line by line. Will you help me learn Latin again? I'm very rusty.'

He was able to laugh easily.

'Go on,' she said, stepping away. 'Get dressed.'

She put on a brassiere and a slip and the same rather tight tan skirt. By the time she had started making-up, Marcus had dressed.

'Go downstairs and wait for me,' she said. 'I'll just tidy up.'

She made a little moue at him in the looking glass.

He did as he was told; returning to the dining room where he combed his hair before the mirror above the mantelpiece, studying his face with a sense of complacent good fortune. He looked at the heavy, overstuffed three-piece suite, the glass cabinet with an assortment of worthless, fairly ugly china, a matching glass-fronted bookcase with standard sets that looked entirely pristine.

135

In no sense did Marcus feel guilty, but he retained enough sensibility to feel rather sorry for Roope. Unless...

Marcus understood that he was very young and that there were many things that it was not possible to discover from books. For the moment, he did not want to pursue this line of thought. He wanted to enjoy his first *affaire*.

On the broad arm of one of the overstuffed chairs, where he had put them down, lay *The Decline and Fall of the Roman Empire*, *The Age of Constantine the Great*, *Life and Letters in the Fourth Century*. On the table were the tea things, with a half-eaten queen cake and an untouched cup of tea. He was still bewildered by the rapidity of their explicitly discovered mutual lust: but gratified. He touched his obliging genitals with tacit approval.

She came downstairs. Marcus hoped, instinctively, that she would not be coy. She was not. She was extremely businesslike.

'D'you drink?' she asked. 'We don't keep a lot. But we have some sherry and gin. Ceiriog would think it was all right to offer you sherry, because you're at Oxford.'

'I'm quite happy, thank you, Mrs...'

'Oh, honestly! Marcus, darling! Virginia...'

'Sorry.'

They both laughed. He noticed she was keeping a politic distance.

'All right. Help me clear away these dishes. Then we'll get down to the age of Constantine. Or would you rather go? You might feel a bit awkward, you know.'

Marcus' entire cultural experience had led him to suppose that such sophistication was essentially masculine.

He was a little shocked. She laughed at him.

'It's quite possible,' she said. 'Listen, darling, if you want to know what happened to us, I'll tell you. Very simply, for the moment; then at greater length when I see you next. I wanted to go to bed with you. It's as straight-forward as that. Why I did is more complicated. And I don't really understand it myself – so we'll leave it for the moment.'

'Thank you... Virginia.'

'We mustn't get sentimental, Marcus. That's dangerous.'

'I must seem very young to you.'

'Of course you do. But I'm not very old. And there are things we both enjoy together.'

She handed him two cups and saucers and began to clear away the tea things.

'Take those to the kitchen,' she said. 'And come back for the plates. The point is that if we want to go on meeting – and I want to – not just for sex, I'd like to get to know you *well* – we've got to behave sensibly.'

Extract from A Coriolan Overture. *Hazel & Sims, 1969.*

Until that last disaster, I don't think he bothered much with any woman who was younger than himself. Most of us were a few years older. I don't think there was anything Oedipal in this – but I'm not a Freudian anyway, so I wouldn't expect to take that sort of view. I think it was quite simply that his first experience of sex was with a woman who was older and very generous – I mean, of course, emotionally generous. This was a woman called Helen and I think he must have loved her very much.

137

Now, when you consider the kind of man he was – and love wasn't something that came very easily to him, as opposed to desire, obsession, a need to possess – this means that it must have been a quite unusual relationship. In Michael's case, I think unique. He never talked about it. I mean, he might make some passing reference to Helen after he'd had a few drinks – but if anyone tried to question him, he'd shut up.

Rose Brandt, novelist and psychologist, in BBC radio programme.

The guilt syndrome is never far away from the central preoccupations of Caradock's work. It is significant that in *A Coriolan Overture*, described by Caradock as 'an essay in autobiographical fiction', the explicit psychosexuality of the central encounter abandons the protective mythic cocoon for the first time in that both subjects are not related to a theomorphic scale on the one hand or to an anthroposophist ideal on the other: they are simply sexually motivated against an ambience of normalcy and, as such, in their freedom to treat such themes simplistically suggest that they are an intellectualisation of a growing need to confess to a repression of life instincts, especially those related to the gratification of sexual pleasure, in an organised attempt to prove that such instincts were never real or in any way significant.

Irving Haller: The Centaur and the Druids. *Heseltine, 1972.*

Autumn morning. The greyish-yellow stone colludes with the lighter grey of a mist that has still to rise, coloured by early, diffident sunlight, as the grass on the lawns begins to fade and the leaves begin to turn colour. The air smells of damp and smoke and it is already cold. The city is going about its business of traffic jams and daily shopping and consequential prosperity and the noise of drills digging up the rubber tiles of Cornmarket Street. And the university is minding its own: with gowns on flying bicycles and large elegant dons striding into a Hall to give Aristotle the best of three games and little female scholars fixing a silly emendation with icicle eyes and old men remembering and medical students plodding to dissections among the leafiest stretches of the Parks. A blonde girl pedals furiously along the High, too late for modesty. An old coal horse stamps patiently in St Ebbs. A preoccupied young man, no doubt composing verses, frowns at a policeman near the old Sheep's Shop. A Junior Dean tells three ex-commandos it will not happen again and fines them a total of nine guineas. Housewives have a cup of tea in the market. People sigh and laugh and grumble and float and gnaw and stump and idle their way through the autumn morning.

*

When I awoke, the first time, the sky was very blue and the sun caught a bird on the very tip of a spire of a church I could see from my narrow window. By chance, or so I think now, another bird was singing in the college garden. And I believed that the metal bird on the spire was real and singing. I took it as an omen and until then I had never been as happy. I got up in a tearing hurry to go out and breathe the air and smell, taste, touch, hear, see a town I had been determined to love and now found that I was already loving.

Extracts from 'Oxford and the Weather: Portrait of a Love Affair', from Metaphors of Twenty Years. *Vortex Press, 1950.*

Michael Caradock's first reactions to Oxford were intensely suspicious and not at all the highly lyrical sensations that he describes in the four sketches to be found in *Metaphors of Twenty Years,* though Michael Beauchamp-Beck and Idris Lewis both remember clearly that Caradock in his first term valued Oxford for its enormous range of activity in the arts and in the dissemination of ideas. He also worked very hard. Otherwise, the social communality of college life held little appeal for him. He distrusted the suave and feared the hairy.

After the first vacation all was different. Both of his closest friends have been recorded as ascribing this new confidence to his relationship with Helen Westlake; but Idris Lewis is also disposed to offer another contributory factor.

'Michael Beauchamp-Beck was enormously kind in many ways. We were all visited by parents and so on, usually in the summer, which I suppose everyone thought was a bit of a bore. I've always got on perfectly well with my family, but I think most young men – even the most sophisticated – are embarrassed from time to time by the older generation. As you can probably imagine, Michael went through paroxysms when Howell and Phyllis Caradock came up to visit. Phyllis was, in fact, rather a silly woman who insisted on telling charming stories about

"Julian", as they called him, as a small child. Well, that can be very wearing. But Howell was a decent old boy – very square and a little dull, but thoroughly likeable. Beauchamp-Beck was absolutely splendid. I tried to help a little, but he was really most considerate. He took them all out to dinner and to the theatre and to watch Eights on the river. And, of course, he was an Old Etonian, so they were enormously pleased and impressed. But otherwise, Caradock would have had, quite unnecessarily of course, an excruciatingly miserable week.

'Then with his second year, he began to involve himself passionately in all sorts of things. He'd already passed Prelims with quite a few alphas, so his academic future looked good. And it was then that he wrote those sketches.'

Perhaps like a lot of good love affairs, there was a pretty uncomfortable period of adjustment, at the beginning.

Extract from David Hayward's official biography.

Acknowledging, therefore, the astounding achievement and genius of James Joyce, his daring and dedication, the almost frightening ambition and technical mastery, the novelist struggling along in his mighty wake is inclined to ask himself rather obsessively how it came about that one who set out to 'forge in the smithy of my soul the uncreated conscience of my race' (no small purpose), managed to forge something very much more immense – a synthesis of the creative intelligence of his civilisation and a different level of consciousness.

I do not know whether Joyce created a conscience for Ireland or the Irish and I am not qualified to make any such evaluation: I do know that his has been the most affirmative voice in relating the myth, thought, literary drive and linguistic versatility of Western Europe. This is a very large claim: but it is not I who make it – it is made in the work of Joyce by its very existence. Naturally enough, another writer begins by examining the resources and essential aims of one whom he greatly admires. Joyce offered us a brilliant commentary on Aquinas' idea of beauty:

> – To finish what I was saying about beauty, said Stephen, the most satisfying relations of the sensible must therefore correspond to the necessary phases of artistic apprehension. Find these and you will find the qualities of universal beauty. Aquinas says: *Ad pulchritudinem tria requiruntur integritas, consonantia, claritas.* I translate it so: *Three things are needed for beauty, wholeness, harmony and radiance.* Do these correspond to the phases of apprehension? Are you following?

If we accept these three requirements as central to Joyce's basic purpose in creating any work of art, we are on the threshold of a fascinating study and perhaps yet another academic tome of intolerable specific gravity. So I prefer, for the moment, to consider three resources necessary to the artist as specified by Joyce: silence, exile and cunning:

> – Look here, Cranly, he said. You have asked me what I would do and what I would not do. I will tell you what I will do and what I will not do. I will not serve that in which I no longer believe, whether it call itself my home, my fatherland, or my church: and I will express myself in

some mode of life or art as freely as I can and as wholly as I can, using for my defence the only arms I allow myself to use – silence, exile and cunning.

Perhaps I may draw attention to the word that I have used in describing these attributes: it is 'resources' – where James Joyce refers to them as 'arms'. But I am in no doubt that he is entirely right in suggesting that 'silence, exile and cunning' are the means of *defence* that an artist – today even more than in 1916 – must rely on if he is to survive in order to work and to believe in his purpose, which may still be to create something which has wholeness, harmony and radiance.

Justifiably, in the context in which it occurs, and because of the weight in the word 'exile', much has been written about this phrase in regard to Joyce's attitude to Ireland, 'the old sow that eats her farrow'. It would be most unwise to underrate the importance of Joyce's voluntary exile from Ireland psychologically and artistically: but I contend that, while he meant the word to apply to that specific and in some way sacrificial act of renunciation, in part, Joyce also wanted it to be understood in a much broader significance – as 'silence' and 'cunning' would almost certainly be understood as part of the limited weaponry available to the writer of serious conscience.

As 'silence' means also 'reticence', and 'cunning' means also 'artifice' – at least in my own reading of Joyce's phrase – 'exile' means more than the abstention from a country, a town, a way of life or religion or of thought: it means a wilful detachment from other people. The cultivation of an isolation that permits total dedication to an art (or indeed a craft) and allows the artist the wonderful solace of receiving and offering love with only a very few people. In that sense it reduces him: he is less privileged and probably less happy than other men. And he imposes this exile upon himself not out of a feeling of superiority to others, but out of a sense of difference. Where most people are content to live their own lives and interfere in the lives of others, the artist wants to live a thousand lives at least. Since no artist has the emotional strength or intellectual energy to successfully identify with the variety of people that he wants to know and be, he must detach himself. He must process feelings and improvise on everything he observes and experiences and he must develop a startling dispassion in order to ever be passionate. This might very well make him hell to live with. Truth (or reality) for a fictionalist – poet, playwright or novelist – is endlessly adaptable. His distortions and liberties are, in his own mind at least, permissible in the names of wholeness, harmony and radiance.

I hope in this limited essay to sketch certain approaches to Joyce's achievement of these three ideals through his practice of silence, exile and cunning.

Extract from 'Silence, Exile and Cunning', an essay from An Elemental Wound. *Hazel & Sims, 1963.*

What is it now? A bottle-and-a-half past reason. Mid morning. The turning of the tide. Yelling birds. See where the kingfisher dives. The winter visitor: flash of colour in the grey, white and pale-yellow light, with the rain and dark

144

cloud holding off. The wind must have changed. Again.

What will they do for the rest of their lives? What is she now planning? Will she have dressed? No, she still lies there, white breasts, white thighs, dark luxuriant hair, still, wicked eyes, red mouth. The rose of Hell who flowered from my poisoned tree.

There are very few who can comfort us by being loved, by letting us love. There is too little.... They are too few....

The cage. The careful construct I made. In which now I must sit terrified and tamed, away from the bars while the wild jungle noises sound – the screams, the slithering and rustling and scraping noises among the steaming, lush vegetation, the roars, howls, snickers, ricane of savage pleasure. Poor tame chimpanzee, in catatonic fear, while the wild ones come around, curious and baffled and some hostile. I dare not move from the middle of the cage.

What hope was there in a bare landscape within sight of the broadleaf woods, the coniferous mountain, the headlands and salt meadow pastures. That is not the dark land I feared, the ant-people in their flurry....

Grey and green and gold. Red, drunk faces, the pointed teeth and slurried eyes; the light through trees on a spring of childish despair; a mob in the street, smoke and thunderflash; howl of someone hunted through dark fields; a glimpse of plump thighs; chestnut trees and stammering insincerity – the pale-haired innocent hurling off the bed with her knickers awry; the Sanctus, the Gloria; Ariel flitting into the veils of scented dark; a poem in the snow by the river; the brush of a tit.... I also feared. I have lived my life in fear.

Silence? Ha. Speak for me Friedrich: Ach, so. The author

145

must keep his mouth shut when his work starts to speak.
The gash of a mouth that no longer smiles or kisses or
speaks. The tragic mask of Dionysian tragic purpose: the
paralysis out of which spews shame and self-pity.

A special cage was built for him out of heavy steel used for
temporary runways. 'They thought I was a dangerous wild
man and were scared of me. I had a guard night and day....
Soldiers used to come up to the cage and look at me. Some of
them brought me food. Old Ez was a prize exhibit.' For some
months he lived caged, sleeping on the ground, shielded from
sun and rain only by some tar paper a kindly GI found for
him. In the cage he wrote furiously, madly, poignantly. The
fruit of the imprisonment was *The Pisan Cantos....*

So Richard H. Rovere wrote a mere six years ago about
Ezra Pound, who was at the time still confined in a mental
hospital in the United States. Rovere's cool analysis of the
long penitence exacted from Pound by the American
nation is truthful, scornful and compassionate. It did not
seek to excuse but to forgive and was instrumental (by the
response that it evoked from international writers) in
helping to achieve Pound's eventual freedom.

Two immediate reflections occur. The first is no doubt
emotional: a great creative writer – one whose entire life
had been devoted to 'making it new', to extending the
range and influence of artistic experience – was put in a
cage and kept as a sort of pet by men infinitely less
intelligent. The man who had tirelessly challenged sterility
and orthodoxy in the name of aesthetic progress and who
had generously helped in energetic and practical ways a

number of other artists (including Eliot, Joyce, Yeats and Frost) was treated as a wild man.

The second is perhaps more rational: Pound did espouse crypto-fascist ideas and vented virulent anti-Semitic sentiments. He did broadcast against his own people on behalf of a barbarian regime in time of war, although he had attempted to leave Italy and had been refused permission, by US authorities. Because of his bizarre economic theories, he identified himself with intellectually barren politics.

Undoubtedly the sober, unimaginative psychiatric report on Pound in 1945 saved him from severe retribution, perhaps from the death penalty; but would imprisonment among criminals have been any worse than incarceration among the insane in a bare concrete ward where many of the patients were restricted within modified straitjackets. In due course, Pound was accorded more privacy and facilities for writing. He worked, he read, he translated. But he was not freed.

The argument against this treatment rests on a premise that liberal democracy must be magnanimous or it is nothing. Vengeance has no part in the politics of toleration. The case against Pound is a case that might be made against many men of genius who dabble in ideas that belong to the life and concerns of the active man – the statesman, legislator or administrator. The artist is often impatient at the torpidity of a self-indulgent mass, angry at the exploitation of this mass by non-productive financiers. And so he fulminates. The man in the street may feel as little appreciated as the artist, but he merely grumbles.

One of Joyce's young men in *A Portrait of the Artist* complains that Aquinas sounds too often like the man in the street. Pound's problem is that he does not, has never done and probably would not wish to. This has made his voice sometimes strident, and stridency disturbs the well behaved whose disapproval only augments its annoying pitch.

If we are to survive, then something of our civilisation, however little we do to protect it, will survive. And in the perspective of history, the great and good writers will be pardoned (in Auden's words) by Time for writing well. It is not too soon to pardon Pound for the aberrations of a busy, impatient and quite unusual mind.

We live in a materialist society in which standards are low and fashions matter more than ideas: energy goes into exploitation and the satraps of art eclipse the true artists. Not the least paranoid of men, it is easy for these to imagine that they will fare better in a more strictly ordered society run on Aristotelian lines. Only when rational considerations prevail does it become immediately apparent that the organised power of the modern state makes the artist of independent mind particularly vulnerable. His remaining strength lies only in silence or inaction. Silence and inaction to the artist are a living death. It is appropriate in these days of so-called commitment to remember that anything that restricts the exchange of ideas, even if they are bad ideas, restricts our opportunity to distinguish the bad from the good.

These observations are intended to delineate a stance in considering Pound's work, rather than to offer excuses for this short study. I shall concentrate on his range, his huge technical ambition and his lyricism. T. S. Eliot states that Pound's ideas, as ideas, are not very interesting; but there is no doubt that his eclectic 'volitional' mind was about the work of amalgamating disparate experience to create new wholes in much the same way that Mr Eliot described in his approbation of the Metaphysical Poets....

Extract from 'The Singer Not the Song – A Note on Ezra Pound', an essay in An Elemental Wound. *Hazel & Sims, 1963.*

Evidence in a sequence of purely literary essays, most notably the 'note' on Ezra Pound, 'The Singer Not the Song', indicates that Caradock was no reactionary. He feared proletarian revolution: but he detested right-wing barbarity and always referred to fascist regimes as barbarian, seeing in them a late manifestation of a long and mindlessly destructive power-principle. The last apocalyptic nightmare was that great art and serious artists would be finally destroyed by apathy as much as by wilful desecration. Passages in the *Laocoön* illustrate this nightmare often, sometimes hysterically. As the silt and sludge creeps higher from the overflowing sewers, the psychopath arrives in his canoe, drugged and blood flecked, to smash and tear and spoil. Caradock was never in doubt that the strong are very often vicious, when they feel strong enough.

His contemporaries at Oxford recall his enthusiasm for Pound's early poems (collected in the Faber volume entitled *Personae*) and most particularly for *Mauberley*. In fact it is not unreasonable to suggest that Hugh Selwyn Mauberley's disillusions and passions were very similar to Michael Julian Caradock's: for Caradock too saw himself as a man of great sensibility struggling to survive on his own terms in a vandal and philistine world. He did not believe that any of his books had succeeded and (according to a close confidant, James

Faber) professed to be hated and a failure in the eyes of the literary world. He showed none of the robustness of Pound in dealing roundly with his detractors, but carried on working all the same with concentration and diligence. Once again the determination to be an outsider or a misfit seems to be manifest: the success of several novels and his acceptance by artistic circles in London was firm and considerable. It was Caradock himself who did the rejecting.

A last word on Caradock's attitude to Pound must underline the difference between the radical and the conservative: Pound was a radical not a reactionary – he wanted to innovate everywhere – and it is my own view that Caradock, who was instinctively conservative, however liberal his theories, was ill at ease in trying to write about the greater and more ambitious writer. He admired Pound but he did not understand him and it is for this reason, I submit, that he evaded the issue of discussing Pound's ideas in favour of a study (albeit a very sensitive and valuable study) of Pound's lyricism....

Extract from Stephen Lewis: The Novels of Michael Caradock. *Molyneux, 1971.*

It was not very long ago that I discovered an aspect of nostalgia that, for me and I suspect for quite a few others, is very important: the nostalgia of hatred. I was walking along a suburban street on a very fine September morning rehearsing in my mind old insults, replaying the outrages of childhood and adolescence and, in the manner of an irredeemable fictionalist, working out different resolutions. Quite abruptly and for no good reason, I became aware that it was a lovely morning, that the trees in the gardens were beautiful, that there were roses and chrysanthemums: and that there was no excuse for this burning acidosis of the soul. I had absolutely no right to feel such resentment on such a clean morning in Hampstead or Mortlake or wherever I was.

Well, it seemed, as soon as I became aware of what had just been going on in my head, that there were many more resentments and furies in reserve. I discovered that I possess enormous reserves of malice, that I stock a library of grudges, that there have been few periods of my life in which I have not nurtured and cherished injuries to my pride, before which (at the time they occurred) I was powerless, stammering, choking back sobs of rage and frustration.

The discovery was useful in that I have since been able to see with more reasoning and discrimination landscapes that I enjoy dwelling upon in memory and places that I revisit. I stood once in the Parks at Oxford, metamorphosed into some youth that I had never been but quite convinced that my bogus trance was genuine. (I was, I suppose, very happy at Oxford.) I have since, anonymously, walked through the village where I lived as a child, diligently recalling my boredom, my insecurity, my early conviction that it was some kind of transit camp in which my stay was unavoidable but finite.

It came as something of a shock to me to realise that my pleasant fits of nostalgia were simple indulgences – obviously necessary escapes into a better, happier time from some transient discontent but that my journeys into hatred were psychologically more necessary in that, through my fictional analyses of past slights and savageries (real and imagined), I was equipping myself for those that are still to come and are coming.

Soon after I was able to isolate the nostalgia of shame: the appalling recollection of some foolish phrase, or gesture, or action that makes one squirm or shudder in the most complete privacy. Not the funny howlers or mistakes or simple embarrassments: the unguarded confidences or asides that reveal the triviality and basic meanness of oneself.

Beginning of 'Going Back', essay in An Elemental Wound. *Hazel & Sims, 1963.*

I do not know whether, indeed, 'the truest poetry is the most feigning'. (I suspect it is so: because it seems to me that direct personal experience requires the discipline and reticence of metaphor not so much to spare the reader embarrassment but to involve him at a more universal level.) In my experience, the writer of prose fiction certainly 'feigns' all the time, because it is far less dangerous to invent circumstances and people than to attempt to report on events and those who took part in them. There is less opportunity for spleen or sentimentality and experience is purified by the imaginative process of distillation into fiction: so that the prose fictionalist who proposes to write a number of books usually translates ideas that he has formulated, characters that he has met, situations that he has confronted, feelings that have moved or disturbed him, into an entirely unreal condition. But then comes the sudden upsurge of intense lyrical pleasure released by a chance association and an unexpectedly urgent desire to set it down: to say to whoever cares to hear or read 'Time was indeed away and she was there and if it was not Arcadia, it seemed for a few hours to resemble it' as an act of belated thanks to her and to the 'most high gods who watched that sunlit hour as it passed'.

As a young writer, I should have tried to put such an impulse into a poem, or even into a prose sketch. Now, in what passes for maturity, a little nonplussed, I am trying to catch that unattended and sunlit moment, while trying to explain something – I am not quite sure what – to myself.

Camus' cynical judge-penitent in *The Fall* says: 'Of course, true love is exceptional, two or three times a century, more or less. The rest of the time there is vanity or boredom.' I'm not sure that I am, by those criteria, prepared to claim that what I once experienced was 'true love': but it was something I knew to be rare, something beyond the possibility of boredom and something in which there was no vanity and something completely different from the excitement of a happy sexual interest that is successfully shared.

Whatever it was that spring afternoon, in an absurdly ornamental garden of a country palace that neither of us particularly wanted to visit, with the normally gentle landscape of Oxfordshire across the river seeming wild in comparison with the formalities of Duchene, it was something that both of us understood without speaking a word, without even touching: it was commitment, it was trust, it was mutual desire, it was a will to take and to give, it was the relief from pain and anxiety that comes from the unconditional surrender of one's own existence, however briefly, to someone else: what one would dearly wish Death to be and fears that it is not. Perhaps this is the last extreme in self-love and what seems to be the most complete abdication of vanity is only a deliberately sought martyrdom. I did not think so then, watching her

153

walk ahead of me, in a light flowered dress which swirled a little as she moved, waiting for her to turn and smile as I knew she would. And I do not think so now. And I do not think that it was a magnificent work of my imagination. The moment was, for me – for us both, so perfect that there was no time for sadness....

Extract from 'An Idea of Remembered Love', a lyrical essay in the collection The Philosopher's Stone. *Hazel & Sims, 1965.*

The ceaseless and graceless and debasing pursuit of Cunt. And, like so many others, I have dedicated myself to it with a pathetic slavering avidity. Ambition! What is ambition next to the sweaty wallowing of a nurtured Lust? The obsession with one that will do the deed, a well-turned tit, a plushy crutch luxuriously adorned. Capability's Natural Garden! And I to sigh for her! To watch for her! To pray for her!

And then the achievement. Oh, great master, the simpering dame goes to it, but it is we who are the soiled Centaurs, rising to the sour scent of appetite. We are the weakly pursuers: and what they are – they are the required accomplices in the crime. Merci, cher semblable... the crime? To give it the name of love. The sugar'd game...

What energy and what absurd waste: the obsessive importance of coupling, the close animal straining after flesh for flesh. Too hot! To thee, to thee, my heaved-up hands appeal....

The disgrace is absolute. The brothel is a clean and disinfected place compared to my memory: spreadeagled bodies, whimpers, shrill grunts of boarish fury out of my own loaded head, the thresh of their titillated thighs and my

own taut silken fetishes of madness. To the whipping house?
No, never that, at least! A bitter little joke if you like. Say
rather a kind of besotten suffocation between sheer silk and
velvet flesh. A kind of loveless vampire fury to possess and to
debase and to be debased. The worshipful enslavement to the
great pulsating Cunt of them all... all since the first time....

What did Helen want after all: love, affection, to give
herself to a mere boy? No. She wanted the itch of her own
lust assuaged, tickled, and flourished and thrust into
quiescence. At a hint, Helen too delighted in lewdness and
display. And after Helen, the others...

Now this hellcat... out there, you on that hill in the
greying noon, still darkening, you have been my final
humiliation.... And I am now finished. I was never whole....
How rare is that man's speed! How heartily he serves me!

The bitter day is at its height now and the ruffling grey
waters subside in the newly falling rain. There is a terrible quiet.

Good apothecary, an ounce of civet...

160. Ext. Glanmor. Day. Leighton Rees approaching camera, along the rock-strewn path below Caradock's house...	MUSIC: R. Strauss: *Tod und Verklärung* (7a and b)
... Rees passes camera, climbing, which...	Peak music
Pans to follow him onto a rocky outcrop to the left of house, some hundred feet below. Rees	Begin to fade music but hold under Rees...

pauses, glances round...

161. Ext. Caradock house. Day. Rees (head and shoulders)

Rees (Sync.): So much that is beautiful: the ever-changing light on the water, the delicate colour of the Welsh countryside, the wild and haunting cry of seabirds...

Rees indicates house above and behind

Above which that embittered, lonely man brooded over his life of rejection and contempt. When he was offered love, he spurned it; when it was forbidden him, some demon in what might have been an artist's soul of genius goaded him into crazy determination to dominate and possess, inevitably to corrupt....

162. Ext. Estuary. Day. Cut to view from Caradock's house over estuary, panning round from right to left – the White Crow hill, with the wood below, village and harbour, along the jetty to the White House and headland

(V/O) *Rees*: The fatal flaw in a man of high talent who rejected first of all his heritage, only to find a vacuum, a void, which he sought to fill with the ersatz febrility of London Bohemianism: trying himself to live up to a dandified image of an *âme maudit* whose debauchery was sad and anachronistic.

Zoom across widest part of estuary to headland and cut to

Bring up and hold music

163. Ext. Caradock house. Day. Long shot of the islet with Caradock's house in sunlight: end of day...

Fade music. Bring up birds and sound of water

Creep shot to left, discovering Emlyn Savage in shot, looking out at scene (back to camera)

Lose birds and water.

(V/O) *Lloyd*: Leighton Rees who knew Caradock in London for many years admits that he did not like him as a man and thinks that he allowed his talent to be eroded.... Emlyn Savage is a gamekeeper at Glanmor and was a friend of the writer....

Medium shot, Savage contemplating same view of islet and house

(V/O) *Savage*: At least I like to think so now... I like to think I was a friend of his. He always treated me as one. (*Pause*) He wasn't a happy man and he drank quite a bit: but that last business wasn't his fault. No good will come of it now, but he just wanted to be left in peace. And if he had been, then it wouldn't have happened. I miss him a lot. He was a decent, quiet man....

Sequence from television programme on Michael Caradock, 'Landscape of a Prophet', narration by poet Trevelyan Lloyd.

Throughout his life Michael Caradock enjoyed and sought the company of attractive and intelligent women. In an early chapter I described him as a passionate puritan and this is in no sense too exaggerated a label for him. Living among artists, whose standards long before the liberating influences of the last five years or so have always been permissive or progressive, according to one's point of view, Caradock enjoyed several close and intimate friendships with women of his circle, who were themselves painters, writers, or else involved in the arts or the mass media.

At the same time his early upbringing, the shadow of the Capel, encroached upon his enjoyment of a free-and-easy, uninhibited way of life. And time and again in his work, as well as in confidential testimony given to me by men and women who knew him well for many years, there are examples of a perennial conflict between his passionate nature and a dark capacity for brooding about pleasures proved – which quickly become guilts suffered. Over and over again, Caradock's young men find themselves involved in affairs, sometimes gentle, sometimes torrid – only to experience some form of revulsion.

It is at once facile and mistaken to assume because of the circumstances attending Caradock's premature death, that his was a life much given to womanising and to debauchery. This is emphatically not so: it is important to emphasise that Caradock's obsessions were artistic and ethical, where his day-to-day preoccupations might have been less rarefied. Nevertheless, when a man and his mistress have both been murdered brutally, it is essential to ask questions which are not necessarily within any principles of tact and decorum. It is necessary to look at the way a man lives his life in the context of his art and of his contending passions. The irony of his death in a place where he had obviously sought rejuvenation and reconciliation is stranger than any fiction.

Derek Parnell: In His Own Country. *Guildenstern, 1970.*

And suddenly I believe again in innocence. Something that I have scorned for many years. It certainly isn't the Innocence of the English Romantics – children are, on the whole, blatantly animal in their self-interest, however cunning – but it convinces me (if that matters) that there is something good, unspoilt and generous to be discovered, sooner or later, in most of us. I think that in a few hours we not only learn, but wish to give ourselves entirely to someone else; that we are briefly vulnerable; that, immediately after, we reconstruct the elaborate systems of defence that protect us against attack, against slurs upon vanity, against boredom. We become ourselves again. We put away those few hours – whenever they happened.

Then one day, by chance, they come alive in memory. And they are so clearly the best few hours lived.

Extract from 'An Idea of Remembered Love', lyrical essay in collection The Philosopher's Stone. *Hazel & Sims, 1965.*

4

Unquestionably the most important event in Michael Caradock's life at this time was the departure from it of Helen Westlake.

The lady in question has cooperated willingly and generously with me in providing information about Caradock during those years. The nature of Caradock's death and the unhappy welter of speculation that followed it made her anxious to offer her account of the true facts as she knew them and as they concerned her. Understandably, since she has been married for fifteen years, she does not wish any further incursion into her private life and has asked that her present name be withheld. Anyone who has met or talked to her for any length of time will not be surprised that her influence, particularly on a younger and highly impressionable man, should be considerable. Helen Westlake is above all an extremely gentle person, though without sentimentality. Her judgements are governed by a well-trained, alert and very well-stocked mind. It will emerge clearly that so must they have been at the time of her relationship with the young Caradock.

This relationship, she confirms, was sexual and fully consummated, although it began as a particularly warm friendship. In Helen Westlake's opinion, Michael Caradock (whom she refers to as Julian) was a boy of outstanding gifts and an original mind. He was also lazy and not prepared to put in the necessary work to master the subject that she taught – Latin. She realised that the only way to make him work was to, in some way, make the language and the texts come alive for him, so that it was no longer an academic chore necessary to get him to Oxford. She offered to take him and two other pupils for special extra classes, during school hours, at free times. The other two pupils dropped away but she read with Caradock several texts which were outside their immediate curriculum – Tacitus, Juvenal, Martial, Ovid and Suetonius. In so doing, he discovered an enthusiasm for Latin and she discovered a growing affection for him. She says that he had an interesting mind; because he was relaxed, secure and natural with her, she (unlike most of her colleagues) thought he had an attractive personality. She found him very much more sensitive than the usual run of pupils at the school. She is quite adamant that during those two years, neither of them imagined that they were anything other than teacher and pupil on unusually good terms, though she admits that there must have been some sense of sexual attraction between two people of relatively similar ages. The headmaster had not allowed Caradock to sit for Oxford in the same year that he took the Higher School Certificate examination. He was supported by Helen Westlake and Howard Paul in their private advice to the boy, who was anxious to leave as soon as possible. Mr Paul thought that it would be wise for him to go up a year older to a university with a high proportion of ex-servicemen; Helen Westlake thought it would do him no harm to read a lot more outside the school syllabus.

Caradock left school aged nineteen. Helen Westlake expected to see him occasionally and was certainly interested to hear how he was getting on. She was pleasantly surprised when he asked her to teach him Greek, and, looking back, wonders why she had not proposed the idea during the previous year. She was pleased to see the young man regularly again and inclined to laugh at herself. Caradock returned to Cwmfelyn on the long Oxford vacations well before the school broke up. Helen Westlake, who took her holidays with her parents in Shropshire, was prepared to cut them short. They were discreet but spent more and more time together.

Helen had had one happy love affair some years before, but the man whom she might have married was killed in action while serving with his regiment. To her consternation she began to think that she was infatuated, even in love, with this ex-pupil, whom she had still thought of as a boy until a few weeks previously. She is quite candid about what happened: 'Neither of us seduced the other. Quite honestly, I don't think that either of us would have known where to begin. We just looked at each other one afternoon and gave in. It was very simple.'

The love affair continued until the following summer, by which time Helen had decided it must end. All villages are a sympathetic medium for cultures of gossip and Helen was aware that it had already started. She realised the extent of any ensuing scandal and, a practical lady, the harm that it would do to her career and reputation, as well as to Caradock who would have to deal with the reaction of his family. There was no question of marriage at that time between a man aged twenty and a woman almost ten years older in those particular circumstances; a long relationship would in many ways inhibit Caradock's development in that he would rely more and more upon her for love and encouragement at a time when he should be risking himself emotionally and discovering as much about life as possible. She said in conversation: 'I was intensely ambitious for him. I knew he was very, very good.'

She spent two weeks with him near Oxford in that summer, during which time she tried to convince him in every way that she was deeply in love: then she explained that she proposed to go away and never to see him again. She told him her reasons gently and patiently. Of course, the young man argued: Helen was firm. She had resigned her job at Cwmfelyn. She was going away and she would not say where. Caradock's emotional upset was clearly going to be considerable for a time, but she thought he would recover quickly, believing in the resilience of youth and in Caradock's own capacity for detachment. And she evidently knew him very well indeed. While that first love affair was always remembered in his work with kindness, Michael Caradock applied himself immediately to recovering from it. He worked very hard, he wrote a great deal, he showed increased interest in the activities of small, elitist literary groups. He said little about Helen to anyone.

For her part, she went on to London where she taught for some years, before moving on and a few years later meeting her present husband. She is one of the most honest, sincere and good people that it has ever been my privilege to meet. It is hardly remarkable that Caradock remembered her with such love: but whether or not her decision to finish their love affair decisively had as limited an effect upon him as she supposed it would is doubtful. Some of his friends (especially those women who knew him intimately) suggest that thereafter he became watchful, quietly isolationist, never prepared to surrender himself; that he made detachment and irony a personal creed of behaviour. What would have happened if Helen Westlake and Julian Caradock had met in the late sixties in the same circumstances as they met in the late forties is a matter for conjecture, as is the question of how they would have lived, and whether a happy and fulfilled Caradock would have written the books he did.

Extract from David Hayward's official biography.

I think it's a very beautiful place in the summer. Perhaps it's because I've worked in so many godforsaken climates that the decent English watercolour image became irresistible – cows in Merton fields, pretty girls in Parks

Road, people in gowns in Broad Street: very seductive in Buenos Aires or Calcutta I promise you. And it used to be a term when most people who weren't taking some kind of examination were able to relax a little. That is to say, of course, the ones who weren't relaxing anyway. Michael did very well in the previous term at his first examination, but he always worked hard. I remember it quite well for some reason: he was reading Chaucer, Langland and Gower and several other Middle English odds and sods who convince one that life is worth living: but he didn't let up.

When he came back up in the Michaelmas term, we were no longer sharing rooms, but we saw each other quite a bit. And he was a lot more assured. As though he knew exactly where he was going.

As for women, I don't think there were any really serious things going on. I don't honestly think that one can avoid this: he had already had a very complete love affair and he wasn't much interested in what Oxford could offer. Obviously he took various girls out but I don't think he was very ardent and I doubt if they cared. He became fiercely ambitious.... Apart from that one big incandescent thing, he scorned delights and lived laborious days.

Michael Beauchamp-Beck in BBC radio programme.

The air of a July evening in London was, for Marcus, like a breath off Olympus – an intoxicant composed of fumes and fug and sweating bodies and cheap frying oil and hotdogs; hot roads, dust and rubber; sickly gushes of warm flatulence from underground ventilation outlets. Marcus, wearing a charcoal-grey suit with a rose in the lapel, breathed with the self-conscious satisfaction of a valetudinarian on an Alp, standing there outside Swan & Edgar, sniffing appreciatively. The prostitutes – or, at least, the girls whom Marcus assumed were prostitutes – did not bother him. This pleased him because it implied that he did not look provincial. He felt debonair. The lights began to glow, flash and twinkle more brightly, there was a queue outside the Pavilion, a discreet trickle of West Enders entering the Criterion, further along the bright running neon sign outside the Prince of Wales, crowds moving along Coventry Street past Lyons Corner House to the dusty greenery of Leicester Square. Marcus felt at one with London, and quite sure that London would soon feel at one with Marcus.

Virginia Roope came out of the Underground exit on the other side of Piccadilly and stood for a few seconds looking flustered and nervous, but remarkably young and pretty; much more fragile and delicate than the well-built and respectable married lady at home. Marcus felt an untoward stirring at his loins, rather ashamed that her uncertainty should thus excite him. He waited for her to find him in the crowd, setting his face in a confident smile and brandishing a rolled umbrella. If *she* had once possessed the initiative and sophistication, here, in London, it was he who would be dominant. After a brief flicker of relief, she regained composure. She came rippling towards him in a soft, wafting summer dress: smiling now, trying to reassert authority that she usually exercised over him with such astounding economy. But Marcus had seen her revealed in that moment. He looked forward to the night – beyond the evening – ahead.

Virginia kissed him.

'Hullo, love,' she said. 'I hope you haven't been waiting long.'

He noticed her accent: the liquid Welsh lilt undulating like an electronic wave: very melodic, nevertheless, against the surrounding discords of the cosmopolitan and Cockney crowd around them.

'Virginia!' he said. 'How wonderful!'

She looked up at him quickly, her eyes widening very slightly. For a moment he thought that she was going to smile or even laugh.

'Darling,' she said.

Marcus put his arm around her waist.

'Where have you left your bag?' he asked.

'In the left-luggage,' she said.

'Let's have a cocktail in the Criterion bar before we pick it up and go back to the hotel.'

Tactfully she detached herself.

'That would be lovely,' she said. 'Where are we staying?'

Marcus had given much thought to the matter: he had wanted an hotel that was bored enough by adultery not to pay attention to the difference in their ages but which was yet suitably elegant and fashionably placed. There had been an uneasy moment when he had thought that they would be given away by having to produce ration books, but discreet inquiries among his worldly friends had reassured him that these were no longer necessary for short stays. He had accordingly chosen a place in Mayfair, which was probably too expensive, but which must impress her. He did his best to sound casual:

'The Embassy,' he said. 'Just off Curzon Street. In Mayfair. Not far. We'll get a cab.'

He was not able to stop himself looking sideways at her quickly to see the effect. She smiled. But Marcus thought that there was a twinkle of untoward amusement in it. He began to think that Mrs Roope was seeing their clandestine meeting in London less as a passionate but suave occasion than as a romp. He had an uneasy feeling that she thought he was funny.

'I have tickets for *Coriolanus* at the New Theatre,' he said, as he guided her across the street. 'We've plenty of time and we'll have a spot of supper later.'

Again she smiled – almost politely. Marcus wondered if she could not trust herself to speak, for fear of being unable to disguise the laughter in her voice. But in the high-ceilinged bar of the hotel she sat close to him, pressed her thigh against his knee under the table and called him 'Darling'.

And they did not see *Coriolanus* that evening. When they went back to the hotel in Mayfair, he turned round from unpacking to find Virginia sitting on the edge of the bed. She had crossed her legs high up the thigh and arranged her dress so that it fell just above her stockings. She knew already the effect that this sort of display had on Marcus, but the expression on her face alone would have excited him violently. She smiled, slid the top leg slowly away from the other and said: 'When does the play start?'

*

168

The three days that Marcus and Virginia spent together were happy, without being remotely idyllic. Relieved of the impending Feydeau farce of their liaisons in the village, Marcus enjoyed the leisurely hours of relatively elegant sin. The actual sex was as dynamic as the urgent sequence of meetings during his last vacation, but now the *encadrement* of conversation and visits to theatres and galleries and serious films made the whole business more appropriate and satisfying.

It was also fascinating to watch an attractive woman at close quarters. Marcus understood why painters and sculptors could become obsessed by their women in unguarded moments, as they dressed or washed or made up. When the need to possess was no longer immediate, he enjoyed watching Virginia; and when he became aware that she merely tolerated this scrutiny, without much liking it, he enjoyed it all the more. At a rather different and more sensitive level he knew a real and profound pleasure in waking up in the middle of the night to find her beside him. She wore soft silky nightdresses in pale colours, one blue and one yellow. He would touch her and wake her and they would make love.

There was no doubt in his mind that now they made love. It was no longer a coition that satisfied some vague sexual want: it was an act of love – far removed from what had happened on their first afternoon when they should have been talking about the Emperor Julian. She was unfailingly kind: Marcus thought that she gave herself to him and believed that he was (most of the time) able to please her. At the same time she enjoyed all the erotic interplay for its own sake: she liked the teasing that aroused him and the caressing that awakened her. They walked about in London, went to four galleries, saw *Le Diable au corps* and *Les Parents terribles* as well as Sartre's *Crime passionel* and *A Midsummer Night's Dream*.

They laughed a great deal and talked easily together. As Marcus dropped his pretensions of sophistication – or as they fell away from him – she acquired a dignity and an assurance that he had never suspected; qualities well beyond her sexual confidence and her female integrity. He became aware that he was living, however briefly, with a mature woman: it was she who was conferring the favours and it was she who was likely to become bored before he tired of her. Long before, perhaps. He was pleased when she suggested they spend one more day together. She telephoned her sister, with whom she was staying for her short holiday – spending a day or two shopping in London first, with a plausible excuse.

On the next day she bought a present for her husband and told Marcus that it all had to end. He was astounded that he took it so calmly, but gallantly pretended to be upset.

'It was probably all very foolish to begin with,' she said, her soft Welsh voice almost stroking the words, 'but I don't regret any of it. I've been very happy and I've wanted you so much. But now we've been all we could ever be to one another. And honestly, Marcus – please believe me – in bed that's much more than most people ever are. Now it has to stop: before someone gets hurt, before there's a scandal. I have my husband to think of and you have your future. I was a silly girl looking for a final passionate love. Well, I'm a woman now. Thank you for that.'

'I shall never come back there again,' said Marcus. 'I hate the place anyway. The idea of you there and not being able to touch you...'

'You'd learn to live with it, love,' she said.

Marcus wished she had said 'Darling'.

'So these few days have meant nothing,' he said, in a bitter tone.

'You know they've meant a lot. There are things that I couldn't have pretended. You must know that.'

She sounded troubled: but perhaps she was cleverly and considerately playing out the scene, in exactly the way that he was. Marcus knew quite well that he was going to be miserable, while at the same time recognising that it was all for the best. A scandal in *that* place would be unbearable. His frowning father, hysterical mother, the old chapel crows and the taproom pack. And he did not want to hurt Roope, break up a marriage, when there was no chance of any permanent relationship with Virginia.

'There's no question, I suppose, of us – in due course – marrying...' he said in a quiet, lame voice.

Virginia laughed.

'No,' she said. 'I'm thirty. You're nineteen. We come from the same little mining village in South Wales. There'd be a nasty divorce. Months of uncertainty and misery. What would we live on?'

'You come from Cardiff,' he said, irrelevantly.

'Not any more.'

She paused and took his hand, walking in St James's Park beside the lake.

'One more night together,' she said. 'And that's all.'

'What about Latin? Won't your husband be suspicious if you suddenly lose interest?'

'Why should he? I've picked up a lot of Latin. I can still read. And why should you care? You're not going to come back. Don't look so miserable. Think how lucky we've been and let's not waste any more time.'

Extract from A Coriolan Overture. *Hazel & Sims, 1969.*

... The book that gives you the most accurate idea of what he was like is the one that is supposed to be a send-up and even that has a presumption of arrogance in the title – *Coriolan Overture*. Forget the nauseating love affair thing. Personally, I don't believe that he'd have been up to it. And read the rest of it. The Coriolanus pose is flattering. I know he got a first, but he was a snob and a dilettante for all that.

George Shelley in BBC radio programme.

67. Ext. High St, Oxford. Day. Mobile tracking shot of High Street, Oxford, beginning at Magdalen Bridge past tower, early morning: bicycles, occasional cars, stragglers on pavements, following sweep of street around to Queen's College and University Church...

MUSIC: Wagner: *Siegfried Idyll* (8b) Hold under...

(V/O) *Lloyd*: At Oxford, the city of dreaming spires and lost causes, Caradock found at last a kind of freedom and perhaps assumed forsaken and unpopular beliefs that were to remain with him for the rest of his life. It was still, by contemporary standards certainly, a conservative place:

68. Cut to still of group of Oxford undergraduates, some in academic dress, others informal, talking in street (circa 1950)

the ex-servicemen had returned more radical than they had gone away – but there was none of the political commitment or activism found in today's students (even at Oxford). They were a serious generation, there to get degrees.... To make the most of their time, and yet to enjoy themselves in a boisterous sometimes destructive way. They were men who had already seen something of life and they took themselves seriously and expected to be taken seriously.... *Lose* MUSIC.

69. C.U. one of faces in above group: mature, laughing, with pipe

70. C.U. another face in above group: serious, bespectacled: in academic dress, with white tie and square

71. Still of bump-supper night with blazing boat and boisterous, laughing faces

(Tape:) Drunken singing of bawdy song (First verse of 'Little Angeline') Fading under...

(V/O, *Lloyd*: They burned their expensive boats on bump-supper nights, but not many of the bridges between themselves and the placid, stable society of the welfare state.

72. LIB: Cut to film: Demonstration by students, 1968 outside Clarendon Building

(Tape:) Students chanting. Peak and take down.

173

| 73. Cut to still of College Photograph 1949 and close up to Caradock and faces around him | Lose chanting. |
| | Creep in Wagner: *Siegfried Idyll* (8b). Hold under... |

(V/O) *Lloyd*: Who can say how the young and obviously impressionable Caradock would have responded to the Oxford of today: whether it would have made him a different writer with a different outlook? Whether he would have been a writer at all? Whether the sense of freedom and release he experienced in an age where youthful emancipation occurs earlier and more comprehensively would have been anything like as dramatic and intoxicating...

C.U. Caradock's face

74. LIB: Contemporary students, fairly scruffy, kissing in College Quadrangle

Lose MUSIC
Nowadays the colleges are mixed and sex is taken almost for granted....

75. LIB: Mix to: Very glamorous Commemoration Ball (Magdalen Coll.) (circa 1950) in colour. (See Note A7)

Creep in dance music 'L'Âme des poètes' (Charles Trenet) ('At last at last, you're in my arms') and hold under...

(V/O) *Lloyd*: In those days the men who had fought in a war and those who succeeded them, who had seen service if not action, were restricted to precise hours in which they could entertain women in their rooms. And not long before girls who had male visitors had to move their beds into the corridors...

Lose dance music.

76. Ext. Broad St. Day, looking towards Magdalen Street. Late afternoon sunlight.	MUSIC : Wagner: *Siegfried Idyll* (8b) Hold under... (V/O) *Lloyd*: But this was not the freedom that Caradock had yearned for, when, rightly or wrongly, he had felt stifled in
77. LIB: Students working in long sunlit library	his native valley. As well as the opportunity to spread his wings intellectually, he was looking for some kind of literally physical escape, certain that with it would come a spiritual release....
78. LIB: Undergraduate entering tutor's room for tutorial	(Tape:) Conversation and pleasantries. Fade, but hold MUSIC throughout and after...
79. LIB: University Parks with cricket match	(V/O) *Lloyd*: And he found it. Caradock loved the place....

80. LIB: Snow scene on towpath with swans and eight on the river and undergraduate wobbling along on bicycle...

Bring up MUSIC

81. Ext. St Ebbs. Day. Poor streets in sunlight

82. Int. Ashmolean. Day. Dept of Western Art. Long shot tracking along gallery, dwelling on Ucello 'The Hunt'

83. Ext. Botanic Gardens. Day. With punts on river beyond

84. Ext. Worcester Coll. Gardens. Night. Open Air OUDS Production in Worcester Coll. Garden.

(Tape:) *Midsummer Night's Dream* performance

85. Ext. St John's Coll. Gardens. Day. Cut to James Faber in gardens of St John's College.

(V/O) *Lloyd*: James Faber knew Caradock for many years at Oxford....

Faber approaches camera and stops to look around gardens

Faber: (Sync.) I don't think that the sense of relief and release that Michael Caradock experienced has been especially exaggerated. I've gone on

176

Move in to Faber on gesture to
C.U. (head and shoulders)

Track away from Faber and
follow as he moves on right-
hand arc around lawn

record before as saying that he
was an unusually melancholy
man and I should guess that the
years at Oxford – interrupted as
they were by National Service
(and *that*, as a result of this
curious quirk of character that
I'll say something about) –
those years were perhaps the
happiest in his life.
These gardens were one of his
favourite places and my own
opinion is that he would have
been wiser to stay here than to
move on, as he did, to London.
But here we have the strange
restlessness of spirit that
always seemed to move him on,
as though he could not bear to
accept or be accepted for long.
I did not know him until he
came back here from the Navy
and we were both young men
in the same Senior Common
Room. He was by no means a
'confessional' character, but I
think I might claim to have
been offered some of his private
opinions during several late
nights of chat and argument.
The arrogance that some people
have chosen to point out was

177

not especially remarkable. He was a clever young man: but only one among many and Michael was the first to admit that there were several minds better than his own among our

Cut to Faber with his back to college buildings, medium shot

colleagues. Academics generally are not celebrated for their humility, but Michael Caradock was in contrast rather diffident and, on the whole, offered opinions only when they were solicited. At the same time, he had published three (or even four) books by the time he left Oxford the second time and this gave him a certain confidence which some people probably resented. There was no question that he had been glad to get away from Wales, glad to

86. LIB: Aerial view of central Oxford receding

get away from the Navy; (V/O) and I think, sadly as it turned out, there was little doubt that he was eventually glad to get away from Oxford, much as he loved it.

Extract from television programme, 'Landscape of a Prophet'.

Caradock was thought by most of the members of the Senior Common Room at his college to be a reasonably clever, hard-working, polite undergraduate with a talent for words. They were pleased that he should have already published a book, but did not regard him as intellectually outstanding. He was quite well liked but, perhaps because he lacked the vitality that seemed to endear even troublesome students (in those days) to the average don, he was not one of the most popular figures of the college. At school he had been reticent with most of the staff and he kept a similar distance between the Fellows and himself. Some were irritated: Walter Hansel, Senior Tutor until 1965, found him supercilious and intellectually arrogant – since this arrogance was not based, in Hansel's view, on any great academic talent, it was sufficiently offensive for him to oppose Caradock's appointment as a junior lecturer to the college some years later. Other Fellows, however, found this reticence agreeable and modest: among these were Professor George Harrington, who had known Caradock's grandfather, J. L. Rabone. Others again, Richard Rose and Keith Olafsen among them, were eager to encourage the young man's writing and made a mild fuss of him when his book was published, which Caradock enjoyed.

Rose, his tutor, did not expect Caradock to take a first, although he thought it might be a close-run thing. When they discussed possible themes for a D.Phil. thesis, he was surprised by his pupil's dispassion: 'For the first time, I began to think that Michael might make a good professional academic, because the things he wanted to do were all concerned with writers or ideas that I knew he didn't care passionately about. Topics at that time tended to be much more restricted than they are now and it would have been very unlikely that he'd have been allowed to do anything on Joyce or Ezra Pound, even if he'd wanted to. Other writers that he liked – Proust, Thomas Mann and so on – were out of the question for someone who had taken a degree in English. In three years, I knew quite well that his enthusiasms were for Dickens and Fielding, Swift certainly, and rather more recondtely Clough. So I expected to have to put up a bit of an argument because I didn't think that any of these people, with the possible exception of Clough, would have been acceptable to the Committee. But not a bit of it. He proposed an idea based on the influence of silver age Roman satirists on Elizabethan and Jacobean writers. This took me by surprise. I put him on to Lucian Soames at New College, who was immediately very impressed.'

Lucian Soames is still enthusiastic in his praise of Caradock's flair and imagination. He writes: 'The trouble was that he gave up and I think that something outstanding was lost. Certainly, he came back and finished it off and was awarded the degree: but that spark of divine fire wasn't there. Dick Rose and I supported him very strongly and recommended that he be given some sort of lectureship so that he could do a little teaching and not have time to brood. Some people opposed it, because he'd thrown it all up: but fortunately Martineau, who is a wise old owl, threw all his weight behind us. I don't know what went wrong the first time. It had no effect, of course, on our friendship: Caradock and I were always on the best of terms.'

The reasons for this abrupt decision to leave Oxford are not immediately clear. Caradock knew quite well he would be immediately liable for conscription and it is unlikely that he viewed this with much enthusiasm. There have been recent attempts to suggest that there was a sensational even a violent love affair with scandalous overtones that precipitated this sudden departure; but without exception Caradock's friends state that his relations with women at Oxford were entirely casual. Idris Lewis suggests another theory, but emphasises that there is no substance behind it. It is that Caradock was reacting belatedly to the death two years earlier of Phyllis Caradock. At the time (Lewis says) he was annoyed by the exaggerated callousness that Caradock seemed to show towards the woman who had, after all, lavished affection, however misguidedly, upon him. 'Michael harped a great deal on her selfishness and the iron-clad self-interest of her family. He knew by now that he had been adopted by them and that Phyllis and her family were not blood relatives. I remember losing my temper with him. And then, I think, he came to his senses when he saw that poor Howell Caradock was very badly shaken. The old chap had really loved his wife, however silly and demanding she had been. Michael Beauchamp-Beck and I went to the funeral and he was almost pathetically grateful: meanwhile Michael Caradock stood around looking cold. Eventually, although he never admitted it, I think he decided he had been a disappointment. And he was filled with remorse and shame – as we all are from time to time about something or other. So he decided to do something which he thought would please Howell by going down from Oxford and doing National Service. And

Howell *was* very pleased. He'd have preferred the infantry but the Navy was acceptable enough. I must add here that Michael Caradock did not do this to ingratiate himself for the sake of money. He was already a rich young man. It was conscience.'

Perhaps the last word about Caradock's defection should go to the retired Master, widely regarded by the under-graduates who came under his benign but uncompromising eye with affection. C. R. Martineau remembers the young and green freshman in his first nervous weeks, the young man he appointed to an enviable teaching position and the almost established writer leaving the University with a characteristic show of dispassion: 'Caradock's problem was that he read all the great Continental writers in quite the wrong way. He was a young man of irrepressible enthusiasms and he became far too absorbed in Dostoyevsky, up to a point in Flaubert, and in due course in the *Parnassiens*, who – if I am any judge – proved to be a lasting influence. My point may appear to be obscure: but I think it was no accident that the hero of an essay in auto-biographical fiction, as he chose (somewhat ponderously) to call his novel *Coriolan Overture*, should have been a scholar reading Greats. (Incidentally, that is a very amusing book, in my opinion.) Now, Caradock himself would have liked to have been a classicist. His capable mind was wayward. And he was aware of this. So he strove after the Hellenic ideal of "nothing in excess". In this, Caradock might have been unwise in that he was tampering with his own natural psychology. For all that, the Russians (particularly Dostoyevsky) and the French (particularly Baudelaire and

Rimbaud) are no substitutes for Plato or Marcus Aurelius. In due course, Caradock was very well aware of this: or so I am led to believe by his later work, which I think is extremely interesting. As a young man, he was aware of an imbalance, a lack, in himself. Rose tells me he was very fond of Dickens and of Fielding. It is a pity he didn't take to Jane Austen and Sir Walter Scott; or even George Eliot. I feel they might all have been *very* helpful to Caradock.'

Extract from David Hayward's official biography.

This first book is interesting because the stories, probably all written in Caradock's first year at Oxford before he had adopted the affectations to which many of his contemporaries testify, show us what he was capable of. (The *Angry Sunset* novel, while exploring some of the seminal poses of Caradock's later myth-making, also shows us glimpses of warmth and sympathy towards ordinary people that were effectively stifled by an effort of will.) Interesting also because in some of the sketches, and most of all in the essays, we begin to see the triumph of that will, the snobbism and lust for privilege that thwarted a genuine lyrical talent in a welter of social and political prejudice. The preciosity of the 'Oxford Sketches' is forgivable in a young man, awed and impressed by the well-oiled rituals of an ancient and reactionary community. (Not everyone who spent some time at Oxford in the post-war years was as easily seduced: though few in their hearts despised the place as did young men from poor backgrounds in previous generations.) What is really nauseating are the airs and graces that Caradock gives himself in the four essays, notably the ones entitled 'Portrait of the Artist as a Young Turk' and 'The Cloister and the Cadena'. The verbal dexterity of these pieces may delude an unsuspecting reader into supposing that he is participating in some profoundly witty irony, but, in the perspective of Caradock's later work, we see established the conceited youth with an inbred sense of superiority setting out premises that were to be adopted not only against working people but against the true inheritors of the manners and attitudes that Caradock chose to admire. Compared to the famous chroniclers of privilege rooted in school and university and leisured tradition, Caradock stands revealed as an *arriviste*. The ostensible objectivity of the review of literary Oxford in 'The Cloister and the Cadena' shows us a waspish, envious young man sneering at facilities he yearned to take up: juxtaposed to the sentimentality of the 'Sketches' we have a full-length portrait of a very unpleasant person, even less likeable than the glamourised Marcus of the *Coriolan Overture*. But Caradock did not want to be liked: that was part of the myth.

   Richard Snow: The View from Lemnos. *Medusa Books, 1972.*

Oxford is a great place for poets, sprouting like beans or spawning like tadpoles out of jam jars on the classroom window ledge, effortlessly, wonderfully, monotonously. Unlike the beans and the tadpoles, however, the poets will not be ignored. They proclaim themselves. This is all very well, perhaps, in the privacy of their rooms when they conclave solemnly to praise each other's musifying: but in public places, it evokes – especially from the threadbare and patched writer of prose who knows he has years of labour ahead – a yearning for Platonic proscription or at the very least the diatribe of a Gosson, preferably something stronger. They are encouraged by visits from divers ancients, already occupying the jobs in literary journalism, provincial universities or the British Broadcasting Corporation that will be the lily pads for our own metamorphosed tadpoles to hop onto in due course. Sometimes these shamans import with them a whiff of Fitzrovian Bohemia, which, too, has its own characteristic odour – but for the most part the visitors hold court in the cafés, being great eaters of cake.

These atrabilious observations are not entirely malicious or frivolous, but based also on a sincerely held conviction that the work of any writer is a lonely and comfortless business in which he should never count upon the opinion of others or the safety of like-minded numbers. Fame and recognition have very little to do with the obsessive need to write. James Joyce said that he wanted to be famous when he was alive: but it would have made no difference – he would have gone on writing, anyway. Gide told Camus that when he was asked by young writers if he thought they should continue, he replied: 'What! You can stop yourself writing and you hesitate?' I believe that there is too much urgency about getting into print, sidling along to the literary coterie, too much elevation of banality, too often the remarkable is made commonplace. Any literary endeavour should involve long and patient preparation: contemplation. This is especially so of verse, where the great writers will invest their thought with a vibrance and excitement to thrill the reader and the not-so-great will engage him by a less exciting but no less valuable seriousness. The prose writer, too, must think and think hard. Stories are as important to him as images to the poet, but they are not everything; variety is perhaps more significant, and intensity less. Technically they have to beware of quite different traps – the poet must not become so fascinated by his repertoire of devices as to forget the vital importance of his ideas; the novelist must not become so absorbed by his ideas and the characters who express them that he becomes satisfied with some routine format. All this preparation requires the discipline and isolation of the cloister: the sense of present vitality, the apprehension of past tradition, the silence of contemplation, the cool draughts of reason.

Extract from early essay 'The Cloister and the Cadena' in Metaphors of Twenty Years. *Vortex Press, 1950.*

Yes, I suppose I *did* encourage him. But no more than Rose did. And in due course Lucian Soames. I found him interesting and amusing. Interesting because, although he had an unremarkable mind, he had a really exciting talent for language. And there are enough people about with remarkable minds, very few of whom can talk or write well. Amusing because there was behind a veneer of sophistication a primevally cunning mind at work. I can imagine Caradock in his Cro-Magnon gyre, working out ways of pleasing everyone, securing a comfortable hide, scribbling on the walls, avoiding the actual boar's tusk without actually appearing to. It takes art. And he had it. Why not? I'm reprehensible and I'm sure you are and I'm sure our listeners will agree that they are. In certain ways, of course. But we admit it only when we have a hangover, or have perpetrated some act of meanness, or have made someone unhappy, or in our most private shame. Caradock admitted it all the time. And if it is paranoid to expect no more from others than you offer, I suppose he was paranoid. He was, at the same time, diabolically clever. And as he would have said himself: This is the excellent foppery of the world.... Expecting one *not* to know how the speech went on and thereby scoring an ironic point. I am by this time, of course, confusing the young lad who first came up, when I (for my sins) was Junior Dean, with the very engaging junior lecturer who shared the same Common Room. What I liked in the undergraduate was enterprise: playing to strength: knowing where strength was. What I liked about the older man was enthusiasm: the passion for art made up of pride and of prejudice: the dedication from weakness. Has anyone asked, by the way, how many divisions Michelangelo has? Caradock knew how terrifying the statistic would be.

Keith Olafsen, Fellow of Caradock's college and erstwhile Junior Dean, in BBC radio programme.

As Mandrick talked, Marcus leaned forward eagerly. But he was not listening. It was summer and the windows were open. Five or seven or nine flies circled in the middle of the room near the ceiling. The curtains fluttered like a girl's dress. Out of the corner of his eye he could see the wistaria on the wall. Behind Mandrick's austere head was a blue sky with a single puff of cloud. And Marcus was waiting for a decent pause so that he could speak.

He admired Mandrick: very tall and thin in his unseasonable suit, sitting upright in his chair with his hands folded demurely on one knee, the lines of his face in repose. They were so often in repose that Marcus came to wonder how Mandrick's face could have acquired so many lines – lines furthermore which enhanced his bearing and personality. Most of all he admired Mandrick's assurance: his sardonic humour, the way he could turn barbs into carnations, his fastidiously acid wit flicked at difficult young men to scald but never to stain. Somewhere there was Mrs Mandrick, whom Marcus had never seen, perhaps lolling gently on a daybed as Virginia had with him such an age ago. Probably not: she was no doubt shopping or seeing to the children or busy at some academic chore. Marcus realised with a very mild but unpleasant shock that he was almost certainly just that to Mandrick and started listening again.

'... the liberties taken by the rich are more destructive to the state than those of the people,' Mandrick said.

Fortunately Marcus recognised the axiom.

'Perhaps so,' he said, 'but Aristotle was surely misguided in equating aristocracy with riches.'

'Not if you consider privileges to be invisible riches.'

'I don't think he meant that. Rightly or wrongly, I've always thought of riches in terms of a bourgeoisie: as a principle rather than a fact. The landed gentry and so on, I suppose, must count for something as well. But that's not what I mean by an aristocracy.'

'I don't think it matters, Conrad, what you think of as

an aristocracy. To many people a congeries of politicians, film stars, business magnates and songwriters gathered together in Monte Carlo will form an immediate aristocracy, in that they are assumed to be especially endowed with talent or beauty: they become a focus for admiring envy. Your own idea of an aristocracy based upon exquisite sensibility and high intellect is, I respectfully suggest, based upon envious admiration. Is it Sickert who says that an artist has no time for preference?'

'That is exactly my point,' said Marcus, delighting in the meeting of minds. 'The artist has no time, because he is too busy: but the case for an aristocracy is that it has time to appreciate all that is worthwhile, to encourage and to...'

'Subsidise, Conrad: the word is "subsidise". In return for flattery. Think of the sixteenth and early seventeenth centuries.'

'Why not? I'll play that hand.'

'If it is a question merely of subsidies, why not accept the Britain of Mr Attlee and post-Beveridge good intention, which requires neither flattery nor indulgence. Now, tell me: while your aristocracy is hunting, shooting and patronising, who is governing?'

'You're playing games with me, sir,' said Marcus alertly. 'I'm talking about a responsible aristocracy whose main function is government, but which guarantees the free development of art and ideas. And which elects itself.'

'On merit?'

'Yes!'

'Are the freely developing artists and thinkers to be incorporated in the aristocracy?'

189

'Where appropriate.'

'I congratulate you, Conrad, on devising at last a bureaucracy of the spirit. Has it ever occurred to you that conservative systems produce conservative art? Admirable as it may be, it is not the exciting and rejuvenating force that you have in mind. I think all this brings us appropriately to Plato again. An interesting digression, however...'

As Marcus walked back along Longwall Street towards his own college, he felt pleased with himself and at the same time dissatisfied. Mandrick had a disconcerting facility for reminding him in the most civilised terms that he was only semi-civilised. Marcus had some idea of himself as a champion of his cause – but he was aware that he must achieve his purposes in a lonely and essentially aesthetic way. In his own country, it was quite easy to define his position: puritanism and corrosive political resentment made his own position clear enough. But confronted by one of his own kind, Mandrick, ironic and unemotional, he found himself often doubting himself and his ideas. In the pleasant dappled sunlight of early evening he found himself, at the top end of Hollywell, approaching the King's Arms wondering whether Mandrick thought him to be an innocent. The memory of Virginia was very comforting.

Extract from A Coriolan Overture. *Hazel & Sims, 1969.*

Major Ganz pushed the beautiful crystal decanter towards Ganuret, who had never in his life tasted such wonderful liquor. He poured more into his glass and held it as carefully as he might have held some infinitely precious goblet between his palms, letting the bouquet drift upward. The room was pleasant in the dim summer's night, cool and dark. Ganz leaned forward and took a cigar from the steward who offered the box to Ganuret in turn. Ganuret shook his head.

'No thank you. I'd like to concentrate on the brandy,' he said.

Ganz smiled. The steward walked across to the high windows and drew heavy red drapes across. When he switched the lights on the dark panelled room glowed, the crystal and silver glittered. Ganuret felt completely at ease, if a little surprised that he should take so readily to unaccustomed luxury. Major Ganz was still smiling as he prepared his cigar elaborately. Ganuret thought that in the artificial light which had created a new set of shadows the lean, accipitrine face with its long, jagged scar under the left cheekbone was less sinister; the pale blue eyes were kinder.

'You look as though we have at least compensated you a little for the discourtesy of Fountains,' said Ganz.

Ganuret laughed.

'An extraordinary place for you to visit,' Ganz said.

'Don't tourists always make for the red-light districts, the wicked square miles?' Ganuret said.

'Oddly enough, I have never been a tourist,' said Ganz. 'My visits to other countries have been usually as a soldier – or a prisoner. But I suppose you are right. Bourgeois men and women seem to have an irresistible delight in the prospect of vice when it offers mild, safe frissons of shock and no more. This age has specialised in voyeurism. I have made inquiries and I'm told that it is a favourite practice in the Fountains district to pick on a young innocent tourist such as yourself, to put some kind of drug into his drink, and at leisure to rob him. He usually finds himself in his underpants on one of the waste lots to the north of the city where they dump refuse. Your admirable constitution almost killed you. You were able to resist the drug until you crashed your car when it finally overcame you.'

'I have no recollection for some time before that.'

'General Waldeck is impressed by you. He has not met many poets, especially not young poets, in recent years. He would be pleased if you would stay. We should all be pleased. You would be doing us a service.'

'In what way?'

'The General, as perhaps you were aware a couple of evenings ago, is subject to attacks of hypertension. You see, he is a man accustomed to vital action – a truly remarkable man of great intellectual power and unusual resources of physical and emotional courage. When young he was a brilliant scholar and thought of a literary career: but with the war that followed he had to abandon such ambitions. In that war, he served with such distinction that it seemed natural for a while to continue a military career. At the same time it became apparent that Axel Waldeck's qualities of leadership and vision were needed in the political direction of our affairs. As the youngest colonel, ever, in the army, he was persuaded to resign his commission and to take an important post in the Office of the Interior, where once again his decision and his astounding ability to grasp disparate facts rapidly made him a valuable servant. During the next war he achieved a world reputation for his courage and international military statesmanship and when it was over astounded even his enemies by his honesty, his unfaltering faith in his compatriots, whom he misguidedly believed to favour and value Freedom in much the way that he did. Soon after he was rejected by them. You will understand that his dreams and ambitions, all turned outward from himself towards his people to whom he wished to bring Utopia, to whom he wished to bring the sovereign knowledge of truly equal Freedom, remained turbulent inside him. While he, brought down by scandals that were meaningless and trivial, was consigned to obscurity – to brood here about his frustrated plans. Understandably, the intensity of his vision and thought, in conflict with the impotence of what he can achieve, has led to bouts of psychological illness that manifests itself in acute depression or in rare moments of mania. He is, as you are aware, loyally served. But by soldiers, by politicians. Quite frankly, by some who are leeches and caterpillars. You would be doing us a service if you were to stay?'

'But I couldn't afford to.'

'You would be able to write poems here.'

Ganuret was amused that the subtle Ganz should be so ingenuous.

'I don't make a living by writing poems. I work in a library.'

'The General is in need of a librarian: someone to catalogue his papers and documents, who will help him in the writing of his memoirs.'

'It's a good offer. But...'

'We should make all the necessary arrangements with

your employers. They have already been informed of your accident and subsequent indisposition. You may think it over.'

Ganz was smiling and puffing at his cigar, most amiably. Ganuret sipped the superb brandy, leaned back in the deep leather chair and looked appreciatively around at the room.

'It would be most valuable for the General to have someone as... refreshingly different as yourself... to talk to from time to time,' Major Ganz said.

Ganuret smiled under his benevolence and then quite suddenly wondered what would happen if he refused. Perhaps they would insist. Compel. Perhaps he had already seen more than he should.

'I would want to return home in due course,' he said.

'Naturally. You are not one of our own countrymen. But you would be performing a valuable service. Just in talking to the General. And once the cataloguing is complete, the time would be appropriate for you to return, suitably rewarded, to your own country.'

'Then I accept.'

Major Ganz's face creased into a warm smile, except around the scar on the left where the skin was frozen and immobile. The effect of this broad goodwill, as distinct from the usual courteous set of his features, congealed about that mutilated segment of his face, was grotesque; but Ganuret thought that his twinge of alarm was childish.

'You are most welcome,' Ganz said, pressing a bell and rising to offer Ganuret his hand.

The steward came in almost immediately and with surprising speed. Ganz gave him instructions. The man listened impassively, inclined his head and went out again.

'Please take some more brandy,' said Ganz. 'Tell me, do you believe in greatness?'

'I don't understand.'

'In our modern age. Do you believe that there are any more great men and visionary men: or are there only councils of ministers, party committees, national executives, congressional sanctions?'

'I believe in Democracy,' said Ganuret.

'Of course, of course. But when has there been effective, real democracy without great leaders dedicated to a democratic ideal? Do you understand greatness?'

'I know that there have been great men. Some of the men whom I think of as great were certainly not statesmen or soldiers.'

Ganz laughed. It was an unexpected noise. Where his smile was warm and encouraging, the laugh was rasping. It sounded oddly as though it was seldom used.

'You will be very good for the General, young sir,' he said.

He went on laughing for another few moments.

'So what of destiny?' he said, his face returning to curved-lip politeness.

'I'm not sure I understand what you mean.'

'Do you not believe that you, for example, are destined to be a great poet? Have you not dreamed of becoming one?'

'I do not think that greatness is a matter for poets,' Ganuret said seriously. 'They are too busy being poets to think about it.'

Major Ganz began to laugh again and this time went on laughing, the same curious rasping noise, until Ganuret was becoming embarrassed. He took some more brandy to cover his confusion, nervously. Then the doors were opened and a neatly built man with sleek black hair and humorous dark eyes stood there, smiling, already participating in Ganz's laughter, which quickly faded. The polite smile took its place.

'What a very good joke,' the newcomer said in a somewhat guttural baritone.

Ganz rose.

'Allow me to present a young friend of the General's, Your Excellency,' he said. 'Piers Ganuret, who is to be the General's own aide and to catalogue his archives. His Excellency, Søren Claudian. An old and valued ally of General Waldeck, and our ambassador here.'

Extract from Promethead. *Hazel & Sims, 1967.*

There can be little question that Michael Caradock belonged among the European writers whose inspiration is derived from an amalgamation of Indo-European Myth that underlies the ethical and political framework of North Atlantic society, fundamentally different in character from Mediterranean or Nordic cultures in that it is an uncomfortable synthesis. Its cement is compounded of ingredients which have to be blended in exact proportion if they are to become firm: otherwise substance crumbles, the foundations collapse, the building falls. The idea of tottering towers which is so much an apocalyptic nightmare of Western literature in the last hundred and fifty years underlies the apprehension of the precarious equilibrium of liberal-democratic civilisation as it is known and which is now beginning to go through a crisis which will worsen and perhaps not be resolved until the next decade. Hegel, Wagner, Nietzsche, Mann, Joyce and Eliot are all men of genius who have contributed to the nervous tradition of a civilisation in imminent danger of collapse unless a spiritual sickness is overcome. Pound, more than any other, saw that a society based on trash entertainment and commercial profit must be doomed – but unlike the other great artists mentioned was bold enough to prescribe economic and political measures (however unacceptable), where the others offered at best spiritual panaceae, or passively stated in marvellous and architectonic works of genius (*Der Ring des Nibelungen, Finnegans Wake*) a tragic and irreducible case.

Much of the thematic imagery in Caradock's work derives from the ideas of these great men: his pessimism and his sense of ultimate destruction which will not give way to futility is stoical in the most orthodox sense of the word. But Caradock was not able to match the intellectual coherence of his great predecessors and there creeps into the themes he pursues a notion of hope that the inevitable catastrophe (not, of course, a question of nuclear holocaust) will be avoided because of something noble in man. This is difficult to reconcile with the desperate and bold posture of the dying wolf beset by the craven hounds of envy, greed, resentment and sloth. It is Marxist and neo-Marxist writers who are able to be optimistic, who *must* be optimistic. There is ample evidence that Caradock's instinctive enthusiasm for one aspect of thought arrived at spiritually was tempered by an intellectual respect for another entirely different aspect arrived at emotionally. So many themes and thematic images in his work appear to me to be contradictory, though at varying levels of significance.

Yet another confusion arises from Caradock's cosmic preoccupations concentrated upon the foreknowledge of death and (as I read it) his painstaking catalogue of innate response mechanisms in man to this foreknowledge which occur in the conscious mind that distinguishes man from other animals. So that where the newly hatched chicken has no foreknowledge of death and reacts to the shadow of a cardboard hawk, the newly born human is helpless and unable to react to the agent of its destruction, but within a year or so becomes adept at producing responses to the idea and certainty of Death. Religion, philosophy, art and science are all born of the certain foreknowledge that a man must die; the notions of happiness and misery belong to the fact of finite mortal existence not possessed by the mayfly or the young turtle or the fledgling. This is the most important thematic strand in Caradock's work: born directly of a need to justify and dignify the pursuit of art as the only means of discovering the purpose of intelligent existence: where religion sought to offer solace through mystery, philosophy explanation through rigorous investigation of data, and science to amass data beyond theory, art alone offered an answer to the puzzle of Man. The idea in itself is unremarkable and in fact thoroughly ingenuous: but the passion with which it was held and pursued is worth examination.

H.-J. Kastner: Patterns of Despair. *Hazel & Sims, 1973.*

The amusing aspect of Michael's famous European culture was his rather less well-known loathing of foreigners. He read French and German and Italian avidly: but if he was shown a Frenchman or Italian, he bristled all over. Before his foster-mother died, he didn't get about much, because she wanted him to spend his vacations in Wales and she managed various stratagems to take him back there. But I think it must have been in our second long vac, we persuaded him – Jeremy Philbrick, Idris Lewis and myself – to come with us on a tour of France and Italy. We bought an old Bentley for some absurdly low price and had it tuned up. It was a very funny trip. Philbrick and I had both travelled a lot, quite apart from our National Service. Idris was a tremendous enthusiast about everything and spoke atrocious French very loudly and insistently. Michael, who was the only one who didn't drive, harangued us about Baudelaire and Racine and Sartre and Proust, at the same time keeping up a scurrilous commentary on France and the French which was uproarious. They were an interesting contrast: because Idris liked everyone and everything and was a great buttonholer of unsuspecting chaps in bars, most of whom thought he was an amiable Visigoth; while Michael distrusted everyone and detested the cooking and the lavatories and even the wine.

Michael Beauchamp-Beck in BBC radio programme.

An extraordinary belief seems to have grown up, fostered by Marxist writers and evangelised by their critical sutlers, that it is only the extreme left in literature which has any faith or belief in the future of man and in the idea of progress towards a better human condition. For my part, I believe the future of man seems to be grim and the idea of progress illusory: things are falling apart and anarchy is already loosed upon the world. But I admire and envy the faith and goodwill of one of the great liberal writers – Albert Camus, who put the situation neatly:

> It would appear that to write a poem about spring would nowadays be serving capitalism. I am not a poet, but I should have no second thoughts about being delighted by such a poem if it were beautiful. One either serves the whole of man or one does not serve him at all. And if man needs bread and justice, and if we have to do everything essential to serve this need, he also needs pure beauty which is the bread of his heart. Nothing else matters. Yes, I should like them to take sides less in their books and a little more in their everyday life.

Camus is for me the writer who more than any other displays affirmation and courage in the face of despair; and, furthermore, an affirmation that is repeated throughout the various stages of his work with increasing conviction, without ever refusing to take cognisance of the evidence of positive evil and inhumanity in the world. As Camus' own delight in physical existence, the exultation in the body, was impaired by his health faltering, so was his exalted and exalting hedonism inhibited by his awareness of injustice and cruelty which achieved its zenith under the Nazis in the thirties and forties but which still rides high in the firmament. Camus describes with tragic dignity the tragedy of the happy man in this century.

> A day of sunshine and clouds. The cold spangled with yellow. I ought to keep a diary of each day's weather. The

fine transparent sunshine yesterday. The bay trembling with light – like a moist lip. And I have worked all day.

and:

Beyond the window there is a garden, but I can see only its walls. And a few branches flowing with light. A little higher, I see more branches, and higher still the sun. And of all the jubilation of the air that can be felt outdoors, or all that joy spread out over the world, I can see only shadows of branches playing on white curtains. There are also five rays of sunlight patiently pouring into the room the golden scent of dried grass. A breeze, and the shadow of the curtains come to life. If a cloud covers up the sun and then lets it through again, the bright yellow of the vase of mimosa leaps out of the shade. The birth of this single flash of brightness is enough to fill me with a confused and whirling joy.

This evident rapture fills me with a sort of whirling joy, too, that is saddened because I don't think that I have ever been able to experience it at first hand. I think I have noticed in the French a capacity for living for the moment (which perhaps explains in part their egocentricity) that is unknown to the Anglo-Saxons and the Celts who toil reluctantly out of a swamp of nostalgia like hippopotami who, presumably maddened by the intense sunlight, imagine themselves to be gazelles and leap towards a golden savannah of the future. Intensity of experience is in the Nordic peoples only possible through brooding, seldom through living. With what envy do I read:

... In a sense, it is indeed my life that I am playing out here, a life which tastes of warm stone, is full of the sighs of the sea

201

and the rising song of the crickets. The breeze is cool and the sky blue. I love life with abandon and wish to speak of it with freedom: it makes me proud of my human condition. Yet people have often told me: there's nothing to be proud of.

Yes, there is: this sun, this sea, my heart leaping with youth, the salt taste of my body, and the vast landscape where tenderness and glory merge in blue and yellow. It is this conquest that requires my strength and resources. Everything here leaves me intact, I give up nothing of myself, I put on no mask: it is enough for me patiently to acquire the difficult knowledge of how to live which is worth all the arts of living.

Existentialist philosophy always seems to me at its most convincing, as well as at its most attractive, when this kind of affirmation is being made: when it is finding meaning in a godless universe through man's intuition of joy in living, rather than when it is solemnly enjoining us to do our duty to one another in Chaos. Of course, Camus in his finest work has often reminded us of this duty:

I have chosen justice in order to remain faithful to the earth. I still think that the world has no final meaning. But I know that something in it has meaning, and that is man, because he is the only being to demand that he should have one.

This commitment to individual dignity and responsibility – or more accurately: the dignity and responsibility of the individual – is courageous and it is also cheerful. Cheerfulness is not trivial and it is something underrated by those who possess enough of it, though not by the melancholic. T. S. Eliot hints in his essay on 'Shakespeare and the Stoicism of Seneca' that cheerfulness is an important component of stoicism. So it is. It requires an effort, which for some is too great, but it distinguishes the relatively fortunate Epicurean (in the real sense of that word) from the Cynic or the orthodox Stoic, whose moral certitude at a time of social and economic uncertainty may sustain him but is unlikely to offer him much hope for improvement. My contention is that Camus' hedonism was natural – something he was born with and did not achieve by rational meditation. While he knew that...

> ... In 1933 began a period that one of the greatest among us rightly called the days of wrath. And for ten years every time we were informed that naked and unarmed human beings had been patiently mutilated by men whose face resembled our own, our heads swam and we wondered how such a thing was possible....

he was also terribly aware of the darkness of his and our age...

> ... In the year the war began, I was to take ship and follow the voyage of Ulysses. At that time, even a penniless young man could form the sumptuous project of crossing the sea in quest of sunlight. But I then did as everyone else. I took my place in the queue shuffling towards the open mouth of hell. Little by little, we entered. At the first cry of murdered innocence, the door slammed shut behind us. We were in hell, and we have not left it since. For six long years, we have been trying to come to terms with it. We now catch glimpses of the warm ghosts from the islands of

the blessed only across the long, cold, sunless years which are still to come.

At the time when Camus wrote those words, I doubt that he could have imagined how cold, how sunless and how very long those years were to be. And as I have already hinted, I can see no end, although the tantalising ghosts flicker somewhere beyond everyday life, taunting us with promises that we shall never see fulfilled. Nevertheless, the salutary reflection occurs that Camus was living through horrors and dangers that so far, in Western Europe, we have since been spared. The torturers and executioners were strutting in the marketplace, clacking their heels on the cobbles that hurt the thin-soled feet of the innocent, hands behind their backs, leers at the ready, making sport of insult. Now this outrage was taking place before a man who had no solace in religion, but who was able to write in *Noces*:

> If I obstinately reject all the 'hereafters' of the world it is because I am also not prepared to renounce my immediate riches. I do not choose to believe that death opens onto another life. For me it is a closed door....

and who in this philosophical context was able to recall in the 1957 Preface to *L'Envers et l'endroit*:

> As a writer... I started to live in admiration. This, in a sense, is paradise on this earth. As a man, my passions have never been 'against'. They have always addressed themselves to what is better and greater than I.

I know no other writer who has put his case so simply and so honestly and I know of few others whose affirmation is as loud and (for the melancholic) as reproachfully stirring. Shakespeare – in the vastness of his genius; Joyce – in the spiritual assurance that arises from the textual contortion and the unremittingly factual observation of his great works that enables him to be certain of the individual and pessimistic about the crowd and the way they choose to manage their affairs or to have their affairs managed. But Camus speaks more directly, I feel, to more people. He awakens in me a kind of shame, when he writes:

> When I lived in Algiers, I always waited patiently throughout the winter, because I knew that on one night, one single, pure, cold night in February, the almond trees of the Consuls Valley would cover themselves with white flowers. I marvelled, then, at seeing how that fragile snow resisted all the rains and the winds from the sea. Yet every year they endured, exactly the time required to prepare the fruit.

This, indeed, was the man who learned:

> In the middle of winter... I carried inside me an invincible summer.

This is a lengthy preamble to a comparatively short study of Camus' four major works of fiction – *The Outsider*, *The Plague*, *The Fall* and *Exile and the Kingdom*. I excuse it by claiming that it defines an admiring but uncomprehending attitude. Many will know the story of the church dignitary who on a progress through Italy sent a servant ahead to test the wine in the taverns where he might stop. Where the wine was good the servant was to scrawl 'Est' on the wall. The dignitary came upon a place where there was written: Est! Est! Est! And the wine bears the name. I feel like a privileged servant before whom the dignitary went leaving on the sunlit ancient wall the message: Sum! Sum! Sum!

Extract from essay, 'Sum! Sum! Sum!' in An Elemental Wound. *Hazel & Sims, 1963.*

No man is an Iland, intire of it selfe.... No: perhaps not. And perhaps it is true that any one man's death diminishes me. But certainly such an intimation of mortality makes me more and more aware of the diminishing ice floe on which I am adrift and alone. The skies are uniformly grey and the sea or lake on which I am floating is grey and calm without any shore in sight. Pascal's vast and silent heavens remain impassive. So my existential problem is to reconcile a will to act and a sense of purpose with this overpowering awareness of a nothing in which my own insignificance is startlingly obvious.

Some readers will remember the photograph of the nuclear scientist on such a block of ice and the purpose of the picture – to draw attention to our predicament in a world apparently bent upon self-destruction, where the only certainty is our inevitable death. The existentialist implications of the composition were underlined when it was used to illustrate a magazine article on Sartre: and it is these that I want to examine in relation to my own conflict of depressive futility and manic faith in human art, of a sense of isolation and the memory of offering and taking love, of despair and duty. None of these themes is original: except that such conflict presents itself differently to each individual and may therefore be reflected in some glancingly original way, modified by temperament, experience, knowledge, reading and historical circumstance. It is very difficult in these middle years of the twentieth century to be an optimist, difficult not to bear a cosmic grudge on behalf of the Continent from which the individual scrap of ice has become detached, difficult to hold that No man hath *affliction* enough that is not matured, and ripened by it, and made fit for *God* by that *affliction*. It may seem a paradox to be attempting an apology for Stoicism: but that is my purpose in this speculatively dismal tract....

Extract from 'A Private Iceberg', one of the moral essays from An Elemental Wound. *Hazel & Sims, 1963.*

Now that the rain has stopped the one-colour grey sky overpowers the imagination. I turn my back on the land and look out to sea: nothing stirring it seems a grey corrugation of water merging into the sky. The seabirds are silent and it is only the middle of the day; quite easy to imagine an unpeopled world as though turning from the wall of the cave where the images and shadows move to look at the panoply of the real world, the poor cave-dweller found only an abyss swirling with mist, a sheer drop and no path on the pageant of faith and fear and futile energy was thought to have passed. Think now of the echo of a girl laughing. No, not an echo: a distant rippling sound filtered through a grey silk as though the sound ruffled the delicate texture like the stroking fingers of a summer breeze. Who?

Helen, Brenda, Fay? My mother whom I do not remember and do not know and never knew. How much do I remember that I do not even know? That strain of laughter. Sunlight. An idea of sunlight on a very green landscape with trees and a strong hand lifting me as I fell. Panic for a second and relief. The strength of the sustaining hand. Nausea at the mouth of the cave, vertiginous, gut-racking, hollow... return, return, philosopher into the cave....

'The soul is like an eye: when resting upon that on which truth and being shines, the soul perceives and understands, and is radiant with intelligence; but when turned towards the twilight of becoming and perishing, then she has opinion only, and goes blinking about, and is first of one opinion and then of another, and seems to have no intelligence....'

How much is left of that one year? No strong-sinewed hand; no ripple of laughter; the dimming of the sunlight and the fading of the green summer landscape. Blank misgivings of a creature.... Was it her voice? Vanessa? The grey silk, the long silk dark hair, the smiling mouth and wide grey eyes.... And a strong brown hand, brown eyes, good teeth; laughter...

And do I delude myself? Or do I delude myself? Only my own shadow, strange prisoner. I never did belong and yet I cling for protection. Alone. The grey coalescence of sea and sky. Poor Howell Caradock, alone in a desert of missed glory. Captain. Phyllis Jenkyn in her fen of wraithed pain and self-pity. Alone: bumping against each other in the drift of currents working well beneath the placid surface of the lake. Or do I delude myself? Do I not remember calling her by my mother's name and holding tight and hiding and being glad of love I did not have it in me to repay. Do I remember? The monster struggles to get out....

Vanessa and Edmund in their racing car in France. The mind straining to call up one single image: not the laughter, not the reassurance of the gripping hand: not an image – some fact of memory.... Blood trickling between the grimace of good white teeth, her grey eyes staring wide in a twist of gaudy metal and below the mutilation of their crushed and severed and distorted flesh that made me....

Grey black and mud ochre: coal track, clay walk. Fiery skies above the slag triangles. Grey rain sweeping up the sullen valley. And being quite apart, outside, separate. Kicking about, without thought, in a damp garden when the rain stopped, watched by vague people in the gleaming-windowed house. Aware of them. Playing the part assigned. Little boy in a curious loneliness. Poor little chap needs loving. Needs... needs... needs... Needs?

Quite apart. Not belonging. Reaching back to a vague impression, a dim face. Strong hand. Laughter. Grey veils of silk rain.

A flight of birds. Chevron of duck. Too small for geese, thrusting into the still rainless grey. I drink to you Vanessa and Edmund who left me behind the wreckage. I have not since I first knew you had existed been able to escape your loving: I am a voyeur in your bedroom: you are romantic thirties film stars in chiffon and elegance gliding through a mist of pale colours and blurring shapes. I watch alone and drunk.

... How far Caradock's relationships with women, often rather older than he was, were an unremitting search for his lost mother is an interesting area of investigation for a critical biographer. Michael Caradock's own parents had died when he was very small and he was adopted and brought up by an uncle and aunt.

The shock he experienced when told that the people who he thought were his parents were, in fact, not really his mother and father must have been traumatic. In my own view, after much conversation with people who remember the writer as a young boy, this sudden revelation was responsible for Caradock's lasting insecurity and contributed much more to his sense of not belonging than his unhappy experiences as a schoolboy. It is not too fanciful to argue that these unhappy moments were the direct outcome of a timidity and insecurity, which made him vulnerable to the normal robustness of children from a less shadowed background. Caradock's life had begun on a note of deep family tragedy which pervaded his entire subsequent life.

The retreat to Wales I see not so much as a self-imposed exile from literary and artistic London, as a positive attempt to escape from the lifelong search for the love that Caradock had missed so intensely as a child and a bold move to establish self-sufficiency in a hermit-like withdrawal into his own considerable resources of intellect.

Extract from Derek Parnell: In His Own Country. *Guildenstern, 1970.*

Someone really should lock people like Parnell up, in order to prevent them spreading their childish candyfloss over the books. As I've already told you, Julian was a reticent boy and on the few occasions when we met after he left Cwmfelyn the last thing he would have told me about was his private life. But I am quite sure that there was no nonsense about looking for his lost mother. It's surely not all that unusual for some of the women in a man's life to be older than he is. Anyway the fellow doesn't get his facts right.

I know for a fact, and his Oxford friends will tell you the same thing, that Julian did not know anything about his adoption until he was just about to go up to Oxford. It was one of the few things he talked to me about concerning his family. They had told him what had happened to Edmund and his mother in what I gathered was a fairly emotional performance. Now, the point is that the boy was excited. The news was a shock, of course. But it was not a traumatic shock or whatever Parnell wants to call it. He was enjoying the game of being a foundling. I daresay a lot of others would, if the truth be told! And it is also nonsense to suggest the boy was starved of affection. If anything there was too much of it from Phyllis Caradock who tended to coddle him. And I would have guessed that his relief was partly derived from a sense of being justified in breaking away from that intensely possessive fuss.

John Morris in BBC radio programme.

Poor old Parnell comes in for a lot of stick from various people, but curiously enough I think that he often has some glimmer of the truth in what he says, overstated as it all is in colour-supplement language. I think the theory that Michael

211

was always looking for his dead mother is sheer moonshine. And when he develops all that through the various characters in the novels, he forgets one very significant thing that I should have thought was fundamentally necessary for any critic to bear in mind. What is it that Camus says: 'A character is never the author who created him; but an author may quite likely be all his characters at once.'

Idris Lewis in BBC radio programme.

The girl turned and smiled at Baldwin. In the light of her room he saw that she was much younger than he'd thought in the street: not more than about nineteen. Her eyes were made up but they were very bright and clear, laughing eyes, lovely grey and eyes full of fun. She had a small pretty mouth covered with vivid lipstick. Her hair was mousy but soft and it fell prettily around her face.

She took her short jacket off and hung it up tidily on a coat hanger hooked onto a chipped wardrobe, ancient and faded. Then, she turned to face him. Baldwin took in her high breasts, small waist, the curve of her hips and the line of her legs under the cheap blue cotton dress. He felt himself begin to stiffen and rise with eagerness for her: but at the same time she looked so young and fresh with those nice eyes smiling at him, full of youth and health.... She held out her hand.

'Come on,' she said. 'Don't be shy.'

Baldwin's heart pounded and his guts quivered. His skin felt hot and tingling. He did not move.

'All right,' she said. 'There's no hurry. Sit down and have a fag. I won't be a minute.'

She smiled sideways at him as she walked past towards a door on the other side of the room: a sexy, wicked smile full of practised allure and suggestive promise. She also unbuttoned the top of her dress and swung her hips as she went out. Baldwin felt panic rising and glanced towards the door, wondering if he dared run away. Down the steep stairs, out into the alley into the street and away from bloody Soho and his wickedness. He could be out of the room before the girl noticed so there would be no chance of any pimp getting him. It had all been mad. What a stupid notion? That he could learn anything about the act of *Love* from a prostitute. But he found he couldn't go. He was ashamed at the thought about the pimp and sickened when he thought of this girl run by some oily Soho thug with flashy manners and a hidden arsenal of viciousness.

He looked around the room. A big bed in one corner. Baldwin felt a flutter of hysterical laughter rise, hiccupping, somewhere behind his nose. The furniture was cheap. Make-up on the dressing table. All strangely tidy. A few trashy magazines neatly stacked on a bedside table alongside a pink light. No books. The same unpleasant laugh choked again in the back of his throat, an unnatural laugh that did not begin in the belly (or in the head) to come out naturally; but some paroxysm of the larynx almost like a sob.

'Well,' the girl said, 'will I do?'

He turned round to see her in a sexy pose, framed by the door. She had taken off her dress and was standing there in a lace bra and a scrap of frilly pants. She was still wearing stockings and a suspender belt. The stockings were an orange colour with very shiny tops. Baldwin's mouth began to salivate excessively. He felt his jaw slacken and his face stiffen as though the eyes were drawing down at the corners. He was trembling. For a moment the girl looked uncertain, then she assumed the professionally seductive face again and came a few steps towards him.

'Well?' she said again.

This time when she stopped she chose a more brazen stance, no longer with one knee bent in on the other, but thighs taut and apart, hands splayed over her loins. Baldwin heard himself moan and sank to his knees in front of the whore clasping her thighs and burying his face in the flesh and nylon of her crutch.

The girl remained still for a few moments. Then she laughed.

'It's like that is it?' she said. 'Aren't you a naughty boy, then? And me thinking you were a shy one.'

She pushed him away gently and began to slip off her pants. Slowly. Baldwin did not know what was happening.

'Go on, then,' the whore said. 'You should have told me.'

She kicked the pants aside and posed again a few inches away from Baldwin's face. He looked up at her and saw her laughing: the same good, clear eyes: young, full of fun.

He felt the vomit rising and began to gag involuntarily as he struggled up. The girl evidently recognised the symptoms and rushed to the door, with a resigned, obscene comment.

'Quick!' she said. 'And don't spew in the sink.'

Baldwin was violently sick, still trembling, completely horrified. It was not that such an idea had never occurred to him, it was just the casual way that this girl had immediately acceded to a perversion as part of the transaction. This young and pretty girl, younger than he was himself. And he was ashamed and humiliated that he had reacted so pathetically, that he had been unable to carry the thing off. He felt ill but the nausea had receded. Baldwin bathed his face in cold water and looked at his flushed, puffy-eyed reflection in the mirror, full of self-pity and disgust, thinking suddenly of his parents. He cursed again his straight, decent upbringing.

The girl had put her pants on, but had not bothered to dress.

She was sitting on the bed, looking bored, pretending to be looking at a magazine, her legs relaxed, but without any hint of seductive intention. The small pretty mouth was pressed into a peevish line.

'Have you made a mess in there?' she said.

Baldwin heard for the first time a north country accent. Somehow that made it all the worse. Baldwin felt himself near to tears. He shook his head.

'All right,' the girl said. 'Get a move on, then. I don't suppose you feel like it, now.'

'I'm sorry,' Baldwin said. 'I didn't want...'

'No. I could see that. I don't know what you were doing in the first place. Why doesn't a nice lad like you go home to his mam?'

Baldwin wanted to ask the whore why a nice girl like her chose that way to make money, but he restrained himself. It would be cheek. He looked at the girl sitting on the bed, her face cold and bored but still pretty. She crossed her legs. The stockings rasped. Baldwin was drained of all lust.

'What do I owe you?' he asked.

She laughed and the eyes brimmed over again with mischief and innocence.

'You're a funny lad,' she said.

He put three pounds on the dressing table. The girl shrugged and stood up. Baldwin looked at the good body he had had no pleasure in.

'Sure you don't want to try?' the girl said, expecting the answer no. 'Then, if you don't mind, I'll get on with it. The night is young.'

'So are you,' said Baldwin, before he could stop himself.

'Oh don't be bloody silly,' the girl said. 'Let yourself out. I'm going to get dressed.'

She walked by him, this time without an exaggerated movement of the hips, brisk and businesslike. Baldwin would have guessed that in such a situation he would have wanted to stay and talk. If he had been writing a story, he would have had a long, touching, almost painful exchange between the girl and the young man in which they discovered things about one another. He was a fool. He had been a fool. He did not want to stay. He wanted no more of the girl who was already corrupted. He wanted to walk the long walk home and work out his failure and disgust.

Extract from The Low Key of Hope. *Alvin & Brandt, 1954.*

Jeremy Philbrick describes himself as much the most practical of his contemporaries and was instrumental in helping several of his friends in their early careers. He was always intent himself on a parliamentary future and has already served as a Junior Minister in Government and a Front Bench Spokesman in Opposition after enjoying a successful business career. Philbrick says that he appreciated early in life the value of making and maintaining contacts, and adds, with a certain self-deprecating humour, that his brand of social pragmatism paid off very well. Others are more disposed to suggest that Philbrick's efforts, on behalf of friends or of people whose talent impressed him, were entirely unselfish and motivated more than anything by an essentially practical dislike of wastage. He met Michael Caradock through Beauchamp-Beck towards the end of their first year at Oxford, thereafter belonging to the same closely knit circle of friends, drawn from several different colleges, who met frequently without forming themselves, in the manner of undergraduates of that period, into an exclusive and pretentious little club. After reading and liking some of Caradock's stories and prose poems, Philbrick met the eccentric and irascible independent publisher, Reginald Webber, who was responsible for introducing (over a couple of decades at least) a dozen new authors of subsequent eminence to the public. In his own words, he says: 'Immediately my hackles of thrift rose and I told him about this interesting young man at Oxford with what I thought was a delicate and inventive gift. "Fed up with snotty-nosed cleverbuggers from universities," he said. Which was quite typical. But I managed to prevail upon him to read some of Michael Caradock's stuff and to engineer a meeting. Well, Webber liked Caradock who, while he was eager to be published, was certainly not going to be bullied about what he wrote. And he agreed to take on the first book, which Caradock wanted to call *Stories and Essays* for some reason. Webber chose the other title which Caradock never liked: but they got on quite well and Webber was prepared to encourage him in writing the first novel *Angry Sunset*. Webber liked young men to be lyrical: he wanted them to be positive and optimistic and to enjoy life. But he recognised, long before Caradock himself did, that they must inevitably have a big row and this came with the novel about the journalist who repudiates his past. Webber used to say that Caradock was potentially a very dishonest writer, in that he was capable at the drop of a hat of thinking himself into some persona that would be fictionally profitable. I hasten to add that this "dishonesty" was only in Webber's own eyes because he was the sort of editor who believed that everything should come from deeply felt personal experience. And he very much disliked the character of Baldwin in that particular novel with all his resentments and hatreds; he also disliked the explicit sex, which seemed to him to be pretty irrelevant. I certainly would not subscribe to the view that a writer of fiction has to stick to his immediate, direct experience, but Reggie Webber was adamant about that sort of thing and I think he rather liked quarrelling with his authors after he'd started them off. It allowed him to be marvellously vituperative and then he could go away and look for something or someone new. The fact is that he did put a lot of faith and energy into Michael Caradock's work when it was most useful and the book was very well received. It meant a great deal to him and he was a lot more upset by the break with Vortex Press (who were in pretty severe financial trouble at the time of the Baldwin book, anyway) than Reginald Webber was.'

Extract from David Hayward's official biography.

The long and lasting lie. Years put to a purpose that is purposeless; the self-aggrandisement, the great act, serious silences and overplayed furies. Words, words, words. How much better to have loved unselfishly and to have turned away from the tangle of hatred and envy and self-interest that enmeshes the artist. The itch of the creative ego, which will be momentarily placated or soothed by flattering lotions, the balms of praise and possibility: only to start up again, asking to be scratched until it blisters, suppurates, erupts into a hideous and inflamed infection. Not contagious. The everlasting allergy.

And to have thought for so long that my purpose was so serious. To have laboured over huge and wasteful tasks that were folly. Now to see, now to know that all the skills taught to me were useless, that my wounds were self-inflicted and kept open by myself alone and not by the defied gods, that my part in the war is a futile part because it is a war that no one can win and there is no good end for which to strive.

219

All those words, images, metaphors, fantasies, even ideas...

An empty sky...

Stillness. Receding waters...

A whore sheathed in grey silk to comfort me, against whom I rub off my craving and come in a mighty rush against – without penetrating. I see the still eyes in the empty, white face as she watches me with contempt. My lady of fiction.

While she, now neatly dressed, goes about preparing the midday meal and he suffers silently, watching her... the points of her nipples in a thin white blouse... madame of the real world, smiling and her soft voice, low with caresses....

The old lies, the same old lies. The deceit and betrayal of the scullery kiss and car-park fuck: pitiful little acts of gratification involving insult and wounding and the slighting of souls. Sordid little actions quickly expiated in disgust....

Not so the noble lies of art....

93. Studio interview with Angela Petrov (Trevelyan Lloyd off camera). Camera moving in quickly to close up

Petrov: (Sync.) Well, you must have heard people say – you should read poets and never get to know them. It's absolutely fatal, because you'll be very soon, very sadly, disappointed. Well, it's exactly the same with novelists, if not worse. I mean, the thing about

Take in Angela Petrov's gesture with cigarette holder

poets is that they say all kinds of splendid things and do quite the opposite: the thing about novelists is that you never know what they are. It was very difficult to tell with Michael what exactly he was up to and indeed who he really was. But he always gave me the impression of being totally ruthless. It was like watching someone dissecting frogs....

94. Cut to studio interview with Fay Mackail. Close up

Mackail: (Sync.) I'm not sure: ambition was certainly very noticeable, and dedication. His seriousness was really impressive, you know? And he did not make a terrific fuss about it. Never when he was working. But as far as I was concerned, he was endlessly interesting to be with. Very kind and considerate.

Medium shot Fay Mackail

Lloyd (o/s): Always? That's not, if I may say so, the most general view....

Close up Fay Mackail

Mackail: Perhaps not. But I loved him for a long time. I think I still do....

5

I didn't like the chap. I thought from the beginning that he was no good. Any decent officer gets to be a pretty good judge of a man and this fellow Caradock always seemed to me to be a thoroughly unreliable type. We were given to understand, of course, that he was frightfully clever and that he wrote books and what have you: but this was part of what I found objectionable. It's no secret I suppose that many officers disliked National Service intensely and the Royal Navy had no recruiting problems. We were the first service to abandon conscription, and not a moment too soon. There were many reasons: but quite apart from anything else, it's obviously desirable to have a highly trained, entirely reliable *professional* service with one hundred per cent professional officers. By the time one of these National Service fellows was trained, he had a few months left to serve and was very little use. Caradock, as a matter of fact, was a case in point. As I remember, he was a sort of assistant to the Captain's assistant secretary. He could have had very little to do. But he was a calculating young man and he had certainly ingratiated himself with the Captain. Clever chaps are often erratic and unreliable.... I did, as a matter of curiosity, dip into one of his books, which was in the wardroom library. But I didn't get very far. I think it was a set of stories about a place in Wales and some stuff about Oxford. I understand he wrote a book about the Service, but I certainly wouldn't be bothered to read it.

Rear-Admiral H. Van den B. Ralph, Royal Navy, formerly Commander's Assistant at HMS Calypso, *shore establishment at which Caradock finished his National Service, in BBC radio programme.*

'So you're not interested? Is that it?'

Fleming was most alarmed. Roberta Calloway's bosom heaved unavoidably under his very eyes – but he was able to cope with this form of temptation. What he was not able to understand was why she had singled him out as a confidant.

'I don't think it's appropriate. Do you?'

'Oh for Christ's sake, why don't you learn to unbend a bit? Must you always be so stiff?'

Fleming disposed of the prurient irony without shifting his frown. He offered her a perplexed and concerned seriousness that he sincerely hoped would be adequate for her slightly drunken mood of frustration and humiliation.

'I'll tell you, Paul,' she said. 'I'll tell you all about it.'

She let her shoulders sag for a moment in an involuntary contraction of defeat, so that the bodice of her dress fell forward and he saw her splendid breasts held up very lightly in a lace bra. The unhappy woman looked at her drink. And talked.

Fleming thought that she was, indeed, as she said she was, very pretty. No; more than pretty. In different circumstances she would be beautiful: her mood and the place and the events conspired to detract from her beauty and to make her merely an unhappy, disconsolate girl. He did not exactly register what she was saying because he was able to guess the story. Her debonair husband, as a young sub-lieutenant, had pursued her relentlessly. She had no reason to hurry, but had given in to an almost puppyish importunity. In the course of two happyish years she had grown to perhaps love him: then he had started on a course of haphazard and callous lechery.

'I don't know why,' she said. 'God knows, I did all I could reasonably have been expected to do....'

Fleming showed no embarrassment, but fortunately the girl stopped this particular line of complaint. He glanced across the bar and saw Calloway talking to a young, blushing guest. Fleming was not an emotional man and even when his emotions rose he was mercifully not the victim of any kind of physical disturbance: yet on this occasion he experienced an acid salivation at the back of his throat and an accompanying nausea. If they were usually merely contemptible, in some ways they were sickening. Fleming thought about his bitter, intelligent, spiteful mother. He shrugged.

'Why do you think I can help?' he asked.

'You! I don't think you can help! I just thought you'd...! I'm sorry. I'm drunk, Paul. No... you deserve a decent answer.... I thought that you hated them all as much as I do... and we'd just cuddle up together. Because you're one of them and I'm one of them and we both loathe them.... Oh God, I wish I was just stupid....'

Extract from Carcases of Tall Ships. *Alvin & Brandt, 1956.*

D'you know about Upper Yardsmen? No. Well, if there have been particularly good keen chaps joining as ratings at any given time, the Navy has always had a scheme for hurrying their careers along a bit. Good officer material, so instead of plugging away over the years, we lay on special courses and they become sub-lieutenants in a much shorter time. Obviously when we had National Service (Christ knows why) we extended the scheme and had these chaps known as National Service Upper Yardsmen or NSUYs. And I was Training Officer for a year or so on the old *Arundel* in charge of these chaps. And they weren't a bad lot! On the whole fairly bright, well-educated lads, but obviously without the drive and motivation of the kosher Upper Yardsmen.... This chap, Caradock, was a year or so older than the others, having already been to university, and he was jolly useful. Unlikely to make a silly ass of himself. I took him aside early on and said the necessary and I must confess I rather liked him. You see (Joanna, is that your name? Jane, sorry) you see Caradock was not athletic, in fact he was rather clumsy, and he wasn't particularly good with his hands and I think he was often frightened: but he was bloody determined. I think it was crazy to put him into the Supply and Secretariat Branch. He should have been put into the Executive Branch and then he'd have had some time at sea. It would have been jolly good for him.... Well, I'm certainly not going to sit here and pass judgement on a chap who's a famous writer, especially when I haven't read a word he's written: but I remember clearly what he was like scrambling through an exercise that didn't bother most of the others which was difficult for him, scared stiff but absolutely determined to hang on. And while I wouldn't necessarily have wanted Caradock around when all about were losing theirs, so to speak, he most certainly wasn't a ... I'd better rephrase that if it's going to go out on the wireless... he was a very decent type.

Commander R. G. Abernathy, Royal Navy retd, formerly NSUY Training Officer during Caradock's National Service on HMS Arundel, *in BBC radio programme.*

A number of theories have been put forward about Caradock's reasons for leaving Oxford before completing his research, some plausible and others less so. Howell Caradock was certainly, on the evidence of several people who lived in Cwmfelyn, pleased by what he saw as a manly action of someone prepared to do his duty; and, at the same time, Michael Caradock was certainly becoming more and more aware of his limitations as a scholar and of his positive ambitions to be a serious novelist. His tutor, Richard Rose, who had himself served with distinction in the Royal Air Force during the war, did nothing to dissuade him – quite sure that the experience would indeed do his pupil the world of good. Lucien Soames, who was supervising his research, did argue; but took the sensible view that if the young man was jaded and irresolute about his work, not much good would come of it and there would be further opportunities in two years' time for him to resume his studies. C. R. Martineau talked at length to Caradock, pointing out that his decision might seem to many wasteful, even prodigal, and reminding him that there was no guarantee that the college would take him back should he wish to continue after the service interruption. Practically, he also drew Caradock's attention to the fact that the Korean war was still in progress and the possibility, however remote, that he might be sent to that theatre of operations. He was impressed, however, by the young man's sincerity and seriousness, which was certainly crucial in later years (when Caradock *did* wish to return to his college) in securing him a position which enabled him to finish his doctoral thesis. I am inclined, however, to go a little further in explaining the idiosyncratic move. In the first place, Caradock was quickly and easily bored and the intense but necessarily narrow focus demanded by serious scholarship might readily have made him restless; secondly, he had (in my view) become afraid of belonging to any place, any group, any person. He had deliberately and without difficulty cut himself off from his native valley and upbringing. His experience with Helen Westlake (as many of the women who knew him intimately in later life are prepared to say) made him wary of committing himself to any other person. There remained his great love of Oxford – the place, the University, the way of life. It is, therefore, my contention that he cut himself off, partly to prove that he could do so, partly as what he saw as a necessary procedure in preventative therapy.

Richard Snow, in his uniformly hostile critical study of Caradock *The View from Lemnos*, says that Caradock may have had style and considerable technical ability, but he had no passion and no purpose. He claims that his work is sterile and that this is because Caradock belonged nowhere and to nothing and chose deliberately not to belong. Stephen Lewis has refuted this point of view fairly comprehensively in his own study, insisting that Caradock *did* belong and arguing his case at length, but (with more conviction) also pointing out that such an argument applied to a novelist, or indeed to any writer of imaginative literature, is irrelevant. I am inclined to go part of the way with Snow: but it is my view that this isolationism was intellectual in its origins rather than emotional. I am not sure that Snow does not suggest that Caradock's attitude was the result of an inverted snobbery – in that he felt socially inadequate at Oxford until he cultivated entirely ersatz manners and assumptions. This was emphatically not the case. Caradock was entirely confident that he could be accepted by any group to which he bothered to make himself agreeable. The fact was that he seldom made this effort and that this was a coldly cerebral decision.

For the moment, let us return to his years in the Navy. Caradock was recruited at Portsmouth in October 1952 as a Coder (Educational), having talked his way out of becoming a Coder (Special), which would have involved learning Russian. This is again consistent with his temporary resolve to break away from all things academic, since the Russian course, after a fairly gruelling initial period of training, afforded most of those who were successful to any degree a fairly comfortable time, as well as the perquisite of learning a new language. To his amused surprise, Caradock enjoyed his basic training: he was clean, competent and relatively mature, friendly enough to his messmates but sufficiently aloof to attract quickly the attention of his Chief Petty Officer Instructor and his Divisional Officer, both of whom thought that he was worth recommending as a National Service Upper Yardsman – in short, good officer material. So he never did serve in the capacity that he was recruited, as a Coder (Educational), where his duties would have been clerk and general dogsbody to the Instructor Branch on a shore establishment or perhaps (if he was lucky) a ship. He was transferred from basic training immediately to the rigorous and physically demanding NSUY course on board the training ship, *Arundel*, an ancient cruiser given over to various instructional and training courses which were ultimately transferred to the aircraft carrier *Ocean*.

Caradock applied himself diligently to becoming a good Upper Yardsman and earned the approbation of Chief Petty Officer Topkiss, in charge of that particular course, who says: 'He was by no means outstanding, wasn't Caradock: not like Bridgemont and Wills, for instance. But he was a good trier. And I formulated the same idea of him as Lieutenant-Commander Abernathy, the Training Officer, did: that he was a good worker, a decent trier digging in hard, and that it was more difficult for him because he was scared quite a bit of the time. He would go white, sir, in fact, and you'd see the sweat under his cap band. It worried me at first because I thought he'd go and lose his head. But he always mastered it. Well, of course I pointed it out to the Training Officer, and he said that that's what it was all about. Fair enough. His attitude was always good and very respectful. He never came it as some of them did. But he was never in the class of people like Bridgemont on that course and a few others I could name as don't concern you for this purpose, who could have been *real* officers.'

J. S. Bridgemont, now a bank manager in a pleasant suburb of London, was by general consent the outstanding member of the course. He thoroughly enjoyed it all and subsequently served as a sub-lieutenant on a destroyer. He is now a Commander in the RNVR who enjoys what he calls 'playing at it' but had no ambition to achieve a permanent commission. Of Caradock he says: 'He was rather a reserved man, older than most of us, except I think for Joseph and Barlow. We were certainly not bosom chums, but we got on well. I remember being very surprised to find out (after being demobbed) that Mike was a writer. He said nothing at all about it. I read a couple of his books some years ago, but I don't remember much about them. And then, of course, there was that awful business in Wales.... Terrible pity, that. Anyway, to get back to the point, I remember him as a studious type. If he went ashore, he usually went alone. I think he drank quite a bit, but he was never the worse for it. And in the Mess he used to read a lot. He was an interesting chap to talk to, knew a lot about politics and current affairs which was useful for the rest of us, since we were expected to know more or less what was what and who was clobbering whom.'

Vernon Joseph, now an executive with a multinational electronics firm, and a member of the same National Service course, did not find Caradock as agreeable. 'I found him supercilious: always prepared to lecture from a position of superiority, but never prepared to argue the toss. He was very patronising in that way. Of course, when it came to any sort of physical effort, it was a different story – because he was a bit of a dead loss. Bridgemont and Wills and one or two others virtually carried him through. But he was quite a good actor and that fooled the relevant people.'

Extract from David Hayward's official biography.

One of the duties of the second Officer of the Watch was to walk around the establishment at midnight accompanied by one of the Duty Petty Officers to check the security of all doors and windows. Fleming usually chose to make this tour alone. There would have already been a check on all important buildings carried out by the Duty Lieutenant-Commander on his rounds, and since the station was pleasantly situated among wooded hills, Fleming enjoyed a leisurely late-evening stroll, preferring his own company to the routine banalities of the conversation he would have been obliged to make to his escort. For his part the Petty Officer concerned did not in the least mind not having to turn out.

On this particular evening, in July, Fleming was listening to the trees, watching the clouds and in a thoroughly un-officerlike way experiencing the moonlight on the Hampshire hills. There were the curious noises of country night and the flight of owls and shadows where they were least expected.

Fleming did not much care whether a pretty Wren was being suitably pleasured by a goat-bearded Leading Seaman, but when he arrived at the Camp Cinema he found a door open and a shaft of dim light. It was unlikely that the Russians had penetrated this centre of the North Atlantic nervous system, but Fleming knew that the ship's dramatic society were rehearsing Nöel Coward's *Hay Fever* (with the First Officer, WRNS, as Judith Bliss). He thought it was conceivable that some gentle and vocationally misconstrued sailor in the cast might have forgotten to switch off and lock up. Or indeed that the appropriate nymphs and satyrs were finding arcadia as and when it occurred. In either event, the First Lieutenant would not be pleased and more preoccupied officers than Fleming might bring such subversions to his notice. Fleming looked inside the cinema.

There on the empty stage, set for the Bliss ménage, Fleming saw the First Lieutenant himself, lit by a single working-light, contemplating a cigarette box. It was a satisfying sight and fanciful images of Euripidean, Senecan and Jacobean tragedy flooded into Fleming's well-trained mind. He coughed.

The First Lieutenant started. And offered a blustering cough, in return.

'What's that?' he said. 'Who is it?'

'Officer of the Watch, sir,' said Fleming. 'Midnight rounds.'

232

'Is that you, Fleming?'

'Yes, sir.'

'Arrhum.'

Fleming advanced into the darkened cinema with feline certainty. The First Lieutenant groped his way down from the stage.

'I noticed a light on. DLC must have missed it.'

'I think the cast were here late, sir. It was their dress rehearsal for the Drama Festival.'

'Suppose we'll have some poof from Basingstoke telling us that One O is another Gertrude Lawrence.'

'It's conceivable.'

'Bloody slack all the same, Fleming. I'll have a word with Harper about it. Look, here's the key in the lock. You're going back to the main gate, aren't you? Take it back.'

'Aye, aye, sir.'

The First Lieutenant looked at Fleming with morose suspicion and went off without another word in the direction of the wardroom. Fleming returned the key, mentioned the incident to the first Officer of the Watch, on duty at the gate, and thought no more about it.

The following evening, in modified Mess Dress, he understood more about what had been going on as he sat among the loyal audience for the first night of *Hay Fever*. The First Officer, WRNS, was not dissuaded by her somewhat solid and square figure from acting in the *grande dame* manner; she was also firmly disposed to believe in her flair for light comedy. Fleming had followed with interest the diplomatic manoeuvrings whereby the timid Instructor Officer in nominal charge of the production had steered her away from Amanda in *Private Lives*, while failing to have her accept the role of Madame Arcati. The compromise had been Judith Bliss in which part her substantial presence and natural histrionic bent were more or less accommodated to reality. To polite laughter from the audience, the First Officer swept and swanned through the play until there came a moment of farce. While talking to someone down-stage, she went over to the silver cigarette box and with a flourish took a cigarette which, as she moved flowingly away, she intended to fit into a suitably long holder. The flourish was efficient. And out of the handsome box floated a streamer of cigarettes, all presumably sewn together. Whatever the collective emotions of the audience had been, they were relieved in a loud, spontaneous and delighted laugh. The bemused actress stood in the centre of the stage trailing her banner of cigarettes like a forlorn slogan on a humid day, struggling for composure. Fleming searched the rows in front for the First Lieutenant and found him sitting diagonally from him. In normal circumstances the First Lieutenant was no admirer of amateur (or indeed any) theatre, but on this occasion his sullen face was creased in what was almost pleasure. The First Officer's interpretation of Judith Bliss did not recover its buoyancy.

Extract from Carcases of Tall Ships. *Alvin & Brandt, 1956.*

Caradock's melancholy preoccupation with forces of cruelty and violence just beneath the normally civilised even pleasant surface of life is perhaps most dramatically noticeable in his fourth book, *Carcases of Tall Ships*. The ironic title comes from a passage in *The Merchant of*

Venice and relates to a description of the Goodwin Sands – 'a dangerous flat and fatal where the carcases of many a tall ship lie buried'. Caradock uses his metaphor for a double purpose: first as a vitriolic figure for the state of the modern Navy, and second for the wasted and profitless lives that Fleming sees around him.

In the early part of the book Fleming looks on with disdainful amusement at the concerns and obsessions of these others with as little compassion as someone studying the behaviour of ants while idling in someone else's garden. Against the generally comic undercurrent three separate skeins of plot become apparent: the harmless but absurd territorial rivalry between the Wren officer and the First Lieutenant; the savage jealousy of the pretty young wife of a lecher; and the bitter quarrel between an unstable but brilliant officer and the less able Lieutenant-Commander whose career, according to the system of zonal promotion in the Navy, he has thwarted finally and absolutely. Caradock has his hero observe these people with a dispassion that is well inside the bounds of credibility but which is nevertheless frightening: the laconic wit, the irony, the contempt.... Until suddenly the reader finds that Fleming himself has been drawn into the web of triviality he so much despises. Caradock will not allow a character to get away with invulnerability. In the earlier novel, Baldwin cuts himself off ruthlessly from hometown and family, renders himself immune to the ills that his translated flesh was heir to: and in a moment of impulsive folly (which is also one of sheer bad luck) takes on a group of thugs who paralyse him. Fleming's paralysis

235

is achieved more slowly in that his infatuation for Christina Finch builds up progressively. The reader is aware that Fleming himself has become a character in one of the burlesques that he has been observing with such sardonic calm.

The transition is all the more effective for being gradual: when Christina first appears, Fleming hardly notices her; then she amuses him; soon after he is mildly interested in her flirtations with younger officers. And then he is crazed. His jealousy drives him to manoeuvres of humiliation that he, least of all, can support.

This merciless purgation of the central character who imagines himself to be whole and untouchable is characteristic of Caradock's work from the early stories (the happy blackberrying boys who find a murdered girl) to the complicated and deeply tortured Axel Waldeck in *Promethead* (who sees himself destroyed by an electoral whim and who is *almost* destroyed by his own ensuing paranoid obsession). No one, in Caradock's landscape, gets away with anything: least of all with getting away. And the retribution is harsh for those who make the attempt.

At the same time, it is worth noting that in the two novels which are regarded as satires, Caradock's point of view is very different. In *Carcases of Tall Ships*, the satire is strictly objective and Fleming becomes involved in a situation which he can no longer deal with objectively; the impact of the novel is acidic. In the succeeding book, *Broods of Folly*, a genuine comedy, the satire is entirely subjective: in that Laertes Jones is openly amused by the truly extraordinary people that he meets, but also entertained by his own reactions to them. Whereas Fleming might have thought himself safe from insult or injury, Laertes Jones seems never to have thought that he is not the central innocent character in someone else's farce. He watches himself watching the action. And his own surprise is (for once in Caradock's work) pleasant.

The women portrayed by Caradock (as already noted) tend to be gentle, very feminine and unfailingly kind to men who are usually less experienced and less emotionally mature. There are two exceptions: the upper-class secretary in *The Low Key of Hope*, who disturbs the young journalist, Baldwin; and the WRNS officer Christina Finch, who virtually destroys Fleming. Fleming's bitter realisation is entirely consistent with Caradock's severe chastisement of all those people (invariably his central characters) who think they can live separately or apart and who are ultimately humbled by the realities of living. The miner Rhys in the early story 'Kingfisher' sobbing in pursuit of vandal children is also Fleming hurling a billiard ball at the girl who has deceived him and is, at length, Waldeck sacrificing himself for an impulsive moment, ideologically excusable, in order to purge himself of private guilt.

From the comic war games of the First Officer and the First Lieutenant, which include the very funny scene where the Wren takes revenge by painting the naval officer's gaiters with a tincture of aniseed when he is officer of the guard and also looking after the absent padré's bitch, to the personal drama of the young wife whom Fleming contemplates with alarming dispassion, while being alive to her evident sexual presence, to the bitter anger of Commander Rattray and Lieutenant-Commander Fraser: in all these circumstances Fleming is able to retain his good sense, to assert his feeling of superiority. He can watch, he can help, he can sustain. But we gradually realise that Fleming is no longer himself. His *hubris* has been discovered. His bluff has been called. Consistently with the rest of Caradock's work, we are presented with a character for whom escape from trivial human contact seemed possible, and even easy, but which resulted in personal humiliation if not defeat.

Extract from Douglas Rome: Michael Caradock *in Writers of Today series, 1969.*

I was a Communications Officer, at the time, and I suppose he was really rather attractive. He had a lot of dark hair, always very well looked after, and nice blue eyes; and he was a big man without being disgustingly hearty or anything like that. I think there were two things that I *did* notice: he was always especially smart – probably because he was National Service and hated the idea of people thinking he was scruffy; and he kept very much to himself. As far as I remember he talked to young Doc and one or two of the Schoolies and otherwise he was terribly reticent. But I think he did rather fall for Chrissie Dove, who was a terrific ball of fire, very unlike Michael Caradock in temperament, and also the daughter of an Earl or something. Well, as you can imagine, she had not much time for a young officer merely getting through his National Service. He wasn't dynamic, you know.... She was very attractive. And she knew it. She was always very kind to him. But you must know yourself, the sort of spaniel look, panting away and waiting to be kicked. And there was – in the loosest possible way, if you see what I mean, and it mattered more then than it would now – a sort of class thing.... Because clever as he was, he was *not* in the sort of address book that she kept. I don't think it was important because I don't think it came to very much – but from odd things she said I think he'd rather gone overboard and she wasn't having any. In the nicest and kindest way.

Mrs Anne Dryburn, formerly 3/O Anne Sage, WRNS, Communications Officer on Flag Officer Defence Liaison's staff, HMS Calypso, *in BBC radio programme.*

The evidence, already quoted, that Caradock enjoyed his initial training is borne out by friends who met him on leave. Michael Beauchamp-Beck and Jeremy Philbrick, both of whom had completed their National Service before University, were mildly surprised that Caradock should have buckled down so well to routine and discipline. Eventually, he was commissioned as a sub-lieutenant in the Supply and Secretariat Branch and worked in the Captain's Office at HMS *Calypso*, a shore training establishment. There is very little factual proof that he did not find it agreeable, though rather less so than his service as a rating: but it was during this period that he obviously gathered material to be used in his next book, *Carcases of Tall Ships*, which marked a departure in style and outlook from the earlier works.

Senior Nursing Sister Sara Vernon served as a member of Queen Alexandra's Nursing Service on the same shore establishment as Caradock and knew him fairly well, though she qualifies this by adding that it was not possible to know him well: 'He was sociable enough and he would chat around the bar in a friendly enough way, but if you ever asked him anything personal the shutters came down. Not with a snap, but evenly and firmly. I had a pretty jaundiced view of the Navy, as did one or two of the Schoolies (Instructor Officers) who were taking a soft option on National Service and serving an extra year to have the guaranteed commission. And so on *Calypso* did the Surgeon Lieutenant whom I saw a lot of, of course, being in the same business. He was a very joky, thoroughly indiscreet character. And we were all fairly bright – anyway a lot brighter than the average run of naval and Wren officers, so we used to have a spot of ribald fun at their expense. Michael never joined in this and I think he was a bit embarrassed. Then occasionally, because he had a very sharp mind, there would be some aside or some flash of exasperation which was very funny and often very cruel. There certainly was no Christina Finch in real life. I think he did fancy one of the Wren officers quite a lot and I think he took her out once or twice, but she was very upper and she tended to behave as if he wasn't there. But there was no drama at all. The only person I recognise in the book is a minor character, the one called Bobbie, which is a fairly merciless caricature of one of the people on *Calypso*.'

Extract from David Hayward's official biography.

Most critics, including those who admire Caradock, admit that the portrait of Christina Finch is unusually vicious. Although the girl bears some resemblance to June in the previous novel, who spurns (so understandably) the pathetic Baldwin, she is presented with a unique savagery. It is noticeable that most of the women in Caradock's books, all of whom are sexually overactive, offer themselves to his heroes. Very seldom does the man begin the process of seduction and it becomes apparent after serious scrutiny of his work that he held women in very low esteem, regarding them as intellectually inferior to men and useful only as sexual objects. Much of the evidence about his private life supports this view. It is feasible to suggest that Caradock may indeed have had his advances rejected by a real 'Christina', perhaps for very different reasons, and so, with characteristic venom, he took his vengeance (as he did on his native village and people) in fiction, where there was no possible opportunity of retaliation. We are incidentally spared none of Caradock's obsessions, which I shall deal with later, relating to female underclothing, especially stockings and suspenders, which recur in very many different episodes in succeeding novels.

Once again Caradock's considerable ingenuity and literary facility were turned to his own literal advantage: to present himself through his central character as a man apart, a noble, supremely clever man misunderstood and grossly ill-used by people of grosser sensibility. I would also suggest that it marks a development of his contempt for women into irrational hatred, compatible with a man who admired Nietzsche and de Vigny among others, which from this novel onwards takes increasing prominence in his writing.

The main impression left by *Carcases of Tall Ships*,

however, is one of the type of social failure (however little some of us might esteem such so-called social success) that marks the eighteen-carat snob. Unaccepted by a group and class of people that he envied, Caradock was as usual taking selective revenge, while totally unable to disguise a yearning to belong among them.

Extract from Richard Snow: The View from Lemnos. *Medusa Books, 1972.*

Lieutenant-Commander R. W. A. D'Artagnan-Fogg entered the wardroom anteroom with a swagger that dated at least from the events subsequent to St Bartholomew's Night. He glanced at the occupants of the bar with his usual look of blaring scorn, midway between the gaze of a fish and a basilisk, his mouth set in something between a smirk and sneer. He nodded at Fleming, wrote out a chit and in due course spoke in a languidly creamy tenor:

'Not much social life, Fleming?'

'Oh, I get by, sir.'

There was a snort of pleasure from the little knot of Schoolies, SD officers, the Nursing Sister and one of the recognisably human Wren officers at the other end of the bar.

'I meant in the Mess. Pretty dank.'

'Decidedly moist, sir.'

'The name's Bobbie, by the way. D'you play cards?'

Fleming knew the name was Bobbie, because the name had been floated and fluted around ever since Lieutenant-Commander de Fogg had arrived at the station, additional for special training. He was the scion of a naval family with a tradition dating back almost to the time when Pepys was

Secretary, in the years following the revocation of the Edict of Nantes, which Fleming was disposed to view in a strictly non-sectarian way as a disaster. 'Bobbie' de Fogg was regarded as a character, as assured as anyone could be of attaining a high rank, endowed with a congenital contumely, whose eccentricities since he had proved himself to be an entirely adequate officer in the Executive branch were indulged within the limits of the protocols of seniority which de Fogg scrupulously observed.

'I once played a game called gin rummy with our American allies in Montevideo,' said Fleming. 'And I have forsworn all such activity.'

De Fogg, untypically unsure of himself, looked at Fleming with an unblinking, baleful stare, his mouth set in the same expression, now slightly congealing, which in his case effortlessly expressed contempt.

'Really?' he said. 'How boring.'

Fortunately a Commander appeared and de Fogg was able to reach for the chit book and turn his back upon Fleming while they engaged one another in conversation more suitable. Fleming did what he could to avoid the wasteful nuisance of hating people, but 'Bobbie' de Fogg represented all that he (and no doubt his waspishly clever mother) detested about the Navy: the assertion of a mindless tradition that leadership was inherited, the insolence of generations distilled into a few egomaniac relics slavishly imitated by the middle class and the bourgeois.

To see R. W. A. D'Artagnan Fogg walk across the parade ground was in itself to know immediately the assumptions of authority that he had accepted prenatally and which he would no doubt carry beyond the grave into the relevant bowge of damnation. He was a very tall and thin man who kept his shoulders back and straight without bothering to adjust his lower thorax accordingly: in a fat man the effect would have been absurd, but in de Fogg it was highly individual. At the same time he seemed to sag at the knees when he walked, but only slightly. Fleming, as a young officer in Gibraltar, had once seen him aboard ship wearing his hat tilted over his forehead as he walked along the deck of an aircraft carrier, and had glimpsed the spirit of Caligula.

*

Soon after the girl had first appeared, creating something of a stir amongst married and single officers alike, Fleming had the opportunity of watching her at the opposite table during a Mess Dinner. She was unusually pretty with vivid blue eyes and dark, naturally curly hair: but most impressive was her effortless slender grace of movement that made the modified steel-blue tarpaulin that WRNS officers were obliged to wear as Mess Dress seem almost elegant. She had been placed between a promising lieutenant, who combined the unlikely interests of boxing and amateur drama, and a habitual guest of the Mess who lived locally. She blushed, Fleming noted, in all the right places; laughed moderately without performing the teeth-baring rocking convulsion usual among her sister officers. Once or twice she caught his eyes. And they both looked away: she demurely, he deliberately.

When she subsequently came to the Mess in the

evenings, in a dress or a suit, he often watched her and placidly undressed her without much more than the usual pleasant chit-chat. Fleming liked to keep his sexual initiatives well apart from his daily routines as the member of a closely knit community. Yet he knew that she was aware of his appreciation: anyone as pretty and as alert to such things could walk into a room and spot the men who were avid, interested, interested in spite of themselves, and non-starters for whatever reason. Sometimes, always accidentally, he found himself in a position where he was able to admire her long, well-shaped legs suitably disposed as she sat on a bar stool, watch the beautiful movement of her nearly perfect hips as she walked by, take pleasure in the swell of her breasts above a small waist as she made some trivial gesture with her arms. Their relationship was delightfully cordial.

Then, one day, Fleming returned to the Mess early at lunchtime after attending Commander's Requestmen and Defaulters where there had been no takers. It was the eve of some weekend function and he found the splendid Christina Finch on a stepladder, trying to fix some Tyrolean decorations to a wall, in accordance with the theme of the party to be held.

'Can I help?' Fleming asked.

'No. I can manage,' she said. 'But you could hold the ladder. I get a bit tottery at the top.'

Fleming tokenly braced the contraption. Christina, who was a tall girl, climbed to the platform at the top of the ladder and stretched upward. She stood with her legs apart, no doubt to be sure of balance. Fleming glanced up casually and saw under the uniform skirt the really superb legs in black stockings, the firm thighs and delightfully round arse in pretty white pants. He went on looking, suddenly and shamefully aware of a total, absolute lust for this one girl.

He was excited and disconcerted at once. Then as she came down the ladder and he, most delicately, helped her off it, he saw something in her eyes that was sure indication that she knew exactly what was in his mind.

'Let me buy you a drink for that,' she said.

*

'It's all very simple,' said the Surgeon Lieutenant.

He had an unusually long jaw which seemed to wobble at the end when he was serious and eyes that seldom smiled, although his face was usually arranged in an amiable pattern. Now the eyes had that professional earnestness of which only doctors are capable when talking off duty.

'It's all sex,' he said.

Fleming was aware that the Surgeon Lieutenant had ambitions in the direction of psychiatry, but he was well prepared to listen to any such diagnosis in the context of the latest phases of conflict between the First Officer and the First Lieutenant.

The Surgeon Lieutenant's grey eyes scanned his audience of three as keenly as those of a consultant, about to reveal a new facet of medical truth.

'Fiercely repressed sexual urges often manifest themselves in forms of aggression,' said the Surgeon Lieutenant, earnestly.

His grey medical eyes lighted on Fleming who nodded with gravity.

'What about Konrad Lorenz?' asked the Surgeon Lieutenant. 'It's all there if you look, you know. In the study of beasts.'

'What? Painting people's gaiters with aniseed?' said Instructor Lieutenant Woodthorpe.

The Surgeon Lieutenant's face adapted itself into deep lines of science and mockery. His eyes squinnied, becoming impatient and mean at the same time. Fleming thought that he had never seen the man really laugh.

'For Christ's sake...'

'No,' said Woodthorpe. 'You tell me, Doc. Is painting gaiters in all this rubbish about grooming ritual and the rest of it that you've been going on about?'

'My dear bloke,' said the Surgeon Lieutenant. 'I could quote a hundred examples where the male or the female and sometimes both indulge in aggressive display before they get down to mating. It's all part of the courtship ritual.'

'We've no established proof that Harriet did paint Number One's gaiters with aniseed have we, Paul?' said Lieutenant-Commander Grimm.

Fleming shook his head solemnly.

'Nor who sewed the fags together in the play,' said Woodthorpe. 'It stands to reason, Jack. Look at it: first the fags – and she looks daft; then the dogs on parade – and he looks dafter; then the fire extinguishers; then the fire picket in Wrens' quarters; then the rule about no Wrens allowed in his part of ship; then her orders that Wrens mustn't speak to officers so that the Captain comes in for a pint and the girl behind the bar won't say hello.... It's bloody farce.'

'Never,' said Fleming, 'in the field of human conflict have the lives of so many owed so much entertainment to such futile ingenuity.'

'I must say, I wonder what they'll think of next,' said Grimm.

'It's not futile, though,' said the Surgeon Lieutenant. 'It's sex. Elaborate love-play. *Unusual*! I'll admit that. It's extremely unusual. But that's what it is.'

'So we'll find them under the billiard table any night now, will we, Doc?' said Woodthorpe.

'Jesus! You can be bloody childish, sometimes, Woodthorpe. Do you know that?' said the Surgeon Lieutenant.

*

'It's very nice of you to come and talk to me, Paul. In the circumstances.'

Fleming looked at Roberta Calloway calmly. He smiled. She refused to. Her eyes were big and dark, without humour and without bitterness. He apprehended the danger of the situation without in any way understanding it.

'The circumstances are that you are a lovely young woman and that I would like to talk to you.'

'All right,' she said. 'All right. Where's your pretty Wren?'

'Who is that?'

'The new one. Christina Something.'

'Not mine, Roberta. Emphatically not mine.'

Mrs Calloway swung on the bar stool in a limited sector, so that there was a moment when her legs were provocatively apart.

248

'Ah, who cares!' she said. 'It's ridiculous, isn't it. Here we are on the threshold of annihilation. The bloody Western World, all democracy and liberty and human rights. And look at us. Niggling at little personal vanities and sniffing around each other like animals. Oh, there are a few who don't. Nice married men like Frazer and the DSO and the three or four young men who want to be good. But what about the rest of us?'

'Some already proven,' said Fleming. 'Others waiting to prove themselves.'

'You make me sick.'

'Why?'

'Because I'm as clever as you are. And I know what that kind of fatuous remark means. Which is nothing!'

'I'm sorry. I was being relatively serious. I think I'd prefer to be commanded by any of these people – within reason – than a lot of others who are more intelligent, more sensitive, more politically shrewd.'

'Like my bastard husband.... You know, I wonder what happens: one day you really love each other. Or so it seems. Tenderness and little jokes and private games: and then the next... or it seems like the next... he's after everything with a round arse in a skirt. At first he makes jokes about it... which you pretend are funny.... And then he stops bothering. And you stop bothering. And you watch. It's undignified and it cheapens everything. All the quiet, silences, peacefulness that you used to have together... I believed in "making love". Is that funny? Well, I don't any more.'

'It would be the same the other way round.'

249

'Oh don't be clever, Paul. I'm too tired. What does *that* mean?'

'Do you remember suggesting that we should...'

'I think you're a shit for reminding me.'

She repeated the precise swing of the bar stool, with the exact provocation, this time holding the pose for a moment or so.

'Perhaps. But don't you think it's a matter of self-pity?'

'So what!'

'You have me, there.'

'I don't care about self-pity. And you understand. You wouldn't take me because it was inconvenient and you didn't want me enough. Well, I don't care about that. I was randy and you were handy. My God, did I invent that? Surely not! And you know very well in your elegant way, you behave as badly as he does. All neat. All on the side. No strings. Why don't you sign up at a good brothel?'

'I don't know of any.'

'There you are. The big joke. The glib reply. Do you know what it feels like, the shame of watching your husband on the scent...? And when you are young and fairly attractive, do you know the shame of being groped and stroked and fingered by people who you think are repulsive because they think that he's away and you're going to be a pushover.'

She had collected herself, physically as well as emotionally. She straightened her back and the large dark eyes flashed. Fleming thought that she was wasted. All the assumptions made on her behalf by parents (very like Fleming's own) who had sent her to proper schools and

kept her away from appropriate places of learning had
contributed to her state of incarcerated failure. Fleming
wished that he might have liked her enough to comfort
her. And, as he did so, wondered where indeed the pretty
Christina Something was....

'It's not what I thought it was about,' she said. 'I
wonder what might have happened if I'd married a
schoolmaster or a parson or a writer. At least I wouldn't
have been as bored.... Don't ask about children, Paul. I
don't want bloody children. I don't have to have children
in order to fulfil myself. Oh, Christ, here's Woodthorpe....
Look, even if your sexy Wren comes along don't abandon
me to Woodthorpe, will you?'

'He's a fairly honest young man.'

'And boring.'

'Not entirely. Besides, Woodthorpe would not... insult
you. If you understand what I mean.'

'I do! He'd ask permission first. Is that it? Oh my God,
Paul, it's not that I don't feel like retaliating – but he's
not quite... he's not one of us.... If you see what *I* mean.
Do you?'

Extracts from Carcases of Tall Ships. *Alvin & Brandt, 1956.*

Carcases of Tall Ships seems to me to be Caradock's
weakest novel. It has a certain assurance and there is the
technical achievement of virtually concealing the central
plot of the book in no less than three subplots, so that the
reader is genuinely surprised by the violent dénouement of
the last few chapters. It is difficult, however, to be
convinced of Caradock's wholehearted involvement in the

Navy and it was only when Caradock was involved in a community, or a society that he truly cared about, that he wrote well. In the two major novels, *Promethead* and *Laocoön*, this involvement was on a cosmic scale, but in the earlier work one feels that he really cared about the ambience in which his characters moved, however much they are in conflict with the conventions that obtain, however eager they are to break loose. And this is where I take issue with those critics who seek to emphasise Caradock's alleged detestation of Wales and of his native valley, because as we have seen in the early stories, the involvement is close and the sympathy considerable. The same sympathy endures in the novel *Angry Sunset* and is transposed into a fairly, but not entirely, convincing Northern industrial landscape in *The Low Key of Hope*. The inference must be that Caradock really cared about, first, the locality, and, second, the situation of young people at odds, as most young people are, with their immediate traditions. To be strictly fair, however, it is essential to note that Caradock never wrote fiction about the place that was undoubtedly very dear to him, which was the town and University of Oxford. This tends to support the view that his most imaginative writing was invariably the result of his own conflict with the community or society in which he found himself. At Oxford, Caradock felt comfortable and happy: so he was only able to write commentaries about the place and its people. In Cwmfelyn, later on in London, and finally at Glanmor, he was so irritated by environmental factors that he must make fictions.

252

In the Navy, however, he was neutral. He did not really care one way or another about the people amongst whom he placed his curiously ambiguous hero Fleming. Caradock has been accused of choosing to hate from the inside: and Fleming in *Carcases of Tall Ships* is the most frequently cited character in support of this view. Fleming is an accepted member of the officer class – not, as Caradock was, a National Serviceman, not even a member of one of the less elite branches of the Royal Navy – and yet he is intensely critical of his inheritance and of his circumstance and colleagues. Caradock's most vehement detractors have pointed out that Fleming's indignation stops well short of action and that the laconic shrug is no substitute for a bold man speaking his mind. What is interesting about *Carcases of Tall Ships*, though, is not its picture of naval life – comic and pathetic and realistic as it may be, by turns – but of Caradock's dawning realisation about the nature of his central character: the determined misfit who is unaware of his own hubris and who is ultimately humiliated, as much by his own vanity as by any force acting from the outside. Caradock not only makes Fleming vulnerable, but he makes this vulnerability the central and painful point of the novel. The humiliation, after the scene in the billiard room where he has savagely hurt the promiscuous Christina and is rescued from her lover by the execrable de Fogg, is complete. De Fogg uses the opportunity to make things as unpleasant as possible for Fleming and his shame is intensely conveyed to the reader.

Yet, *Carcases of Tall Ships* is an objective book. Fleming is a cypher, in the way that Baldwin and Tudor (in *Angry*

Sunset) and the figures in the early stories were not. The whole novel is a clever equation which works out well enough and equals nought. Perhaps it is essential that a novelist obsessed with structure should formulate equations that never work out. With all their imperfections, they suggest new ideas for new equations to the readers. And so the process goes on. At no time, however, are we convinced that Caradock is in any way involved: the novel is satirical in intent, but the satire is cerebral, distant, carefully balanced.

Stephen Lewis: The Novels of Michael Caradock. *Molyneux, 1971.*

The General got up and began to pace up and down, the heavy leonine head weighed down upon the deep chest. Ganuret looked uneasily in the direction of Major Ganz, who was untroubled, the mouth curved in the affable and imperturbable smile that Ganuret had come to know so well. With one index finger Ganz traced on the unmutilated side of his face, almost the exact line of the scar which cut jaggedly across the other cheekbone. He repeated the compact gesture over and over again, but his face remained utterly calm, even contented.

'I was never one of them, you know,' Waldeck said. 'I was a scholar by inclination and I had an ambition to be a writer – a poet like yourself. I do not think I would have been a very good poet, but I think I might have written some usefully reflective essays. I loved the Classics and I was most fascinated by the time of Tacitus and Pliny and Epictetus and Juvenal. In my trivial, juvenile way, I almost wished that I might live in evil times, under the sombre tyranny of a Domitian, so that I could test and prove my worth. I did not know what was to come a mere twenty years later. But those times, you see, Ganz, were not evil: they were vain, unjust, imperious and chauvinistic but not evil. And we all believed that ours was a free society in which men of principle agreed to disagree. Not much to test the mettle of a stupidly intelligent young man. The diplomatic seismographs were already registering the first tremors of earth movements: and so, instead of pursuing an untroubled career of scholarship and idealist thought at various institutes of learning, engaging in colloquia with the gentle ephebics of my persuasion and gradually attaining a more sonorous respectability, my good family thought it wise and patriotic for me to join a good regiment. The traditions of my family had always been exemplary.

'Rather to everyone's surprise, there was a war. Those diplomatic rumbles should not have fulminated into catastrophe, but they did. And I recall the confidence and elation with which the news was received in my regiment. I shared neither: but I do not pretend that I foresaw the extent of the degradation and suffering that I was to follow. By virtue of my family's influence, I was given a staff job in the capital. I was required to look splendid in my uniform. Gracious and sometimes lovely young women, in the manner of the times, flirted with me and pretended that I was heroic. I knew quite well that I was not heroic and had passing through my mind an interrupted but consistently running cinema of the major acts of carnage from antiquity to the Napoleonic wars.

255

Before my eyes, I saw the shattered bodies, lacerated limbs, the distortions and mutilations of the flesh; in my ears I heard first the screams and then the groans and the delirious mutterings of the wounded; in my nose there would be the stench of dead or decaying flesh and I seemed to sense upon my hands the tacky and unclean stain of blood, my hands were filthy and I thought they would never feel clean again even if washed in acid. I would look down and see that they were merely sweaty. I would accept another glass of champagne from the orderly. I would incline to the General's daughter or the Admiral's maiden aunt. The elation and confidence persisted. It should not be possible.

'When things started going against us, I applied to be returned to my regiment – a cavalry division which was held in reserve for the time being. Things were far from uncomfortable in the garrison some seventy miles away from the front lines. And my conscience was no longer as troubled. But I was aware as I shared in the lives of my brother officers that I was not one of them and that I never should be. And yet, Piers Ganuret, here you see me now. A discredited Marshal and you wonder what else I could ever have been except a soldier. Perhaps, you even think that these are the delusions of a disgraceful and disgraced old man. But Ganz knows. You must ask Ganz. You are one of them, aren't you, Ganz?'

The Major smiled and Ganuret heard the slight rasp of an ironic laugh. Waldeck was himself grinning broadly.

'Ganz was born into the military elite. He accepts its premises and assumptions. He knows that a high-born self-perpetuating officer class is essential to the maintenance of good order and liberty. We will not go into the eugenics of the matter, Ganz, we will accept this hypothesis.'

Ganz went on smiling, the one sector of his face rigid and immobile, so that what would have been an expression of warmth and joviality was, in effect, a grotesque distortion. He showed no resentment at Waldeck's teasing.

'So Major Ganz will keep his gaiters polished and his buttons brilliant and his uniforms impeccable – or, at least, his orderlies will – and he will dress himself up in all manner of archaic finery for the benefit of quite futile ceremonial in memory of this or that memorable act of carnage. And he will maintain the false legend of brotherhood and loyalty and inter-reliance; and he will preserve the elaborations of behaviour, protocol and ritual, which have long been out of date. He will. Ah, but I should say he would have. Major Ganz, you see, Ganuret, is blessed or cursed with a sharp intellect, a very good mind. He has also what is rare, except at the most infantile level, among officers: political acumen. So Major Ganz has renounced not the tradition, but the benefits that might accrue to him from the tradition. He would now certainly be no mere major: a colonel-general at the very least. If we achieve the ends that he and I are working for, constitutionally, if our people ask us to return to govern them, then as my Chief of Staff Ganz will see to it that the excellent tradition, to which he belongs and I do not, is maintained.'

'You digress, General,' said Ganz easily. 'I am sure the young man is not interested in me.'

Ganuret noticed again that no one ever addressed Waldeck as 'Marshal', the honorary title bestowed upon him, by a régime that he despised – to render him, as he well knew, obsolete.

Waldeck nodded.

'Perhaps he is not interested in any of us. He is a poet. And you are an innocent, Piers Ganuret. I do not know how much you have read about the great slaughters of the past, the great tyrannies and genocides. I suspect little. I had read much, but I had not seen with my own eyes.

'That early war began in an illusion of past gallantries that were never, *pace* Ganz, gallant. It ended in a smell and taste of foetor that, once experienced, may never be escaped. It is no mere question of mud, putrescence, commonplaces of excrement, the horrid, spiked fur of fat rats, the indignity of lice – think of that, Ganuret: a poet like yourself would probably have been a private soldier, think of how you would endure lice. No *mere* question, I say. God knows it was enough? Fear, shell shock, shit; screaming. A question of trying to keep things together. Not quite so bad in the war we shared together, was it, Ganz?'

'In some ways, General.'

'In some ways. True.'

The General began to pace again, great heavy steps. Ganz stroked the smooth side of his face again. The corners of his mouth were now turned down, but his expression was still placid. The heavy fauve head went up as Waldeck stopped, the thick body turned.

'Slow small flies, the unclean itch, the degradation of men...' he said. 'And I, Ganuret, kept thinking of the elegant scene and the decorum that I had left behind. The solemn orderly with his tray of glasses at my elbow. An eternal footman of sorts, I suppose. Some might have been, some *were*, able to return to the library and the cloister. I admire them for that. I could not do it. Do you know the work of Barna of Siena: the darkness of the faces, the irretrievable anguish of a generation that has seen despair's own decayed face, the veritable skull beneath the skin drawn tight. Think of that, Ganuret; and think of those people in the bustle of a scene of Brueghel, and think of such a scene consecrated by an artist of genius to an act of carnage. Now, take out of your picture all colour that is not dirty, polluted, adulterated. If you see reds, greens, blues, purples: you are in close up and it is the process of putrefaction. The vaster canvas is yellow streaked with brown, streaked with grey, streaked with beige, streaked with black and highlit with dirty white. All this is pitted with craters and holes, filled with noisome water, deliquescent bodies, the dank fumes of death. It is crisscrossed with mantraps and corrosive wire upon which hang fragments of clothing and strips of flesh as the shriking trophies of a cosmic butcher-bird. And the noise is incessant and terrifying. Both ears shriek and throb in the silences, so there is no respite. Everything you touch is sticky, mucilaginous and indescribably foul. Can you eat with that hand again? Can you taste anything that does not reek in your throat of corruption?'

Major Ganz was listening as though transfixed. His face was still, the eyes on Waldeck, without expression.

'And behind the lines, when we were withdrawn for a

259

rest period: there were the whores and the camp-followers. There was disease and pusillanimity and the meanness that flesh is heir to. I thought of the gracious young women when I was a staff officer and I wanted to see them outraged in the same way. No. You see, I was never one of them. But having seen and committed myself to responsibility, having survived, I could never return to Theocritus or Virgil or the great aristocratic tradition of my learning. I had heard men laughing on the other side of something worse than hell by then. I saw them, when ordered, shoulder their kit and go back to it. I had to stay with them. When it was over, I had to stay. For the soul of every dead hero that was not carried away to Valhalla, in the name of defeat for every idiotic notion that death in battle is glorious or honourable, to spit in the face of the political little men at their ceremonies and receptions. I was not one of them, though, ever.'

Extract from Promethead, *Hazel & Sims, 1967.*

Leslie Chambers who saw more of Howell Caradock at their golf club after the death of Caradock's wife testifies that this reticent man, who had taken no particular pride in his foster-son's achievements at Oxford, was very pleased about his ephemeral career in the Navy. 'He seemed to take it that the fact that Julian had gone in earlier than he needed to was almost the same as volunteering. And then, he was delighted when the boy got a commission. Very pleased about that. Howell always thought of himself as an officer, you know.'

Both Mr Chambers and J. Rudmose Bowen suggest that

Howell missed his wife very much. He had arranged with a childless married couple that they should take over part of his house and look after him, but was apparently at a loss much of the time with what to do with himself. Mr Bowen writes: 'He was prepared to forgive Julian all his previous negligence, however much it might have hurt Phyllis, now that the boy was doing so well in the Navy. He came up to the club on Wednesdays and sometimes at weekends. Not that I was always there myself, of course, but I usually had a round on Wednesday and most of the members called in on either Saturday or Sunday – so that we coincided from time to time. He was having quite a bit of pain with his back, I think, though he never said much about it – and so he used to drink a fair drop of whisky. And I remember being astonished when he told me that he was glad Julian had joined up when the Korean war was on, because there was always a chance that he might see active service. My own kids were about twelve and nine at the time, so I was hoping that the whole thing would be finished with before there was any question of them being conscripted. And National Service as well, if it comes to that.'

Leslie Chambers adds an interesting footnote: 'Howell would nod his head and say: "Well, of course I was keen for him to see a bit of life and knock about a bit: but the important thing is that he should get his doctorate. I can see a young fellow will get pretty restless at a place like Oxford, but at the same time I've always impressed upon Julian that a man has to finish what he starts on. And he must get down to his research again, once he's finished his service."'

Extract from David Hayward's official biography.

The bitter and bolted plant run riot. Accidie: the pernicious enemy of those who dwell in the desert.... Aha! Bringing its highest tide of inflammation at definite, accustomed hours to the sick soul. He shall deliver thee from the snare of the fowler, and from the noisome pestilence... the pestilence that walketh in darkness, the destruction that wasteth at noonday... aversion, boredom, scorn and contempt. État de siege.

What is the way the old story goes: when a man is no longer affected by the drink he takes, his soul is already decayed....

The other half...

But, dear boy, you have turned yourself into a hermit. Eremite, doctor Faber, the derivation is from the desert. And I am the deluded sage or the wise madman who has chosen to inhabit the desert of the spirit. No plump cushion...

Dear Lord! It hath a fiendish look!

I see no ship. Outside the gates of Calypso. Duty watch, thinking of her in the most intricate frippery, shifting her this way and that. And all the time that pretty little bored face, magnificently unconcerned. Thrusting her tits towards me in the taxi and looking out of the window. Reverential hands inside unbuttoned dress. A devastating and total calm. Nothing in her face...

There was no humiliation. It was a joke and I should have seen it long since. But I needed the grudge, the anger. It had always been a lie. Some goad out of the jelly state of accidie. Strike the poor stranded thing on the high rock where it lingered in the pool and was deceived by the tide.... No, no, no. There is no deceit in Nature. The questing hand gets no

further than the stocking top and then a guillotine falls, the
thighs close. She offered a blank mouth to be kissed. It
opened routinely, flaccid lips and tongue. Dress still open.

I barely remember her name.... Christina? Was it
Christina?

No humiliation, certainly... a need to be despised by
someone hardly there. Futile months in a fatuous life.

Patches of clear blue in the sky now. The weather
clearing as the tide recedes. And someone rowing against
the run of the water.

As we have seen, in his early novels Michael Caradock
relied upon the observation of actual situations and circumstances upon which he brought to bear the focus of his
individual experience and conscience. Consequently, these
early books, where they have (as we have noted) consistent
patterns of imagery (the industrial landscape, the wise and
tolerant old men, the impatiently ambitious youth, are the
most significant among many recurrent themes) do not rely
upon any sources outside the author's own responses for
their energy and their structural cohesion.

With *Carcases of Tall Ships*, Caradock turned for the first
time to the use of myth and in his subsequent novels this
reliance upon the powerful thematic strands of North
Atlantic cultural heritage in this respect was crucial not only
to the development of his work but, as Richard Snow has
pointed out, to his own involvement with the process of
writing fiction. It must be added that Snow's Marxist stance
often blinds him to the nature of Caradock's intentions, but
he has drawn attention usefully to the obsessive significance

of the Philoctetes and Heracles myths. His 'mythopoeic' argument, though oversimplified, is often shrewd: but he strives, time and time again, to jam into a preordained mould of conclusion the purposes of Caradock, thus distorting them to conform with his own interpretation. In the course of this investigation, we shall consider in more detail this complex aspect of the integration between Caradock's life and his literary preoccupations.

What is interesting about *Carcases of Tall Ships* is that it is a transitional novel. The three stories about the various naval officers observed by the cold and supercilious Fleming are all aspects of myths concerning the Greek god, Poseidon: these are ingeniously and most comically used. Poseidon is surly and quarrelsome as is the First Lieutenant in the novel, and disputes with the goddess Athene, the most belligerent of the female pantheon, on various occasions; Poseidon's mate, Amphitrite, had viewed him with some indifference until she was won over, whereupon she became increasingly jealous of his infidelities – as does Mrs Calloway, the pretty young woman, who resents her husband so deeply; the third strand of the plot is perhaps less immediately obvious – but the feud between the wilful Rattray and the experienced, diligent though sometimes rash Fraser may well be seen as the most famous of Poseidon's campaigns, as waged against Odysseus. Nevertheless, to his novel and to this comedy, Caradock has added the much more serious and humiliating destiny of Fleming himself, at the hands of the woman Christina. This has nothing to do with Poseidon and some critics have mistakenly assumed that it reflects some resentment in

Caradock's own life. Nothing of the sort: it is the first expression of a new theme, to be of vital importance in more of his works.

H.-J. Kastner, Patterns of Despair. *Hazel & Sims, 1973.*

The title of this essay is unintentionally misleading. It has very little to do with the poet Alfred de Vigny, from whose *Servitude et grandeur militaires* I have borrowed it, except in so far as it concerns stoicism and the literary 'ivory tower'. My main concern is the work of the great American poet, Wallace Stevens: with the way in which he was able to reconcile one of the most subtle and sensitive poetic intelligences of modern times with his career as a serious and prosperous businessman; but more importantly I should like to consider Stevens' hedonism as it occurs in his celebration of the Imagination and to ask the question whether this was not an original version of Stoicism, cleverly adapted to the needs and circumstances of the twentieth century. The servitude and grandeur is of two distinct kinds. In the first place I have quite arbitrarily chosen to describe Stevens' lifelong career with the Hertford Indemnity Company as 'servitude', though there is no evidence that this is how he saw the connection himself. And against this, of course, there is the 'grandeur' of his vocation as a poet. And few poets have taken their vocation more seriously or arrogated to Poetry the claims made by Stevens for whom it is the Supreme Fiction which replaces the Supreme Being. In a world without God, Stevens finds his substitute in Poetry. In the second place, the 'servitude' is of a different kind:

it is what we all share – the servitude of mortality and the essential bewilderment at being alive; the 'grandeur', in the case of Stevens at least, is the way in which he was able to come to terms with this mortality and bewilderment in poems which celebrate the living world at the most intense level, declaring the true reality to be the reality of the imagination.

Some writers have held that it is desirable, even necessary, for their work that they should be involved in some other kind of full-time employment: such activity is disciplinary and concentrates the mind admirably towards the serious purpose. Stevens, however, carried things too far in that he enjoyed his other job and was obviously very good at it: surely the writer must chafe a little at the laboursome duties that keep him away from his struggle with his art. I have been lucky in that I have been able to pursue the craft of novel writing single-mindedly throughout my life, except for one short period of military service (servitude in my case without the slightest hint of grandeur) when I have to confess that my creative acumen (such as it is) was considerably sharpened by the routine I was obliged to observe. I wrote very little in that time that was subsequently published: but I was able to try a number of experiments which at the time I found fascinating and which in later years were useful, as well as to sketch ideas for projected work and to read in the vampiric way of the dedicated or compulsive writer.

But let us return to the much more important matter of the well-dressed man without a beard, the amiably bulky Jocundus with the uniquely elegant manner. Stevens rose to a high position in his firm and used his extremely comfortable means to live well – in reasonable luxury, buying good pictures, presenting to the world that most uncomfortable persona, a rich poet. In so doing, he acquired a reputation for insouciant hedonism which infuriated many critics, some of whom were sternly censorious that anyone in such dismal days should dare to pursue pleasure in a way that was at once highly individual and rarefied, others of whom were offering the doctrinaire reflex kick of egalitarians in an age of imbecile fashion described as 'pop' culture, against taste that was refined, discreet and expressed in an art which is demanding, difficult and invariably subtle.

This short study will suggest that many of Stevens' critics have perhaps misunderstood, or incompletely realised, the nature of Stevens' hedonism and (as I shall contend) its close relationship to ideas which are essentially Stoical.

Stevens' hedonism was ethical – in that he took the moral view that the only thing which is good is pleasure, a roughly Epicurean stance: a view that might suggest that it is a mistake of intellectual judgement to believe that anything else except pleasure is good, while recognising that it is possible to desire things other than pleasure and certainly to describe other things as good. In Stevens, I suggest, this view is modified by a Stoical ideal: that of living in harmony with nature. So that far from withdrawing into a particularly well-appointed ivory tower (of which more later), Stevens was always striving to adapt his 'mundo' to the actual world in which he found himself: he wished to establish a relationship between individual integrity and the integrity of prevailing circumstances. Unlike the Stoic, however, with his emphasis

on a moral intellectual attitude of unimpeachable correct-
ness, he was concerned to make this adjustment through the
imagination. And this more or less philosophical paradox
seems to me to be consistent with the way in which he chose
to live his life....

*Extract from 'Servitude and Grandeur', an essay by
Caradock on Wallace Stevens in* An Elemental Wound.
Hazel & Sims, 1963.

... But I wonder how much of our discomfort, if not our
positive misery, may be ascribed not so much to an
inability or a failure to communicate: but to a wilful
determination, only partly realised, not to express our
purpose in words, not to explain what we are about. And
for me communication is essentially a matter of words,
not of gestures, postures, grooming rituals and the like. I
can by using my face, hands and body suggest to someone
else, or for that matter to another animal, what my
intentions are; but once I start using words I have either
to try to make myself clear, or I am bluffing – that is I am
deliberately trying to disguise what my intentions and the
true nature of my self-interest may be.

The inability to communicate is clearly frustrating and
must attract a certain sympathy in that it implies a desire
to make contact which fails for reasons beyond the control
of the would-be communicator. The failure to communicate
is somewhat different in that it suggests that where the
ability to make contact exists, one or other of the parties
involved is preventing an efficient transmission of
information. I am suggesting that these situations seldom

obtain and that as often as not, sometimes without knowing it, sometimes fully aware of what we are about, we are unable to communicate, or we fail to communicate, simply because we are quite inflexible in the defence of our own private identity: to establish communication would be to surrender something of ourselves and this we are eager not to do. This is quite a different matter from bluffing when we try to present ourselves as we are not and when there is no danger whatsoever, providing the bluff is successful, of revealing what we truly are and therefore of diminishing the private identity.

When I was quite young, there was a general idea that sooner or later in adolescence, a solemn-faced guardian would appear and expound what were known as 'the facts of life', a homiletic on sex and sexuality. Mercifully, I was spared any such experience, and so, it seems, were a great many of my acquaintances whose knowledge was acquired sketchily, but not all that inaccurately, from hearsay, observation, living and fictional models. Nowadays, amid the fads of sex education, this seems to be laughably inept, if not psychologically potentially damaging. Again, I wonder. Privacy, the integrity of our own personalities, as only we understand and know them, is something I suspect that we hold very dear: and the inability or failure to communicate on the part of so many of a different generation was perhaps a device to protect a necessary privacy. This, of course, all runs counter to the therapeutic or cathartic benefits of much psychological and psychoanalytic theory, now a matter of general acceptability, and I am certainly not arguing that the repressed or disturbed personality should not be helped by confessional and self-revelatory systems of treatment. I am saying, however, that the apparently balanced individual, whoever or whatever he may be, is entitled to the maintenance of his private individuality by withholding from communication.

I served briefly in the Royal Navy during the years of conscription and had the opportunity, in a thoroughly amateur way – very much that of the fictionalist rather than the sociologist – of observing the ways in which the different members of a stratified closed community chose or did not choose to communicate: the rituals, codifications, rules and charters which obtained. The Senior Officer addressing an equal whom he liked as opposed to one whom he did not like, addressing a subordinate of either category, ordering a drink from a pretty or plain Wren steward, from a male steward of whom he did or did not approve; relationships between junior officers of different specialisations and between officers of different specialisations and ratings; the air of conspiracy or hostility that obtained between senior ratings and most officers – conspiracy when specialisation or duty coincided (for example, in matters of executive duty or discipline), hostility when they did not (there was often open contempt on the part of certain Seaman branches for the Instructor and Medical branches, though the contempt for the latter was invariably tempered by superstition): all these were forms of elaborately contrived communication. In the confines of the wardroom Mess, however, apart from necessary codifications between officers and ratings, or between officers on duty, a much more complex set of systems obtained. Many people, especially officers living in, chose deliberately, though invariably politely, not to communicate. Things would be different aboard ship because of the disciplines imposed by being at sea and rehearsing the urgencies of action. But ashore, especially in the presence of women, wives, sweethearts and Wren officers, elaborately contrived forms of *non-communication* were established. There was very little bluffing because the community was too small and defined to allow for its effectiveness: but was always fascinating within the presupposed limits set by that society, to watch the instinctive physical communication that took place between a man and a woman, of whatever age, status or rank, who attracted or repelled one another, and at the same time to listen to the elaborately wily conversational structures that defended individual privacy. I have tried to apply a few general theories I formulated at the time intermittently to other groups and found they work quite well. I am now inclined to believe that we give ourselves away physically, in the case of heterosexually persuaded people, whether we like it or not: we surrender by degrees *something* of our privacy to people whom we call our friends. And friendships wane, after a lapse of years, when people who once shared such communication meet again and are no longer prepared to make any similar sacrifice of individuality – having in the interim developed, or changed, or in some inevitable way been modified by experience. Only with a person whom we love are we prepared to make the effort that leads to an intellectual and spiritual communication which matches the instinctually physical revelation of purpose and desire. Self-interest becomes unimportant.

Extract from 'Facts of Life', essay in An Elemental Wound. *Hazel & Sims, 1963.*

She leaned back against the bar, with both elbows resting on it, like a tart in a film who knew what she was about. The gaudy fabric stretched across her breasts. She smiled and Fleming found himself almost counting the small wrinkles around her eyes and noticing for the first time the tiny vertical lines which were beginning to appear above her upper lip.

'It's a pity about us, Paul,' she said.

Fleming was obscurely irritated by the assumption of intimacy in her voice.

'What's the pity, Roberta?'

'Oh, you know. We might have made it. But then I suppose I couldn't offer what the avid little Miss Finch does.'

'Please, Roberta. I don't think it's necessary.'

'Well, you should know, my feathered friend. You are not, if I may say so, looking your formerly unruffled self. Is she giving you a bad time?'

Fleming tried to look cool. It had, after all, once been easy. His face and shoulders and arms knew what to do, how to compose themselves, in order to register the required impression: but he was quite well aware that there was a rigidity of feature and muscle which Mrs Calloway was too astute to miss. He took a sip from his drink and offered her a cigarette from his slim gold case.

She laughed. And shook her head.

'Poor Paul,' she said.

Fleming managed to lift one eyebrow.

'You're very kind,' he said.

'Not at all. I don't want to be kind. And I'm not being kind. But, obviously, I like you. Otherwise I should not have... well, let's forget that. I'm sure it embarrasses us both.'

Fleming lit his cigarette.

'Is she?'

'What?'

'Giving you a bad time.'

'Roberta, I'm not really sure what you're talking about. And whatever it is you have in your mind, I'm not sure that it really concerns you.'

'It doesn't! Why do you have to be such a bastard? Listen. I once asked you for help. I didn't much care what sort of help – which is why I made it quite clear I'd go to bed with you. You gave me nothing at all. But I still like you. I suppose I still fancy you. That's the nasty little phrase, isn't it?'

'And I think you're a very attractive woman....'

'How can I live with it! Get me another drink.'

'Are you sure?'

'I am f****** sure.'

Fleming lifted his chin at the Wren steward, who appreciated his unfailing and correct politeness, and came over smiling. He wrote out a chit. Mrs Calloway kept her back turned to the girl, who glanced at her sideways with resentment. Fleming thought he knew quite well most of the forms of scorn and hatred that existed between men – which were open, often ribald, invariably coarse: the furies of women were quite different. Mrs Calloway showed no sign of noticing that the girl was there. The steward went away.

'I suppose,' Roberta Calloway said, 'that you're too high-minded to understand: which is why that silly little alley cat is giving you such hell. All I wanted was someone to want me. Really want me. I wasn't proving anything to *him*. Who the hell cares? I wanted to prove something to me. I suppose it was silly going for you....'

'I'm not quite sure what I should say....'

'What should you say?'

'Well, there were certainly others who... admired you....'

'Yes. And I was never quite sure that their socks were clean. If you know what I mean.'

'I suppose I should be flattered.'

'Yes. You should be! It doesn't matter. I don't think I'm oversexed, but I'm thirty-one and I've got a lot of... oh for God's sake, it sounds ridiculous. But I have ordinary female urges. I want physical sex. And if there are any substitutes, I'm not getting those either.'

Fleming saw the room swirl a little to the right. It was a strange sensation for the straightforward reason that he had not experienced it since the age of seventeen. He did not like being drunk. The woman beside him was entirely desirable. But he had not wanted her and did not want her. It would have been much too simple, after all.... Commander Rattray came in, confidently. Mrs Calloway composed herself slightly and smiled. Rattray wrote himself a drink and joined the First Officer, who blushed and was pleased.

'There you see him,' Roberta Calloway said, unexpectedly. 'Very much his own man, Paul. But, my God, you'd never believe it!'

'You're drunk, Roberta. I don't think...'

'*You*? You never think. Don't patronise me, little man. Just listen. I have been to bed so far eleven – no, fourteen – times with Rattray. And you are stupid! Do you know that? You are really so stupid.'

'Well, I'm sorry....'

'What have you to be sorry about? I wasn't asking for absolution. Rattray makes it quite clear that he wants *me*. Not anyone else. Not your tatty little Miss Finch. Who is *Anybody's!*'

Fleming knew that the stiffening of the muscles of his face had nothing to do with the bout of dizziness that he had experienced a few minutes before. Yet it was like that first idiot experience of being drunk: stupidly vulnerable and no longer in control. It was, however, worse – in that he must respond. A slack-mouthed grimace was not going to be enough. Malicious and stupid as Roberta's intentions were, he must not show the panic that he felt. She anticipated him.

'Oh, don't be shocked, darling. You've got it coming to you. She's a tart, as I said she was. She has been had in various locations and I've no doubt positions by Mathieson, Rutherford, Powell, Holme and Watson. Not to mention the five-star pig of them all, Calloway. And don't be in any doubt about that! I saw them on our vile married-quarters bed. Such a pretty little face, hasn't she?'

*

275

The nonsense seemed to Fleming to be complete. He looked around the elaborately decorated Mess, taking in the equally elaborate and artificial mood of bonhomie. On other occasions he had always found time to be amused by the assortment of the shapes and sizes of the wives in their finery, to take a cool, elegant view of the jollification, to enjoy himself alongside a girl at least as pretty as any other present. And she had changed all that. He did not still understand how an easy and important attraction had become a feverish infatuation and in due course a raging jealousy, but now he detected in eyes turned on him sometimes sympathy, sometimes satisfaction as they sensed his distress. The aloof, contained confidence had departed. He thought bitterly that the pleasure of others in the discomfiture of those who try to keep apart from the general crowd always far exceeded even the delighted response to bad news of an enemy.

Now he saw the First Officer glancing nervously along the bar to the corner where the First Lieutenant sat sombrely over his pink gin and he thought there was something like pity in her expression, a softening of her features that made her look younger and more feminine. On the dance floor Lieutenant-Commander Fraser's wife was being charmed by Commander Rattray, while her husband placidly smoked his pipe with one or two of his older, soberer brother-officers. And Roberta Calloway, wearing a very becoming low-cut dress, listening to her dashingly attentive husband, caught his eye without any flicker of sympathy or satisfaction. Where was Christina?

Suddenly it became intolerable. Fleming left the bar with

as much discretion as he could and walked along the corridor to the other public rooms – the television room, bedimmed and decorated as a sitting-out room with a totally unconvincing intention of romance; the guest room, where the main buffet was laid out and waiting; the WRNS officers' anteroom, arranged as an annexe to the buffet; the games room....

Christina had been wearing a very tight-fitting white dress of some sheer material and quite evidently nothing underneath. Fleming could recall much too exactly the excitement he had felt on first seeing her, the immediate physical arousal, an almost impossible desire for her. She was now wearing the dress in an ugly swathe around her hips, lying on some cushions on the floor, pressing her thighs together and hunching her shoulders as she tried to draw her arms together to cover her crutch. Fleming was hardly aware of Mathieson struggling with the flies of his trousers to her left. Someone had left a few billiard balls on one of the tables. Fleming, without realising what he was doing and without the slightest idea of what he intended to do, picked up one of them and hurled it with all the force he could at the shocked face of the girl, the mouth opening to speak, the make-up smudged, the dark hair disarranged. It was fortunate that he missed, but he hit her painfully above the breast on the right shoulder and the girl cried out. Fleming was trembling with fury, trying to speak....

'You cowardly bastard!' Mathieson said, and hit him on the side of the jaw....

Extract from Carcases of Tall Ships. *Alvin & Brandt, 1956.*

The owl cried again in the clear night. He experienced a sudden start of pure elation which he could not have explained, standing there above the silvered wood surrounded by the softly rolling southern hills, listening to the stillness. Again the sharp ke-wick of the owl in the silence and the same kick of delight in his stomach, alone and awake and alive on the hill at midnight in the mild October night.

The bird of Athena. He remembered a summer night in Athens, gazing in similar clear moonlight at the shadows of the Parthenon on the great rock of the Acropolis and how he had, then, felt at peace, in harmony with the night and with creation: but none of this present elation. It was a teleo- logical paradox that in the symmetry of the Acropolis, the zenith of anthropurgic control now in ruins, he had felt the calm of being at one with the vastness of the timeless, spaceless universe, whereas here among the trees and hills he should suddenly experience this wild flair of individuality, this joy at being himself and alone, a man outside the rest of Nature, somehow in control of his destiny.

He thought again of the ruins....

It was a question less of symmetry than balance. Counter- poise. Thesis and antithesis, perhaps: but never synthesis. Unless synthesis was the still moment of equipoise: the stasis between being and non-being that might be the ineluctable and infinite state of becoming. 'Reason – the conscious certainty of being all reality.' The rational participation. But that could not be, because becoming was ceaseless regeneration, the ceaseless correction of errors of delineation – and as such could have nothing to do with equipoise, perfection, stasis. The mechanical image was wrong. And critical intelligence denied participation in the whole.

The cry of the owl.... The ruins.... A still, moonlit night.... Landgrave began to think about the ruins. Plague and panic in the streets. The recorso of civil and national violence. Opposed forces of reason and unreason, the chaste and the unchaste, the warrior and the artist. Owl and Nightingale. Grave and gay. Or Blodeuwedd and Philomela. Unchaste and chaste. There, somewhere, was the clue: somewhere in the violent turbulent organic process of lust: power, possession, territory, domination. Barbarous and sacrificial kings, violator and victim. Kewick again. The cry of the owl. And this time he saw the low swooping flight of the bird, his eyes now accustomed to the dark, and strained his ears to hear the squeak of the bird's prey. He heard nothing. Landgrave shook his head. Participation in the whole must be a matter of intelligent choice. Man was part of, but outside, the rest of Nature and the whole was not a matter of integration but reconciliation. Landgrave conceived a vision of total calm, universal entropy, the ultimate, gradual and total state of Death and for a moment of profound fear seemed to understand part of the equation in the horrified contemplation of pure existence as Nothing, the nothing of dreamless sleep before birth and after death.

He began to walk quickly down the gravel drive, trying to fill his mind with images of crowds and colour, noises and movement. The sylvan moonstruck landscape was still frozen in that instant of transported imagination: there seemed to be no movement in the trees, the owl was silent and in a fit of crazy fancy he thought he dared not look at the sky for fear he would see the moon still and fixed above a motionless world.

He reached the small cluster of low buildings, the roofs frosted with the moonlight, and paused, almost laughing at his panic. Perhaps more accurately it had been the antithesis of panic. But it had filled his whole being with a terrible fear....

The cry of an owl and an image of moonlight on broken pillars....

Well, then he had been much younger and had made the mistake of supposing that metaphysics was an authentic science: that its terms were, by means of reason, measurable. Once again a paradox.

Poetry is a divine instinct and unnatural rage passing the reach of common reason.

And Landgrave had believed that he was a true poet, blessed with common reason. The images that had reassured his mind in the chill moonlight were still astonishingly vivid: versions of Brueghel and of Bosch. It seemed not to matter how cruel the nature of existence as long as existence denied the glimpse of nothingness which he had seen so vividly.

He stretched out his sullen, stiffening limbs in the sunlight of the Forum and looked fancifully up for the bird of night to descend and sit, hooting and shrieking. It did not come. He looked around at the fastidiously cherished ruins and thought of Tiberius, Gaius Caligula, Nero and Domitian. The bird of Athena – goddess of wisdom and goddess of battle, queint Bellona in her equipage of power, possession, territory, domination.

Landgrave got up painfully, chronicler and sutler of that

equipage different from the Dionysiac train only in its armour, threatening Vulcane or Hephaestos for their saucinesse. It was October and the sun in Rome was warm enough to soothe the stiffness away. Catherine, who had been watching children playing further away beneath the arch of Severus, noticed him move and came over. *She* moved superbly. Her yellow skirt swirled as she walked. As she became aware of Landgrave's pleasure, she smiled. Tears of delight sprang at the back of his eyes.

'Balance,' he said to her. 'I traded in a divine rage for balance.'

'That was rash,' she said. 'I was watching the children playing.'

'So I saw.'

'Little beasts.'

Landgrave laughed at her.

'What was all this about trading in something?' Catherine said.

'Well, do you know, young woman, I once set out to be a poet. And then I had doubts. You must not laugh. It is as bad as being a seminarist who discovers Babylon is fun. The art was and is held in contempt. Mecoenas is yclad in claye, And great Augustus long ygoe is dead. So I became what I am.'

'I like what you are. Do you feel like eating?'

'Yes, I think I do. Something suitably balanced.'

'Of course. And was Babylon fun?'

'No. It was hell. October is a violent month, my dear: a time of terror and massacre. And I have seen too much of both in Babylon. There is a kind of corrosion in my veins.'

'Think about the good times.'

Ah yes. Landgrave began to move away as she adjusted her own pace, gracefully, to his: so that they might seem to be leisurely, enjoying the moment and the sunshine.

'I always thought and it was my mistake that I could remain apart from it,' he said. 'Whatever "it" was. Then dispassion hardens into discontent, which becomes hatred. The always delicate equilibrium is upset....'

Landgrave shivered in the chill moonlight as he remembered the moment of equilibrium so many years before. Catherine did not understand and must have thought that he was ill. She looked anxiously at him, but said nothing and took his hand.

Extract from the 'October' episode of the Laocoön *novel, provisionally titled by Hazel & Sims, which appeared posthumously.*

6

My initial impression was that Caradock was rather shy.
Of course, he knew that Hansel, who was a pretty
formidable figure around the place, and one or two others
had strenuously opposed his admission to the Senior
Common Room; but, equally well, he knew that Rose,
Olafson and Martineau were all behind him. So his
diffidence was rather odd. He was perfectly well aware
that he had an original rather than a brilliant mind, but I
think, quite simply, that it was nothing to do with any
shortfall of intellectual confidence: I think he was simply
overawed at being a don.

I was in an interesting position as a spectator, because I
had been an undergraduate at a different college and saw
the other Fellows with an unclouded eye. I was also a few
years older than Michael and I'd been a submariner

towards the end of the war so that I thought myself fearfully experienced and quite able to look after myself in any company.

The SCR was in some ways rather curious: there were no absolute heavyweights with an international reputation in scholarship of the sort you might find in some of the other colleges and who exist as presences that disturb with the joy of their elevated thoughts, whether or not they choose to be obtrusive. The older Fellows were good, straightforward dons, interested in the administration of the college, in making a decent fist of teaching, occasionally publishing a learned article. But not really very ambitious, and dedicated to a comfortable life. It was a confident college and they lived very well. Then, there were the younger men who were brilliant and ambitious and who did not think that civilisation ended at Magdalen Bridge. Rose was one of these and so was Olafson and there was a very sharp economist called Manchester. There was, accordingly, quite often a conflict of viewpoint between these boisterously questing intelligences racketing about in a placid landscape and the denizens of somewhat longer establishment. Martineau had the presence and academic distinction to rule the roost effortlessly, but the rest of us chickens sometimes had squabbles in which the feathers flew.

Hansel was a fiercely conservative scholar with a waspish tongue and a very brittle temper. Oxford is full of lazy clever people who've missed boats they didn't care about catching as well as occasional stowaways and pier-head jumpers. But there are some clever men who have worked hard and diligently and yet have never somehow quite realised their potential. It's difficult to guess why: perhaps they lacked an indefinable spark of inspiration which is necessary to make scholarship outstanding. Hansel was one of these, well respected within the confines of his field of learning, but missing the reputation and authority that I think he believed he deserved. He detested, perhaps in consequence, anything showy or spectacular. And quite honestly I believe that one of the things he held against Michael was that he wrote fiction. Hansel simply could not believe that a decent scholar, of Caradock's age, would have time to bother with such frivolities. All very well as recreation for established professors, perhaps: but reprehensible in the young who aspired to academic laurels.

He was too independent a man to be the centre of any clique, but he did represent the essentially non-radical aspect of the Common Room, along with the chaplain who was an enormous craggy patriot who'd been wounded in the battle of Arras and a rather splendid old chap called Mundy who was Tutor in Chemistry and a member of the Athenaeum.

I suppose that Michael and I were drawn to one another *faute de mieux*. We had both, after our fashion, been at the ships at Mylae, we both enjoyed good food and drink, we did not want to enlist in any social or political crusade and we enjoyed fanciful and rather elaborate conversation. I relished his satirical gifts and the capacity that he had of making blind intellectual leaps and landing gracefully in some interesting and original place. I suppose that he enjoyed what he took to be my worldly wisdom (which I'm afraid I tended rather to advertise) and he was very interested in Philosophy, which I taught. I'm not sure that I was all that successful with Michael, I must say. Some of the ideas in his later books strike me as frightfully muddled.

James Faber in BBC radio programme.

After his National Service, Caradock spent two years at Oxford during which he completed his thesis on Silver Age Roman poets and the late English Renaissance, for which he was in due course awarded the degree of Doctor of Philosophy. Lucien Soames, who supervised his work, was impressed by his industry and application, which was considerable. When we recall that Caradock was also teaching about a dozen pupils, partly to justify his place in the Senior Common Room and partly so that (as Richard Rose put it) he had little time to 'brood' and that he was working on the novel *Carcases of Tall Ships*, published in the spring of 1956, it was obviously an energetic time of his life in which he succeeded in throwing off the accidie, which James Faber, Beauchamp-Beck, Idris Lewis and others have noted characterised so much of his behaviour in later years. Faber, who knew him well at this time, says that he sometimes detected the symptoms of incipient melancholy even then, but ascribed them to restlessness that was partly sexual in origin.

Quite apart from his academic and creative work, Caradock was beginning to widen his circle of friends. Michael Beauchamp-Beck who had taken a spectacularly good degree in the school of Litterae Humaniores had become a Fellow of All Souls, but made regular visits to London, on some of which he was accompanied by Caradock. Idris Lewis was already working in London in the Ministry of Housing, having done almost as well as Beauchamp-Beck and having also excelled in the Civil Service Examination. James Faber, who is laconically self-deprecating about himself in those years, was another acquaintance who went regularly from Oxford to London to visit a number of friends whom he describes as 'a rather louche selection of people living on their wits at the peripheries of art and literature'.

Among these people, who worked in journalism, broadcasting, politics, in the administration of the arts, in publishing, in museums, in the Civil Service, some of whom were working writers, painters, sculptors, musicians and actors, Caradock seems to have, for a while, enjoyed himself. It is doubtful whether he would have achieved a Fellowship at Oxford and unlike many of his younger colleagues he would not have contemplated an academic career anywhere else, but in any event he was sufficiently welcomed by the friends of friends to move to London. He was personally rich enough to take a comfortable flat and to live discreetly on his private income and on what he earned from his published novels (which was little enough) without having to undertake freelance drudgery.

Caradock was not seduced by London life. He was an experienced drinker and a quick talker. His early confidence with women, given to him by Helen Westlake, may have been slightly eroded by later encounters: but it was soon to return. He was not overawed. He took stock of situations and in due course produced the satire *Broods of Folly*.

Extract from David Hayward's official biography.

287

Well, I remember one thing very clearly: he was absolutely terrified of All Souls. He would never come there. I'm not sure why: but I think it was a facet of the original fear, perhaps even the feeling of inferiority, that he had when he first came up. And which he was quite determined never to show. He would accept invitations and then find some excuse to duck whatever it was. It was naturally enough exasperating at the time, but not very serious. By contrast, he was entirely at ease in London, where at that time it was fairly fashionable to praise his first three books, especially *Angry Sunset*. When I look back on it, I think the novel called *The Low Key of Hope* was rather an extraordinary achievement, because he wrote all that before he had any experience of the London literary-journalistic arts-and-flowers scene. And it really isn't bad for a work of imagination. Anyway, be that as it may, he took to the sub-bohemians pretty well. And I think he used other friends as a respite from them, which I didn't mind. Idris, however, was furious that he was wasting his time and talent on such worthless people and a sort of coolness developed between them which took quite a long time to unthaw.

Michael Beauchamp-Beck in BBC radio programme.

Oh my God, we had dozens of furious rows. Basically I could not let Michael get away with this nonsense about loathing Wales and his thoroughly unjustified resentment. And he could not forgive me for having no such resentment. And it took a long time before we began to understand one another. But I didn't like the novel about the Navy when it came out and I didn't like *Broods of Folly* some time later – because, I suppose, I don't care for satire. Michael didn't like it either. He used to fulminate about it, later, in the sixties. Yet he wrote that very nasty book. Have you read a book by an American scholar called Highet, about Juvenal? No...? Well, he says something in that which is relevant to Michael. He was not trying to change or improve anything. He has no pity for the poor who are being exploited or the middle class who are being insulted. He is just yelling at the top of his voice that what is happening to him is *wrong*! That's a paraphrase. But I think it obtains.

Idris Lewis in BBC radio programme.

'Who is the tall person fidgeting?' asked Laertes.

'That,' said Leydon Wells, 'is Meurig Bowen-Powys who is unbelievably important at the BBC. That is why I have brought you here. If your little sister has gone astray in *le monde de télécommunication*, there are at least a dozen people in this very room who have only to flicker a tiny finger and have the man (or woman) – it has been known – who done her wrong quivering like an electronic jelly.'

Laertes Jones was flummoxed. A rubefact woman of some seventeen stones with the face of the emperor Galba smiled at him with what he took to be sinister invitation. He offered a timorous half-smile and turned rapidly to Leydon Wells. But he was fluting some kind of love-call across the room and when it was echoed went off in pursuit of the sound. The acrolithic dame had tacked four-square onto him: Laertes Jones burrowed into the mass of people around the bar which was in the charge of a single wisp of a woman with tangerine hair, who was filling glasses at amazing speed.

'What you want, love?' she said.

'Whatever you've got there,' said Laertes.

'Welsh, are you, bach? Don't have any of this. I'll give you a nice drop of whisky. Rot-gut this is. They always serve it. On the cheap, see. Mean as muck. There. That will warm you up. You don't look well at all.'

'I've lost my sister.'

'I'm not surprised with all these hooligans. This is no place for a nice Welsh girl. I'm surprised you bringing her here.'

'I didn't. She's disappeared. She came up to work as a secretary in the BBC and we haven't heard of her for six weeks.'

'Do you see that tall man there making shapes? He's in the BBC. That's Meurig Bowen-Powys. He's Welsh as well. Perhaps he knows your sister.'

'My sister was only a secretary.'

'Oh they're all very close in the BBC. He's bound to know her, what with being Welsh and all.'

'Here you are!' said Leydon Wells in exasperation. 'I see you've met Dolores, little mother of all the Mabinogion.'

'Dolores Davies,' said the little woman, smiling. 'From Dyffryn.'

'*Una bottiglia di vino locale, per favore, carissima,*' said Leydon Wells.

'Oh, he's a case, isn't he?' said Dolores. 'Mr Wells here. You are a case, Mr Wells.'

'*Carramba! Ha sudo una tarde estupenda, amada.*'

'He never stops,' said the delighted woman, pouring white or red wine unerringly into a score of outthrust glasses. 'A real case, yes?'

'The staggering news is,' said Leydon Wells, 'that I've met someone who knows your sister.'

'Hey,' said Dolores Davies, urgently. 'You see that one over there with the lockses. That's Selwyn Crosswell, MP. He's Welsh. In the Environment.'

Leydon Wells drew Laertes away from the bar in the direction of the huge porphyritic woman of Roman aspect. At the first token of Laertes Jones' shrinking back from the encounter, Leydon Wells' hand constricted firmly upon his forearm.

'Who is she?' whispered Laertes Jones.

There was no need to whisper. There was a babel of shrieking and hooting all around and the woman was some distance away. It was sheer awe.

'Bella Fontenoy,' said Leydon Wells dramatically.

'Is she at the BBC or an MP?'

'She is not. She is headmistress of a comprehensive school.'

'Not Welsh?'

'I suspect that she would garotte you at the suggestion. She makes her very knickers out of Union Jacks.'

'How does she come to know my sister?'

'Through a literary rivulet that feeds the proud main stream of contemporary culture. Have you noticed that when doctors inquire into the intimacies of micturation, they talk of a good *stream*? I suspect it is the same thing. Your sister was, however, briefly, it seems, secretary to J. P. Waitrose, the novelist, who as Pearson Waitrose is frightfully important at the BBC. Brace yourself, Laertes. We are on the trail.'

The lady Galba seized Laertes Jones' hand and crushed it in a nutcracking grip. She boomed. Laertes was appalled but did not know whether from fear or revulsion.

'Leydon, darling. I have the most dastardly news. Dickie Simeonov has been arrested in Northern Thailand for smuggling idols. Who is this charming boy?'

'This is Laertes Jones who has lost his sister.'

'What sort of idols?' said Laertes.

'Odd name. Laertes. What exactly do your thoughts and wishes bend to?'

'I don't think they do, in fact,' said Leydon Wells.

'Siamese idols,' said the lady Galba, 'or so I assume. I have no doubt, knowing the young Simeonov, that they will be rivetingly obscene. As an anthropologist he lacks finesse. My God, I see the resemblance. You must be the sibling of Amelia.'

'She was briefly Pearson Waitrose's secretary at the time you...'

'Don't be tiresome, Leydon. I know quite well who she was. A charming little thing with a beautiful body and large dark eyes. Men are such beasts.'

'When did you last see my sister?' said Laertes.

'At a meeting of the Islington Gynaeceum to which I introduced her. A young girl on her own in this wicked place might very easily find herself in quite the wrong company. But alas she came only the once to a paper given by Dr Unity Spence. I do not think your sister was at all high-minded.'

'No, you couldn't say that,' said Laertes.

'But such a sweet little face and glorious...'

'Bella...'

'What a tatty little man,' said the monstrous woman, indicating a slight and morose poet, famous enough for Laertes Jones to recognise. 'The world is full of tatty people and he is one of the tattiest. There was a time when parties were fun, full of wit, sparkle and high-minded repartee. Now look at us.'

The imperatorial features set in noble scorn as the woman assumed a pose of majesty. She held it for a moment and then her dark eye lit on Laertes Jones again. 'You, however, are rather dinky,' she said.

'No,' said Leydon Wells hurriedly.

He stepped up on tiptoe and whispered something to her. The flattish, mauve face was vacant for a moment as she listened and then the entire grotesque bulk of the woman began to quiver and shake and then heave in vast bellows of laughter. Wave after wave of sound bellowed around the anxious ears of Laertes who felt like a light skiff in a fog being dashed against the cruel rocks on which stood the groaning buoy intended to warn the benighted and rudderless.

He slid away into an alcove....

Extract from Broods of Folly. *Alvin & Brandt, 1960.*

The subjective satire of *Broods of Folly* is almost picaresque. The aptly named Laertes Jones is full of rather ostentatious concern for his 'lost' sister, Amelia, who has disappeared in London after taking a job as a secretary with the BBC. Laertes turns up at Broadcasting House where he is befriended by a serpentine young man, Leydon Wells. In the manner of the two virtuous and staggeringly slow-moving brothers in Milton's *Comus*, they set off in search of the sister who is surely the victim of some depravity. Characteristically, Caradock added his own acid embellishment to the plot in that the oily Leydon Wells hopes and intends to seduce the thoroughly innocent Laertes. (He does not succeed.) On the trail of the sister, they encounter a whole sequence of monstrous people from all walks of life – notably the arts, but also broadcasting, journalism, education, politics and even science – until the novel ends in an outrageous and disturbing dénouement. Professor H.-J. Kastner has already written two very illuminating articles on Caradock's preoccupation with certain themes and symbolic figures which he is expanding into a full-length study. Kastner identifies many of the monsters in *Broods of Folly* with their Greek originals, and shows, to my mind conclusively, how Caradock worked invariably in his later writing inside a mythological framework. The title of the novel is taken from the poem *Il Penseroso* in which Milton banishes 'vain deluding joys / The brood of Folly without father bred'. The title suggests the mood of disgust with which Caradock eventually came to regard the life he had rather determinedly set out to enjoy in his years at London before returning to Wales.

Stephen Lewis: The Novels of Michael Caradock. *Molyneux, 1971.*

Among the most loyal and important friends that Caradock made upon his arrival in London, when he settled himself in a comfortable flat in South Kensington, was Fay Mackail. In many ways, Miss Mackail was the spiritual successor to Helen Westlake: she was about ten years older than Caradock, a gentle, generous, reassuring woman who was prepared to offer him love without compromising his or her own independence. I am indebted to her for her entirely frank and unselfish help in piecing together these interesting and confusing years in Caradock's life.

Fay Mackail is a successful writer. With typical modesty, she describes herself as a hack: but she enjoys a successful career as novelist, columnist, journalist and reviewer. She was Michael Caradock's mistress (her own term) for some time although they never actually lived together. 'That was my decision' (she writes), 'which didn't particularly please Michael at the time, although he saw the wisdom of it all in due course. I didn't know anything about his work when I met him – at someone's house – but we liked each other. It was the kind of immediate thing when a man and woman know perfectly well without having to spell it out that they are mutually attractive. In due course, we went to bed and went on being lovers intermittently for five or six years. I don't think that Michael loved me but I think that I loved him. At the same time he would have been impossible to live with, because he was a parasite. Not emotionally and certainly not intellectually: but he would at the drop of a hat rely on anyone who lived really close to him to do everything for him. And I was too old and too set in my own happy ways for that. So we always remained good friends and we occasionally had wonderful and happy days or nights or weeks together. I also got to respect his work and his seriousness and what he was trying to do. The arrogance (which I must say I rather liked when I first saw him) was almost entirely a mask. He was really very dedicated and almost – though it's a silly word – humble. Some of the most rewarding evenings of my life were just talking to him about literature. It sounds ridiculous. But we were completely easy together and we were interested in what the other was trying to say and, I suppose, ultimately, in who the other was. I think one of his major frustrations was that he thought himself to be formally limited. He had no vital, new formal ideas and he would dearly have liked to be an innovator. During these years he did a lot of experimental writing, which he never showed to anyone and which he must have destroyed. And he read. So that he was really preparing for the two long novels and for the essays.'

Miss Mackail also explains the genesis of the comic novel *Broods of Folly*, which some people, including Stephen Lewis, think is a transitional novel. 'I think' (she says) 'that it happened more or less as an accident. Michael could be waspishly funny after, say, a party or something of the sort and he didn't like a lot of people he met. He was a fairly comprehensive misanthropist, in fact. But it made some of us laugh. And I forget who, but someone, it might even have been me – I certainly agreed that it was a good idea – suggested that he put some of his sketches into a novel. He hated what he thought was meretricious and what he called "Sunday-newspaper culture", but curiously enough he got on far better with journalists than he did with other serious writers, most of whom he despised. Some people have the completely mistaken idea that the innocent Laertes Jones in that book was Michael's own impression of himself. Not a bit of it. Michael thought himself very sophisticated, which he wasn't – though at the same time he wasn't an innocent. And Laertes Jones is a somewhat oversimplified and quite unfair portrait of Idris Lewis, who is an extremely intelligent and brilliant man. But there was some sort of coolness between them at the time and Michael was being what Idris himself would call "jocose". After a while he began to impose one of his famous structures on the material and fitted it all neatly together in what I think is a funny, if rather a cruel, book.'

Extract from David Hayward's official biography.

As you can imagine we were never actually buddy-buddy, but all young men in a group talk about sex and so I heard him, at least in public, on the subject. The point was he hated Lawrence, and most of us, in the group that I used to chat and drink with, revered the bloody man. I still do. And Lawrence was essentially for straight, happy, naked sex. Caradock was a fingerer, if you know what I mean. Like Joyce and one or two of the others, it was all a matter of frilly knickers, and black stockings and a sort of deliberate, lewd display. Masturbatory stuff you find in these porn magazines at the moment. You know the old chestnut about the girl in the burlesque and the coarse audience shouting: 'Get 'em off, get 'em off'? Well, Caradock was the type of bloke who'd be shouting: 'Keep 'em on, keep 'em on.' But in a very careful voice.

George Shelley in BBC radio programme.

In the BBC Club, Leydon Wells was describing with malice a ballet about Proserpina. Ponsonby, half-turning his back upon Laertes, took up the theme and embroidered upon it. J. P. Waitrose said something in Latin. Maxwell Burdock compressed his lips and said 'Ham!' Ponsonby proclaimed the death of the theatre, but pointed westward to the bright lands of television. No one offered Laertes Jones a drink, but he stood politely by. Leydon Wells changed the subject to opera and a gaunt production of a story by Hans Karossa recently staged by a new company under Arts Council subsidy, which was to be broadcast. Ponsonby forecast the death of opera, radio and the Arts Council. J. P. Waitrose said something in Greek. Burdock was tight-lipped. Ponsonby pointed to the practice of politics as an art form. Laertes Jones was, by now, quite thirsty, so he edged his way a little nearer to the bar, confident that he would not be missed. No word had yet been spoken of his sister, but he thought he must be patient and polite. Ponsonby was now obituarising the novel, poetry and finally God: his optimism about the future was unbounded, however, based on the living drama of news and current affairs. Waitrose said something in Russian. Burdock snorted. Leydon Wells uttered a sort of hissing purr.

Laertes Jones worked his way around to the bar, where he was noticed. All four men in the group immediately emptied their glasses and allowed him to buy them large glasses of spirits. He became aware of a fifth smiling presence at his elbow and turned to see a small, precise man smiling at him. The man bowed and said: 'Fockemall.'

'I'm inclined to agree with you,' said Laertes Jones.

'No,' said the precise man, with something suspiciously like a clicking of his heels. 'I am Fockemolle. Ze Cherman representative of ze EBU. You are Appleton, are you not? Yes?'

'No,' said Laertes Jones. 'I'm nothing to do with all this.'

'Excuse me, you are Appleton. I remember when we are in Schweitz. Ohohohoho. Ze joyful women. Yes?'

Herr Fockemolle's hands described elaborate and generous curves in the air.

'Haha, Appleton. What larks, as your novelist Charles Dickens says, old chap. Yes?'

'Leydon,' said Laertes Jones.

'My dear boy.'

'Will you please tell this German gentleman that I am not someone called Appleton.'

'Appleton's in prison,' said Maxwell Burdock in a staccato burst.

'Excuse me, no. I am Fockemolle. Here is Appleton.'

'No, no. This is a Welsh person,' said Ponsonby. 'Appleton is a Wykehamist.'

'Haha. Yes. He is certainly so,' said Herr Fockemolle, delightedly. 'More than anyone I ever meet.'

He clapped Laertes Jones happily on the shoulder.

'Is it not so, Appleton? Hohoho.'

Laertes Jones was never exactly sure how, subsequently, J. P. Waitrose, Maxwell Burdock and Ponsonby faded into thin air: but they did. He heard a fragment of what he thought was Portuguese, but that was all. He was beginning to feel exasperated.

'What about my sister?' he shouted at Leydon Wells.

'Hush, dear boy, hush. We'll go immediately to Lime Grove. I have a very hot tip. Goodbye, Mein Herr, we are looking for a young woman and we must go urgently to Shepherd's Bush. You'll excuse us won't you?'

'Hahaha. I shall come with you. Oho. Appleton, you are

always for ze joyful ladies. Yes? Where is this place? It is most fortunate zat we are so meeting, Appleton.'

Extract from Broods of Folly. *Alvin & Brandt, 1960.*

Why should a city breed monsters in such profusion? The vain and chimerical illusion is that the fear of such marvellous predators is purged by laughter. Laughter is merely a shout of fear in a dark room where there are the scrapings of rodent feet, the imagined shuffle of the quick arachnids so that the muscles tighten, the neck becomes rigid and the whole body seems to tremble as in an epileptic spasm, when it is entirely still. The clammy fear upon the limbs, the deep single pulse of blood, the impure amniotic clothing of sweat in the womb of despair and fear.

Is it any better here...? The same empty bottles, the same emptiness, the same sense of fear and failure. Clear sky of early afternoon. The flying birds against the pale sky. Grey heron slow and strong, indifferently cruel...

There was someone rowing but now there is no sign of a boat. Savage on some inscrutable countryman's task.

There is no peace.

There is no peace.

And the laughter soon becomes a roaring in the ears, a ceaseless chafe and chattering of harsh, woodland birds who krank and scrape their notes out of sight. Laughter that echoes in hollow bone. The crash and splinter of violence. A joke, Herr Friederich, is, as you have said, an epitaph on an emotion. And most often the emotion was ignoble and base. That is my feeble contributory footnote.

And now I pace again that maze of stews and alleys and

foetid conduits, unable to rail and hate, for they are peopled only by my fictions. Breath infects breath.... Oh thou wall that girdlest in those wolves....

Well, it's something very difficult to understand if you've never felt this kind of boredom and I haven't experienced anything of the kind myself. I thought *Broods of Folly* was funny but pretty superficial. It's much too easy after all in London literary and broadcasting circles to find targets and to pick them off at leisure. But, of course, it was a very successful book.

Michael Beauchamp-Beck in BBC radio programme.

I think it always has been and still is an underrated danger for people who live in that sort of feverish world to drink too much. So part of his depression was, in my opinion, post-alcoholic. I sometimes think that his older friends should have tried to do something more positive round about this time, but I got married and we had our first child – and as often happens, one tends to drift away from former acquaintances as one settles into a new way of life....

Idris Lewis in BBC radio programme.

You have to remember this tendency that Michael Caradock had towards obsession. He made up myths about himself and, as you might expect, retained accordingly an elaborate equipment of symbols and personalised imagery which he saw as motifs, if you like, in his life. Some of these motifs were intellectual ideas which he was always worrying at and attacking from different points of view, others were about human relationships and attitudes, but the process extended right down to paradigm situations or to images.

Most novelists, I think, move forward by a process of observation and distillation, modifying their ideas as they go. A great many of the very best novelists have only the broadest-based ideas from which to work. Others who are writing sagas to a particular plan may be working out some elaborate theory, whether political, ethical, psychological, what have you. Michael belonged to a third type which is rarer: the kind of writer who has a central nuclear pile of ideas which he dares not approach too directly, so he circles around it and occasionally makes a quick dash towards it; he may even build deliberate labyrinths around it. He knows more or less what the pile is but not entirely and there is much that he does not know about the way it works and he is rather afraid of irradiation.

So you have on the one hand the theme of the Promethean sufferer who has some kind of physical or psychological wound that poisons his attitude to the world, or the theory of the artist as a persecuted necessary evil, or the notions of charity and chastity as essential but opposed forces. There are many others, of course. And then, on the other hand, you have the detail – the sort of seduction rituals he describes usually follow a pattern, for example. And then there were specific instances of repeated scenes almost, though treated very differently, with which he obviously had some private association. One of these is the party with an outsider looking on and working out some plan of campaign. Another is the tennis match, which occurs two or three times. I don't know the precise facts but I should guess that

Michael had once been to a tennis party and hated it, so that
it became his shorthand symbol for a particular form of one-
upmanship and arrogance.

Rose Brandt in BBC radio programme.

As he watched Major Ganz come striding from the house,
carrying a couple of rackets, Ganuret was once again
impressed by the man's vigour and energy. Ganz must
have been forty-five or six, but he had the lean hard
physique of a much younger man with strongly muscled
arms and shoulders, powerful forearms. He was gleaming
in immaculate tennis clothes. He saluted Ganuret with one
of the rackets and ran onto the court to adjust the net.

Another group came from the house – three men and four
or five youngish women. Two of the men were wearing
tennis shirts and shorts, the one a gaunt thin man with
gangling wiry limbs who was unusually tall; the other was
square and bullet-headed. As they approached the tennis
court they were both talking gravely, as though approaching
a council chamber where some momentous decision was
about to be made. The third man was Søren Claudian,
dressed in long white flannels, his sleek hair immaculate,
the dark eyes faintly amused. He too had a trim, fit
appearance, but he looked in some way the least likely of
the tennis players. Two of the girls were also dressed for
tennis, but the others were wearing light flowery summer
dresses; they were all laughing together in the manner of
people who want to seem to be enjoying themselves.
Claudian was walking alone, paying no attention to them,
the two other men were still deep in conversation. Beyond

them, Ganuret saw a couple of younger men appear and then, dramatically alone, a slim girl in a scanty black bathing costume. She was in no sense opulently curved, but her figure was perfectly proportioned. Her hair was black and shining and her skin very white. The two young men turned and waited for her, smiling and swinging their tennis rackets, but she walked past them without turning her head or smiling at their badinage. She walked around to the far side of the tennis court where there was a canvas chair and sat down, beginning to rub her white body methodically with oil. The young men grimaced at each other and chuckled after the manner of their kind.

Finally, two servants emerged from the house with an elaborate drinks trolley which they lifted down the flight of stone steps and wheeled around the stone path towards the bench where Ganuret was sitting. Ganz was approaching.

'I'm glad you could join us, Piers,' he said. 'Do you play? I could lend you a racket and some kit.'

'Thank you, no. I'm still a little unsteady.'

'Of course. I must introduce you to my friends. Claudian, of course, you already know. Patrice, may I present the General's young secretary who is reorganising our library. Piers Ganuret. Monseigneur Ladvenu, Ganuret, who is the Papal representative here.'

The gaunt, tall man took Ganuret's hand in a heavy grip and spoke in a growling voice. Ganuret tried to imagine him in his clerical robes in some dim cathedral, the sepulchral voice in a confessional, the gaunt face emerging from shadows to terrify idling tourists....

Ganz was presenting him to the square man who was a

judge, Maître Linz, an examining magistrate with jurisdiction in an important area of the city. He was a slow-speaking man with wary watchful eyes that moved slowly around the group from one face to the next, palely observing, never darting quickly or obliquely. The younger men were, as Ganuret had expected, easy, charming, privileged: the one a junior officer of good family, the other a young politician. Both spoke in indistinguishable voices and accents; they even looked alike although one was fair and the other dark – with straight hair, brushed to the side, greyish eyes, slightly mocking grins, earnest frowns when required and well-kept teeth.

The women, Ganuret thought, had been chosen for decoration (or perhaps athletic prowess) rather than anything else. The two dressed for tennis were chunky, well-muscled girls with taut, lightly tanned limbs. The others were self-consciously feminine, fresh, smiling, sweet smelling, appropriately pretty, suitably shy and quite sure of themselves.

Apart from all these was the suave, sardonic figure of Claudian, joining in the good humour without ever belonging to it or to the rest of the group.

And out beyond the tennis court, alone, was the white-bodied witch in the black bathing costume, now fully reclined on the long canvas chair.... Ganz made no reference to her.

It was agreed that the first tennis match should be played by Ganz and the Monseigneur against His Excellency Søren Claudian and the Maître. The young men were charmingly self-effacing and Ganz explained that other people were to join the party who would undoubtedly give them a more vigorous game.

'Schmidt is here to provide drinks when anyone feels thirsty,' he said, smiling.

As usual, Ganuret's eyes were drawn to the frozen scar on the left cheekbone and the sinister twist it gave to the Major's face. One of the girls, a curly and fair-haired young woman, wearing a delicate, flowing dress which discreetly emphasised her figure, gazed at him adoringly. Ganz appeared not to notice and led his group onto the court. Play began after a fairly vigorous knock-up, with everyone except the priest looking suitably and seriously dedicated. The priest remained gaunt and stony, hitting the ball with controlled ferocity at great speed.

All the players were surprisingly proficient, but in very different ways: Ganz and the priest both played a vigorous, blustering game, serving fast and following up quickly to volley at the net. The Monseigneur used his enormous height and wiry arms to smash at every opportunity. The Maître was perhaps less expert but made up with energy that was astonishing in a man of his age for his comparative lack of skill. He was never beaten and rushed or charged to retrieve (sometimes successfully) shots that the other three would have been content to let go. Claudian was at once the player possessed of most finesse and the least comfortable of the four. He played elegantly: his ground shots were sure and accurate; in the air, he used subtle deflections and exact placings to win points. But he was unhappy about the force and brutality of Ganz and the Monseigneur.

Ganuret noticed that Ganz, who must have played tennis against Claudian before since they were both such significant members of Axel Waldeck's court, at the earliest opportunity smashed the ball directly at Claudian. The velocity of the shot was considerable and the ball would have struck Claudian somewhere about the shins. He was thoroughly discomposed, beat at it ineffectually with his racket and skipped in an ungainly fashion to get out of the way of the ball. One of the girls laughed.

Thereafter in later games, Ganz repeated this tactic several times and the priest, quick to notice the invariably timid reaction of Claudian, imitated his example. The Monseigneur's whipcord arms projected the ball even more savagely and Claudian's game very soon went to pieces. It was evident that he was afraid of being physically hurt. He remained composed – his hair remarkably unruffled, his clothes immaculate, where the other three were panting, sweaty and unkempt – but Ganuret saw two hard lines appear on either side of his good, firm mouth, realising that these were usually masked by the winning or sardonic smile that the Ambassador habitually wore.

The young people at the side of the court, watching, ignored Ganuret. He made one or two attempts to take part in their conversation but they all knew each other, shared the same kind of social diary which was of endless interest to them, and while they were polite enough, they were soon able to exclude him effectively. He did not very much care: the young men were snobbish and not very intelligent, the girls uniformly affected and quite simply stupid. Ganuret watched, undistracted, the psychological battle on the tennis court.

'What's the matter with Angela?' one of the girls said in a light tinkling voice.

'Just being herself, surely,' said one of the young men.

'Why on earth does she do that?' said a second girl.

'Obvious, isn't it?' the same man said.

'It's a bit much.'

Ganuret was interested, as they were clearly talking about the girl in the bathing costume.

'We could all show off if we wanted to.'

'Some of us have rather more to show.'

The two girls in tennis clothes giggled a little.

'Neurotic bitch,' said the second young man.

It seemed that only then did they remember the presence of Ganuret and perhaps they thought they had committed some breach of loyalty to one of their set, because the two men and one of the girls turned and stared coolly at him as though he had been deliberately eavesdropping at a private conversation between friends. From that moment, any pretence at polite good manners vanished. It was the hostility of the well-heeled and exclusive raised in the inviolate confidence of their own apartness, superiority based merely upon a community of interest and background that was never questioned. Ganuret flushed in anger and discomfort, but did not move away.

At that moment, the Monseigneur succeeded in hitting Claudian with a particularly powerful smash. Claudian jabbed the racket in front of him and performed the same ungainly skip, but the tennis ball hit him painfully on the inside of the thigh. Almost involuntarily he doubled in pain, but as soon as in two huge strides the priest had gained the net and the Maître had bustled across and Ganz had paced anxiously from his own base line, Claudian was waving them aside, his head in the air, pretending it was nothing. The game was halted as he paced around, briskly massaging his leg. Among the spectators, there was a certain amount of suppressed mirth, smirking heads turned aside to conceal contemptuous laughter.

Extract from Promethead. *Hazel & Sims, 1967.*

Beauchamp-Beck at All Souls, and Philbrick making his way as a newly elected Member of Parliament, kept in touch with Caradock during his first years in London, when he did quite a lot of broadcasting on radio, appeared abortively twice on television, a medium which he detested, and wrote very occasional reviews. Idris Lewis, however, who disapproved of Caradock at this time on several counts – his association with people whom Lewis thought were worthless, his relatively promiscuous attitude to women and most of all his decision not to take a job and to live on his private income – allowed a rift to widen between them which was only bridged when Caradock returned to live in Wales and took the first steps towards rapprochement. Lewis is disposed to ascribe the estrangement to several contributory factors, among them his marriage to a girl who disliked Caradock, his own puritanism ('more to do with work than sex, if you can believe that'), and Caradock's complete failure to understand how someone like Lewis could be happy and fulfilled in the Civil Service. 'There was never any major quarrel,' he writes, 'just a sequence of verbal scuffles and a few high words; but I thought he was wasting his time and talent. I still believe that if he had stayed at Oxford or taken some suitable job in London the course of his subsequent life would have been significantly altered. We might not have had the essays, or the *Promethead* or the *Laocoön* book, but who is to say that we would not have had something as good. Surely, it is as important that Michael would have had some more stable foundation on which to build his precarious emotional life than the rickety foundations of those wasted years in London. I suppose there was this erratic streak in his character which even now I do not understand. And I have to admit that this kind of speculation is sadly futile.'

Extract from David Hayward's official biography.

... I return again to the question of ambition. Let us consider three separate statements. First Stuart Gilbert writing illuminatingly on Joyce:

> It must not be forgotten that Joyce regarded aesthetic beauty as *stasis*; kinetic art, pornographical or didactic is, for him, improper art. The artist does not, like the rhetorician, seek to convince, to instruct, or to disgust. He treats his subject matter, grotesque or transcendental (or both at once), as he finds it. The value, for him, of facts or theories has little or no relation to their moral implications or their ultimate validity (if any).

And now Sartre in *What is Literature?*:

> The artist has always had a special understanding of Evil, which is not the temporary and remediable isolation of an idea, but the irreducibility of man and the world of thought.

Next Camus:

> An artist... goes to Port Cras in order to paint. And

everything is so beautiful that he buys a house, puts his paintings away and never touches them again.

Such a reply and such an attitude as I am attempting to express may well seem to the reader, who has no urge or commitment towards writing, to be mere affectation, particularly at this present time when artists are expected to be increasingly committed to things which have nothing to do with art. I contend that the artist's commitment is so complete when it is sincere that it is as psychologically and physiologically disturbing as an addiction. My point is that the artist who went to Port Cras and who did not paint was not very serious anyway. It is an existentialist posture that life is a substitute for art: for the artist his art is life and nothing takes its place except death. When I wish that I did not want to write, it is the expression of a death wish. When I pretend that I could be happy cultivating my garden, or scribbling diagrams on the sand, I am lying. And so, if I am committed entirely to my art and craft, I must be ambitious: I must try all the time to contribute not only to its scope but also to its freedom; I must not only probe into the preoccupations of art which are traditional and inalterable, focusing upon the definition and relationship of what is Good and what is Evil, I must also extend the limits (in so far as I am able) of the art that I live by. Abstraction is not to be dismissed, not to be derided: but abstraction is most useful when it is applied to themes which are by no means abstract. It is the 'Pure Science' of Art: quite beautiful in itself and for its own sake: but meaningful to a larger audience only

311

when it is elegantly and properly applied to ideas that are in some way relevant to this audience. This, of course, does not mean that the artist has to write erotica, crime fiction or comedy for television. It does mean that he must set himself serious tasks in terms of his subject matter and in terms of formal invention. Much is said, quite properly, about the responsibility of the artist to an audience that he knows nothing about; but we hear less these days about the artist's responsibility to his art. In this respect an artist must either satisfy himself that he is contributing something and something that is all his own, or he might as well buy his ticket for Port Cras.

At the heart of the artist's purpose and preoccupation is the problem of Evil since it is an attempt to explain the nature of Evil and the inescapability of Evil in man that leads him into his investigations and labours. It is a Heraclean task and to undertake it requires Heraclean drive and ambition, at the end of which the artist may well – he does not know – suffer the excruciatingly painful apotheosis of a Heracles. Even art which is concerned with the Good and the Beautiful, even great art so concerned, relates entirely to this special relationship of an artist to Evil so admirably described by Sartre.

But here the form taken by the ambition varies in tackling the problem. I do not know whether Sartre would wish to talk about 'kinetic art' but he certainly does talk about commitment. Although my own convictions are very much those of Joyce (as set down by Stuart Gilbert in the passage quoted), I am not sure that Sartre's ambition does not even transcend that of Joyce which was formidable enough. And I shall not pursue this particular argument in this essay, since it occurs over and over again in other parts of this book. All I wish to suggest at this point is that the magnitude of the task, the seriousness of the purpose, the sheer weight of labour, whether a matter of stasis or kinesis, that such an artist sets himself demands an ambition that in its self-confidence is arrogant almost to the point of hubris. The saving grace of humility occurs in the artist's respect for his art and the inevitable knowledge that comes to him that he will never be its master.

The stern stuff of which ambition is made, however, is the losing battle any writer or artist must at some stage of his career fight with this mastery of his chosen art. A young man may enjoy a little success and be far too readily satisfied with himself and with what he is doing, but sooner or later he will have to serve the apprenticeship that in this profession does not necessarily come at the beginning of a working career. At some time or another, if he is any good, the artist will find it necessary to re-examine his ideas, the themes he wishes to pursue, and to re-examine 'the way in which he is disposed to say it'. If, as Eliot said, each effort is a raid on the inarticulate, in any writer's life there is a period when these forays are fruitless, apparently wasteful and very damaging to reserves of pride and confidence. It is only through making them, most of all during the period of attrition when nothing will go right, that the artist may find out what he can do. And perhaps equally important what he cannot do and never will be able to do. This knowledge is essential to him. Its achievement is a fierce struggle. I know of no better description of it, nor of the ambition that makes such a struggle necessary than this by Wallace Stevens:

313

I want, as poet, to be that in nature which constitutes nature's very self. I want to be nature in the form of a man, with all the resources of nature: I want to be the lion in the lute; and then, when I am, I want to face my parent and be his true poet. I want to face nature the way two lions face one another – the lion in the lute facing the lion locked in stone. I want, as a man of imagination, to write poetry with all the power of the monster about whom I write. I want man's imagination to be completely adequate in the face of reality.

Extract from 'Sterner Stuff', essay in An Elemental Wound. *Hazel & Sims, 1963.*

The Dog-Star month. Landgrave's rage of disgust was accompanied by a wave of nausea, though this was perhaps because of the noisome mound of garbage piled in an alley as a result of the strike. So intense was the feeling that he had to pause, leaning against the low wall of a church, in the forecourt of which a group of filthy derelicts with swollen inflamed faces and befouled mouths were passing from one to another a thick brown bottle.

> Dogge of noisome breath
> Whose balefull barking bringes in hast
> pyne, plagues and dreery death....

And the corruption of the city he had once loved, or thought he had loved, overwhelmed him.

In almost every window of the next street into which he turned were photographs of girls in lewd positions, partly dressed with silk stockings stretched over splayed thighs, scraps of flimsy nylon taut over fleshy crotches, huge breasts pushing out of tiny brassieres. Or else there were bookshops catering for every kind of deviation and perversion. The sensation of defilement and impurity was overpowering, bringing back into Landgrave's own mind the memories of his grovelling lusts, the humiliations of his past lecheries, slavering for the favours of some silk and fleshy waste of shame. The rank hypocrisy of his nature during those years, the goatherd among the bushes ranke, pretending aloofness, the high ambition of his calling and privately tumescent over the lewdest imaginings, searching endlessly for the Circe who would bring him most finally down.

That was past and he had chosen his austere life only to find a despair that was infinite. Landgrave had never found much reason or cause for hope, but he had cherished the illusion of some kind of Promethean defiance and dignity, an idea of service and nobility, an ideal of stoical energy. And yet this high ambition had always been sullied by human appetites. The dignity was only attainable, the cosmic imagery of his ambition, in the mind. Physically, emotionally, spiritually he had succumbed to the pleasures of our ladyes bowre and when at last by a supreme effort of will he had achieved the true austerity of the mind, he had found only this despair. It was not just the disease in his body that nourished it, it was the dispassionate contemplation of himself and of other men. The black farce of the sage sitting in thought brayned by a shellfish

> For sitting so with bared scalpe
> an Eagle sored hye,

315

That weening hys white head was chalke,
a shell fish downe let flye:
She weend the shell fishe to have broake
but therewith bruzd his brayne,
So now astonied with the stroake,
He lyes in lingring payne.

Landgrave smiled bitterly to himself: and a whore who was leaning against a doorway, straightened up languidly and spoke to him. Suddenly there was the same spurt of desire that he had fought down. The girl had a superb body. Landgrave stamped onward, furious. He had been destroyed between the crab's claws of lust and ambition which had left him with a barren mind in a decaying body.

Extract from 'July' sequence of Laocoön. *Hazel & Sims, posthumous.*

I have already remarked on Caradock's obsessive preoccupation with various items of female underclothing, notably stockings, which occurs in even the most serious and portentous novels. Even Landgrave, Caradock's most gigantically presumptuous mythopoeic creation, drools in the sequence entitled 'The Crab's Claws' over past sensualities, while at the same time ostensibly despising his 'human' weakness, having opted for chastity. Caradock describes this particular projection of himself as destroyed by lust and ambition and the particular sequence is worth detailed study because it exposes the central hypocrisy in Caradock's work as well as demonstrating his mythopoeic technique, very like what anthropologists call *Bricolage*, and setting out in plainest terms his notion of the superior being and this ichorescent creature's relationship to ordinary men and women.

The culmination of Caradock's contempt and hatred for the female sex occurs in certain passages from this sequence: but it is a fascinated hatred because he is at the same time honest enough to realise his own enslavement to sexuality. What is displeasing is the way in which he tries to excuse this weakness by his favourite device of deliberately complicating simple issues through allusion, cross-reference and arbitrary association of one impulse or idea with another. There is no question that Caradock, using as he does throughout the novel parallel moments from Spenser's *The Shepheardes Calender*, sympathises more with the attitude of Morrell than with that of Thomalin. (According to the Glosse this is 'that albeit alle bountye dwelleth in mediocritie, yet perfect felicitye dwelleth in supremacye'.) This is certainly not Spenser's intention and is a typical example of the way in which Caradock was prepared to distort other texts or exemplars for his own purposes. This association of 'Promethean ambition' with unbridled lust as a spiritual destroyer is entirely arbitrary; as is this same example for the destruction of an individual with the crab's claws that tear apart the noble and just city – crime and exploitation of sex. When Caradock, with great ingenuity, works in the appropriate month from the *Très Riches Heures du Duc de Berry*, which is an innocent portrayal of sheep shearing and harvesting – which become symbols for pimping and criminal racketeering respectively – and when these activities are associated with Abel and Cain, the bogusness of this method is transparent....

The purpose of the mythopoeic process is a flight from reality, in order to create a structure on which the uncommon man of untypical experience may be, Prometheus-like, strung up to suffer. This at a time in world history when it is the commonplace concerns and sufferings of ordinary people that should be most important to the artist. Political commitment apart, art today seems to me a matter for dignifying tears on a street corner.

Richard Snow: The View from Lemnos. *Medusa Books, 1972.*

... This whole question of ambition seems to me to be crucial and I would claim has little or nothing to do with commitment. Sartre commends the writer who is an outsider (quite a different case from Camus' Outsider) as long as he is outside bourgeois society and bourgeois values, but this writer is expected to be inside Marxist society and do his duty there by that society. Man is free and there are no moral judgements to be made except upon one's own account until society makes these and other judgements on everyone's account. This paradox is something that Sartre himself is brilliant enough to use as a source of creative energy, but in the hands of less able 'thinkers' of the left it becomes feebly transparent.

The notion that man is what man does is obviously tenable, but commitment is not exclusively a matter of left-wing idealism, let alone putative terrorism. Quite apart from the fact that the left do not have a monopoly on ideals – there is, after all, such a thing as liberal idealism, or indeed social democratic idealism. If I, a nauseated art student, throw a petrol bomb into a museum so destroying irreplaceable pictures, furniture, artefacts, tapestries, am I good and just because I am in revolt against bourgeois society if my viewpoint is left wing, but evil and anti-social if my viewpoint is right wing? The gesture is the same, its effect is the same: I have destroyed something worth preserving in order to assert my own feeble and pathetic freedom. And a democratic society has every right to pass judgement on my action, my moral discernment and my thoroughly undesirable and egomaniac conduct.

It is obviously not difficult to understand that in a situation of war, particularly against a force as manifestly evil as Nazism, issues are relatively clear-cut: but even then it is surely not axiomatic that not to resist actively is to collaborate. Outside this state of war (in which collaboration is, after all, as positive a decision as resistance) where choices are more varied and variable, it is not possible to lay down such hard-and-fast rules. And my contention is that a writer, any artist, must be firmly outside all systems of society. He must resist any kind of commitment other than his commitment to his art and to his own private morality, which is not the morality of a party or a faction or a religion. He must observe, he must record and if he offers judgement it must be personal – valuable only in the context and accuracy of what he describes. His moral standpoint will be a distillation of ethical precepts and the teachings of many wise and illuminated minds (one of which would be that of Sartre): but it will not be a politician's book of rules, the articles of faith of some theorist, let alone a committee of theorists.

My admiration for Sartre the writer is unbounded. *The Reprieve* seems to me to be one of the greatest achievements in the novel in any century. The massive achievement of *Les Chemins de la liberté*, the versatility of his work in prose fiction, quite apart from the verve, energy and dramatic salience of his many plays, makes Sartre for me and for so many others, who cannot accept his prescriptions and proscriptions for the conduct of a writer, a towering giant in literature. I am not equipped to comment upon his technical philosophy, but I have found it profound and profoundly stimulating, which is surely a function of creative thought communicated in its purest form. Sadly, it is where Sartre has been most consistent in his increasingly political preoccupation, achieved at the expense of his arts, that I find the alarming inconsistencies that seem to me dangerously threatening to the function and dedication of the individual artist.

Passage from 'Je suis que...', essay on Jean-Paul Sartre in An Elemental Wound. *Hazel & Sims, 1963.*

'He is a barbarian,' Leydon Wells said. 'And I think you must be protected from him.'

'But he is the brother of the man my sister is supposed to have gone off with.'

'I do not believe it, Laertes. I do not believe that that individual has any relatives of ordinary flesh and blood. He is Attila and Ghengis Khan and Alaric the Goth all rolled into one. One would think it would be enough to eke out a parasitic existence as a book critic, but to write about the theatre *and* about television as well... his sadistic instincts are unbounded. He savaged a really sensitive novel by Peregrine Wracke the other week, not to mention a brutal assault upon a quite hilarious comedy by my close friend Emmerson Jebb and the very last word in butchery was his notice for Zara Anstruther's wonderfully imaginative production of *Lysistrata* in drag at the Edinburgh Fringe. Take it from me, dear boy, that man has come here straight from the abattoir.'

'He looks miserable. I don't care. I'm going to speak to him. If he can help me find my sister, I will put up with a bit of rudeness.'

'Then it is a matter for you and your conscience,' said Leydon Wells in a sinister voice, before turning petulantly on his heel.

All the same it was with some trepidation that Laertes Jones approached Perceval D'Arcy. He had the head of a very large, very grumbly boxer dog: large, weak, rather protrusive eyes and a great prognathous snout set in steady gloom. Laertes Jones had once known a boxer dog who had looked very like him and was not in any way disturbed by this appearance.

'Good evening, Mr-er-D'Arcy,' he said. 'My name is Jones. I believe your brother knows my sister.'

'Then God help her,' said D'Arcy. 'The man is a beast.'

Laertes Jones looked alarmed. D'Arcy scutinised him morosely.

'You seem concerned, Mr Jones. I have nothing to do with my brother. The last I heard of him, he was a bookmaker's clerk or something of the sort.'

'Oh. I thought he was a trainer of horses.'

'I said something of the sort. Is your sister horsy?'

'She is very fond of animals.'

'I wish I were. Look at this menagerie.'

Perceval D'Arcy swept his glass of wine before him in a gesture that comprehended all the roomful of writers and artists.

'A carnival of animals, Mr Jones. A Noah's arkful. Are you an author?'

'No. I'm a teacher. But I do write poems in my spare time.'

'Then spare your time, Mr Jones. And yourself and the public. Desist from writing poems. You may start off with sincerity and zeal, even with talent, you will end up as a literary hooligan performing gratuitous acts of vandalism, travelling to all corners of the country in order to tangle with rival hooligans, chanting imbecile slogans and revelling in obscenity. *Si testimonium requiris, circumspice.*'

'Oh?'

'What sort of poems do you write?'

'Harmless lyrics.'

'You are not a satirist laying bare the nervous system of a sick society with a merciless scalpel of neo-Marxian wit?'

'No. I write about the beauties of Nature.'

'You are not a rocking and rolling poet with an over-simplified idea of the extraordinary poetic uplift that lives in the souls of laundry workers and publicans, convinced that social, economic and constitutional evils would be righted if we were all herded into arenas for purposes of community singing and if we were all nice to one another?'

'No. I'm not a bit like that.'

'You are not tough-minded with a searing scorn that you bring to bear upon anyone who does not share your circumscriptions upon thought, technique and imagery?'

'No. I wouldn't like to think I was dogmatic.'

'Then you are lost in this present company. Commitment to the left of you, commitment to the right of you. And those people over there believe in themselves as apostles of a rejuvenated popular culture.'

'You don't say.'

'That simian apparition is Elmer de Pugh, Junior, visiting these shores from America, where he assures me it is all happening. A man of teak sensibilities and mahogany discretion. He tells me that nothing of significance is being written on this side of the Atlantic. And the sadness of things is that he is right.'

'He doesn't look well.'

'Woodworm.'

Laertes Jones noticed the critic's glass was empty.

'Shall I get you another drink, Mr D'Arcy?'

'There you see the distinguished Russian Kamikazurian who is a disappointed gymnast. His stance of defiance against the bulldozer is purely because of this failure and a disposition to arthritis after the rigorous callisthenics of his adolescence. I am drinking this unspeakable yellow soup.'

Extract from Broods of Folly. *Alvin & Brandt, 1960.*

A succession of crowded rooms. Alcohol and tobacco fumes and overheated bodies, sweat, soap and perfume; oeillades and becks and wreathed smiles, robust grinning, perfect teeth, painted idiocies; the furtive hand, the frotting of tit against forearm, belly against belly; the trade of second-hand intelligence, jokes about masturbation, the earnest penetration of blue-rinsed curiosity, cavorting of the queer mice, serious jowls of the personalities in obtrusive economic council; the yellow of the wanton spirits ambling lechery, lechery: wars and lechery, nothing else hold fashion; the crimson of the dayglow copywriters; the purple of the cardinals which use such tyrannical colours and pompous paynting.

There was a terrible knot of fury tightening inside my skull, tightening, tightening... until it must split itself. A terrible tension that would one day part with a cracking sound... a sort of cracking sound. And that will be the end? What a sorry end. When I listen I can hear that crack as the strands fly part and see behind my eyes the blood suffuse my brains....

This room – high and airy with the great windows staring blindly out over the receding waters, the declining day. Still light and the rain has stopped. This comfortable, dark, battered furniture which has no associations, debris of other people's lives. Expensive faded wallpaper stained and scuffed. The empty bottles, one rolling on its side into a corner. A few spent books attempted in a last feeble effort of the will to survive.

Alone. At last. The real sense of isolation, the consummation once devoutly wished, the ideal of chaste, self-reliant reflection, a communion with the self that admits only of truth.... And what is it? It is cold, it is empty as the sky out there is now empty of birds and evenly covered by the dull, pearl-coloured cloud. A padded cell of sky. The *recessional into myself has led to this state of disgrace: no heroic stoic on his melting block of ice outstaring the even sky, but an inward shrinking, frightened casually crouched in a corner, his barren mind that desired quiet peopled with the phantoms of a succession of crowded rooms, the snatches of banality, the nightmare smilings. The silence is crowded....*

98. Int. Party scene. Night. Dramatisation of novel, *Broods of Folly*. 'Laertes Jones' (played by James Maple) gazing around crowded room.	MUSIC: Noisy party music of period. (Elvis Presley: *Hound Dog*. (8a.))
Panning shot of variously fantastic faces, the fat headmistress, the actors, the BBC executive, the red-haired barmaid, etc., etc.	(V/O) *Laertes*: My God! I'll never find her in this. Where do they all come from? Such self-possession, such confidence. A poor shy creature like Amelia could never survive in this. She would wilt.
Hold briefly over 'Peregrine' and 'Sir Bruce Dumbrell'	*Peregrine*: My name's Peregrine. Who are you? *Sir B.*: Sir Politick Bloody Might Have Been. Sod off!
'Laertes' reacts	Music up.
Resume panning shot with	Music loud

faces becoming masks as in
Ensor *L'Intrigue*....

'Laertes' reacts, his face
showing increasing surprise,
mouth and eyes opening wide

Cut to one of the three she-
centaurs dressed in a black
body stocking with horse's
head, lingering over her
figure

Laertes: God in heaven!

Track back to include the
other two she-centaurs
dressed respectively in red
and purple

Laertes: May I ask, miss, what
you are supposed to be?

First Centaur: I am a chess-
piece.

Second Centaur: I am a figment
of the imagination of Jean
Cocteau.

Third Centaur: I am a horse of
a different colour.

The first she-centaur comes
close to 'Laertes'

Close up of the she-centaur's
torso from thighs to breasts,
she holds out her arms to
embrace him

Music very loud.

326

Close up of the she-centaur's
head, grotesque, flared nostrils

Close up of 'Laertes' looking
horror-struck, mouth opening
in a soundless scream

Music loud, deafening chatter,
snickering laughter.

Ensor *L'Intrigue* group

99. Int. Party set. Night. Cut
to Leighton Rees on party set
among remains of celebration,
bits of food, bottles, dirty
glasses, one of the horse's
heads. Rees looks around....

Rees: (Sync.) Well, of course it
was nothing like that. Caradock
and I moved for a while in the
same circles and the parties to
which we went were perfectly
ordinary gatherings of people
who more or less liked each
other. The conversation was
often quite intelligent,
sometimes very good indeed;
the people were on the whole
gentle and decent. There were
none of the grotesques that he
put into his satire and none of
the sub-orgiastic, self-conscious
Bohemianism that he affected
to remember. And certainly

Move in on Rees to medium
close shot.

Michael Caradock was no
innocent. Some of the portraits
in that novel, *Broods of Folly*,
are vicious and vindictive, but
there was never any question of
him being victimised by a

sophisticated and cruel society
of urban intellectuals. It was
he who was the emotional
gangster. I doubt whether he
would have had the courage to
become a real one – I never
saw much evidence of it – but
he was callous and had no
compunction at all about
spiritual assassination.

Extract from television programme, 'Landscape of a Prophet'.

Throughout his London years, Caradock's relations with
his foster-father, Howell Caradock, were cordial enough
but maintained at a distance. From the evidence of Mr
Caradock's acquaintances at Cwmfelyn, Michael Caradock
appears to have written to the old gentleman fairly
regularly. Fay Mackail says that Caradock regarded it as
an obligation: he had no particular affection for Howell,
but he realised that he must be very lonely and felt sorry
for him. She adds that the letters were a considerable
labour, because the older and the younger man had very
little in common. Caradock's serious preoccupations at the
time were entirely literary and stylistic and his social
activities would have seemed either uninteresting or
shocking to Howell. J. Rudmose Bowen recalls that on his
visits to the golf club, Howell Caradock sometimes
mentioned that Michael had met some celebrity or other
in London, or offered some opinion or other upon an item
of news that they had discussed in letters. He agrees with

Leslie Chambers that Howell Caradock probably longed for the occasional visit from Michael, none of which were forthcoming. 'Not' (says Mr Bowen) 'that the old boy ever complained. He was much too reticent to share anything of that sort with casual acquaintances. He was obviously in a fair bit of pain around this time, but I don't suppose Julian (or Michael) was told much about that.'

Mr and Mrs Timothy Rogers, the couple whom Howell Caradock had engaged to look after his house, grounds and himself after Phyllis' death and to whom he left Dan-y-graig in his will, were very fond of Howell. He kept himself at a distance from them, which they did not find strange and which they certainly did not resent, but he was unfailingly generous to them and called upon them each day for a brief chat about general matters. They take a sternly critical view of Michael Caradock's behaviour: 'He was no good, if you want my frank opinion,' Mr Rogers says. 'Mr Howell Caradock was a gentleman and a very tidy man. He enjoyed his glass of whisky, but so do we all; but he was a thoroughly decent man in his morals and attitude. And I am only thankful myself that he didn't live to see the shocking end that that fellow came to. It would have grieved him very badly. Fortunately, too, the way of life of Julian didn't come out until after all that business at Glanmor, so Mr Howell didn't know anything about it.' Mrs Rogers adds: 'Quite apart from that, Mr Rogers and I both thought that the son could have spent some time with his father. I know Mr Caradock was only his foster-father, but as anyone who lived in this village could tell you, they had both been very good to him and he was lucky that they had taken him in as a child when his own parents had died. Mr Caradock was very lonely, as my husband and I could see. He used to come in every day for a little chat and he used to go up to the golf club occasionally, but he missed Mrs Caradock very much. And this is where I blame the son. He should have had enough feeling to see this. We often asked Mr Caradock if he'd like to come in to sit with us in the evening. He did sometimes, but we could see he didn't want to impose. If ever there was a special occasion, we always invited him to join us. And he was generosity itself, of course. Nothing was too good for Mr Rogers and myself.'

Howell Caradock died in December 1958 after a heart attack. He left the house to the loyal couple and a few minor legacies, but the bulk of his considerable capital he left to Michael, who was already extremely comfortably off. The funeral was held at Cwmfelyn and Michael Caradock attended it. Many people saw reason to comment on his general demeanour, which was stony, but without any appearance of grief or mourning. Mr and Mrs Rogers remarked bitterly that at no time did he show the slightest sorrow at Howell's death and certainly no remorse at his own filial shortcomings.

An interesting sidelight upon the funeral of Howell Caradock was that it widened the rift between Idris Lewis and Michael. Lewis had read about the death and, as he was visiting Wales at the time, had driven over to attend the last ceremonies. Caradock spoke to him briefly and coldly, but did not invite him back to the house and at no time after did he communicate any word of thanks to

Lewis for a considerate gesture of condolence. Fay Mackail says that Caradock was angry about 'Idris behaving as usual like a self-conscious Sunday school superintendent. He doesn't have to be a good chap, he must take damn good care that he is seen to be a good chap.' She feels that Lewis' appearance had aggravated Caradock's sense of guilt. Contrary to the opinions of Mr and Mrs Rogers and others at Cwmfelyn, Miss Mackail (who knew Caradock intimately) thinks that he was upset and that his remorse was considerable. He would not, she adds, have shown his friends in London any such emotion and in Wales he would have been at great pains to disguise anything that might be construed as weakness.

Extract from David Hayward's official biography.

I have little patience with those writers who make a great deal of money churning stuff out for television who give themselves airs about their intense social conscience and their commitment to connecting with ordinary men and women. The implication, of course, is that they themselves are not in the least ordinary. Perhaps they are not. Their work most certainly is. I have even less patience with the besotted egalomaniacs who think that a television serial is more valuable than *Finnegans Wake* or the *Four Quartets* because it gets through to more people. And I believe that people who are writers (or for that matter film-makers), and who tell themselves that what they are doing is worthwhile because of the size of the audience they are serving, are writers who could do nothing else. They could *not* write *Finnegans Wake* even if they wanted to, they could *not* compose the *Rite of Spring* or the *Apollo Musagetes*. They succeed at what they are doing, admirably no doubt, because they are incapable of doing anything better. Shakespeare would *not* have been a television hack, if he had been alive today, and it is grossly insulting to his memory and achievement that glib Sunday journalists think that they are being amusing and alert in suggesting such nonsense. Bach would *not* have been a composer of 'pop', or even progressive jazz. These great giants might not have written *King Lear* or the *B Minor Mass* in quite the same way, but the greatness of their minds, the magnificence of their ambition, their technical mastery, the nobility of their art would have triumphed as the art of Stravinsky triumphs, as the art of Joyce and Eliot and Proust triumphs.

To the diligent, hypercritical, self-doubting novelist, the abiding and sometimes depressing problem is one of responsibility and inheritance. After the enormous labours of Proust, Thomas Mann and most of all Joyce, the unproved writer is under an obligation to follow, to try to contribute to the development or expansion of the form: the novel did not end with *Finnegans Wake*. And it is up to the conscientious novelist of sensible ambition to try to learn and exploit the technical innovations of greater minds and great geniuses. It is idle to suppose that everyone who sets pen to paper seriously could hope to write *Ulysses* or *The Guermantes Way* or *Dr Faustus*, but Camus and Sartre have proved what can be done by the application of serious and coherent philosophical ideas to a sensitive perception of events. The great work does not have to be long. In his bleaker moments the novelist might feel a little fed up that he can never hope to emulate the massive achievements of those who have gone before, but he should feel not more than fed up. He should not despair. He must try. And this means he must attempt to do things which are technically daring, if not in language then in structure; he must work under intense imaginative pressure; he must traffic in ideas. For too long, especially in England, novelists have been content with beautiful writing, what is known as 'characterisation', the exposition of sound, well-knit stories. Of course, a novel should have all these things in the sense that it should be well written, in the sense that it should present a variety of characters and a variety of 'characterisations', in the sense that it should tell a story or describe events that are coherently relevant: but the language and the characters and the story must make demands upon the reader. The novelist must surprise and startle, he must make efforts to achieve an imaginative state of excitement which will awaken responses in the reader (from his own experience) that the novelist cannot know anything about, but which he guessed must be possible.

The so-called 'new' novel in France promises works of some considerable interest, but so far the intricate and wonderfully conceived labyrinths built by our predecessors and masters have been abandoned and left untenanted. They must be occupied again, restored, maintained, developed and if possible extended.

Extract from 'Labyrinth To Let', essay in An Elemental Wound. *Hazel & Sims, 1963.*

102. Studio interview with Fay Mackail (Trevelyan Lloyd off camera.)

Mackail: (Sync.) Yes, it was a bad time for him. Because he was ambitious in the best possible way: he wanted to achieve something. And it had nothing to do with being famous. At this stage he thought he would never achieve it.

Close up Fay Mackail.

Lloyd (o/s): And around this time, Howell Caradock died.... It is said that he behaved rather contemptuously to others at the funeral....

Mackail: He might have given that impression, because he liked to be aloof. Nobody cares about that in London, but obviously in a smaller community (especially one where they make rather a fuss about warmth) it would be noticeable and resented. The trouble is that very few people knew him well and he hated giving himself away, which is why I think it was only to certain women that he behaved completely honestly.

Profile close up Fay Mackail

He hated put-downs and especially of unpretentious people. I remember once being at the Regent's Park Open Air Theatre with him and after the show – *The Dream* or *Twelfth Night* or whatever it was – we were going away and there was an elderly north-country woman who was clearly having a lovely time. It was all magical. A beautiful summer evening and this lady started enthusing about the Post Office Tower across the park. And some clever young idiots, adolescents, started sneering.

Move away from Fay Mackail to medium shot.

And Michael was furious and he went for these kids savagely – he called them 'tatty little brats of a shabby magazine subculture'. They were very surprised and so was everyone else. Well, it was easy enough, I suppose, but I can think of many other examples and so could Brenda Thackeray, I'm sure, if only she would talk at all....

Lloyd (O/S): Why is it that she won't? Do you know?

Zoom in to close up of Fay Mackail, very serious.

Mackail: I don't think I can speak for Brenda. And I very much respect her silence. It's just that I think some people – and I'm one of them – can adjust the perspective on a very sincere artist and a basically very nice man. I told that story simply to try and give some idea of Michael's respect for enthusiasm and a real response to living. Most people have an idea that he was frightfully cold and cerebral, but he could show a child... no that's the wrong word, a very young and totally unaffected delight in quite commonplace things and recognise this delight in others – like the Post Office Tower on a soft and fragrant July evening.

Track slowly away to medium long shot...

Extract from television programme, 'Landscape of a Prophet'.

... We never did see the comet. It was either too low in the sky, or the turrets and domes and spires of Whitehall were in the way, or we were looking in entirely the wrong part of the universe.

What we did see was morning, just after dawn, on a cold day in late autumn in St James's Park with light pink cloud in the eastern sky, and ripples on the water, the bright wet grass seeming to sparkle, the water birds about their purposeful lives. The streets were empty apart from the occasional rushing car or cruising taxi and there was about the often shabby West End a really solemn stillness.

Not solemn enough. We were laughing. Not because what we had to say was particularly funny or brilliant, but because we were up and alive, tingling with the cold and feeling a little stupid. A very young policeman with a lugubrious moustache that didn't quite work regarded us with the utmost suspicion. People of our age and pretensions had no right to be so happy at that time of the morning....

Extract from 'Urban Lyrics III', in The Philosopher's Stone. *Hazel & Sims, 1965.*

7

Michael Caradock met Brenda Thackeray in 1960 at the party given by his publishers to launch the novel *Broods of Folly*. According to friends who knew them both well, their physical and emotional attraction for one another was immediate and mutual, but the relationship that followed was often as tempestuous as it was undoubtedly passionate.

Unfortunately Miss Thackeray is not prepared to talk about Caradock or about these years when they lived together, although many friends have attempted to persuade her of the value of her potential contribution to such a biography as this: so I fear that most of the evidence relating to this crucial encounter and its consequences for Caradock must be based on the observations and opinions of others, which I have tried to balance, relying to a certain extent upon my own memory.

Brenda Thackeray was at the time a freelance journalist and broadcaster who contributed regularly to the *Observer*, the *Guardian* and the *New Statesman* as well as to serious discussion programmes on radio and television. She is a socialist with decidedly left-wing opinions and it was her political conviction that often set in motion the vivid intellectual clashes she had with Caradock. At first, as I observed myself, they both seemed to enjoy these conflicts, but in due course the arguments became increasingly savage and bitter, as Caradock's own social and political theories became more and more isolationist and elitist and Brenda Thackeray felt herself morally obliged to react.

Many people have noticed that Caradock's most intimate women friends were of the same physical type. I am told by people who knew Helen Westlake and who have seen photographs of Brenda Thackeray that there is a distinct resemblance, which also may be seen in Diana Bradley and Fay Mackail: where Miss Thackeray differs from the others is in colouring, having very bright blue eyes and blonde hair. Michael Beauchamp-Beck describes her figure and stature as 'magnificently, opulently anadyomene', referring particularly to the sculpture at the Villa Ludovisi in Rome. He goes on to say: 'I haven't seen her for very many years, because immediately after splitting up with Michael Caradock she went to live in France and, when I last heard of her, was working in either Rome or Geneva with one of the United Nations agencies, but I liked her *very* much. She had a warm and generous sort of personality, rather impulsive and with an alarming temper. This was all the more surprising because she looked extremely cool and pacific. In most ways Michael was besotted with her and it was pretty obvious (as you must have seen for yourself) that their physical relationship must have been unusually passionate, so I don't think it's surprising that their emotional and intellectual interaction would also have been tempestuous.'

The publisher Candida Lee describes the couple in much the same way, though perhaps less sympathetically than Beauchamp-Beck. 'Their first meeting was positively chemical. Brenda Thackeray never made any attempt to conceal anything – physically or emotionally – and she made it quite obvious that Michael could have his way with her right from the beginning. He wasn't usually quick to respond, although he was much more lecherous than many people thought, as I know to my cost, but with her you could see he couldn't wait to tear her clothes off. I had the greatest difficulty – I was his editor at the time with Alvin – in getting him to stay at the party for his own book. And they often behaved in this way subsequently. It was embarrassing and sometimes rather repulsive.'

Angela Petrov, however, read the relationship somewhat differently: 'As I've often said, Michael made a great thing about being fastidious and distant, so that Brenda, who was a fascinating person and tremendously outgoing, was a complete temperamental contrast. She had this cool blonde exterior but as soon as you were introduced you were rather engulfed by her warmth. Obviously a lot of their ideas were incompatible, but so were their personalities. Brenda was fearfully untidy in everything except her personal appearance and Michael liked everything to be just so. So that he was always, perfectly good-humouredly, putting things back in their place after her. Of course, this was all very trivial – except when he couldn't find one of his books. Then out of nowhere they'd have a fearful and quite disproportionately fierce row.'

This view is not generally shared – certainly not by Fay Mackail, who has made many sincere and diligent attempts to persuade Miss Thackeray to describe her life with Caradock and who is the only one of their circle who has remained in touch with her. She says: 'There were passionate quarrels. These were inevitable because Michael was intellectually rather cold and never emotional, while Brenda invariably let her heart rule her head, especially when it was something to do with poverty or inequality or injustice. I don't know that I should say they loved one another, but for a while they were searingly and fulminatingly in love. There was nothing gentle about it.'

Novelist, Rose Brandt, goes a little further: 'I think Michael Caradock was frightened of the intensity of the affair. Unquestionably it was always capable of self-destruction. Highly volatile explosive. Apart from the crisis of values that existed perfectly genuinely between them – and they both held quite coherent and considered views about culture and anarchy and related themes – there was also the added strain imposed by Michael's habit of casting people in certain roles. He had made up his mind that Brenda was Aphrodite (I think you said Michael Beauchamp-Beck said something of the sort) to his Hephaestos. And sensually they must have had a

341

splendid time. But the only thing that really mattered to Michael was his art: and his views and standards, relating as they did to broader cultural issues, were bound to conflict with Brenda Thackeray's intensely committed political ideas. It was always doomed.'

Michael Beauchamp-Beck supports this argument, suggesting that Miss Thackeray was responsible for a Dionysiac release of repressed energy that was merely an interlude in Caradock's determinedly Apollonian way of life – a way of life, he suggests, that was not natural.

Another novelist acquaintance, Frank Adeane, writes: 'Brenda Thackeray was not beautiful, but she was impressive and very sexy and built to generous proportions. She obviously fancied Caradock enormously physically, but I couldn't understand how they ever managed to get on out of bed. In fact they seldom did, so things must have been pretty good when they were there. Caradock was always a bit pretentious, though nothing like as much in those days as he must have become. There was nothing at all affected about Brenda. She was a very female woman and she responded quickly to men. Caradock was often furiously jealous and I think he used to go to all kinds of ingenious lengths in order to trap her. Well, naturally, no relationship could survive that sort of performance.'

Extract from David Hayward's official biography.

A convulsion of real and appalling pain writhed in the General's face. Ganuret was alarmed at the way in which the massive head seemed to shrink into the heavy shoulders so that there seemed to be a massive knot of painful taurine muscle about the old man's neck. He did not know whether the General was actually experiencing a real physical spasm of agony or whether it was something that Claudian had said, obviously calculatedly, which had jabbed some goad into a nerve centre. Claudian appeared to be calm and serene, Ganz was anxious but determined not to overreact. Ganuret was pushing back his chair to get up but Ganz reached out and restrained him. The General appeared not to notice. He shook his head slowly and painfully from side to side and his shoulders sagged a little, but there was still that bunched, tortured set to them as he walked from the room.

'I suppose that was necessary,' Ganz said.

For the first time Ganuret heard in the normally pleasant voice, the rasp that he had noted in Major Ganz's laughter. His face was impassive, the eyes steady, but the hostility was barely concealed. Claudian turned his head towards him, smiling.

'My dear Ganz, the rehabilitation must begin sometime and it can only be achieved by a resolute examination of the disagreeable past.'

'It is nothing. It is not relevant.'

'I don't think that you can really believe that, Ganz. And it is idle to pretend to in the circumstances. The truth is that it is not merely relevant but vital. The man cannot be allowed to indulge this self-disgust any longer. When the moment comes, he must be seen to be sane, the iron-willed, right-minded giant that he was supposed to be and will be expected again to be.'

He glanced at Ganuret. The smile had faded but the

look was one totally without interest. Ganuret realised that for Claudian he simply did not exist other than as a physical presence. If he was overhearing secret or important conversation, it did not matter – because *he* did not matter.

'We must act carefully and kindly,' Ganz said. 'You have neither the right nor the medical authority to take these things on yourself.'

The smile returned.

'Events do not wait upon caution and kindness, Major Ganz. You are a soldier. The General always reminds us how admirably you have always conducted yourself as a soldier. You must appreciate that.'

He rose elegantly from the ornate chair and bowed to them both, an ironic, patronising bow, wearing on his face the same small pleasant smile. His dark eyes alive with a faintly contemptuous humour. Ganuret stood up but Ganz remained seated.

'I shall speak to Dr Ranke,' he said.

Claudian made one of his exact charming diplomatic gestures, repeated the ironic little bow and went suavely out of the room. Ganuret looked towards Ganz, wondering whether he should stay.

'Sit down,' Ganz said, his face still without expression. 'I expect you wonder what that was all about.'

'I assume that it is not any concern of mine.'

'You really astound me,' Ganz said. 'I find it difficult to believe in your innocence. I can think of no better word. Innocence. Do you not wish to know what could so abruptly bring that look of pain and despair to such a man? Now that you know him. Now that you have perhaps some idea of his greatness of intellect and spirit.'

'There are many things I should like to know, but I am not sure that others want me to know them.'

Ganz stared at him, the same blank stare. Ganuret's eyes rested on the scarred cheekbone, avoiding the grey steady eyes.

'It is so trivial,' he said. 'Waldeck was once married. The woman was an actress. Beautiful, highly intelligent, but emotional. For a while their life together was extremely happy, but she did not understand her responsibilities. That is to say she was not able to see herself in the context of his career, his service to his country, or in the perspective of his greatness. It is a common fault among such women. They are unable to adjust the demands of their own personality to the needs of an ideal, a process of history. The General was an ambitious man making his way in the difficult political labyrinth that somehow emerged out of the chaos of that appalling war in which he first proved his distinction. Their life together was fragmentary, of necessity, until the woman began to feel that she was neglected. Her own career which she pursued was not enough. Rather than devote herself to him, she demanded that he offer more of himself to her. Their sexual rapport deteriorated. The marriage, now of convenience, held up: but it was a poor thing. As is perhaps not surprising, since Louisa Waldeck mixed with artists and poets who are often possessed by what they imagine to be progressive ideas, she became interested in libertarian politics. I do not know how much this was part of a wish to disengage herself totally from the life and values of her husband, but she was an embarrassment to him, although only privately. Her stormy character precipitated endless scenes between them, although publicly she remained silent, apparently unconcerned.'

An expression that was almost one of uncertainty crossed Ganz's normally confident, composed features. He had been looking and speaking straight ahead of him, now his eyes wavered to Ganuret who listened as neutrally as possible.

'Some men are less able than others to live without sensual diversions,' he said. 'Waldeck was once such a man. Perhaps it is inevitable that when a relationship based on love falls apart to be replaced by a mere gratification of carnal lusts from whichever source it comes, this degenerates into fantasy that can only be realised in brothels or by prostitutes. Waldeck, under intense stress, succumbed to this kind of distraction. He has always been as rich in enemies as friends and so it was arranged that Louisa should discover him in a humiliated circumstance with two women at a flat he used for such purposes. Her anger was savage, whatever the reasons. I do not imagine that she had lived chastely but it is not inconceivable. Although it was possible to prevent the scandal becoming public and although Waldeck was not in a position of authority where it would have damaged his career at that time, his wife made his life intolerable and there was an ugly dissolution.'

'It must have been a very long time ago,' Ganuret said quietly.

'Long enough,' Ganz said. 'The General renounced pleasure of the flesh. For some years, the domestic political situation and his responsibilities and then the war that followed occupied him and all the ferocious energy that he is able to bring to bear upon an issue. And out of that renunciation, that self-disgust, has grown his obsession with chastity. From that revulsion with his own weakness he has extrapolated his ideas of equanimity and service – but (as you know) he is sometimes not well. And even here he is a prey to enemies. I do not know, Ganuret, what temptations you are open to but Waldeck is still vulnerable and there are those who will exploit him.'

Ganz got up.

'I do not know,' he said, 'whether Claudian is right and that this is a question of rehabilitation. But I think you might help. The General likes talking to you.'

'I couldn't,' Ganuret said. 'I wouldn't know how to approach the subject. Unless he talked to me...'

Major Ganz stared at him blankly.

Extract from Promethead. *Hazel & Sims, 1967.*

Quite frankly, Brenda was never really at ease with the rest of us. For that matter, I don't think Michael ever really adapted to our particular circle – although he was accepted readily enough. And he was eager enough to *be* accepted – he wanted to make it at the socially intellectual level, if you know what I mean. Of course, my brother, Nicholas, and I were more or less born into a literary and artistic ambience. My ex-husband, Leighton Rees, came from Wales but he adjusted very quickly – very quickly indeed. As did most of the others. We were cosmoplitan, pretty bright, rather amusing and on the whole attractive people – oh, John Preminger in the Arts Council, Trevelyan Lloyd the poet, Candida Lee in publishing, Peter Lindsay who does the television arts programme 'Camera Oscura', Josh Stanford who's into pop music – those sort of people. Brenda didn't fit in and made very little effort. She was a formidably warm person but not particularly sophisticated, although she looked it. And the warmth could be rather overpowering. And the amusing thing was she was frightfully untidy. When one went to their flat – the place they shared together – it was quite amazing. You could almost see demarcation lines where Brenda lived and where Michael did....

Angela Petrov in BBC radio programme.

It's absurd to pretend that two such intelligent people could and would not adjust to each other's way of life. And I am less inclined to think than others that there was any kind of intellectual intolerance. Brenda Thackeray was left wing but she was entirely rational – not an extremist, and there is a lot of nonsense talked about Michael Caradock's politics. He was a perfectly orthodox, right-of-centre liberal. He was interested in, but did not accept, the ideas of Nietzsche as *philosophic* ideas. But if people paid a little more attention to his essays, it is quite evident that he was more worried about the effect on cultural standards of fashionable political and social trends than he was about politics. He also believed passionately in the independence of the artist and, consequently, disliked the idea of any kind of commitment. I suppose his attitudes were broadly paternalist, but so were Brenda Thackeray's.

The real problem was that they lived together at an artificial level. As I've already said, love did not come easily to him – apart from that early relationship with Helen. But in his life with Brenda, he found a kind of emotional release which surprised him and, in due course, disturbed him. After the physical part of the relationship was sated, they both had time to think about their differences and to realise that it simply wasn't possible to live at that pitch of sexual expectation. Nevertheless, when Brenda left him, Michael Caradock was seriously upset. He had lived a fairly promiscuous life before meeting her and I think he experimented a little after they separated. Then there followed this revulsion about sex which occurs in the later books (not the *Coriolan Overture*, the other two) and in some of the essays. The really important theme of the *Promethead* is the way in which Waldeck's altruistic ambitions all seem to stem from a basic self-disgust, from the reaction against the sensual of a man who has explored sensuality fairly comprehensively. Given Michael Caradock's capacity for self-dramatisation I think that this was a deliberately exaggerated metaphor for his own experience. The sort of remorse that Caradock must ultimately have experienced after that *last* disastrous affair is beyond my imagination. He must have been at the depths of despair....

Rose Brandt in BBC radio programme.

The passionate puritan at last had found his white goddess. The description is not entirely fanciful: Brenda Thackeray –

a tall, superbly built young woman with a pale complexion, brilliant blue eyes and fair hair; a woman of impulsive good nature and generously immediate response; furthermore – as many of their friends will testify – someone with whom Caradock found the kind of sexually ecstatic realisation which so often eludes his characters and must have for many years eluded him; a complete and self-reliant woman.

Their early years together were, it seems, blissful. Caradock brought to her the kind of vivid intellectual challenge that Brenda Thackeray demanded: she offered to him the fulfilment of a rich and unrestrained relationship that he had been seeking for so many years, after that first éclat of self-discovery when he had been little more than a schoolboy.

But such passion brought with it tornadoes of jealousy, resentment, anger. Brenda Thackeray in her own right was a formidably good journalist, who had written several well-respected stories. She saw no reason to live in the shadow of Caradock's prospective reputation. And there were long, loud political arguments. On the one hand, the generous, impulsive liberal woman; on the other, the scathingly eloquent would-be patrician. For his part, Caradock had found the physical perfection that would not renounce her individuality or intellect. She would play with him in his sexual fantasies, but she would not indulge him in any way outside the bedroom. She remained all the time her own woman.

It would be invaluable to hear from her. But Mrs Thackeray will not speak....

Derek Parnell: In His Own Country. *Guildenstern, 1970.*

... Of course, Brenda was not going to sue anyone. It has nothing to do with that. I don't suppose she ever read the book.

Fay Mackail in BBC radio programme.

Much of the misapprehension – if indeed it is current at all – about Michael Caradock being a puritan full of repressed passion must be attributed to that rather sad book by Parnell which was rushed onto the stands while the newspaper ink was still drying on the murders. That was quite disgraceful as we all know: but it happens. There was a sort of Shavian paradox in Michael Caradock, in that he was a sensual man who enjoyed sensual pleasures – but he disliked, if not despised, himself for enjoying them as much. Now, this had nothing to do with revulsion or repulsion. It was a question of the recognition of a weakness. I eat rather a lot: but I have to put up with indigestion sometimes and I sometimes think that I indulge myself untowardly. And most of us know someone or other who is remorsefully drunken.

Michael was a heavy drinker and he did not have any puritan feeling in this area. In some curious way, he seemed to think he was quite moderate and always made jokes about the English obsession with pubs and opening times and the dry Welsh Sunday – as it used to be. But he was puritanical about sex: and in the traditionally rather hypocritical way of the rascal beadle. He used to thunder about what he called the Maltese falconers of Soho preying upon the presumably innocent indigenous species, but he was always fascinated by the porn shops. (Not that they were anything like as explicit in the early sixties as the emporia that we now enjoy.) I don't think this is especially unusual: sexual fantasy, excepting the genuinely deranged minority, has little to do with real life for most people. And they accept it. I can walk along the street with my wife, whom I love, admiring the thighs or ankles of some unknown girl, whom I momentarily desire in the rapturously careless confidence of never having to meet her. Michael Caradock was promiscuous by nature and ashamed of it. He wanted to be a thoroughly moderate man. Nothing to excess. But he did have this blind spot about heavy drinking.

James Faber in BBC radio programme.

The satirical novel *Broods of Folly* was a success. Caradock's earlier novels had received their share of attention and a fair measure of critical approbation, but the new book made him known to a much wider audience.

The rift which followed between Caradock and Alvin & Brandt, his publishers at the time, began much earlier than is supposed and there were more ramifications to their disagreement than Caradock's desire to write critical essays instead of novels. Certainly, there was a quite serious difference of opinion about Caradock's choice of epigraph, characteristically from Juvenal:

> Quiquid agunt homines – votum, timor, ira, voluptas
> gaudia, discursus – nostri farrago libelli est.
> et quando uberior vitiorum copia?

(*Whatever men do – their hope, fear, rage, pleasure, their commerce and frivolity – this book is a farrago of all that. And when were we so well off for vices?*).

Candida Lee, who worked as an editor with Alvin &
Brandt, records that the publishers felt, as she did, that
the epigraph was unnecessarily portentous and much too
heavy for a good 'knock-about satire'. 'Of course,' she
adds, 'none of us were aware at the time that Michael
Caradock wanted to branch out in a very serious and (in
my view) pretentious way. I thought it was a pity because
Caradock had a gift for comedy and could have achieved
more by writing other books in the same vein as *Broods of
Folly*. But he was an abnormally gloomy man: and it was
almost an insult to his image of himself. He wanted so
much to be taken seriously....'

It must be worth noting that Caradock, who took Juvenal
so *very* seriously, could not have seen satire as a light
literary form and that his reasons for graduating from it to
the absolutely 'straight' essay and then to the later
ambitious novels were much more complex and the result of
a deep self-examination. Caradock won the argument about
the epigraph by conceding to the publisher's insistence that
he make himself available for valuable publicity. This
became the subject for scathing comment by Brenda
Thackeray at moments when she and Caradock were less
than enchanted with each other, when (as we are told by
Frank Adeane) she taunted him with one of his own
favourite polemical quotations: 'No man can be a lover of
the true or the good unless he abhors the multitude.'
Adeane adds that this was very far from Brenda Thackeray's
own attitude, but that she welcomed 'the chance to beat
Caradock with one of his own cudgels'.

Broods of Folly may have enlarged Caradock's audience,

may even have enhanced his reputation, but it certainly also made him a number of enemies. He pretended not to care. Fay Mackail says that the puritanical wrath was real enough; but unlike James Faber, who stresses its sexual origins, Miss Mackail suggests that it was entirely cultural. Or to be more exact – aesthetic. 'He loathed the sixties: first of all television, colour magazines and then *pop*. The last straw was the vogue for what was at the time called "satire", which was sometimes quite funny and played to the rather uneasy smart middle classes who were profoundly unsure of themselves. For Michael it was the cavorting of a lot of undergraduates who hadn't grown up, abetted by an older generation of intellectual bullies who weren't very clever. Rightly or wrongly, he saw the sixties – the Beatles, those television programmes and all the rest of it – as a period of aesthetic decadence in which standards were irrevocably debased. I wonder sometimes if he would think we were now seeing something of a regeneration – but I very much doubt it. This fury (which was not always understood, even by people who knew him well) with what he thought was artistic rubbish was often confused with his political viewpoint, because pop and so on was (spuriously) identified with increasing liberalism. Michael wouldn't have minded if it had not all been taken seriously. He regarded television as the single most significant force for triviality in life. True, there were some personal problems. But his acknowledgement of no religious faith, his ethical doubts and this conviction that the one saving source of human inspiration – art – was betrayed and corrupted, combined to produce the despair that made him on the one hand try to isolate himself and on the other to take up intensely pessimistic and misanthropic ideas.'

*

Although Caradock's novels had been published in the United States (*Metaphors of Twenty Years* under the new title *Paradise Terrace*), it was not until *Broods of Folly* appeared there that he went on the first of three lecture tours. His academic credentials were more than usually impressive, so he was soon invited to take up short appointments as a visiting lecturer – or author in residence – on certain campuses. He declined. Caradock's notorious dislike of foreign places has already been described by some of his friends and his opinion of the United States, especially New York, was no more favourable than his early view of France and Italy. Fay Mackail persuaded him to go to France with her on a holiday, hoping to cure him of his xenophobic tendencies by showing him architectural treasures and splendid landscapes. Wryly, she admits she had no success. Nor, she adds, had Brenda Thackeray who insisted, early in their relationship, on their going to Florence and Rome.

Caradock's reluctance to take advantage of the potentially lucrative and prestigious offers from America was another source of disagreement with his publishers, but *Broods of Folly* was doing very well and they were anxious not to let relations deteriorate too far. The novel with its picaresque adventures – the absurd plot by the civil servants to assassinate their Minister, Crosswell; the conspiracy of a group of actors to take over the BBC; the ambition of Meurig

Bowen-Powys to be Archdruid of the British Confederation of Druidical Assemblies; not to mention its wealth of comic detail and richly ironic intrigue – delighted a great many people. But the sheer savagery of certain portrayals – notably the three lesbian sisters and the corrupt married couple who encouraged young artists – disturbed and offended a great many others who were not identified with or concerned with identifying the characters concerned. Once again, Caradock's hero undergoes humiliation at the hands of Lammergeier's mother who, although she detests her son, cannot resist abasing the innocent – by that stage of the novel, not so innocent – young man. But the real token of Caradock's extreme disillusionment, what Snow sees as his utterly nihilistic pessimism, must surely be in the last scene where Laertes Jones at last tracks down his sister to the penthouse of a property swindler and she dismisses him in a brief obscene sentence.

Caradock's disillusion with London life – not the city itself of which he was very fond, but the people amongst whom he moved – was well advanced long before his break with Brenda Thackeray. Although their separation may well have contributed to his decision to move away, my own opinion is that his intense disillusion, compounded of atrabilious and unrelenting observation and a fundamental rootlessness, had already predetermined a retreat somewhere. Stephen Lewis in his critical study suggests that Caradock's restlessness was caused by his refusal to recognise where his roots were; Richard Snow is sure that Caradock's refusal to belong and identify with any community, except perhaps for the small and elite university society of Oxford, stemmed from an inability to adjust, make allowances, tolerate. I must incline to Snow's view: though I do not accept his argument that Caradock's state of mind was the result of reactionary political philosophy and authoritarian social theories. The flaw was in the man himself and without it he would not have been the artist he was.

I knew Caradock personally throughout this period and detected, as did Fay Mackail, symptoms of restlessness years before he retired to Wales. Unlike the character in Camus' *La Peste* (an author whom Caradock deeply admired and, I suspect, envied for his stoic humanity), Caradock liked individuals but hated people. He was a fully accredited misanthropist. There is obviously more to hate in a city than in a village and it is my belief that Michael Caradock, who was always capable of rational-isation, took stock of a situation, in which he found himself increasingly often and for increasingly long periods in a state of hate, and decided he must make the break if he was to preserve his sanity. Fay Mackail will not go as far. 'I don't think there was ever any question of madness,' she says. 'It was more a matter of preserving the balance of his mind. He wanted above all else to be a man of reason, a controlled and discriminating man. I honestly believe that he would have liked his big novels to be positive, big affirmative works – all the people he admired are affirmative but his melancholy worked against him. When he became disillusioned by anything, however slight, the disappointment became a rage and the balance that was precious to him was upset.'

Extract from David Hayward's official biography.

357

In the early novels, the disillusion is pervasive, although *Angry Sunset* appears to end hopefully. Baldwin is victim of a cruel accident which renders him helpless in the town which he hated so virulently, cared for by parents whom he had used so badly: a sudden nemesis after his early display of callous ambition. Fleming is brought down by his own pride and his inability to identify with other people. Laertes Jones, most cruelly of all, loses his own innocence in the complicated process of trying to save that of his sister, is humiliated, recovers from the humiliation resolved to live chastely, only to find that the sister is irreversibly corrupted. She dismisses him with a bored and casual obscenity.

It is in this most interesting novel that Caradock begins comprehensively to work his themes into an elaborate tapestry. As Dr Stephen Lewis in his most helpful study has pointed out, the plot is based broadly upon the Miltonic masque, *Comus*; but Caradock is not just content with the son of Circe. We have Circe herself and a panoply of monsters readily identifiable with their Greek originals, from the delighted hints which Caradock supplies in his text. He refers to the 'youthful Aloidae of Independent Television' and it is an amusing enough description, until we remember that the Aloidae were the giants who tried to pile Ossa upon Olympus and Pelion on Ossa and also the people who imprisoned Ares, the Greek god of war, in a bronze jar. The metaphor for Lammergeier and his television colleagues who are so confident about their pretensions in communication and contemptuous of mere artists is extremely suitable. Of course, Comus was not one of the Aloidae, but here Caradock (on a rare occasion) requires the licence of discriminating between

Lammergeier's public character and his private nature. It is not entirely satisfactory, but it is not too difficult to accept.

The Greek monsters are all there, though some in sympathetic form: Echidna, in mythology the mother of a brood of monsters, seems to be a pleasant enough person in the character of the somewhat libidinous actress, Daphne, until we remember that the original was half-woman half-serpent who ate men alive – and until we detect that it is through her that Laertes meets a selection of the subsequent monstrous denizens of artistic London. The gloomy critic is Cerberus, capable of being soothed but ravening at his work as a defender of what he deems to be High Culture; and the Chimaera is the honestly hypochondriac television 'personality' who nevertheless strives to live up to other people's image of him. Although some of the characters are more significant than others, harpies, centaurs, cyclops, gorgons, greae, titans, Scylla, Minotaur – they are all there in one guise or another. Charybdis becomes a wicked married couple and Typhon, the enormous, cumbersome snake, the management of a broadcasting organisation.

In the later novels, the *Promethead* and *Laocoön*, Caradock profits from his early manipulation of models in developing his major themes using similar mythological parallels as guidelines – red threads – through his labyrinthine argument. These will be examined at length in a later section of this study under the general titles 'Philoctetes' and 'Heracles', but for the moment let us return to the categories of disillusion as presented and explored by this author.

H.-J. Kastner: Patterns of Despair. Hazel & Sims, 1973.

Richard heard Grandfather Watkins' genial booming voice at the door. He always made the same kind of entrance – banging on the wood with his stick two or three times and shouting out some kind of greeting. 'Where's young Dick then?' 'Anyone at home, here?' 'What about a glass of beer for an old man?' And then there he would be, with his white moustache and his blue eyes and his smile.

'I'm not going for a walk,' Richard said.

'What?' Richard's mother said. 'I thought you liked going for walks with Grandfather Watkins. What's the matter? You're not doing anything else.'

'I'm not going.'

Richard heard his father talking to Grandfather Watkins in the hall and tears started in his eyes. But he did not want to cry. He wanted to be firm about it but he did not want a fuss with everyone bullying or coaxing him.

'What's the matter, Richard? What's upset you?'

'I'm not upset. I just don't want to go.'

He heard his own voice quavering and shut his eyes very tight. Once again he saw the long, lean shape of the greyhound with the long leering jaws and the huge bounding stride gaining on the frantic hare and heard the cries of the men, hoarse and excited. And the delighted laughter of Grandfather Watkins saying, 'Look Dick, look at the *milgi* after the hare. Ho, ho! Oh, well done, wasn't it? He's got him, hasn't he?'

Richard had seen the big, fast, ugly dog catch the hare, but then he looked away. Another slower black dog had come scampering up after the first. It reminded Richard of the way bullies at school always had hangers-on. But the horrible thing was the laughter of Grandfather Watkins, who knew about birds and trees and flowers and who thought that Nature was often cruel.

He knew now that there would be a fuss. His mother would start scolding him and asking him questions. Why? What? When? He opened his eyes and saw that she was going to the door leading to the hall.

'All right, Richard,' she said. 'Stay there.'

She got there in time to stop his father and Grandfather Watkins coming into the kitchen. He heard their voices murmuring in the hall behind the closed door and suddenly Grandfather Watkins asking, 'But Dorothy, *why* doesn't he want to come?' And then shushing and murmuring again. He heard his father say in the voice adults used when they were being false and wanted you to believe something: 'Bit cold for a walk today, Father. Come and have a glass of beer in the dining room.'

Then, as his mother opened the door again, to slip back into the kitchen, Richard glimpsed the face of Grandfather Watkins, strangely hurt and disappointed....

Extract from 'The Quarry' in Metaphors of Twenty Years. *Vortex Press, 1950.*

Rhys felt a sudden bar of pain fall heavily across his chest. His breathing became laboured and almost at the same time he tripped on one of the half-rotted sleepers of the disused track. He fell heavily across the rusted rail which dug into his side. The palms of his hands flattened on the rough coal grit alongside the old line. He lay there for a second or two and then painfully tried to lift himself. He looked at his ugly gnarled hand grazed with little gouts of blood and ugly black specks of dirt and shiny coal embedded in it.

And he heard the kids laughing. From a safe distance the children who had killed the bright bird were laughing. Soon after they began to jeer....

Extract from 'Kingfisher' in Metaphors of Twenty Years. *Vortex Press, 1950.*

He was certainly fed up. Bored with a lot of the people that he knew and most of all with himself. But I think disillusion is too strong a word. I saw comparatively little of him because I was in and out of the country, mainly in Brussels and Strasbourg – but I also spent some time in Paris. When we did meet, he seemed much as he always had been. A lot more confident, of course, than the young man I'd first met; perhaps a little arrogant. And restless. I think Idris Lewis is right when he says that Michael should have taken some kind of job, whether or not he needed to: preferably something challenging. It would have helped quiet the restlessness and he probably would have drunk less.

I thought Brenda Thackeray was a charming girl. Very attractive and intelligent and whenever I saw him, she was usually there – because I like to think we got on very well. I certainly think a lot of this business about Michael getting disenchanted with everything because they split up is nonsense. The affair had been disintegrating for some time and I imagine Brenda was more upset about it than he was. You must remember Michael Caradock was a tremendous emotional pragmatist: he was quite capable of using his own experience as a base for fiction in this respect, so that a lot of people think that Waldeck's wife is Brenda (in *Promethead*). The truth is she is and she isn't: any more than the sexy woman in *Coriolan Overture* is Helen Westlake. (Incidentally, David Hayward, who did the biography, told me that Helen very much disliked that particular novel.) Anyway, it is an oversimplification to identify any of these fictional people with a real person in Caradock's life, though unquestionably he used them as models.

Another thing about the move from London to Wales was that soon after the break with Brenda Thackeray, he met the painter Diana Bradley, who lived in Glanmor. A further aspect of this pragmatism I've been talking about....

Michael Beauchamp-Beck in BBC radio programme.

What a boast it is to have survived the dawn and early morning of the new age of barbarism! A vain and absurd decade of affluence and licence and steady cheapening of standards in the name of equality, all lived in the shadow of destruction. Anarchy and the brutish state achieved in the death of art, the infection of culture. Liberal democracy tittering gaudily as the deceiving virus multiplies and takes hold and controls one decisive organ after another until there is the sudden realisation that the organism is paralysed: the ears roar, the eyes stare into a creamy blur, the mouth drools. All the ingenuity that went into the making of that accursed Bomb there was so much fuss about was not necessary after all. Yet when were the divine and heroic ages that preceded this the all-to-human colon of time in which we wait breathtakingly and in vain for the voice of God to reduce the milky whorls of chaos? Well, did I survive it? This weary, aching body drags itself from chair to bottle to window, fevered and ague-ridden. Alas the mind has long gone.

There was a moment when I thought I saw her and there was that desperate hint of hope and the clear pool of happiness, which receded naturally and inevitably from my lips. The sage warned us, after all: we suffer less from having to renounce our desires when we have trained our imagination to see the past as ugly. Is that all that I have accomplished? To sit here now on a pale winter day in a sweat of self-pity, anticipating the alcoholic shadows of remorse and fear, the premonition of my nothingness, the vacancy inside the centre of my sinful earth.

The eyase screech of their music, the bedlam jabber of their words, the smug smirking faces when tolerance became a fashion and charity a trend and lechery a way of partly living. Mean schoolboy japes and jibes in the name of satire. Barren indulgencies in the name of liberation. I suppose they cannot burn all the books and their own chance of survival is small. I take comfort in the Dark Ages. Something must survive out of which will come a new, another, Renaissance. The New Barbarians will go down simpering and posturing and attitudinising.

Meanwhile, I slaked my thirst, also, on the green mantle of their standing ponds. It is no wonder my wits are unsettled.

Only three o'clock. I wish it would get dark. I have begun to crave for darkness.

As he climbed up to the rock where Mr Jones sat, Tudor wondered about the old man's stoicism: to be a man of such sensitivity and such brilliance of intellect and to have been cheated twice of his right, condemned to work as a meagre clerk in the Council Offices when he might have been a fine academic or an artist because of ancient economic injustice and then because of an ailing, whimpering wife. And not to mind. Tudor felt his cheeks flush as he thought that his own family's relentless pursuit of money and possessions had had something to do with the economy that had deprived men like Jones of opportunities: but the old scholar did not seem to hold it against him. There was the odd twist of the mouth on a certain reflection or remark, the occasional sly look or irony: that was all.

Tudor plodded up the uneven path hacked out of the rough mountain grass and leading to a mineshaft long since out of use. There were astonishly beautiful rocks – old bits of ore, pyrites that in certain slants of light seemed almost as beautiful as fire opals. Walking back with Mr Jones from the rock, once, Tudor had rather affectedly picked up one of them and said as much. Mr Jones had taken it from him and studied it gravely. 'Clinkers,' he had said. 'Take it home and polish it, if you like. It's still a clinker.' Then the grim mouth had relaxed. 'So I suppose are opals.' Before the gaping mouth of the drift shaft, Tudor paused and looked in at the darkness. He had never read Dante Alighieri, but he knew about the meeting with Virgil at the mouth of Avernus and stood there for a moment in a self-conscious trance. Virgil did not appear and Tudor felt ashamed of himself. These literary affectations were childish and since meeting Jones every so often on the mountain he had begun to realise how pretentious and stupid they were. He looked around at the ugly mutilated hills and the sprawl of the industrial valley with its stacks, condensers, sooted brick sheds and humped buildings, the drab winding terraces layering the opposite mountain, the tips and holes and wasteland, the few smudges of green, dusty and ingrained with coal and stone and broken brick and clinker....

Once again a warm feeling of admiration for Jones glowed somewhere inside him. The way the old man had accepted not only the ugliness of the place, its defeated and shabby surrender to industrial depredation and human degradation, but also the drabness of his daily work in the brown council building, that smelt like all such places of poverty and anxiety and old clothes and distant disinfectant. It was amazing that, in spite of all that, Jones should speak with such fire and poetry. He had read so much and understood so much of what he had read. When he spoke bitterly, it was in generalities – about the incurable crassness of human folly, ambition, lust, avarice; it was never about his own disappointments, frustrations, the slights that he must have endured, the patient merit that he must know he had, which was so lavishly unrewarded. Whenever he talked about his own life, it was factual and dry, circumstantial; but then some association of ideas would take him off on a flight of wonderful rhetoric or lyrical pleasure or thunderous dissent about the works of God and man.

Until he had met Mr Jones, Tudor had known only of

stoicism through the character of Brutus in *Julius Caesar* and he did not think very much of Brutus. Then Jones had talked of Epictetus and Zeno of Citium and Marcus Aurelius and what it was really all about. Tudor hadn't had time to read them because of the syllabus and the Oxford entrance examination but, by God, he was going to....

Only then, at that moment, did it occur to him that it must have been a bitter experience for Jones when he had told him about the scholarship. He had been very full of himself: he had never thought about the feelings of the clever, eloquent man with his questing and unrequited intellect. And Mr Jones had jumped up and clasped him by the hand with the most jovial and sincere smile. No performance, no emotion. Just plain delight and goodwill.

Yet, surely, as he sat there in the spring and summer and autumn there must be some real anger in the man, as he thought of all that might have been, all that he might have achieved, places that he might have visited, women that he might have loved, discoveries, revelations, ecstasies: instead of shuffling through grubby forms and returning to a poky house in a row of houses and his pale, cloying, sickly wife. He must have known moments of acute despair. Tudor knew certainly that he would have fled, absconded, given up, even killed himself. But Jones had fought back out of disillusion into a kind of tranquillity. As far as he was concerned, the valley was peopled with salty, funny, worthwhile individuals and the phantoms of the past. And Marcus Aurelius, Homer, Erasmus of Rotterdam, Shakespeare, Jonson and Leonardo. It was odd that he had no love of music: odd in such a very *Welsh* person. And no liking for religion. He claimed that his life was very full. Yet, Tudor thought, there must be still times of paralysing desperation....

*

There's a fair strain of poetry in you, Tudor lad, that they haven't killed yet with their glosses and their cruxes and their variorum editions: but give them a chance and they will. Not because they are envious or destructive or malign. Far from it, they want what is best for you as your poor benighted parents want what is best for you: a nice degree and a nice little wife and a couple of brats crawling all over your epic novel and a good job at a university where you can squeeze the juice out of other unsuspecting kids in your turn. And the trouble with you, young Tudor, is that you are a bit of a snob socially and you are intellectually arrogant without being all that bright – so you will trade in the precious gift of your imagination for acceptance in the right circles by already acceptable and accepted people. That and money. You're in danger of mistaking a high finish for style, my lad. And that is disaster. There you are, now, talking about the Classical spirit and I can hear through all the flair, already, the academic modulation creeping in.

Well, it's not for me to tell you, to disillusion you now. After all, it might have happened to me and by the grace of something it did not. So I'm prejudiced. But I hope you will not wake out of a trance in your nice Oxford room in thirty years' time, as some youth drones away at you about Alexander Pope's terrible personal uncertainty, wondering where it all went so bloody wrong. And I hope too, on the other hand, that you don't let your imagination run riot and become one of the lost boys living in a never-never land somewhere in Soho. But I have my doubts. I'm not sure how tough the fibre is.

And I do not have the moral courage to actually tell you. Tell you what? To go on picking up clinkers thinking that they're opals....

Extracts from Angry Sunset. *Vortex Press, 1952.*

Suddenly the great clatter and squawk of noise as the light starts to fade. I cannot see it yet, but the birds know and the sea is out again beyond the mudflats. One or two people out there against the spongy green banks. Poking in the swamp for something. Savage will be checking his coverts and attending to his mysteries. Where was he rowing to...?

Lapwing, plover, grey heron, gull, dunlin, redshank... he lists them all.

Ah now. The first cry of the owl. Kweek. Again... kerweek. Somewhere above the house.

All the things I want to know; I would like to have known...

The confusion that tightened in my head. Let it break. Let it be dark....

Dew-bedabbled wretch scampering from the Gabriel pack inside the skull.

Much has been made of Caradock's professed hatred of Wales, but once again it is possible to quote one of his own admired sages, Nietzsche, in explanation of what must have been a convenient pose. The German philosopher wrote: 'When we talk in company we lose our unique tone of voice and this leads us to make statements which in no way correspond to our real thoughts.' I contend that this was so in Caradock's case and that his true and unique voice is to be found in the sympathy and imagery of the early stories and in the underrated novel, *Angry Sunset*.

There are three main branches in Caradock's work: the first and most important is the reflective, brooding pre-occupation with man and God and a hostile universe in which man's attempt to organise and rationalise meaningless and haphazard cosmic event is forever thwarted by his own basically ignoble character – manifest not only in war, oppression, cruelty and injustice, but also in the meaner and more personal faults of lust, envy, greed and commonplace selfishness. The universe, which in any case is indifferent, does not have to work towards man's destruction because he will achieve it gradually, or at a stroke, by his own efforts. The second aspect is the satirical investigation of human flaws as they occur at various levels of seriousness and importance. Here it seems obvious throughout Caradock's work that he regarded the blind pursuit of self-interest at the expense of the lives and feelings of others as the most grievous of failings. A determined outsider himself, he nevertheless castigated the attitude unmercifully in novel after novel, as we have already seen. Third, but not by any means unimportant, is the lyrical and sympathetic man who, almost in spite of himself, *has* to identify with others – and this is the Caradock of *Metaphors of Twenty Years*, of the five moving, sometimes beautiful, stories all set in his native

Wales; and of the gentle and perceptive *Angry Sunset*. It is also the Caradock of the lyrical essays, published in the mature, often demanding volume of essays *The Philosopher's Stone*, and the same kind of lyrical and compassionate grace may be found in many passages in the two major novels, *Promethead* and *Laocoön*.

It is also worth noting that Caradock's return to Wales was marked by the light and elegantly funny sketch *A Coriolan Overture*. Richard Snow, in his painstaking but hostile work on Caradock, consistently uses this book as an example of Caradock's elitist contempt for his origins. It is nothing of the sort, it is a comic but merciless satire on the affectations of a young man who is far too above himself and the background portrait of the community against which he plays out his harlequinade is essentially sympathetic.

Caradock went back to Wales, I submit, because he had rediscovered in himself the certainty that this was where he belonged and for a while he was very happy there. He was accepted by the local people at Glanmor and, in his distant way, he tried to be as much as possible one of them. That it should all have ended so violently and tragically is one of the strokes of fate that Caradock himself saw as part of any man's impersonal doom. It is obvious that the events which led to his death could have occurred anywhere and had nothing whatsoever to do with the place in which they occurred and did not affect in any way the writer's reconciliation with the country of his birth.

Extract from Stephen Lewis: The Novels of Michael Caradock. *Molyneux, 1971.*

I think, quite obviously and naturally, the various critics have found in Caradock's work what they wanted to find. And I suppose it suggests a certain richness that they should have been able to do so. For my money, the very diligent Stephen Lewis is quite wrong about Michael's motives in returning to Wales: there was certainly no question of a desire to reconcile himself to the land of his fathers or anything like that. I used to visit him there quite often in the last few years of his life, admittedly with a view to trying to persuade him to return to Oxford, because he was obviously sinking further and further into the Slough of Despond and drinking much too heavily. He maintained his loathing of the place and the people – and used to draw parallels between himself and Nietzsche, which he was (incidentally) very fond of doing. These were of course all superficial. But you know how Nietzsche always professed to detest Germany and Germans to the extent of claiming to be a Polish aristocrat. Michael did not go *that* far, but only because there was no one identifiably Polish in his family.

There was, if you like, a brief period of temporary rapprochement on his part, shortly after he moved there, but this was directly connected to his real reasons for going – he was bored with London and he had just met Diana Bradley. I think Beauchamp-Beck has already said something about what he calls Caradock's 'emotional pragmatism'. And I agree with him. Michael wanted to be absolutely certain of his own comfort: that is to say, on the one hand, the satisfaction of his sensual appetites; and, on the other, the reassuring knowledge that there was someone around who would see to his needs and administer his life. Brenda was quite happy to do the one but not the other, but Michael was very skilful at enlisting others. In Diana Bradley he found someone who was capable of both requirements and willing to apply herself to each.

However, to get back to the critics: Snow obviously reads, in his paranoid way, a lot of things into the novels that were not intended and which he would see refuted if he bothered to study Caradock's essays. Haller – well, I must say I don't quite know what to make of Haller, but it is vastly entertaining. The best of them all is Kastner. But the one thing he is confused about, in what is otherwise an excellent book, is Michael's attitude to two of his most important influences – Wagner and Joyce. Quite early on he seems to equate the general purpose of these two enormously different men of genius in *The Ring* and *Finnegans Wake*, which seems to be a fairly impenetrable association – if you remember, this all relates to man's need for some regenerative shock if total and ghastly doom is to be avoided. Well, it seems obvious to me that there is an enormous difference between these two works. Wagner's is, in human terms, essentially nihilistic. True, there is a sort of recorso in that the Rhinegold returns to the river nymphs, but only after the fall of the gods themselves and the destruction of the new white hope, Siegfried. Joyce's great book on the other hand is affirmative. That is what is so attractive about Joyce, however episodically pessimistic he can be: the outlook is always affirmative. He deals with the central and recurring theme of the fall of Man, but in Joyce this is followed by a regeneration and a real recycling of forces that must be essentially optimistic. Where this concerns Caradock is that Kastner tries to find in him an amalgam of affirmation and nihilism based on Caradock's own interest in the divine, heroic, human cycle broadly after Vico, which is catalysed by the voice of God breathing over chaos. The difference is that Michael Caradock was convinced that the voice of God was silenced, or had gone off somewhere else, and that there was no hope. There weren't even any Rhinemaidens in the long term: only entropy – the breathing down to nothingness of the entire cosmos – as an end. He was envious of Joyce's power of affirmation, as he was envious of Camus', and deeply admired *Finnegans Wake* as a huge technical achievement and also as a massive synthesis of regenerative myth.

This pessimism of his began to envelop him, which is why – as I say – several of his friends tried to persuade him to move back to England out of semi-reclusion. He was, certainly, quite happy there for a while, with Diana Bradley: but then events began to move in certain directions and served only to convince him of the malignity of chance and the certainty of man's ultimate humiliation.

James Faber in BBC radio programme.

Diana Bradley, when she met Michael Caradock at the London flat of the Welsh painter Leighton Rees, was seven years older than him. Once again the pattern is a familiar one and we find Caradock drawn to an older woman of unmistakable maturity and intelligence, corresponding to a particular physical type. Michael Beauchamp-Beck describes her as: 'Tawny-haired, quite tall, strongly built – very much the kind of woman that attracted Michael, with a not-quite beautiful, rather serene face and a full, accommodating figure. She is, as you know, a very intelligent woman indeed and an extremely good painter. As far as I was concerned, and I think Idris would agree and so would Fay, who has always been characteristically honest and unselfish about these things, she was absolutely ideal for Michael and he was almost so for her. They were complementary in so many ways and Diana was blessed with a really authentic serenity which was capable of adapting to Michael's vicissitudes of gloom.... He worked very much, cerebrally, by intuitive or imaginative leaps which he then tried to explain to himself: he did not have a logical mind and he was not spectacularly intelligent. Diana was (and of course is) wonderfully clear-headed and thinks things through quite ruthlessly. I don't mean that she is ruthless to other people but she refuses to distort fact for anyone's convenience, least of all her own. She prefers to adjust to factual exigencies. Now, given that, the balance of their temperaments was most of all apparent in their attitude to art – even to pictures. Michael was dispassionate and she was involved. If he looked at something, he saw it always in a kind of perspective in which he was included – with the same dispassion. Diana tried to get inside the mind and, indeed, the spirit of the artist concerned, so that she became emotionally involved with what he was trying to do. Michael was never emotionally involved in a work of art, except perhaps in music at the most naïve and superficial level. So there was an equilibrium. There was also emotional understanding and physical attraction. What happened was an appalling paradigm of waste and folly.'

Diana Bradley lived in a cottage near the Welsh seaside village of Glanmor to which she invited Caradock. He was impressed by the beauty of the place – the variety of the scenery, the light on sea and river, the profusion of wildlife, revealing (to the astonishment of old friends such as Beauchamp-Beck and Faber) a childhood enthusiasm for natural history. Even more he was delighted by the way in which Miss Bradley, an Englishwoman, was welcomed, respected and absolutely accepted by the country people whom they met together in pubs to which she introduced him. Observing his restlessness and his disenchantment with London, she suggested that he stay indefinitely with her, being totally indifferent (even in Wales) to convention and gossip, until he sorted out some important ideas relating to his work and what he wanted to do with himself. Caradock accepted the invitation, saw the empty house on the small islet in the estuary near Glanmor, and made the significant, indeed fateful, decision to return to live in Wales. Rose Brandt comments illuminatingly: 'It's too easy to suggest that this decision was all a mere question of convenience because Diana Bradley was there and they were sexually compatible. Apart from disparaging the quality of their relationship which seems to have been full and mutually satisfying, it discounts the quite natural desire of Michael Caradock to stop hating irrationally, to find out the truth, as a mature and better equipped person, about his real relationship with the place and the people he claimed to have renounced. I think that when he left London, he was very hopeful. After all, he had been working on his essays and he had a lot more that he wanted to write and he was thinking about *Promethead*, the *Laocoön* book and a couple of other ideas. Diana's tranquillity – it's the best word I can think of to describe it – would see him through his own crises of doubt.'

Extract from David Hayward's official biography.

7. Ext. Glanmor. Day. View of Glanmor estuary and bay from western cliff (Cefn Wrynach). Slow panning shot taking in Caradock's house and island, traversing estuary to eastern headland (Glanwydden) with village and harbour in the foreground...

MUSIC: Richard Strauss: *Tod und Verklärung* (7.)

Camera dips in on returning panning shot over White House and resumes slow even shot...

Fade music and hold under

(V/O) *Diana Bradley*: Michael Caradock came here originally because he felt that he had lost his sense of purpose as an artist.

Camera travels back across island, over western district of village and woodland to Cefn Wrynach

Hold MUSIC.

8. Ext. Bradley Cottage. Day. Diana Bradley looking out to sea from garden of cottage on Cefn Wrynach

(V/O) *Bradley*: This was something he believed was all too easily achieved in the company of other writers and artists and he had determined

377

to try to discover in comparative isolation the real impetus behind his desire to write and to explore certain themes that were vitally important to him....

Diana Bradley, with her back to the sea, looking directly at camera. Cottage partly in left of shot	*Bradley*: (Sync.) We lived together here for a brief but happy time until he moved to the large house on the little island at the mouth of the estuary. Michael Caradock found, at first, the kind of quietness he needed in order
Move in on Diana Bradley slowly	to take stock of his own ambition and particular talent. While here, he completed the last draft of his novel *Promethead* as well as a book of essays and the draft that remains of his last novel, generally called *Laocoön*. He also began work on two other projects and worked on sketches for longer literary essays and, I think, a
c.u. Diana Bradley	collection of aphorisms. These he appears to have destroyed, since there is no trace in his papers of any projected work. And this perhaps is an

378

indication of his despairing state of mind at the time of his murder. That he might have been helped by many people, who respected his work and who loved the man, is possible but not necessarily certain. He was a proud and secret man, bitterly critical of himself in almost all respects: many of those who knew him best believe that he could no longer find the drive or energy necessary to complete the kind of work he would have wished to attempt. He believed that the struggle (as he saw it) was already lost and there was no further point in battling on.

Profile shot of Diana Bradley looking towards estuary with house and island

9. Ext. Caradock islet. Day. Tracking shot past Diana Bradley, zooming in on Caradock's house on islet, the huge blank windows reflecting the light off the water

(V/O) That he should have died so suddenly and so cruelly is, nevertheless, an irony that would have made him nod in sardonic recognition of a purposeless universe quite without pity or love.

10. Ext. D. Bradley in garden. Day. Cut to close up of Diana Bradley on cliff

It is unfortunately too late for those of us who cared to try *again* to disprove his case.

11. Ext. Caradock house.   Peak MUSIC. (*Tod und*
Day. Cut to windows of   *Verklärung*)
empty house

Sequence from television programme, 'Landscape of a Prophet'.

'One thing that you must never allow yourself, Ganuret,' said the General, wheeling suddenly in mid-step and pausing. 'And that is the luxury of despair. You must keep going whatever the doubt and however certain you may be that what you are doing is wrong or unworthy. You can repair mistakes – even mistakes which have brought suffering to others. You can *not* restore the breaches in the thin sea-wall of confidence that keeps out the turbulent, blindly destructive torrents of chaos and cerebral anarchy. In your case, my boy, I suppose it is a matter of a blank page or a false start: but it can be otherwise. It is even true of people that you allege you love. And while despair is a luxury, love is a necessity of life. Charity. Love. Call it what you will. It is more important than pride, chastity, the sanctimonious self-congratulation of the pure in heart.'

Once again there was on the old leonine face a flicker of remembered pain. Not an actual spasm any more of real suffering, but the shadowy recollection of something that had once been almost unendurable. Ganuret said nothing. He felt he should ask some question, prompt the General: he was certainly anxious for Waldeck to go on talking, to learn more. The old man looked across the room at him and came ponderously towards the dark, highly polished

380

table with its gleaming accoutrements, the heavy expensive silver, used for the ritual dinner of the whole staff every so often, now scattered at random along the long table.

Waldeck sat down heavily and leaned on the table. He looked up at Ganuret from beneath his eyebrows: but with the uncertain, almost pleading expression of someone who awaited justice after a particularly heinous confession. There was in his face, in the face of this once powerful, almost indomitable, still unbroken, man, something innocent, pathetic and childlike.

'Some details are not important,' the General said. 'Let me warn you about the dangers of self-prescribed catharses. The feeling of guilt is luxurious sometimes and the diagnosis is exhilarating. After the last war when I was the leader of my nation, at peril and despised by my own allies as an opportunist, I stood out against enormous forces that seemed certain to crush us. When it was over I could have seized power. It would have meant a short, bloody civil war which I should have unquestionably won: because I was still more attractive to my perfidious friends in other countries than any of my rivals. I was approached by various agencies, within and without. I treated them with equal contempt. And I was rejected by my own people. Hubris if you wish. When things began to go wrong, I was approached again. And this time, Ganuret, I was tempted. And therein, my boy, lies the impurity. I submitted to the insanity of the moment, in that for three days I struggled with my conscience. I desired so much to serve. I was absolute in my conviction that I could render service and that I was fit to do so. Any means would be justified by my own inevitable justice. At the end of the struggle I believe I was really insane – although I was able to resist the temptation, the lure of the vengeful and the rapacious. I produced feverish physical symptoms, tiresome aches and disorders, a bunching and knotting of muscles so that I believed I was quivering uncontrollably. I used to gaze at my perfectly steady hand waiting for it to jerk wantonly in some spasm of nervous defection. To this day I feel here, about my neck and shoulders, a terrible tension....

'Ganz was a young officer at the time. About your own age at this moment. We did not know each other, but by chance it was he who drove me in an army vehicle to the mountains. We talked. I do not remember what I said. Years later, he approached me and asked to join me.'

He paused as though waiting for Ganuret to speak, without ever shifting his gaze, steady and cavern-eyed, from Ganuret's face. When nothing was said he went on.

'I am afraid of mountains,' he said. 'I do not understand why but they fill me with a kind of awe that is only another word for terror. It may be a simple transferred vertigo: in that I am able easily to transport myself to the edge of some abyss in imagination where I know I shall fall. As a child, I used to pass a spire that seemed to me very tall and imagine myself placed at its pinnacle, knowing that I must unquestionably smash to earth. But I do not think so. Mountains that seethed into their dead mouldings, as this very earth took form and went on seething in the primal darkness, are not – for me – dead. I sense their power, their capacity to seethe and bunch and contract or melt and stream sluggishly across forests and pastures rendering a temporal desert. The richness of the soil in subsequent ages is, for all we know, an irrelevance.

'I went up into the mountains to a village. Ganz drove me there because he was aide to a brigadier who had served under me and who did not want me eliminated. I was terrified, Ganuret. I used to walk out in the morning and stare across a huge bowl pinnacled and buttressed with peaks of ice. And there, suddenly, out of the mist of the morning, I would see towering, kilometres, hundreds of kilometres, away, the terrible face of God in some immense congealment of frozen time. I stayed there in isolation. Of course, I exchanged daily politenesses with local people who thought I was strange and a little mad, but that was all. In a state of permanent fear, I took the opportunity to examine my spiritual chaos.'

Ganuret was profoundly uncomfortable. The intensity of the old man's speech and expression disconcerted him and he wished that Ganz or even Claudian were there to share in this apparently agonising disclosure. At the same time he felt sure that had they been present, the General would have said nothing of this sort. He would have contributed to argument and even led it, he might even have been in a rhetorical mood – prepared to speak authoritatively and compellingly to a willing audience, or he would have listened, smiling and almost relaxed, interjecting only with little grunts and chuckles which nevertheless immediately drew attention away from whomsoever was speaking. Ganuret knew that this was highly privileged conversation. The old man was trying to tell him something of importance and the sadness of it was that Ganuret, even if he had understood what the message was, would have been unable to act upon it, and that the General was not able to see that this same message was being directed at someone ineffectual – in Waldeck's own terms, impotent.

'If you are a true poet, Ganuret,' the General said, 'you will understand this in spite of yourself. It is not my experience. It has little to do with politics or ethics or law. It is the unformed question in the mind of the most simple man, however inarticulate, however brutal, however dimly vegetable in his perceptions – why should we suffer, why should I survive? It is more basic and more despairing than the existentialist casuistry about suicide. It has little to do with power or ambition or philanthropy.'

The General pushed his chair back and with short, heavy arms began to rub the powerful muscles of his shoulders near the base of the neck. He winced once or twice as he did so and then made a perceptible effort to relax. Nevertheless, his thick, strong neck seemed to remain painfully immobile and there was the same bunched tension about the set of his massive torso.

He got up and began to walk about the room again, but more freely. The obsessional pacing – eight steps to the angle of a sideboard, right seven paces to one of the dining chairs set under the pastoral landscape, seven paces back to the point (at the edge of the table) where he had started – now became an aimless, restless movement from one article of furniture to another. As he spoke, Waldeck picked up objects, studied them, weighed them, in the case of a small porcelain figure seemed to consider smashing it before replacing it exactly and gently.

'Do not think that I merely reacted to my political humiliation, my disappointments, my own weakness and foolishness and baseless vanity. I experienced despair at a loveless, Godless universe in which I, most of all, found it impossible to believe and in which I was condemned to live without the gift of being able to love. Of course, I had tried to drown myself in the illusion of loving – passionate love of women when I was so intensely myself, a ferocious compassion for others when I thought I was so much part of them. An adolescent episode, false as May-morning religious fervour with sun striking onto the stone floor through the holy colour of the windows. Then, alone in the mountains where I was frightened by the closeness of the sky, there was no escape from my own emptiness. I understood only scorn and I felt for the most part hatred – not for this or that individual, but for all the *works* of men. And I mean the works, Ganuret: the ticking and tocking, cog-fitting technology of mechanical science and psychology. Not the thoughts, the works. Not the pure, neutral, inalienable truth, not the imaginative madness; but the rational organisation of genius into power. It does not matter what sort of power. And what I hated was the greed and envy and lust and pride that in their orgiastic multiple coupling and quadrupling bred the Spirit of Man. My God! The cosmic sufferers are not the political or religious martyrs, but the few dozen great thinkers who are studied for examinations.

'I was caught suddenly in a snowstorm. It was nothing much. But I was frightened of the abyss across the edge of which I must blunder. I should like to have made some Byronic gesture and stood on a crag with my head bared insulting God or the gods. I was merely frightened, huddled into myself, burbling nonsense like a small child comforting itself, hugging my own grotesque body, this squat, strong corpse.... A man with one of those creased, brown, mountain faces, wrinkled blue eyes, came out of a flurry of the snow and said something gruff and comic in a dialect too thick for me to understand. But he knew I was frightened. It was not hard to see, after all. He took me to an inn, where I was... accepted.

'In due course, someone recognised me from old newspaper pictures. People in little villages, however remote, have old pictures. But they let me alone. Perhaps because I had been found frightened in what for them was a little squall of snow, in those high mountains where the leaden clouds threatened to crush you. General Waldeck? They were somehow not impressed, but impressed in spite of themselves. It took an effort to enter their inns uninvited and unaccompanied, but I did. They did not make a fuss, but they let me drink with them. All that is past, now, Ganuret. There are ski lifts and plastic bars and gift shops and smart little shops and chalets on easy terms.

'It was there I tried, in a week or so of exile, to face up to the loneliness of existence and my own appalling lack of common goodwill. I used them sentimentally as my lungs used their icy mountain air to sear themselves clean. And I think I feared them for never knowing, much less understanding, much less needing to understand, the impurities of spirit that were maddening me. The other impurities seemed as nothing – but that was a deception....'

He paused. Ganuret gazed at him with tears dribbling along his nose and was able to say nothing.

'Do you know the *Parzival* of Wolfram von Eschenbach? I don't suppose you do. Most poets are astonishingly ignorant of things they cannot cannibalise. It is a work of imagination and compassion. The ascetic longing which is in most of us, the disavowal of the flesh that we crave, our frenzy for punishment and mortification, is nothing – nothing. The Grail is something human – a matter for striving now and not for a reward elsewhere in some desert of purity where *also* no birds sing. I could not love, Ganuret; least of all could I love my fellow man. But I thought I could serve still.'

His aimless pacing had taken him to the door, where he turned and looked hard at Ganuret. The heavy shoulders shrugged. Then exasperated he pulled open the ornate double doors and went out, leaving them open. Ganuret's mind was awash with images and suppositions. Only then did he become aware of the clawing tension inside him. He murmured something quite unintelligible in order to make some kind of noise and stirred, a little dazed, in the upright chair, where he had been sitting absolutely still.

When he looked up the dark girl called Angela was standing at the door. She was wearing a black velvet dress, décolletée. Her hair seemed as black and as soft as the dress, her face very white, beautifully structured, the light somehow emphasising the dark hollows below the delicate cheekbones, her mouth seemed very red. Unsmiling, she came into the room, moving gracefully, the skirts of the long velvet dress stirring about her hips. She paused at the end of the table and looked at him, still without smiling, before sitting down.

'I don't know you,' she said. 'Who are you?'

Extract from Promethead. *Hazel & Sims, 1967.*

Perhaps one of the most displeasing of all Caradock's postures is the so-called Charity against Chastity argument which is one of the main themes of the *Promethead* novel. The conflict, at best a fairly ersatz product of German romantic thought, is derived from Wolfram von Eschenbach through Wagner and the sonorous interpreters of Wagner who have insisted so tirelessly that there is coherent and significant thought behind the interminable and turgid effusions of his music dramas. At its most simply stated, it suggests the Grail is not a symbol for a rigorously pure and chaste ideal but of human love and compassion and the highest form of striving for such attainments. What nobody seems to bother to have asked is why the two ideals should be mutually exclusive. It is surely possibly for an ascetic to feel the most intense compassion for his fellow men: at the same time I should be the last to suggest that an ascetic morality and an ethic of chastity are essential to human warmth and brotherly love.

What interests Caradock is not the vague philosophic symbolism but the possibility of identifying himself once again in his familiar mythopoeic manner with yet another bitter, suffering, semi-misanthropic character – this time Amfortas. But before examining the nature of this latest example of image-making, the self-admiring iconoplaticism of which Caradock never tired, it is worth pausing to take a look at this triumphant charity about which Waldeck in *Promethead* goes on at such length, though rather more intelligibly than Landgrave in the last novel, called *Laocoön*. We can ignore the entire theme of chastity. Caradock's life was, as is generally accepted, not remarkable for restraint in this respect; and the whole apparatus of guilt is fairly transparently another melodramatic pose intended to suggest great depths of sensitivity and to build up an impression of spiritual anguish in an essentially barren and arid personality. When we examine the brand of charity that Caradock chooses to advertise, we find however that it had little or nothing to do with the ordinary lives of decent, worried, considerate people who want to do the best they can for their families, friends and neighbours without in any way causing discomfort or suffering to others. Such folk never interested Caradock, as may be seen throughout his work, but it is in the two monsters of self-regard whom we must see as projections of the author himself as he saw himself, Waldeck and Landgrave, that he expresses most unequivocally, through the aloof and nihilistic contemplation of human suffering and doom, the *sine qua non* of the classic elitist apostles of high culture, his massive contempt for the rest of humanity. And the feeling of the two men is not even believable at flesh-and-blood level. They are both literary creations and if they live at all it is some kind of chilled ichor that flows through their bodies, allowing them to indulge in their elaborate fantasies of cerebral pain and torment on their Olympian crags, well away from the inconvenience, the taint, the tears and sweat and smells of the real thing.

Extract from Richard Snow: The View from Lemnos. *Medusa Books, 1972.*

Prometheus and Epimetheus... Twinn'd brothers of one womb, Whose procreation, residence, and birth, Scarce is dividant, touch them with several fortunes; The greater scorns the lesser: not nature, To whom all sores lay siege can bear great fortune, But by contempt of nature. Raise me this beggar, and deny't that lord; The senator shall bear contempt hereditary, The beggar native honour....

Poor Timon ranting in his cave. A cave on an island where he lives with the stench of his own wounded imagination. Are Phrynia and Timandra whores? Perhaps. But do they deserve the black vitriol of his hatred? And do you, I wonder? I think of you now only in the lewdest positions, endlessly on heat, titillating your body and imagination with the discovery you have made, that sense of power. Wherever you are, however you are clothed, whatever you are doing, you are stretched wide in moaning, sobbing, demanding and commanding ecstasy of orgasmic corruption. And was it I who corrupted you, my rose of Hell?

The confused weeping of a clever man here in this room as he described what had happened. I did not want to hear. I imagined it too well. I knew each tremor, the tracing of a sharp fingernail along a twitching nerve, the flicker of the tip of a tongue at some tender petal, the pinch of flesh, the smooth velvet limbs slowly moving under trembling tense fingers, each frisson, each kick and sob of surrender and weakness. So you laughed. That which you would not do you must do. But it is tears that you crave, not laughter. You humiliate. You betray and sow betrayal. Your devilish black hair, and white skin and mocking eyes, your exquisite skin, the fragile bones, the shadows on your face.

Pandora too. Emasculate Timon rants in his cave and the sky clears with the approach of night. Tomorrow the cloud will have cleared. It will be a crisp, winter day. A time to *have once gone out onto the headland and watched the flights of the geese and the waterfowl and listen to the intense excitement of a winter day, so much more live than the routine buzz of summer and somnolent afternoons. Too late. Fitful, nightmare sleep peopled by reptiles and insects, feverish, trembling hand fumbling at the new bottle.... Nothing remains that is fresh or clean.... Timon must rant dumbly at the tarnished mirror.*

The boats – one, two, three, four – all coming in as night comes.

It was a strange feeling of peace. Landgrave sipped the wine which had a dulcet flavour and looked across at the woman. She was tall and full-bodied, a little younger than himself. Her face was serene, lined discreetly by the years; her hair was chestnut coloured with reddish glints in the sunlight; her eyes were greyish blue and calm; her lips were tilted very gently in the beginnings of a smile.

'Thank you,' Landgrave said. 'I really am most grateful.'

'I'm glad that you feel better,' she said. 'I was a little worried at the time, as well as frightened. You know what it's like when you approach a complete stranger....'

'Alas, I do not,' Landgrave said. 'That is something I have never done.'

'No?' she said. 'Well, anyway, you looked very ill and I knew we were at the same hotel. In any case, I recognised you.'

'It was the heat,' Landgrave said. 'It's unexpectedly hot for the time of year, don't you think? And you are quite right: I have not been well. I am trying to revisit everything that moved me or, dare I say, inspired me when I was young – before I become too old to recognise what it was that filled me with such exhilaration or wonder or fear or hope. And I have probably been rushing at it. An intellectual gluttony is the worst.'

The woman laughed. A deep, soft, gentle sound. Her clear eyes were alight and there seemed to pass between them a sensation of pleasure and contentment.

'Your name is...?'

'Catherine,' she said. 'The second name doesn't matter and it doesn't belong to me. But for the record it's Gray. I've been divorced for many years.'

'I've already told you mine.'

'I already knew who you were,' she smiled at him. 'I don't think I need say any more: that I've read your books and admire them?'

He shook his head. The pain seemed to be over for the time being. He felt better – much better for her company.

'And what were you revisiting in Poitou?' she asked.

'Something that I first saw by chance in Angoulême. The west front of the cathedral – the representation of the Last Judgement. It once meant a great deal, as did so much Gothic splendour: the patience and high purpose, the effort and dedication of art and craftsmanship stretching for something beyond pride and profit. I think I rather hoped that something of the same enthusiasm would revisit me. And then I had someone drive me out to Lusignan because Jean de Berry once had a château there, allegedly built by Melusine who was half lovely woman and half serpent....'

Landgrave saw something happen in Catherine's eyes and knew that it was recognition of some coincidence that is delightful, amusing and a little frightening.

'I think I was looking for the same hillside,' she said. 'The peasant ploughing below and the others working on the slopes, tending the vines and looking after the sheep....'

'The brown unawakened landscape and the troubled blue sky.'

'Indeed...'

> 'The ioyous time now nigheth fast
> That shall allegge this bitter blast
> And slake the winters sorrowe....'

'Where are you going to next?'

'I think to Paris. I travel by train or aeroplane so I'm more or less obliged to radiate from some central point.'

'And then?'

'Nîmes, I think.'

'Let me drive you there. I'm on holiday. I have no plans.'

In the late sun of the afternoon, Landgrave felt once again the tranquillity that had eluded him for so long, the dangerous and perhaps fatal dawning of what he had always pretended was love. Yet this was not the love, wherein wanton youth walloweth... follye mixt with bitternesse and sorow sawced with repentaunce. The leaden shaft had not struck him in the heel, at first unnoticeable but rankling more and inwardly beginning to fester. He did not believe so. Yet it would not have been the first time that he had succumbed to the idyllic fallacy only to find after a surfeit of

393

vayne iollitie and lustfull pleasaunce that acrid sauce of sorrow lingering on his tongue and sickly in his memory.

Seeing very clearly, as though on the opposite hill, the turrets and crenellations of the duke's castle and the dun, workable land at its walls, he was once again moved out of time into an Oxford garden at the turn of the year from winter into spring when there was the same feeling of expectancy, the recollection of last year's flowers, the grey stones of ancient walls showing above and through bare branches and the feeling of peace, pleasure, hope. He could no longer remember her face properly, only the impression of serenity, certainty, that he had needed and still seemed to need. It was surely a little ridiculous. But then death had been a long way off and the knowledge of it was a youthful luxury for serious midnight argument, grave unwrinkled faces nodding sagely over eternity.

Catherine was watching him: but tranquilly.

'Well?' she said. 'Do we travel together?'

'I'd like to very much,' Landgrave said.

They smiled at each other. The wine was finished and it was becoming cold as the sun fell away behind the hill.

'Dinner is at seven,' she said. 'I think I'd like to change first. Shall I say that we will be sharing a table?'

'No. I'll see to it.'

As he got up, Landgrave forgot the numbness in his right leg and staggered a little. Catherine had been waiting for him to perform the ritual and pleasant courtesy of moving her chair and escorting her away. She made no fuss about it, but with a small gesture of her hand, she reached out towards him. It was an involuntary movement which she tried to resist as it occurred; but that too was reassuring. Landgrave stood still, recovered and moved around the table to her.

Extract from 'March' sequence from Laocoön *novel. Hazel & Sims, posthumous.*

Caradock's arrival in Wales at Glanmor was peaceful. Although the local people, as was normal enough, gossiped a little about his relationship with Diana Bradley, all but a very few were tolerant enough of the unconventional ways of artists. At the same time, they were more disposed to be indulgent to her, someone they liked and accepted who was English, than they were to him – a Welshman who made something of a point of unWelshness and who could not speak the Welsh language. Caradock, rather surprisingly, made friends quickly with certain of the villagers, notably Emlyn Savage, a gamekeeper who had once served as a Chief Petty Officer in the Royal Navy; and with Anthony Simpson, the local GP. Through Simpson, who had a keen interest in modern literature and who liked to talk philosophy, he met Hugh Morgan – a History teacher, who worked in a town not far from Glanmor but who lived in the village with his young and beautiful wife, Mair. Dr Simpson and the Morgans were friends of Diana Bradley with whom they exchanged casual visits from time to time. In a way that would have astonished Caradock's Oxford and London acquaintance, he showed himself affably inclined to becoming involved in village life. He went, with Diana Bradley, to one or two of the pubs and tried to emulate her own easy association with village people –

something that Dr Simpson did not do, because it would have been frowned upon for the family doctor to be seen drinking in public; and something that Hugh and Mair Morgan did not do because people of their social pretensions did not drink in village pubs, still largely the territory of men. The foreign and 'fast' Miss Bradley was an acknowledged bohemian in whom such eccentricities were only to be expected.

Dr Simpson notes that Caradock seemed to settle down easily: '... which rather surprised me because I'd thought we were very much a backwater, especially for someone who had been in the thick of it all in London. Rather different for an artist – a painter like Diana; but for a novelist, especially a satirical novelist interested essentially in a highly artificial and sophisticated society, I didn't think Glanmor would have much to offer. For the first couple of years, we had some very good evenings, and when he moved out onto the island, I for one was delighted he'd decided to settle in Glanmor. He was tremendously stimulating and very kind intellectually. He let you find your own way and if Voltaire or Plato or someone had already been there once and back again, he told you about it quite gently in some subsequent chat, the way I imagine a good tutor would. Medical students, needless to say, are used to gruffer treatment. At the same time, there was a kind of brooding, melancholy quality about him which I noticed from the beginning. It got worse over the years and when I saw him in later years, I tried to persuade him to consider treatment, as tactfully as I could. I only wish I'd realised all those years ago, when he first arrived here, what a very unhappy man he was....'

This, however, was not the impression of Emlyn Savage, who first met Caradock, while about his work, on the headland opposite the house in which he eventually settled. Caradock was watching the wild geese which occur in profusion along the long mudflats of the estuary. It was mid-winter, a very good time for waterfowl of all kinds, and Caradock was delighted to find someone of Mr Savage's expert and detailed knowledge. Emlyn Savage had always been a countryman. He found in Caradock a ready and eager listener, who wanted to know about everything. 'You see, sir, what Michael Caradock had, which a lot round here couldn't see and which they didn't really have the chance to see, was a really childish wonder at these things. I don't mean childish in the sense of silly – I mean, like a little child. You could explain something to him and he was full of wonder. "Beautiful," he'd go. "That's beautiful, Emlyn." He always called me by my name and I did the same with him. Because there was nothing snobbish about him, as a lot of these around here think. At least that's what they say they think. We spent a lot of time walking, while I was doing my rounds and so on, especially the first year or so he was here. And I got to know him well, I should say. I taught him a lot. But he taught me a few things too. Because he was a deep thinker and he used to say this or that in passing that would make me think. I think he was a good man and I think he would have been a contented man if he had been allowed to be. But he never had any peace. There were always visitors coming from London at first, and they used to upset him considerably. And here too. I don't mean Miss Bradley. But there were others.... Still, the least said about that the better.'

Some of the visitors of whom Emlyn Savage disapproved were Caradock's long-standing friends. James Faber found that Caradock was apparently contented, comfortable and accepted. 'It was really all quite remarkable, because Michael seemed to have mellowed remarkably and there he was enjoying an idyllic and undemanding liaison with Diana Bradley, very much delighted by the readily available resources of natural history and surrounded by admiring but not sycophantic people with minds of their own. Dr Simpson and Hugh Morgan were both intelligent and alert young men. And Mair Morgan was one of these magical Celtic women with exquisite bone structure and a very beautiful pale complexion, who, however slender they are, seem to have this kind of essentially female substance, entirely corporeal, an incarnation of the spirit of fertility. She was extremely demure, but it was unmistakably there. Her husband was, I think, genuinely if a little uncritically religious. One of a long tradition of chapel-goers who had lived in that village and a thoroughly decent man. I remember, on one of my visits, we had one of these complicated discussions (which professional philosophers try madly to avoid) about the nature of God, with Michael protecting the others (Dr Simpson and Morgan) from me. A dramatic change of role, I might say! And we covered – or at least we touched upon – Wordsworth and Blake and Rousseau and Spinoza (a great favourite of mine) and inevitably Nietzsche (a great favourite of Michael's), with these incredibly eager young men. Diana Bradley was appropriately amused and rational and Mair Morgan was very beautifully listening. I started teasing Michael, partly because I could not believe in this new-found calm and tolerance, and partly because I did not trust its veracity. So at the height of the argument, I said something like: "Well, Michael, I see that you are, at last, attempting to live in rhythm with Nietzsche – living as God intended us to live." This after a lot of stuff about Nietzsche's anti-Christian obsessions. And Michael turned most coolly to me and said, if you please: "I may very well be living as Nietzsche intended us to live – in rhythm with God." I was bowled over, because it was the last thing I expected to hear from him and of course I must have looked funny, as one does when bowled over. It sounded a most brilliant riposte and the others all laughed, good-naturedly, of course, at my discomfiture. But not Mair. She smiled and remained poised and watched Michael. At the time, I did not think she had been listening....'

Another of the visitors to Glanmor was Idris Lewis. This was entirely the work of Diana Bradley after a trip to London with Caradock to meet Michael Beauchamp-Beck, on leave from his diplomatic post in Rome. In the course of a warm and happy evening, they had talked about Caradock's years at Oxford and Miss Bradley learned of the deterioration in the once close friendship between Caradock and Idris Lewis. She suggested, in due course, that it might be repaired. At first, Caradock was angry and resentful: but in due course he wrote to Lewis, describing his new life and sending him a copy of his essays (*An Elemental Wound*). Lewis responded with characteristic warmth and arranged to visit Glanmor on his next trip to Wales – in itself a fateful move.

Extract from David Hayward's official biography.

Everything was obviously much worse than any of us had imagined. I was one who certainly underestimated the real problems that were worrying Michael. Perhaps if I'd seen more of him at the time and more of him alone, I should not have been so obtuse. But he had always made the most of any feelings of *angst* and, as I think that Faber would agree, as non-believers it was all too easy for us to discount the real sense of deprivation and depression that lack of religious faith had on someone like Michael Caradock. At college, he had once been quite seriously religious without necessarily being devout, then he had lapsed and it came as something of a surprise to find that he was experiencing this intense spiritual desolation. In my opinion, it was compounded by his isolation. As soon as he began to think that the people in and around Glanmor hated him, he withdrew more and more into a bitter, lethargic corner where he had very little to do but contemplate the Godless and loveless universe which he writes about so often in the last two books.

Around this time I had a very vexed letter from our old friend, Idris Lewis, who had been to visit him. Diana Bradley had managed some kind of reconciliation after quite a few years between them, and Idris, who always understood Caradock better than most of us and was much less disposed to make allowances for him, recognised immediately the symptoms of severe and augmenting melancholy. He wrote to me that Michael was trying to persuade himself that he had found a peaceful and idyllic place where he could fulfil himself. And Idris thought, in spite of Diana Bradley's marvellous presence and influence, that he was utterly wrong and going to be appallingly disappointed. He said that he would do his best to get Michael to return to Oxford and asked me to try to make Faber (whom Idris did not like) help. I'm inclined to think now that it was already too late: all the facile talk about hatred of his origins, guilt, problems with women and so on is irrelevant and obscures the fact that Michael suffered from a pathological melancholy which eventually took possession of him. It was a pity because the young man I first met at Oxford was always looking out of himself, enormously receptive, he saw himself as an *un*important focal point from which to view the rest of the world; and at the end he was only looking in and the world was all focusing upon him, dense, becoming denser, to no purpose until the weight was no longer tolerable.

Michael Beauchamp-Beck in BBC radio programme.

Caradock's friends have all been commendably loyal to his memory and I doubt that they ever received the same kindness and consideration from him during his life. I think, from my impressions of him, that he was a man totally without generosity. I never heard him praise the work of another man who was not dead, or at least so established that his reputation was beyond reach or assault. I see no reason why a writer or a painter shouldn't behave as decently and sensibly as a grocer or a postman. We've heard a very great deal about the torment in Caradock's last year or so of life and it's there, unquestionably, in his books – and make no mistake, I do not dispute that he could write very, very well – but all such torment sprang, I think, from his basic inability to give or offer to others, and the torture, however real, was self-inflicted.

Frank Adeane, novelist, in BBC radio programme.

First the progress as splendid and elegant, eloquent with colour and grace, elaboration of manners and flashing of eyes, as any under the forest of Riom: first the progress, and then the killing. First, the carriages through the streets like so many tumbrils, the sun-sodden, splashed and stained streets, with their plump and mantilla'd heroines, the daughters of the bourgeois and the well born, and then the ritual bloodletting. First the blare of the strutting procession, the absurd pomp of the unequal fight; then the delicate yawns, the girlish squiggles of laughter, the stirring of fine lace on a girl's shoulder and the collapsing beast spurting out its life in snorts and gouts of blooded spittle.

The great black bull had stumbled as it had run into the arena and then gathered itself and rushed at nothing. Shapes and shadows before its blurred eyes, perhaps, in the dazzling light after the dark of the pen. A superb, proud man on a high dappled grey horse pranced out of reach, making the unafraid stallion dance and step up most expertly. The majesty of the horse with a bedecked man on its back: the brute, blind fury of the bull taunted by the precise delicacy of the stallion's footwork, the finessing of the horseman, the bursts of speed and nice calculation of each pass and flourish. And the bulky, relentless, maddened beast in pursuit of the artificial but unafraid horse. Unequal combat. The rushes and retreats, the pinpoint dressage. And roars as he plants the darts using only his knees and thighs to guide the careering animal leaning back and swerving to wound and weaken the black bull.

Roars from the crowd as he retires and a dozen rush from the barriers to distract and confuse the hurt, red-eyed beast, pausing in the ring and tossing its head against the pinpricks in his neck. And now the jinking adroit dandies with more darts to weaken it further. And then the real fear of the picadores' horses, pillowed and cushioned, the squat lumpish men, sullen jowled, driving their poles into the meat of the neck up to the guards. And at last the matador, a frightened boy in a gaudy suit, breaking a sword and missing and then piercing something so that a great spray of blood came from the muzzle and the beast faltered but ran on and pursued the tormentor, who had lost his swirl of poise and cruel assurance, acquired at what cost. Until the black bull died from weakness and out of courage, sinking to its knees and trying still to stand again and charge, falling, the rhythmic sprays of blood spattering the defeated youth. Until too late and against the shrieking crowd the boy lined up his sword and the butcher finished off the job, professional and casual, with a little ugly knife.

Fictio: a figure which useth to attribute reasonable actions and speeches to unreasonable creatures.... De Vigny's dying wolf and that great black bull on a hot afternoon in a poor town far to the south, with beggars in the streets and old women in dark, stinking bars too weathered by time and endurance to brush flies from their faces, black, fat flies.

403

Landgrave knew quite well it was ridiculous to compare the instinct of the beast with the resolution of the man. He had gone willingly to the spectacle and seen, as he saw now again, over and over in his mind, the same pageant and chronicle of a yelling crowd sweating in the safety of their galleries crowing at the combatants; the endless delight of the human kind in the suffering and pain and humiliation of others whether men or beasts, the ageless bloodlust. That was the spectacle. It was natural, he supposed, to identify with the beast, the maddened hunk of sensuall delights and beastlinesse hurtling from the dark into a bewildering circle of noise and dazzling light, ridiculous patterns of conduct and artificial traceries of heroism and glory that meant nothing to its rage and frustration.

It was the audience that he most hated, translating himself to the Circus Maximus or the Stadium of Domitian and hearing the same raucous screech of the plebians and watching the same sleekly grunting merchant class and observing the thin lips, pale eyes and bored smiles of the togati. Meanwhile the emperor, surrounded by the softness and the luxury of his perfumed attendants, unsmiling witness to new excesses of torment....

*

Across the straits, they looked in the fading light at the spur of the Atlas range thrust out towards Ceuta, the twin pillar of Hercules. It was now a quiet and peaceful night after the heat and stench of the afternoon and they were in Gibraltar, restored to the veneer, however false and thin, of Anglo-Saxon restraint and fair play. Landgrave gazed across the

404

narrows. Atlas, brother of Prometheus who (as the Greeks say) did first fynd out the hidden courses of the starres, by an excellent imagination. Atlas his great neck forever bowed and hunched under the weight of the heavens and Prometheus chained to his rock and tortured daily by the remorseless birds and Epimetheus who accepted the endowed woman and her caseload of suffering.... Sensuall delights and beastlinesse. Suddenly and irrationally, he was filled with an unjust hatred for Catherine, who looked as calm and untroubled as always, hating her with the mad beastly panic that he felt for the absentee God who released the animal rage and taunted it to eventual, exhausted humiliation and destruction. At times, there seemed there was nothing but that hatred left to remind him that he was alive.

He tried to pick out and name the stars which were beginning to become clearer in the sky above Africa but he was disorientated. His mind worked in jumps and strange loops of association, like the brain of someone lightly asleep who is dreaming and believes himself to be awake. So that all at once he was aware of a lightening in himself as though the heavy body had fallen away from what was essentially him and he almost laughed.

'The great God Pan is dead,' he said aloud.

And shivered.

Catherine got up and held out her hand to him, her face kind but not smiling.

'We'd better go back now,' she said.

Extracts from 'May' sequence of Laocoön *novel. Hazel & Sims, posthumous.*

405

8

*There sodeinly was such a calme of winde that the shippe
stoode still in the sea unmoued, that he was forced to cry alowd,
that Pan was dead: wherewithall there was heard such piteous
outcryinge and dreedfull shriking, as hath not bene the like.*

*Stillness, the oppressive silence and calm sea preface
madness. A cry that marks the disintegration of reason, the
sudden deluge inside the skull, splitting of the knot....*

*A self-acting weapon, the enfeebling wound in the heel
that brings cold to the loins....*

*Structuralists are trapped in the paper maze of their own
diagrams. The scholarship of soapflakes and canned beans
asserts its ponderous law. The storyteller is stifled in a drift
of his torn-up drafts. Infatuations thrive, extempore acts of
mindless cruelty proliferate, the vicious continue to scheme,
whatever the vice....*

*Outside there is the darkness, the distant cry of the owl,
the moonless sky: and beyond nothing. Chance, mischance:
a meaningless chain of events that has no foreseeable end....*

*The calm of the night after a muddy day in which the
colours failed to hold.*

Apart from their private tempests, there is no reason to
suppose that Caradock did not enjoy the journeys in
Europe that he made with Brenda Thackeray, a broad-
minded and dedicated European – but during the first two
or so years after his move to Glanmor he was ready enough
to accompany Diana Bradley on her frequent visits to the
Mediterranean countries. She spoke fluent Italian and
colloquial Spanish, having lived for many years not only in
Bologna and Siena, but also in Granada and Barcelona. She
attests firmly that Caradock, whose knowledge of Latin
was excellent, read all the Romance languages fluently in
the original and that his inability to communicate in them
was sheer 'bloody-mindedness'. 'Michael *liked* being an
Englishman abroad, and furthermore the kind of
Englishman who froze other people with this eye (as I think
Wallace Stevens says in one of his letters). I'm not sure
why. He used to joke about it – that it had taken him so
long to be accepted by the English that he wasn't going to
give up the privilege easily. And there may have been
something running quite deep behind the joke. Even when
he came to live in Wales, he made a point, sometimes
rather an irritating point, about Englishness. Idris Lewis
had no such hang-ups. He never lost his Welsh accent and
didn't give a damn about it.'

While deeply attached to Italy, Diana Bradley loved Spain and managed to communicate some of this love to Caradock who was still able to recapture some of the enthusiasm that had first attracted Michael Beauchamp-Beck. Curiously enough he was eager to see a bullfight, talking of it as some kind of theatrical reality that must inevitably surpass the ridiculous grimacing and attitudinising of the 'so-called live theatre'. 'I think (Miss Bradley writes) he expected a bullfight to be something like the experience in the Colosseum or wherever it was. Now, this was a man who revered Aristotle and the idea of restraint, Classical purity. So I had a shrewd idea that he would indeed find something of the sort and that he would not like it much. And I was right. He *hated* it. We didn't get, for one reason and another, to see the *corrida* until we were in the South – in La Linea de la Frontera. And it wasn't a very good one. But, of course, as with everything else, he used it....'

Returning each time to Glanmor, Caradock professed to Anthony Simpson and Emlyn Savage that he really did feel at home and that he was always glad to return to the peace of the place. His association with Dr Simpson, with Hugh Morgan and his wife, and various other people keenly interested in the arts offered him an opportunity to listen to original and fresh ideas, untainted by literary fashion or affectation. His life with Diana Bradley, punctuated by visits from friends such as Idris Lewis and James Faber, kept him in touch with his own familiar world of professional theorising. His friendship with Emlyn Savage introduced him to new experiences of Nature and the countryside that delighted him.

Extract from David Hayward's official biography.

I was naturally very pleased when Michael wrote to me and suggested that we meet again. I didn't know, at the time, that Diana had put him up to it, of course, because we had never met. In fact, I had no idea that she was in any way associated with him, although I'd seen some of her pictures and one or two artefacts – vases and so on, which I liked very much. My wife was not particularly happy about it, because she had an almost superstitious dislike of him, but on our next visit to my parents in Wales, who weren't all that far away from Glanmor, I drove over.

At first, in the excitement (I suppose that's the right word) of the renewed friendship and of meeting Diana, I was too euphoric to notice any symptoms of disturbance or discordance. Naturally I didn't want there to be any. Looking back, it's easier to remember what they were and where the obvious pitfalls lay. I was reassured immediately by the fact that Michael had got over all the rather silly affectation about Wales. I thought that he had developed and matured considerably; in that, while he had always known when to keep discreetly quiet, he now genuinely seemed to be much more capable of repose – if you see what I mean. It seems absurd to suggest that someone might have matured after a matter of four or five years: but it's no exaggeration to say that Michael had changed as much in that time as many people I had known at Oxford changed in something like twenty years. He had matured. He was more emotionally subdued, slightly more forthcoming in a way that mattered. What I did not see, at first, was that he was immeasurably more bitter. Irony had turned into savagery; sarcasm into violence. There was only a hint of this from time to time, in some chance remark: but Michael had always been inclined to make flamboyant statements. What was evident was that he was not able to connect at all with the local people. I wouldn't claim that Welsh country people are particularly easy to get to know – unlike the fellows you'd meet in the industrial valleys – but there was a quite definite constraint between them and Michael. He took me along to the Lion, one of the pubs, and he was making quite an effort, but several of them called him 'sir' which is one way of not being welcoming and they talked together in Welsh. One of the men who used to be there was simple-minded, an enormous grinning man, obviously very strong, called Bob. And it was obvious that Michael feared and disliked this poor chap from the beginning. He used to shout and bang things suddenly and it used to set Michael absolutely on edge. I really think he was afraid of stupidity, particularly when it was accompanied by physical strength. Yet he would claim that anything was better than the artificiality and modishness of London. In a fairly typical way Michael did a complete volte-face and deceived himself that he could hear truth – not art, he would never have gone that far, but truth – in these homely, rural accents.

Idris Lewis in BBC radio programme.

'He has done wonders with the miniature in verse,' said Leydon Wells. 'He has a remarkable sensibility for things banal and for finding in the commonplace silt some semi-precious gem of cosmic truth. This is accompanied by a capacity for making the remarkable flatly quotidian. It is, of course, in the best traditions of English verse. The pastel colouring and the effortlessly informal formality.'

Laertes Jones studied, in some awe, the figure of the poet, a short man with a great sweep of hair and a pale, dedicated frown that remained on his neatly arranged face even when he was smiling, giving it an expression of unmistakable or perhaps undisguisable malignity. There was something about the man's stance that belied the apparent humility of his verses. He was hectoring a small posse of people of roughly his own height, occasionally grinning to reveal the most curious teeth.

'They are all poets?' said Laertes Jones, in wonder.

'More or less,' said Leydon Wells. 'Oh, don't be disappointed, you sweet, romantic boy. You didn't expect a roomful of Rimbauds and Walt Whitmans, did you? You won't find that any more. Not in London. Quite a lot of drinking, quite a lot of talk about copulation – some of them actually do make it from time to time – but for the rest each wears his cynicism with a difference.'

'Cannibals!' said the voice of Perceval D'Arcy, near Laertes' left ear. 'They devour all flesh eagerly, but never with such relish as when it is the flesh of their own kind.'

Leydon Wells, at the sound of the gloomy critic's voice, had started virginally like a débutante who had been improperly fondled by a bishop in the presence of royalty. He gave a further discreet little shudder and slid away to the left.

'*They* look quite pleasant,' said Laertes.

He pointed towards three very large young men with round and beaming faces in hairy tweed suits who were laughing uproariously at the jests of a small, dark man with a pointed beard who looked like an apprentice goblin.

411

'Ah,' said Perceval D'Arcy gloomily, 'them. They are all Irish and they go in for ubiquitous public charm. But in conclave together their fangs are as sharp to tear a tender reputation.'

'They seem to be very eloquent,' said Laertes. 'I have never seen so many people talking at once and all seeming to listen at the same time.'

'The age-old talent of the common gossip,' growled D'Arcy. 'At first you might be fooled into thinking it was brilliant and literary: but it is either malicious or self-advertising or self-seeking prattle, ineluctably trivial.'

Some few feet away a bearded man with narrow, quasi-piercing eyes was vituperating in a glottal monotone. At first the expression around his moustache might have been mistaken for a smile – albeit self-satisfied, a smile. On closer examination, however, it became evident that the mouth was set in the same permanent and impervious sneer as the voice.

'Is he a poet?' Laertes Jones asked Perceval D'Arcy.

'Even in this company, God forbid that he should pass for one. He is a Jack of all literary trades and esteems himself to be better than his masters at anything he turns his hand to. He claims to be a critic: but he is not. I am a critic and it is not an ignoble profession when pursued with dispassion: where the only thing to be hated is bad art. Wormtongue there, who trades under the name of Jesse Styche, is attempting to work off a burden of colonial resentment in facile and gratuitous cruelty. He appears regularly on television.'

There was a sudden roar across the room of alarming ferocity and purpose, closely followed by a low snarl that was even more chilling. The roar had emanated from an elderly bull with a red and rugged face, advanced in drink but rocking confidently with large shoulders set in a crouch of ready brutality; the snarl from a huge neanderthal figure of adamantine jib, who was doing his best to loom.

Laertes Jones stepped forward, for it was clear that these two enraged literati were intent upon tearing each other apart. He felt the firm restraining grip of Perceval D'Arcy on his arm.

'No need to worry,' said D'Arcy. 'They will try to insult each other to death. There is no risk of physical contact. The crumpled one is a relic of what must have been the inexpressibly tedious golden age of the BBC. The throwback is one of the new fauves who conceals a barrenness of intellect and insight behind a mask of psychopathic savagery out of which emit harsh primeval sounds. The referee will be that capering jackanapes in gold glasses who has frittered away genuine intelligence in often unspeakable versatility.'

It was as the grizzled old bloodhound predicted and there was no violence. Laertes Jones became quickly bored with the lumbering, dinosaurian exchanges and profited from the distraction by examining the faces of the people in the room. He found it hard to credit that his sister, Amelia, however lonely and distraught, could possibly have been beguiled by any of those present.

'Cannibals,' grumbled Perceval D'Arcy.

Extract from Broods of Folly. *Alvin & Brandt, 1960.*

I did not find him at all unapproachable or cold as many seem to claim, I was very struck by the scale of his ambition. He talked a great deal about the *Promethead* novel and the last book that was published that did not have a title, but also about future plans which weren't properly formulated. One of these was for a sort of *Inferno* in which he proposed all kinds of technical experiments of narrative and I found it very inspiring, though it was sometimes difficult to keep pace with his ideas and intentions. He had come to Glanmor to work and to work hard, as well as to be near Diana. Their decision not to live in the same house was largely because Michael was sensitive to what he thought were local standards of propriety. As most people who live in country districts are aware, these standards are often quite separate from local practice. I think, however, that he was hesitant to live too close to someone again after a previous love affair and, practically, both he and Diana agreed that they would work better and harder if they were not under the same roof. They enjoyed each other's company too much.

At this time – his first two, perhaps three, years at Glanmor – I had very little idea of Michael's darker pre-occupations. I wasn't aware of the despair and all-smothering sense of emptiness that ultimately possessed him.

Dr Anthony Simpson in BBC radio programme.

Idris and Faber offering Oxford as Epidaurus: only sleep in the temple a night or so and the cure will be communicated in dreams. The cure? Anthony Simpson, gentle and sensitive soul, trying desperately to get me off the drink. Savage silent, watching with troubled, reticent eyes, reluctant to invade the sovereignty of another island. And Diana... wise enough to be quiet and so blurting out a pain that I could feel jabbing through the endless noisome ache of my self.

No, physician, I will not heal myself. I will simply dull the ache. This quintessence of dust shall settle with watering. Noble in reason, infinite in faculty, paragon of animals by the sequence of selective accident. I did not evolve: I merely happened. Why should I not lie in the filth of my imagination, brutish and ravening. A beast, indeed, without discourse of reason, to mourn or pity or love. All vanity. The final derangement.

Once I apprehended evil too keenly. And I was aware with each small act of selfishness that what I was doing was wrong. But not evil. Not a wilful effort to hurt which is what evil involves, but a calculated manoeuvre of defence which is necessary for preservation and ignores the existence of others. Oh and that is wrong. Discourse of reason demands a sense of obligation and decency and a desire to serve for some greater good. The healer's calm and patience in time of plague, waiting for the symptoms in his own body. I have seen Simpson of an evening sorrowful over the suffering of an old peasant, feeling myself nothing and without shame.

I do not contradict myself. No longer believing. If art serves at all, it is a feeble thing: commentary as against discovery. The logged, starved corpses, the severed bodies, the desert sunsets, the cry of a nightbird interpreted through the electrochemistry of the impersonation, the wild and naked victim with wreathed hair and ivy-twined staff in all his arrogant defeats. And then discourse of reason... 'What is the end – or worse, what is the beginning – of all inquiry?

Is the spirit of inquiry perhaps no more than fear in the face of pessimism and flight from it? A subtle means of self-defence against – the truth.'

Forlorn wanderer in an unlit room hoping to see the light of stars reflected on the darkness of the still waters.

The essays in *The Philosopher's Stone* are readily classified. The 'lyrical' pieces are on the whole optimistic, based upon experiences that have been lived through which were largely happy. Significantly, two of the sections, comprising what amount to sequences of prose poems, are about places – 'Landscapes' and 'Urban Lyrics'. But it is important to point out, in answer to certain critics who have too eagerly seized upon Caradock's preoccupation with locations rather than with the tenants of such locations and accused him of the most frigid if not inhuman disregard for his fellow men, that these landscapes – wherever they occur – are seldom without people. Admittedly, Caradock does not get close to these people and does not allow them to encroach upon him, but his observation is sympathetic – without compromising his privacy. In the other essay in the section, 'An Idea of Remembered Love', Caradock is most plainly himself writing, with some rueful amusement at the tranquillity with which he recollects old emotions.

The 'philosophic' essays in the same book are by no means pessimistic by contrast – but they are sombrely reflective and concerned essentially with the significance of the artist, the thinker (*not* the professional student and teacher of Philosophy), and the historian in society. In each case, Caradock examines the influence of such dedicated men upon 'men of action and affairs'; in each case, he asks at the end of the essay whether we have evolved at all since the Renaissance, a time which he (perhaps arbitrarily) identifies with the dawn of volitional self-aware human progress, arguing that the superior (in Caradock's view) culture of the Ancient Greeks advanced to its zenith more or less by accident – as indeed according to Darwinian theory human evolution occurred. After the protracted barbarities of the Roman Empire and the Dark Ages, Caradock suggests that enlightened men at least thought profoundly about intellectual and spiritual evolution in a way that did not occur to the Greeks. What they lacked in spontaneity and excitement they made up for in purpose: the determination never to see another Dark Age out of which enlightenment might not again emerge. At this stage Caradock admitted the possibility of a reflowering of civilisation from fragments and relics, which he was later to deny. The final essay in this group, entitled 'Parallax', uses the optical phenomenon to make analogies between the different viewpoints of artist, thinker and historian in a landscape of thought and historical event, ending with an elegant coda on a single man's interpretation of circumstances in his own life, as seen and understood at different intervals.

The last and separate essay, 'The Unmoved Mover', begins with an attempt to elucidate the metaphysical concept of Aristotle – the idea of final cause and purpose behind change; but Caradock moves to a more individual treatment of the phrase, choosing to personify it and to examine, through the metaphor of Prometheus, the dispassionate impetus of the seeker after enlightenment, whether artist or scientist, his hubris, his nobility and his ultimate impotence.

This is the single most important theme in Caradock's work and the final chapter of this study is devoted to an examination of the essay and its motifs in relation to Caradock's output taken as a whole. The ideas were most elaborately explored in the last novel (*Laocoön*) and most immediately put into fictional form in *Promethead*.

Caradock cherished a fascination rather than an admiration for the writings of Nietzsche, whose words and ideas occur over and over again in his later books, as epigraphs or in allusions, usually as a point of conflict or else debate. Waldeck, the ageing warrior-politician outcast of *Promethead*, is a curious amalgam of a Nietzschean and an existentialist hero. He is fanatically altruistic, desiring to serve his people for the greater good; at the same time he is a power fantasist, immersed in theories of warfare and conflict not only as he has lived through them but as he has studied them in the history books. After distinguished service in two wars – in the second of which he was his country's exiled political leader as well as commander-in-chief – Waldeck is rejected. The emotional shock upon a profoundly serious mandarin with strong paternalist ideas, exacerbated by physical illness of which he is not immediately aware, leads to intermittent depression and bouts of apparent insanity. His central problem seems to be how he can live as an atheist in a world that has cheated him of the achievement of the only purpose he can conceive: the service of his country and his fellow men – or more accurately his compatriots. Various historical parallels are obvious but Caradock does not seem to have any one of them particularly in mind. He is interested in the components of Waldeck's predicament: his sense of destiny in an egalitarian, derisive age; his aspiration for government based on enlightenment and high idealism; his despair at the corrosion of the spirit in a cheap and shabby age of artistic and intellectual decline; his personal struggle with his own carnal urges and the significance of the realisation of personal weakness, of humiliation in effect, in converting a theoretical altruism into genuine charity. Caradock seems to take the view that the politics and history of the twentieth century have in many ways vindicated Nietzsche's world view, but in Waldeck he presents a rejected philosopher whose stern and pessimistic premises for government are absolutely unacceptable to the ordinary people. The religious aspect of this argument is a powerful undercurrent throughout the novel: Caradock seems to suggest that the Nietzschean hero-figure, taking on the guilt of the world, enduring pain and torture, magnificently defiant, is all very well in a world where it is necessary to announce the death of God to mortals who are shocked and incredulous, but quite out of place among the succeeding generations who take God's demise as a bland fait accompli.

Caradock worked these motifs, with considerable skill, into his two closely knit plots: the one a clever political intrigue in which the two men closest to Waldeck, Ganz and Claudian, plot against each other – Claudian to use the General's name and reputation for his own, ultimately totalitarian ends; Ganz simply to restore the General in his own right and to protect him from the machinations of Claudian, although Ganz himself is by no means an out-and-out libertarian. The second plot concerns the arrival at Waldeck's retreat of a young poet, Ganuret, through whose eyes much of the action is seen and who becomes an important spiritual factor in the resolution of Waldeck's career. Although the young man is the victim of a bad car accident, he is looked on with suspicion at first and subsequently witnesses one of Waldeck's fits of frenzy. He is persuaded to stay, becomes close to the General and personally involved in his life, while at the same time listening to his past exploits and observing the immediate contest for power taking place around him. Much of the book is taken up in narrative involving past events to Ganuret from one or other of the major characters; but there are many passages of direct observation from his focus, as well as brief impersonal accounts of factual circumstances relating to Waldeck's immediate state of health and mind.

The basis for this particular plot is, obviously, *Parsifal*, where the pure fool strays into the court of Amfortas, who suffers from an incurable wound which he must endure until the fateful question – how the wound came about – is asked by the chaste stranger. Caradock adapts the characters fairly freely to his purpose but sticks quite closely to the original framework and certainly presents the figures from the original myth in recognisable modern shape: Kundry, Klingsor and the others are all there. As in *Parsifal*, Ganuret (a simple mutation of the name of the pure knight's father in von Eschenbach's original) fails to ask the important question, is himself seduced in what seems to be a betrayal of the stricken hero, but is ultimately instrumental in the wounded man's redemption. It is interesting to note here something which will be later examined in the light of the existentialist content in this novel: the observation by a distinguished commentator on Camus that Meursault and Parsifal may be readily correlated. Meursault not only fails to ask the important questions, he fails to ask any questions: and in this he gravely errs. It is also worth remembering that the concept of the pure fool was one despised by Nietzsche. Caradock was, as always, eclectic in his sources and used, like so many others writers, what he needed when he needed it.

H.-J. Kastner: Patterns of Despair. *Hazel & Sims, 1973.*

'There is too much talk of defeat,' the General said. 'Too much meaningless, self-pitying pessimism, too much weakness, too much humility of the wrong strain. Defeat for most of those who talk about it is a mere luxury, an indulgent pose; or it is a literary fashion; or it is a theory. I speak from authority, Ganuret, for I have experienced immediately and at first hand the realities of physical defeat: I do not mean something intellectual, or emotional or philosophical, or even moral – I mean the physical fact of being conquered. Ganz understands. He has been a prisoner, taken when wounded: he will know.

'After a few months of the more recent war, I was placed in command of an armoured division which was reasonably well equipped and suitably mobile, and deployed in support of our south-eastern front. After years in the wilderness, to which I was consigned for a variety of reasons – mainly political – I enjoyed even this small degree of responsibility. I am not vainglorious when I say that I should have been better used on the General Staff or in military liaison with the politicians: but at the time I was content to take part in the battle itself. I pressed that my division should be moved immediately from support into the front line which was obviously in need of strengthening – a few brigades of infantry, backed up by artillery and authentic cavalry (troops, if you can believe it, young man, mounted upon horseback, when any assault expected must come from tanks and fast armoured vehicles). My arguments were rejected, my advice was ignored.

'Inevitably the enemy thrust came in the late spring. Our collapse in the north was sudden and complete. Incompetent intelligence and panic at Staff level demanded the transfer of much of the force under my command from the south-east to the northern flank. The centre seemed to be holding, there was no pressure from the south. My arguments were met with indignation, scorn, even vituperation. I was accused by a senior general of cowardice. What happened is now academic. The main enemy effort came a week later in the south-east. It drove through our front with the ease of a white-hot poker through stretched fabric. There was some resistance, but for the most part panic. The mounted troops, true to some irrelevant code, behaved heroically: for the most part, the soldiers scattered. I heard, bitterly, later of the disintegration of courage and resolution among them. The cries – the banal cliché cries – of defeat, as every man ran for his own life.

'We did our best to regroup, but we were now under air attack and my main strength had been dissipated over too wide an area. I drove, in as fast a car as I could find, to the sector where there was heaviest fighting to see for myself what could be done. To see for myself! The humiliation was appalling. Our own men, dirty and bloodshot and crazy with fear in flight – ready to murder and loot for their own preservation. There was very little rape, only advancing armies have the time for such brief diversions. We stopped some of them and asked them where they were going, what they thought they were doing. Without exception, they were regrouping, they were looking for their officers, they were looking for their men, they were searching for a place to stand and fight. They reeked of defeat.

'Occasionally we met single men whose wits were already turned sitting upon stones in catatonic emptiness, or weeping: some grinning and babbling to themselves. The scene, which would normally have been peaceful and pastoral, the lowland grazing plains and downs onto which the mountain pass opened, was desolate: torn metal, craters, the inevitable mud of battle, heavy guns twisted and crumpled like so much foil paper, burnt-out cars and lorries. Bodies, of course, in the grotesque tortions of sudden death, blown open, headless, the hands reaching; always the hands reaching, clawing, fumbling, pleading. Some burned, others mingling blood with gathered rainwater and mud, one hideously impaled upon the shattered strut of the frame of an army truck. There was a man sitting in the ruins of a farm cart, cradling his comrade – a much bigger man than himself – rocking him like a child in his arms. When we were closer we saw that the other one was dead, his side gashed open by a splinter of steel. It was not this. I had seen worse in the earlier war. Much worse. But this was defeat. The stench of it clung to me for months and years. We had been shattered in a matter of hours, we were in flight. The eroded will of our leaders, the diseased central nervous system of our nation had failed the organs and limbs which were defunct, or convulsed in anarchy.

'We were close to the advancing enemy. We could hear the small-arms fire as well as the big guns. For a moment I think we were almost all possessed with a suicidal fury, to go on, armed only with our ornamental revolvers in their highly polished leather holsters, to certain death. Then a new wave of planes came in and someone – I do not remember whom – gave the order to the driver to turn around. As you know, the enemy's main drive came from the south. He held the northern front where he had broken through and curved around the centre where some of our forces and those of our allies were still fighting every inch of ground.

'The only course was retreat. After one more futile attempt at regrouping, I took the tattered army – what remained of it – to join what I hoped might be a new front based on the north/centre lines of battle. But it was already outflanked. The allies insisted upon retreat. They were met with the scorn of the old and literally diehard, with the protests of men who knew they were about to betray the entire cause. It was obvious to me that withdrawal was our only course. We needed time, recouping of energy, an opportunity to find again a new spirit of defiance. I threw in my lot with them.

'The retreat was terrible. You, Ganuret, will not have seen the distraction of refugees as they swarm along the lanes and highways and take to the woods or fields in fear that is hideous to behold as the harassing aircraft come in. The evil of defeat is that it makes men animals again. It reveals how thin the film of decency and humanity is in most of us. There are hardly any saints. As we drove past those herds of frightened people in whose faces there was as much hatred for us – understandably – as there was nameless, unformulated fear of an enemy, I was alarmed by my own failure to feel pity. The chaos was immediately to be perceived: they did not know what they were fleeing from. It was mindless terror, spread by rumour and prejudice and (of course) the sheer physical furore of bombs and bullets. I should not have so easily discounted the last: but I was a soldier and I was used to bombs and bullets. I should have felt more than pity: sorrow, grief even. I did not. I saw only ovine stupidity for which I felt contempt; and in my soured imagination I knew that those who stayed, the bourgeois and the petty local officials, were for the most part likely to collaborate.'

Ganz made an ambiguous gesture which might have been taken as a mild rejection of Waldeck's last assertion. Waldeck glanced at him but ignored the interruption. Ganz's hand remained frozen in mid-air.

'Other tribulations that I had known, personal or otherwise, were as nothing to this all-pervading consciousness of failure and defeat. When I achieved exile, I suffered all the more from the indignity of toleration. The superiority of the undefeated, who take small account of the reasons for their survival. Their condescension is almost impossible to endure. I had had to face inglorious capitulation and retreat and flight pragmatically, so that these people, my allies, could rearrange their defences by sacrificing that great last battle, a glorious Thermopylae in which the best were to be ultimately destroyed unvanquished; so sacrificing, if only temporarily, the honour of my people. This too was nothing to my own doubts relating to that experience of subjugation.

'I needed to regroup my own psychological reserves and it was not easy. Tranquillity of mind is important in achieving a true purity of resolve, a will to be magnanimous, a prospect of reconciliation with friend and enemy alike. My mind buzzed and throbbed and seethed with resentment and humiliation. In those grey years, I took comfort from the Stoics. I took solace from a sense of age and purpose, a growing commitment to my destiny, an unshakeable conviction of my fitness to serve.'

The General smiled at Ganuret rather wearily, the worn leonine face ugly and benign.

'What does it mean to you? To a lyric poet? I ask you, Ganz, if we do not waste our time. Should we not live brilliantly like dragonflies in the cafés around a half-ruined arena in an ancient settlement, rather than play these endless war games in stuffy, shaded rooms? In so many ways I wish that I could have been an Epicurean or a Cynic; both systems ask for discipline. Or if I was damned to be a Stoic, I should like to have been private and discreet, to defy the crack battalions and the traitors of adversity in my own small, if proud, way. Instead, whether I have wished it so or no, all my gestures, my apparent triumphs, my many repeated and considerable defeats, have been public. And I have struggled again to survive and regroup and fight once more. And I am now very tired.'

Extract from Promethead. *Hazel & Sims, 1967.*

> You think that I suffer from a morbid conscience,
> From brooding over faults I might well have forgotten.
> You think that I'm sickening, when I'm just recovering!
> It's hard to make other people realise
> The magnitude of things that appear to them petty;
> It's harder to confess the sin that no one believes in
> Than the crime that everyone can appreciate.
> For the crime is in relation to the law
> And the sin is in relation to the sinner.
> What has made the difference in the last five minutes
> Is not the heinousness of my misdeeds
> But the fact of my confession.

I am astonished by the critical indifference to *The Elder Statesman*, this very profound reflection from the greatest living poet and one of the most creative thinkers of the century. I do not mean the indifference of those people who write professionally about the theatre, whose enthusiasms seem to me to be as eccentric as their aversions, living as they do in a helical draught of fashion they set out to create. I mean the serious attention of literary critics and scholars who otherwise admire T. S. Eliot's work. It seems to me to be a marvellous and tranquil account of a very wise, very fallible man's reconciliation. And reconciliation, however it is achieved, is one of the inescapable ambitions of the mature writer who has not yet renounced defiance, or who has not been silenced by despair. My admiration for Mr Eliot as lyric poet and reflective poet, as commentator and critic, as sly provocateur in the currency of ideas, as patient guide through unfamiliar, forbidding landscapes, is unbounded – as I must have already shown in this essay. It is, however, in *The Elder Statesman*, a much less spectacular achievement than so many others in the poet's long, integrated, severely self-critical progress, that I find myself most moved by the quiet assertion of affirmative values.

For many years I cherished quite blithely the erroneous belief that T. S. Eliot was a Stoic, playing the impudent but interesting game of guessing at events in the writer's life from his writings and forgetting his own notes upon Stoicism. As long ago as 1927, Mr Eliot himself warned:

> I admit that my own experience, as a minor poet, may have jaundiced my outlook; that I am used to having cosmic significances which I never suspected, extracted from my work (such as it is) by enthusiastic persons at a distance; and to being informed that something which I meant seriously is *vers de société*; and to having my personal biography reconstructed from passages which I got out of books, or which I invented out of nothing because they sounded well; and to having my biography invariably ignored in what I *did* write from personal experience....

This in a short, stimulating essay on 'Shakespeare and the Stoicism of Seneca', full of ideas and illumination about the way in which writers – even of the highest quality – use ideas and events to a purpose that they may or may not entirely understand. Undeterred by the author's own wise counsel, distracted by literary rumour, I searched for evidence of the Stoicism I wanted to find.

Classical refinement has always seemed to me to be the highest achievement in literature. Certainly not the *only* achievement: but the highest. It is not difficult to attain in prose fiction or in dramatic forms, but it is formidably difficult in verse. The refinement I refer to is the elimination of the 'self' other than as a receptive filament, a 'shred of platinum'.

> Poetry is not a turning loose of emotion, but an escape from emotion; it is not the expression of personality, but an escape from personality. But, of course, only those who have personality and emotions know what it means to want to escape from these things.

For 'poetry' here, I should suggest 'literature' obtains equally – especially in an age where much of what passes as literature is material for the clinic or the citizens' advice bureau. The profession of literature is a serious and difficult one: it is as much a vocation as medicine or religion or real education. It cannot be mastered by any casual dreamer any more than surgery or higher mathematics: but where surgery is an applied science the benefits of which are obvious, and mathematics is a pure science capable of application (though some mathematicians tell me it is sometimes so pure that it transcends any art), literature's application is by no means evident and even the greatest writers may not be aware *how* the catalytic influence of their minds may work ultimately while remaining massively confident that what they are doing is necessary.

My tone is apologetic. Sir Philip Sidney's was not:

> If then a man can arrive, at that child's age, to know that the Poet's persons and dooings are but pictures what should be, and not stories what have beene, they will never give the lye to things not affirmatively but allegorically and figurativilie written. And therefore, as in Historie, looking for trueth, they go away ful fraught with falshood, so in Poesie, looking for fiction, they shall use the narration but as an imaginative ground-plot of a profitable invention.

'Profitable invention' is the important phrase, suggesting to me that once begun the creative chain reaction of a true work of literature need have no end. But it seems obvious that if the writing, whether verse, or prose, or in dramatic form, is intensely personal it cannot be a true fiction, an imaginative ground-plot, and therefore denies the reader the opportunity of profitable invention.

In assuming that Mr Eliot's classical discretion and technique were the artifices of a Stoic – and a well-bred Stoic, at that – distilling the experience of pain without self-pity or embarrassment, I ignored not only an important line from 'Tradition and the Individual Talent': 'The emotion of art is impersonal. And the poet cannot reach this impersonality without surrendering himself wholly to the work to be done'; but also a significant passage of masterly brevity in the essay on Shakespeare already quoted in which he writes:

Stoicism is the refuge for the individual in an indifferent or hostile world too big for him; it is the permanent substratum of a number of versions of cheering oneself up. Nietzsche is the most conspicuous modern instance of cheering oneself up. The stoical attitude is the reverse of Christian humility.

It is this humility, whether or not it be Christian, that is the absolute requirement for reconciliation. For the professed Christian, especially one of the intellectual gifts of T. S. Eliot, it is a humility perhaps more easily achieved: but I am sure that it need not be denied to the non-Christian and the atheist. In describing the stoical front of Othello at the end of the play, Mr Eliot distinguishes acutely between an aesthetic and a moral attitude. And I fear that the attitude of the Stoic, redolent of pride and personality, is a self-dramatising performance; a gesture of defiance intended for an admiring audience: an act of public self-assertion which makes reconciliation impossible.

Aesthetic attitudes are much easier to strike than moral attitudes are to attain – *any* moral attitudes. At the same time aesthetic integrity is part of moral integrity, and the moral integrity of an artist – which has nothing to do with moralising or moral posturing – is what ultimately convinces the innocent reader and perhaps startles him into 'profitable invention' on his own account. It is this integrity as much as genius that can permit a great writer the lines:

> Age and decrepitude can have no terrors for me,
> Loss and vicissitude cannot appal me

431

Not even death can dismay or amaze me
Fixed in the uncertainty of love unchanging.

Extract from 'The Elder Statesman', essay in An Elemental Wound. *Hazel & Sims, 1963.*

I certainly did not expect a visit from him. In fact I had no idea that he was living in Glanmor. But one day he arrived in Cwmfelyn and of course I was very pleased to see him. After about twenty years. I'd shaken hands with him at Howell Caradock's funeral, but there had been no time to talk and it wasn't the appropriate moment.

My wife had died some years previously and I've lived alone ever since, but I've never felt particularly lonely. Perhaps this is why I had the impression that Julian, or Michael, was not only lonely but isolated. I suppose he would have been about thirty-nine or forty, but he seemed much older: very serious under a pleasant front. He didn't say very much about Cwmfelyn which has changed a lot over the years – from being a rather ugly industrial place to a somewhat forgotten village reverting uncertainly to a spent rural quietness. But I knew quite well that he had disliked it here and he had not come back out of any nostalgia.

He told me why he had gone to live in Glanmor – to look for peace, to try and do something new, something original that was unmistakably his own. And he talked a lot about integrity and morality. I was partly amused and touched and of course flattered that he should think that I still had anything to say to him. You don't go around thinking of yourself as a 'serene person'; but because of certain circumstances in my private life, Julian had decided I knew about 'serenity'. It was a good talk.

And it was a side of him that people haven't seen fit to comment on. Unaffected, serious, respectful. After all, he was a well-established writer and I was a retired civil servant who'd worked for the District Council. We talked about his books. I told him what I had enjoyed and admired in them. I thought that the satire *Broods of Folly* was by far the best and still think so: but Julian discounted them all except the essays. He said the others were 'mindless'. He gave me a copy of *An Elemental Wound*, which I already had, and a proof of his next book *The Philosopher's Stone*. I was very proud to have them.

John Morris in BBC radio programme.

Out of all these reflections, among the ruins, it is suddenly humiliating to become aware that the focus of them all – of the imaginative effort (for what it is worth), of the sincere speculation, wonder, gratitude and sense of exhilaration, even exaltation – is the miserable self: as though all the suffering and triumph, the whole monstrous, volcanic parturition of history, had undergone its indescribably agonising labour to produce the ridiculous mouse of an individual sensibility, touched by sunlight among pictur-esque ruins in the presence of someone who is deeply, truly beloved. It is so disgusting a piece of arrogance as to be immediately farcical: and like so much farce it has distant echoes of tragedy: because such moments may be all that anyone of us ever knows of happiness. If everything else is an accident, to be happy is an accident. The pursuit of happiness is a vain toy. But out of such moments, such glimpses, has been somehow created a concept of happiness – quietness, harmony, equilibrium, beyond the itches of personal gratification, the hungers of self-interest, the thirsts of a private *Me* – as terrible in a loutish tenement sadist who beats his wife and children, or in a chapel-going usurer who economises on everything except his daydreams, as in a Domitian or an Attila or a Henry the Eighth or a Robespierre or a Hitler. In that wonderful, idyllic mirage – in which the delirious wanderer retains the failing power to ask if there *can* be a mirage without a presupposed, preordained, pre-existing reality – the prospect is tainted by guilt. It is not a great surprise. It is the guilt of having lived and, in so living, of participating in all that is evil as much as in all that is unmistakably good.

Out of all this -- the glories and splendours, the buzzing and blurred trance of what must pass for revelation – steps the reality of a gentle woman, living herself and including others, to say that it is time for lunch and that there is good wine in a pleasant place across the piazza. What is there to do but smile, get up, follow her and enjoy the wine.

Exctract from 'Ruins in Sunlight', essay in The Philosopher's Stone. *Hazel & Sims, 1965.*

It must be the last shame: to know that the wound has been kept open, the allergy nurtured, the cures evaded in order to prove some kind of power. A monstrous act of moral courtesy without meaning. See how I have suffered. See how I have been used. See how I do not forgive. See how I remain my whole indivisible wrecked but unconquered self.

Power. The power of bogus courage. The renunciation of humility and love. A nourishment of discontent into hatred to evince a phantasma of courage. The volunteer ape steps into the cage and closes the gate, waiting to become afraid.

A footfall. Was it? A step out there in the darkness...

If fear were so easily come by! Footsteps around an empty house. Phantoms from that crowded silence kicking the loose stones, unwary crunch upon gravel, around and around the house. The cautious barbarian. An oxymoron for our times. Smash of the spiked mace. Drink to the courage of the berserker in his drugged fury and stinking skins bestriding the threshold, swinging the skull-crunching tool – the instrument of his success...

And you white-skinned Celtic queen, insatiable and treacherous in your lust, sob with soft pleasure as he appears and writhe upon your couch and spread yourself in eagerness. For you have prepared a cup to tame and subdue and silence him. Then he shall be ritually sacrificed....

I stand accountant for as great a sin....

The trees begin to stir. A wind is rising. Somewhere the creaking of a hinge. The rusted grating noise of worn metal and weather-tried wood. Corrosion, sodden deadened fibre, desiccation in the fierce, futile sun....

No. That is not the entire shame. Not the odour of degradation and inspired guilt and the stale sourness of accidie. The shame is to sniff so eagerly the air for that trace of the unclean self, the delight in the pungencies of being. I am foul, therefore I exist. It is fear of dying, it is failure to accept extinction. Life is not such a great thing. Out of all such transient beauty, happiness, quietness that made it seem so, comes only this low-lying vapour of the wasting, fearful self....

A falling branch. The wind clacking. Rattle of a decaying house. Whispers of cloud blowing across the stars. No doubt the dark waters crimping into small waves that will become perhaps a surge, a swell. As a child I was afraid of the dark....

I think it would be oversimplifying things drastically to try and label Caradock's relationship with Diana Bradley as this or that. Quite obviously it began as a physical attraction, but it developed into something much more complex. She was, as I think I've made clear, too intelligent and too secure to allow herself to be used. She believed that he was a very good writer who was extremely unhappy. She found him attractive and she loved him. But she loved him on his own terms: she did not, any more than he did, surrender her entire life to loving him. It was a mature, self-respecting commitment. So that when the emotional crisis with the other younger woman occurred, she was able to react calmly. And throughout behaved with astounding kindness and dignity.

David Hayward in BBC radio programme.

The central crux of Caradock – and the one that makes his case so significant in an area of largely academic speculation – is to be found in his obsession with imageless thought. How capable are any of us of authentic imageless thought? Such total abnegation of the individual *se* or *sese* must demand and achieve a rejection of all the bionomic

436

experiences hitherto registered. The *Se* (so obviously distinct a concept from orthodox psycho-investigative currency) is a placid withdrawal from phenomenological certainties into a cosmodispersal perspective of the selfless personality. It is not an *easy* concept.

Such a conscious substructure on the part of a writer of Caradock's luminal sensitivity, a *will to be nothing* in simplistic terms, must inescapably set in motion an ideo-motive train of action. But here it is essential to exercise care in distinguishing between the ideomotive and the ideoplastic energisations of the subject. Caradock's will to be nothing directed him severally. In ideomotive behaviour patterns, he discovered himself (as is clear from his fiction) time after time in unexplainable situations, that were in no way coherent with the taxonomic *rationabilia* of his self-projection *as a creative artist*. In short, he behaved absentmindedly. But to drastic effect. The ideoplastic aberrancies are of necessity more serious in that formulated intellectual incentives were brought to bear by Caradock upon physiological functions. And these incentives were negative!

Caradock, investigated seriously, is a living proof of the obverse of the James-Lange Theory, in that his physical existence and its attendant emotions were determined by the *cerebral* disturbances that followed upon the *analysis* of an exciting fact or event.

Irving Haller: The Centaur and the Druids. *Heseltine, 1972.*

One of Caradock's most frequent visitors at Glanmor was his editor at Hazel & Sims, Sean Moran, whose impressions of him at this time are particularly interesting since Mr Moran was not a close friend and was principally concerned with Caradock's literary well-being. In the early years of Caradock's move to Wales, this was excellent: the security of the relationship with Diana Bradley and the drastic change of atmosphere enabled Caradock to work as he wanted to. Idris Lewis was a regular visitor now that their friendship was repaired; James Faber, who was also a friend of Diana Bradley, was also often welcomed. But to other acquaintances Caradock was less accessible. Angela Petrov had borrowed a cottage from a friend in Pembrokeshire for a short holiday within comfortable reach of Glanmor, but was not invited over and was understandably somewhat annoyed that the best hospitality Caradock and Miss Bradley could arrange was a fairly brief lunchtime drink in the neutral territory of Carmarthen. Trevelyan Lloyd, too, who was making a film for television in the area, met with a cool response to his suggestion of a convivial weekend. Mr Lloyd was curious to find out how Caradock was settling down in the village and made the trip anyway. As he suspected he discovered that 'the rural Welshman, while as hostile to the settler as he is inquisitive about the stranger, is not like his English counterpart who seems to be wondering sullenly how quickly you would disappear in a lime pit. They did not like Caradock and they thought he was a bit mad; they pretended to disapprove of his liaison with Diana Bradley whom they seemed more willing to accept. But I was directed to that sinister house on the island readily enough, with a wealth of commentary.' On arriving at the house, however, after waiting for a suitable tide to cross the causeway, Trevelyan Lloyd was not able to find anyone in.

Sean Moran, however, who was obliged to spend several days at a time at Glanmor in view of the length of the journey, was always received cordially. Used to writers who enjoyed talking about their projected work, he was at first baffled by Caradock's secrecy and learned accidentally about the projected *Laocoön* novel from Dr Simpson who naturally assumed that, as Caradock's publisher, he would have been told of it. He was completely surprised to be suddenly offered the completed text of *A Coriolan Overture*, when he understood Caradock to be working on a long novel, and a further selection of essays (which were never found). Understanding from Diana Bradley that Caradock was working on several experimental ideas, he asked to see them. 'He refused point-blank and was quite annoyed with Diana. In fact I only heard about some of his ideas, which would have been very exciting, after his death. He was always, in a reserved way, extremely courteous, very diligent about dates and deadlines, and he didn't care a hoot about business matters which is slightly off-putting. He was, of course, quite well off and he didn't have to worry about money, but he was very much against publishing single pieces, or work in progress, or anything of that sort. Tentatively I tried to persuade him *not* to throw away or destroy his drafts, notes, jottings and so on, which would be quite valuable. He nodded and paid no attention. Caradock was always a heavy drinker – but he was neither ebullient nor truculent. In fact, unlike most people, the more he drank the less he talked. Gradually, I suppose, I became aware, round about the time we were settling the final version of *Promethead*, of a serious change in him. The brooding silences were very much more evident, which was worrying. But I found it virtually out of the question to make any sort of approach. And I believe even his few very close friends did.'

Extract from David Hayward's official biography.

After the novelty of bucolic tranquillity had worn off, it was obvious that he would have time not only to work (which was all very well) but to brood. He was thoroughly disenchanted with London; but since his retreat to Glanmor had been in search of some Asclepian sanctuary, I thought that Oxford – the only place where Caradock had been really happy – was a pretty fair compromise. He would have peace to write and there would have been the agreeable annoyance of various friends and acquaintances interrupting his leisure in a more or less constructive way.

At the same time, there was a clear problem of tact and elementary consideration. Michael had moved to Glanmor originally to be with or near Diana and it could not be expected that she would necessarily take too kindly a view of my efforts (and as it turned out Idris Lewis') to transpose him. In fact, as we now know from Diana Bradley herself, their relationship had become deeply affectionate, complementary – but in accordance with Caradock's self-imposed asceticism it was no longer sexual. This sort of information is not readily available to people, however sound their friendship, who observe certain proprieties.

James Faber in BBC radio programme.

Marcus climbed the gradual steady rise of the street, wondering what there had been about the place that he had so much disliked. It was neither as ugly as he remembered, nor as positive. It was drab, a little shabby, patched up –˙ as though the entire community was reconciled to falling into disuse.

A grocer, stacking wooden crates outside his shop, looked inquisitively at Marcus, trying to place a familiar, now altered, set of features. Marcus remembered the man twenty years before as a noisy and ebullient youth perched on piled-up cases of lemonade on the back of a lorry, always shouting at passers-by. The face was thinner and appreciably worn, the mop of bushy hair had become sparse and grey, the ebulliencies had dimmed into the valley caution that seemed to beset most of its men, except for the handful of implacable bastards, about their thirtieth year, after marriage and procreation. He passed a number of people whom he did not recognise, although they were all old enough for him to have known. They showed casual interest in him as a stranger in a place where strangers were not frequent.

The dispersal of industry – steel, tinplate and coal – from the valley seemed to have affected the self-confidence of the village. As a child, Marcus seemed to remember a certain bustle in the main street. It was now listless. Many of the shops were empty. Houses that had once been bright and slick needed a lick of paint and often repairs. There was a dispirited atmosphere as though the village had settled for what it could get: television, regular bingo, social security. Marcus was the last person to feel sentimental about the old days of grime, toil and bitterness

– but there had been defiance, self-respect, pride. Perhaps the place looked different in sunlight. Rounding a bend, he remembered some pleasant trees, three or four horse-chestnuts, that had always looked beautiful in the spring. The trees had been felled and whatever building had stood in their shelter was now replaced by a long, low clinic in yellowish cement with steel-framed windows already showing signs of dilapidation.

Marcus stopped at a newsagent's where he had once made a performance of ordering the *TLS* and two intellectual journals, long since defunct. The contents of the window – a haphazard accumulation of faded children's books, comics, women's magazines, trade papers, forlorn toys, a few bits of stationery, random gadgets – seemed not to have changed. The names and designs of the comics were different. That was all.

He saw his reflection in the glass. He was used to the lines but not the heaviness of his face. There he stood, prosperous in his expensive greatcoat, distinguished and grey-haired, immaculate. He had absolutely no notion why he had taken a whim to come back to the place.

Then, as he turned away from the shop window, he saw coming towards him a tall, well-built girl in a red coat. She was about thirty, calm, sure of herself, carefully turned out. She looked coolly at him and then away, so that he realised he had been staring and felt uncharacteristically flustered. The woman herself was entirely unfussed – the kind who understands that she is good looking (and that men will occasionally look at her) without pudeur or conceit – clicking on down the street on strong well-shaped legs.

She had not remotely resembled Virginia, except in that air of confidence and assurance, the reality of her womanness that gave her a central certainty of being that Marcus had never known in men, however clever or brave, or even good. Men were invariably self-doubting, self-questioning; in need of such women.

He wondered, sentimentally, if she perhaps had a pretentious young lover, if she was bored as Virginia had been, if the circumstances in such a place were still as propitious for such romantically foolhardy liaisons. And where was Virginia now? Where, indeed, was Marcus Conrad? The banal and retrocessive mood that had fallen upon him was annoying – but he found it difficult to shake off. He retraced his steps through the village, remembering in now surprising detail how things had once looked, seeing (suddenly) long-forgotten faces, recalling events and situations that had somehow or other compounded in his adolescent self a tight cyclonic column of whirling hatreds and resentment, that had built up pressure inside until it had seemed unbearable and sure to burst out in some extravagant display of fury and humiliation.

And what had it all been about? A child's awareness that he had already a fierce ambition to be somewhere else, to be something else, to be someone else, and perhaps the deliberate nursing of small incidents until they became massive, throbbing hatred; a means of justification; an excuse for a cold, loveless resolution.

He looked sideways up the street that would have led to the house where he had once lived. He understood that it had been sold to a doctor, but he did not want to look at it again. Across the small square where three roads met, he saw the shop where Roope had had his pharmacy. It was now called Sylvia's Boutique. And quickened his pace.

Marcus could not remember when exactly he had first been so certain that he must escape, when the urgency had, for the first time, built up inside. Instead he thought of the ways in which he had worked out different schemes that would enable him to get away from his parents and from the detested place in which they lived so uneasily, pretending to belong and clinging to a family significance that was long obsolete; and he remembered the great lift of triumph and relief when he had heard of his Oxford scholarship – because not even his mother could brush that away. Anything else, yes. But not an important Oxford scholarship.

The car was parked on the other side of the bridge. As he drove away from the village, probably for the last time, he remembered the wild excitement, the rush of daydream and ambition and sensation inside his head that *first* time. The high optimism of a young man leaving a steamy and damp valley for open, broad and sunlit plains; the anticipation and confidence of intellectual adventure, spiritual revelation, pleasure and pain of self-discovery. He remembered looking forward to the other bold, restless spirits that he would meet on the way, to the excitement of their visions and ideas, to the toil of achievement that was hard and personal.

He stopped the car and sat in it beside the narrow, empty road, looking at an elongated greyish mound out to his right, remembering the young, debonair Marcus Conrad with his airs and affectations on vacation, so clever – so very clever.

444

The young man in his pretty blazer and fashionable clothes looked back over the years, with his inevitable supercilious grin, at the middle-aged politician staring at a woman in a red coat in the high street of the village that had spawned them both. And of course the young man could only laugh. What else was there for him to do?

Marcus felt a tear running down the side of his nose. He snarled in impatience, sniffed vigorously without deigning to wipe it away, and drove the car off noisily and fast.

Extract from A Coriolan Overture. *Hazel & Sims, 1969.*

Once again, *A Coriolan Overture* offers us a key to Caradock's self-knowledge, so rigorously exposed in *Promethead* and the last novel, *Laocoön*. It is not surprising, perhaps, in a writer who admired Nietzsche (himself praised by Freud as one who truly and fearlessly understood himself), to find a ruthless pursuit of a flawed personality. Characteristic ironies flash on the edges of hypocrisy and dishonesty in the character of Marcus throughout the short, lucid narrative: at his most self-regarding he is aware of himself at his most palpably disagreeable. And as Caradock himself seldom disguised his opinions, however rash and sometimes silly, Marcus never disguises an affectation.

Yet towards the end of the novel, the sober middle-aged man returning to his native village understands only that he was resentful of something; but cannot give any kind of habitation or name to what he resented. He realises that he fostered unnatural feelings of hatred and despair in order to justify his ruthlessness – but does not know where these feelings germinated. He will not give in. He will admit nothing. He will not even wipe a tear off his face. But he is (at the end of the novel) beginning to face up to his own rootlessness and his need to rediscover terms of reference that are cultural as much as they are intellectual or aesthetic or ethical in order to rehabilitate himself – or, more exactly, in order to find for the first time his own true nature. The struggle was not easy: and it is my contention that all Caradock's last works: the two volumes of essays, *A Coriolan Overture* by no means least, and the two long novels were a coherent effort at reconciliation with something grander and more profound than has hitherto been realised by critics who have concentrated too readily upon the ephemera of discontent that occur so readily in the lives of artists who are sensitive to, and slightly incompatible with, their immediate youthful environment.

Extract from Stephen Lewis: The Novels of Michael Caradock. *Molyneux, 1971.*

In my view, the writer of prose fiction must be dedicated to invention: the structures of his plots, his characters, his situations must all derive from the imagination and must not be based upon incidents from the author's life, or people whom he has known. The one novel that everyone is alleged (quite erroneously) to have in them would at best be an autobiographical essay, which might or might not be interesting, but which has nothing whatever to do with serious fiction or with the aims of serious fiction.

Nevertheless, fictional invention is inevitably determined by the intellectual standards, the emotional predispositions, the aesthetic and moral judgements, the ethical endorsements and the general psychological outlook of the author. While he will have inherited this or that tendency, much of this outlook will be decided by the nature of his experience; so that the most sincere determination to keep real people and events out of fiction, which would not only distort their reality but would itself be distorted by a reality that was not its own, is always modified by the unavoidable influence of living people and actual experience upon the author's attitude and opinions. One of the most rigorous tasks an author must undertake is to make absolutely certain of the integrity of his fiction: to be sure that there are no impurities of pique or prejudice, to be firm against the taint of self-indulgence and the insidious cult of personality. If he wishes to express opinions or to write about himself, let him turn to essays or to unadorned autobiography.

I have recently been tempted to attempt a short essay in autobiographical fiction and have so far been able to resist. The project is attractive because of the rich opportunities afforded to irony in such an exercise and the pleasant games that might be played with imagery and language: the fiction would be maintained in that precise aspects of the central character would be selectively presented according to structural contrivance and artful arrangement of event, idea and dialogue. An interesting exercise in private and no more: but in toying with the idea, I have found myself remembering things that I thought I had forgotten; reappraising events and people, after perhaps many years during which my own temperament and outlook have undergone changes, *some* of which I know about.

447

Trying to focus upon some event in the past which I think I remember vividly because I was particularly happy or unhappy, or because I was excited in some way, I have become aware of a sort of psychological parallax in myself. The more I have tried to examine this phenomenon by analogy, the more interested I have become in what it implies about experience, the analysis of experience, and the distillation of experience into a kind of spiritual fuel.

The definition of 'parallax' in the *Oxford Dictionary* is: *Apparent displacement or difference in the apparent position of an object, caused by actual change (or difference) of position of the point of observation.* The definition becomes more specific and the metaphor may be accordingly extended: but for the moment I should like to draw attention to this displacement, this change in perspective, as it relates to an experience in an individual's past and its importance, or diminished significance, at later periods in his life.

If I think of myself at the age of eighteen, or twenty-five or thirty-two, I can remember at least one event that seemed important at the time and which probably influenced the course of my subsequent life in that certain reactions bred certain attitudes and prejudices which determined my later conduct, or in that I took certain decisions which (in due course) led to a critical path where I took other decisions and so on. Now I am able to see these events in a different perspective: they have assumed, as landmarks, a different significance – and by relating them to other landmarks, and by a system of psychological measurement, I am able to estimate their importance. I know too that faced with this dilemma or that problem, I should now respond differently, because I like to think that I am wiser, more mature, more readily able to weigh decisions in the balance. At the same time, if I am any of these things, it is because I have learned from wrong decisions, from past recklessness, from mistakes and humiliations which, when they occurred, seemed to be incalculably damaging. The process of change in us is ceaseless, so that any event is always minutely changing perspective in relation to the moment, and the very act of scrutiny from one second to the next contributes to the change.

It is this problematical relationship between indivisible time and indivisible personality, where time is delineated by the instruments of personality, and personality is dissected by scalpels of time, that seems to me to be a central concern for the writer of fiction. It is not the same as the preoccupation of the poet:

> There is, it seems to us,
> At best, only a limited value
> In the knowledge derived from experience.
> The knowledge imposes a pattern, and falsifies,
> For the pattern is new in every moment
> And every moment is a new and shocking
> Valuation of all we have been.

Not the same; because for the writer of prose fiction, there is no question of valuation: it is a question of observation and comparison and a description of compared perspectives, which obtains as much for the events and characters imagined as it does for actual events in the writer's own private life. All writers, poets or prose fictionalists, share one defeat:

449

And what there is to conquer
By strength and submission, has already been discovered
Once or twice, or several times, by men whom one cannot
                                                    hope
To emulate – but there is no competition –
There is only the fight to recover what has been lost
And found and lost again and again: and now, under
                                                    conditions
That seem unpropitious.

The intolerable struggle with words and meanings, however, is what the writer engaged in when he volunteered:
he was not conscripted and, if he decides to desert, he is
free to do so without disciplinary reprisals. So he should
not complain, but get on with his task. It is part of his
nature to grumble though, and to ask himself all the time
about the efficacy of manoeuvres, tactics and strategies,
and in the rest of this essay – in considering certain trivial
circumstances and (in a general way) much more important
events as they might be seen at different stages of a man's
life – I hope to grumble efficaciously about what I conceive
to be an important function of the novelist.

Extract from 'Parallax', essay in The Philosopher's
Stone. *Hazel & Sims, 1965.*

A Coriolan Overture has suffered from the reputation of
being a slight book, dashed off somewhat frivolously
between darker and more ambitious projects at a time when
Michael Caradock was relatively at peace with himself. It is
nothing of the kind and offers us a most interesting key to
certain important themes in Caradock's work as well as an

illuminating glimpse of the author's creative processes.

Caradock describes in an essay on the philosophical and social stance of the novelist, related to his aims and function, his flirtation with autobiographical fiction as a possible form. The essay, entitled 'Parallax', occurs in a collection published in 1965, *The Philosopher's Stone*, and so we may legitimately suggest that Caradock had been contemplating the idea since the early sixties. (*A Coriolan Overture* was eventually published in 1969.)

The fascination of the genre for him outweighed certain reservations that he declared about the inclusion of factual material in works of fiction, though how strictly he adhered to these principles is no doubt a matter of some debate. Caradock liked the idea of a fictional central character based upon himself which would allow him to examine, in ironic perspective, certain youthful attitudes and, in so doing, some of the attitudes of the mature man. He was careful to note in a brief preface that the autobiographical component of the novel was strictly limited to the character of Marcus Conrad and that all the other characters were fictions, but inevitably some commentators have sought parallels in Caradock's actual acquaintance and there has been much regrettable gossip and confusion which has tended to obscure the important place of this work in Caradock's fiction as a whole. The novel was intended partly, no doubt, as an extended exploration of some of the theories which Caradock had put forward in the essay 'Parallax': but Caradock chose his model deliberately for purposes of ironic comparison between the proud and intensely physical Roman leader and the arrogant but determinedly cerebral Marcus Conrad.

Why did Caradock cast himself and the young Marcus Conrad as Coriolanus? Surely not for the sake of rudimentary posturing. The young Marcus distrusts and dislikes the politics of envy that he thinks he sees around him in the Welsh village; he certainly regards himself as some kind of superior spirit: the older Marcus, it appears, is a politician (though we are told little of his career or his status) who seems to be more temperate in his views and a somewhat chastened figure. In neither case are the analogies explored in any detail or depth, as we are accustomed to find in Caradock's work when he was working precisely to a particular model. The political aspect of the Coriolanus story – the patrician who despised the plebeians and destroyed himself playing out the myth of his own intolerable pride – was only of very incidental significance to Caradock's purpose. Where ambition and arrogance were important, it was the decisive rejection by Coriolanus of his own people, his own city and its values and the intensity of hatred so implied, in order to remain true to himself and to his notion of his own integrity, that engaged Caradock's most serious attention.

The ease with which Marcus accomplishes a series of rejections attracts Caradock's most bitter irony – as family, friends, mistress and mentors are elegantly put aside, always with facility, charm and rueful wit, most skilfully used to imply a stinging self-contempt.

The tragedy, if that is not (in the light of Caradock's own ideas on the subject) too grand a word, of Caradock's Coriolan figure is that, having rejected so much and having found it so easy to hate, he is unable to find or accept alternatives. If Marcus is Coriolanus, Aufidius seems to be a protean character who occurs in a variety of guises (as competitor as much as adversary), and the Volscians are all the potential enemies: the strangers who are all barbarians, until proved otherwise, who challenge the absurdly sensitive young man. The British class system with its elaborate and subtle opportunities for insult has been a difficult testing ground for many ambitious young people and perhaps it was so for the ambitious, proud and intellectually arrogant Caradock. When Coriolanus rejects his own, there is nothing for it but to join the Volscians: but he is not accepted by them and persists in his own distrust of them – so that ultimately his destruction is assured. Marcus' own disintegration is only dimly hinted at in the novel, which is deceptively light and delicate in style. What *A Coriolan Overture* does is state in specific terms the rejection theme that is found over and over again in Caradock's work, alongside the apparent impossibility of the central figure ever finding a substitute loyalty for that which has been rejected.

H.-J. Kastner: Patterns of Despair. *Hazel & Sims, 1973.*

Caradock's local friendships helped establish him in the eyes of the local people as an amiable curiosity. He was never popular as was Diana Bradley, but the evident regard of Dr Simpson and Emlyn Savage, a respected if aloof figure in the village, was thought to be to his credit. Another friend, Hugh Morgan, belonged to a family who had lived in Glanmor for several generations who were generally held in esteem.

Hugh Morgan had inherited his parents' pleasant house

above the estuary along with a modest amount of money. He was a handsome, affable young man with a reputation for fair athletic prowess. As a teacher, at an old school recently converted to the comprehensive system, he drove into a neighbouring town each day. His ambitions were sensible: he expected one day to become a headmaster and aspired to some kind of official position on a couple of learned societies to do with local history and the arts.

On several visits to Glanmor, I met this young man and his very striking wife, rather surprised that Caradock should find them such attractive company. Mair Morgan was certainly a beautiful girl with dark wavy hair falling onto her shoulders, very blue eyes and pale, almost translucent skin. The bone structure of her face was exquisite. But she was not particularly animated in conversation and, in fact, beyond her physical charms, contributed comparatively little to any particular occasion. Morgan himself was eager and quite intelligent but startlingly orthodox in his opinions. He was a very good listener and an excellent prompter – so that Michael Caradock quite frequently talked especially well in Morgan's company. I supposed, as did James Faber, that Caradock rather enjoyed being oracular: Diana Bradley was quite content to let him. Dr Simpson was one of the subscribers to the cult, and friends from Oxford and London, close enough to be welcomed, were pleasantly amused. It is quite certain that no one suspected the real nature of his relationship with Mair Morgan for some considerable time after it had begun. The reasons now seem ridiculous: she was a passive, apparently loyal wife of a respectable village celebrity; she was unlike all the women in whom Caradock had shown an interest, physically and temperamentally.

Diana Bradley, not surprisingly, was the first to notice a particular tension between the young woman and Caradock. She hoped that she was mistaken and chose to ignore it, although she did confide in James Faber. Faber was alarmed, understanding the delicate balance of relationships in a small community and the precarious equilibrium of Caradock's own state of mind. He watched them discreetly and tackled Caradock.

Faber expected an immediate rebuff. To his surprise, Caradock admitted the affair and confessed his own responsibility for building quite ruthlessly on an unexpected and accidental embrace, which had occurred one afternoon during Hugh Morgan's temporary absence from the White House. His infatuation was violent and complete. They were obliged to be cautious because it was a small village in which gossip was easy and commonplace, but this only made their desire for each other more passionate and more urgent. Faber took it upon himself, reluctantly, to point out to Caradock the dangers of the situation and the inconsistencies of his own attitude. Caradock did not argue, claiming that this was the first, and only, wildly reckless passion of his life, that he was not able to do anything about it, and that he was not sure that he would have wanted to. In Faber's opinion he was obsessed, already deeply unhappy and disgusted with himself, but for the time being sustained by the new excitement of an entirely unconsidered act, a surrender to furious urges of self and instinct that he had always tried so hard to deny. Once again Faber attempted to persuade Caradock to leave Glanmor and reluctantly he enlisted the help of Idris Lewis.

Extract from David Hayward's official biography.

I remember what was in your eyes: the violet triumph and power that you were beginning to already understand with my own strength ebbing still inside your torrid body, the silk limbs relaxing. I remember looking close into your eyes – at the slightly dilated pupils, the delicately ribbed dark blue irises – and thinking how blank they were, frail organs of sight, nothing more, functional, merely animate. No windows of the spirit. And then a slight shift of focus and there they reveal the winding wraithlike orchid tendril of you smokily, mistily engulfing and devouring and sapping away will and strength.

In another age you would have trafficked with devils for the excitement, not believing in devils but believing in you and your newly discovered power to touch with long, refined fingernails, threateningly stroke the most tender and vulnerable centres of pain and affection. I hear your mocking laughter, too, in the wind as the moon races in the ragged sky, as I yearn for you and plod to you, and the slow peasants long for you, the slyness of your lowered long eyelashes, the violet bedewed eyes suddenly raised to the canting, distorted face of the preacher.

There is no wind. The sky is clear. There is no moon.

There are no sounds.

The villagers click their sombre dominoes, shuffle their greasy cards, tock their thudding darts into the flaking board and taste wryly the soapy beer. They do not think of you.

Except in some darkly kept cranny of mean peasant lust. Oh my God, how would you answer to their rape? I cannot tell. The idiot thrusts back his cap and scratches his meagre skull. The landlord wipes the dark bar with a sour grey cloth. They are not thinking of you. And yet you have poisoned these imaginations. And I release you. It was I who let you out of the chaste bud of unknowing. I do not believe it.

You waited darkly blooming for the kiss of darkness.

And you lie there, now, perhaps... while he stamps in the next room and the blood pounds in his hurt, splintered consciousness. I hate you and you still enchant me. In the darkness. Your white, misty arms – so slender, the sweat and perfume of your body...

'No,' said Landgrave. 'It was not that. The intention was to corrupt. It was quite deliberate. A desire to do something evil, for which he could not possibly take *all* the responsibility.'

Catherine smiled.

'You're sure that this was a friend of yours. It sounds unusually like a confession.'

Landgrave laughed.

'Oh, my dear,' he said, 'I have never had the courage to do anything positively evil. And had I done so, I should now be wallowing in guilt. No. It was not a friend. An acquaintance. A moral philosopher of some reputation with an extraordinary sexual appetite. Now this might quite easily have been assuaged by ordinary and comparatively harmless means: there are, as you know, quite enough available women of various ages who for one reason and another are prepared to accommodate moral philosophers. A slightly more exotic savour from time to time was readily achievable at a moderate premium. This was not enough. The man in question gained some extra frisson of excitement – I perhaps underrate what he felt, it must have been more than a mere frisson – from seducing the young wives of colleagues, of sons of colleagues, pupils, acquaintances. He preferred the husband, also, to be young.'

'Poor man,' said Catherine.

'That is an impressively confident observation.'

'It's obvious, surely.'

'Perhaps. I think too much is excused in the name of insecurity. After all why should we excuse a man or a woman this or that antisocial, hostile or vicious thought, word or deed, simply because he or she is insecure. I prefer to allow that this man – my acquaintance – was excited positively by the business of corrupting: there was some irresistible charm in destroying something for him; better still, about demonstrating to these deluded children that anything they believed was precious and personal between them was false, facilely polluted, a lie in the context of human deceit that is universal and unconquerable. We are of course accustomed to the various refinements which are said to enhance mere sexual pleasure by providing this or that aberrant tension; but this man, a moral philosopher capable of expounding the most grave hypotheses redounding to the discredit of most of his fellows, while prescribing the most rigorous means of amelioration for our deplorable condition, took an unholy pleasure in his perfidy, in his treachery, in the conscious betrayal of his

458

own most sacredly argued tenets. I found it puzzling, intriguing and repulsive.'

'Very unpleasant,' Catherine said. 'Why are you telling me all this?'

'You were talking about innocence.'

'Yes?'

'I was reminded of this corrupt man. You said that you were glad that neither you nor I was capable of innocence any more, because there were fewer disappointments in store for us.'

'Do you regret innocence?'

'No. I do not believe I came trailing clouds of glory from God who is my home. I was never aware of innocence. I have always been a commentator. Only those who do, make or act can lay claim to innocence.'

'What happened to your moral philosopher?'

'He met a wonderfully chaste girl. Forgive me, it sounds like a fairy tale. She was extremely beautiful: young, with long black curling hair and violet eyes; she had very white skin, exquisite delicate bones; she was slender and yet bore in every surge or ripple of her body an infinite promise of luxury.'

'You create a very vivid image.'

'Thank you. She had the gift of silence and when she spoke her voice was low.'

'An excellent thing in woman.'

'She was challenging. Her language was in her eye and in her lip: unmistakable semaphore of the face that skilled lechers read at a glance and respond to and read the answering signals in turn. This and the accompanying

459

command of her body. My philosopher was almost put off. The conquest was too easy. After all, virgins are as plentiful as blackberries. At the beginning of each academic year, he was aware of several. And those who wore their defloration with a difference were, to one of his acuteness, merely boring.'

'And then he found she had a lover? A younger man?'

'Better. A husband.'

'We can only bear so much reality.'

Catherine laughed again, but she was listening carefully. Landgrave knew very well that she was not convinced that this was not a confession, and he was already weaving into the rather trivial anecdote minor details that might exculpate himself from whatever he felt uneasy about.

'I wish you might have known my acquaintance, the moral philosopher. And that he might have known you. I believe you would have frightened him.'

Obligingly, she let her eyebrows flicker a little.

'As it was?' she said.

'As it was, the situation was perfect. My acquaintance was a most confident man. His intelligence was not exactly a topic for breakfast conversation in suburban homes, but it was taken as much for granted as cornflakes. His professional reputation was a matter of envy. He was by no means powerful or handsome in appearance, but the viperish energy of his enthusiasm and potency darted from his saurian eyes. Imagine, my dear, that black spark of life in the puckered and heavy-lidded wrinkles of old skin. He indulged the young males. And flattered the young females with hints of wisdom; the prerogative of the eternal female

– to share an eternal joke with tarnished men. The chaste young woman fluttered long eyelashes at him, glanced suddenly with her violet eyes, minutely puckered her bright lips: always prompting him to discreet mockery, always sharing his joke.'

'The husband?'

'A weakling. Not even physically impressive. He did not think he could put up a fight. And, if the truth is told, nor could he. He watched, quite sure that he was losing a woman he loved, and he did nothing about it. He could not threaten her because he would never carry through his threats and they would not be credible. He dared not plead with her because he would weaken and weep, revealing himself to be feeble, unworthy. He could not reason because she was outside reason and reason had nothing to do with the ancient interplay between her and the predatory philosopher. He believed he must lose, reconciled himself to loss and felt miserable.'

'Whose side am I on?'

'Isn't it obvious?'

'Yes. And he won.'

'Cleverly?'

'It could be, though I doubt it. She humiliated your moral philosopher. I don't know how: but not necessarily in bed. She assumed her husband's inability to act was strength: she allowed herself to feel that he trusted her judgement and was content to leave it to her. And she preferred this to the intolerable condescension of the clever man sharing his eternal joke with her. What were you talking about?'

'Chastity.'

'I thought so. Perhaps it is you, after all, who is innocent. It's not that.'

'What is it?'

'Power.'

Extract from 'September' section of Laocoön. *Hazel &
Sims, posthumous.*

It is not only possible but necessary to argue that evolution is a continuing process and furthermore a progress towards much greater intellectual and moral achievement that will accompany and govern any physical improvement or refinement of the species. But the evidence to support such argument is frighteningly meagre. The evolution of man seems to have been haphazard and accidental, the processes of natural selection involved random. Plato is chance, Shakespeare is chance, Bach is chance. There is no purpose. So given expertise in genetic engineering, should we define a purpose and breed carefully to that end. Is the superman a possibility? And what are the implications for the imperfect in body or mind? Or the less than perfect? The moral questions that immediately pose themselves and answer themselves are obvious: such a purpose would be impossible to define in any terms of liberal decency and true intellectual aspiration. It is the dream of canting, tyrannical ideology and cannot be countenanced.

Yet, as individuals, we are obliged to make what sense we can of what remains of our lives. In the two previous essays, I have tried to sketch an image of life without hope, and without faith. My conclusions (such as they are valid for me) were that hope and faith die hard and reluctantly, but that it is possible to live without either when they are dead. I now ask whether it is possible to live without charity.

If life is an accident and to live at all is a matter of sheer chance, then all experience is accidental and my participation in acts that are evil or good is not a matter of my private will determining what I do: it is simply a matter of individual experience, and whether it is designated evil or good is a footnote of no real relevance to the experience. So that an individual is a unit of cosmic raw material at the mercy of various accidental forces. *Except* that the individual is capable of making those footnotes – value-judgements upon his own responses to various stimuli, moral pronouncements upon his own conduct – by virtue of his intellectual power. This may seem a small thing against the vast forces of chaotic instinct pent up inside our frail bodies, but it is an intellectual power compounded of the intellectual energy and effort of all time and it is the only power that can control chaos. The Universal Will, 'Spirit', is not a matter of force or instinct: it is the discriminating power of the individual human intellect to decide what is evil and what is good. The purpose of this essay is to try to investigate whether it is possible to arrive at such a discrimination – to establish a precise moral attitude – without charity, without the Pauline interpretation of Christian love.

Nietzsche's idea that 'the preponderance of pain over pleasure is the cause of our fictitious morality and religion' is not to be easily dismissed, since much of our compassion is either superstitious or prophylactic. Superstitious where we are made aware of the suffering of others and think: 'How awful if that were to happen to me or to someone I love, I must feel sorry for that person and do what I can to help, so that people will, when necessary, help me.' Prophylactic where we think: 'Unless I help these suffering people, things will degenerate in society (so that disease, famine, or whatever, will spread), the rule of law will fail and there will be savage anarchy in which the Have-nots will grab whatever they can.' It is because we all have some experience of pain, and are able to imagine it as something so much worse, that we frame an elaborate system of commandments, laws, codes and moral guidelines to protect ourselves. Now, there have been and are and will be saintly people who are good and unselfish, without a thought for themselves, and who are often motivated by a religiously inspired love of creation, or else an almost mystically intense commitment to other people perhaps the more admirable for not being religious in its origin. I am asking whether it is possible to achieve a coherent morality where a man stops himself doing the evil that he would not, and acts positively for the general good or the good of another individual – but *without love*. If this were possible, it would surely be the highest, purest, passionless form of what is good.

Extract from 'A Modern Ethic', essay in An Elemental Wound. *Hazel & Sims, 1963.*

I suppose it might be a time to ask for forgiveness. And what else is that but a time to make excuses, reaching for the consolatory bottle. The burning in the gut. Perhaps I shall die painfully and wastingly and then they will forgive.

They will have to forgive. The train of phantoms in the accursed tent. I'm sorry. I didn't know. I didn't mean to. I was only... I had to be firm.... I wouldn't have... but do not blame me. A gift confers no rights.

A shutter clacking in the distance. It is cold now. Very cold.

Huddle into guilt. Phyllis Caradock, Howell Caradock, all those whose confidence was never returned, who believed theirs was the right. Nothing will come of nothing. I ask for nothing, giving nothing. A little darkness, a solemn fading of consciousness. I still fear the pain. The silence.

What an appalling irony!

It probably did not occur to the genial Hugh Morgan that his wife should have been so fatally attractive to the sophisticated novelist in whose urbane, eloquent company he took such pleasure, alongside his friend Anthony Simpson. All the evidence is that he regarded Mair as a decorative, moderately intelligent, entirely fulfilled complement to himself: he did not see her, as Caradock came to see her, as a wild, wayward, gipsy creature in whose demurely violet eyes there was an intoxicating challenge of sexuality and female dominance.

Had she not met Caradock and her pretty head not been turned by the power she so easily exerted over this (to her) astonishingly clever and worldly man, it is doubtful that Mair Morgan would have transgressed far from the dainty path of a Welsh middle-class marriage, distinctly mapped out by rural traditions of behaviour and respectability. Perhaps she would never have realised her own potential, she might never have understood her intense sexual vitality. As it was, there can be little doubt that she was corrupted by Caradock and eagerly allowed herself to be so. Corrupted? Is that not much too strong a word? The facts of Caradock's melancholia and his withdrawal into himself, along with the freely expressed opinions of people who knew both of them intimately, suggest that it is not.

Obviously, we do not know what resistance either or both of them made to their irresistible mutual attraction, but they became increasingly infatuated, increasingly reckless. They were already the subject of village gossip and local scandal before Mair Morgan confessed the affair to her astonished and dumbfounded husband. Hugh Morgan took refuge in a dull, benumbed anger. Caradock, after a furious scene, abstracted himself from the affair and cut himself off from virtually all contact – with the exception of his doctor, Anthony Simpson, and his friend, Savage.

And in the long weeks that followed, the scandal festered and rankled in certain minds. Small communities are close and Hugh Morgan's family had lived in the village for a long time. The stranger, with his alien and bohemian way, was obviously to blame. Already, in some slow rural minds the seeds of revenge and retribution were germinating.

Extract from Derek Parnell: In His Own Country. Guildenstern, 1970.

9

They were both, at first, extremely discreet and I don't think the unfortunate husband had any suspicions. Diana Bradley was not jealous and her motives in confiding in me were entirely unselfish: she was concerned for Hugh Morgan and for Caradock, because she had a pretty shrewd idea of how the local people would react to any scandal. At the same time, it is quite fair to say that Diana was always (quite rightly) aware of her own self-interest. Her relationship with Caradock was one of convenience. She had helped him through a fairly minor dejection, as far as she was concerned; she had shown him the escape route from London and the ephemerality that he quite genuinely disliked; but she bore absolutely no responsibility for him. Why should she, indeed? Caradock and Mrs Morgan were both adults who knew what they were doing.

Once I had been alerted – and I cannot tell you with what reluctance – I thought she was absolutely right. I think it was probably very foolish of me to challenge Caradock, but I think I rather hoped it might persuade him finally to leave Wales, where he seemed to be doing absolutely nothing. He was perfectly calm, quietly icy at first. Then he admitted the affair and said that he was completely infatuated with her. I pointed out what an unholy fuss there would be if the affair was discovered and I also, I'm relieved to say, had the grace to put poor Morgan's point of view. Caradock was aware of all these arguments and knew quite well that he had only himself to blame.

James Faber in BBC radio programme.

I curse myself now for being so stupid, though there was probably little enough that I could have done. Mair Morgan told her husband about the affair after a quarrel about something else. He came to see me, naturally deeply upset. Once he had told me what his wife had said to him, it seemed obvious enough. There are things we all choose not to see. Mair had become a lot more obvious sexually – but she was a pretty woman and I suppose any fairly normal man would be inclined to put a newly awakened interest down to his own instincts than to an initiative on her part – any woman's part.

Hugh Morgan subsided into a sullen fury. Virtually a state of shock. He was fond of his wife, he thought she loved him and he thought their marriage was working. He was hoping to have children. Beyond the meaningless flirtatious chatter with Sixth Form girls, that was completely innocent, he did not look at another woman.

I went to see Michael who was shocked about the way Hugh Morgan had found out. The affair was already over, but not the infatuation. Over the next few months to a year, I was one of the few people to see him regularly. And the remorse and anger was real and considerable. The nature of Hugh Morgan's rage, the dumb and helpless pain and disappointment, made Michael Caradock's guilt more acute. In due course, I was able to piece together what had happened. It wasn't up to me to judge. The gossip had started and I did my best to make an obvious performance of ignoring it. The story was that Mair had become degenerate and went off regularly to a town about twenty miles away where she had a regular clientele. I refused to listen and I don't think there was any truth in it. But gossip and rumour are virulent. I think, now, that Caradock was already deeply mentally disturbed and that this tipped the balance.

Dr Anthony Simpson in BBC radio programme.

The change was obvious and shocking. I had the advantage of knowing none of the other people (except Diana Bradley). The GP was a compassionate, unhistrionic character who was rightly very worried about Michael's state of mind. Michael did not welcome me but he understood why I was there. He was very drunk most of the time. Faber had been completely kicked aside and Diana Bradley had given up. Idris, of course, was the worst failure. His bitterness was extraordinary, but then it was an extraordinary situation and the one that had brought me there from Rome, where I was posted at the time. In some curious way, I think that Michael thought that he had been responsible for corrupting Idris Lewis and I think too that a great deal of latent hostility and contempt towards Idris was rising to the surface. Michael was beginning to understand the extent of the hatred of which he was capable. He was in the process of disintegration.

Michael Beauchamp-Beck in BBC radio programme.

The disastrous intervention of Idris Lewis was prompted as much as anything by Caradock's refusal to have anything to do with James Faber. His reasons are obscure. Faber certainly did not set himself up in moral judgement over Caradock and any lack of detachment (of the sort that Diana Bradley was able to patiently command) was occasioned by his firm conviction that Caradock was a writer of outstanding talent, whose best work was yet to come, who was more or less deliberately allowing himself to go to waste. *Promethead* was in the hands of the publisher, but Faber had not read it and didn't know much about its attempted scale. Caradock was evasive and secretive about his 'work in progress'. He was now convinced that it was essential for Caradock's artistic survival and indeed his abiding sanity to move away from his semi-reclusion where he was so patently free to indulge a strange sexual obsession.

Faber's distrust of Idris Lewis had been long-standing and was entirely mutual. He regarded Lewis as over-earnest, chapel-minded, 'a good brain with a Daddy's

Sauce sensibility'. He thought that Nietzsche's aphorism applied exactly to Lewis: 'Some people do not become thinkers merely because their memories are too good.' Lewis, in his turn, with a highly developed social conscience and sense of duty, who had deliberately turned his back on academic life to work in an unglamorous department of the Civil Service, regarded Faber as a dilettante of a particularly frivolous sort. The antipathy was almost classical in the ant/grasshopper mould and had partly accounted for the rift between Lewis and Caradock some years previously.

Whereas Lewis was primarily motivated by the loyalties of old friendship, he too agreed that Caradock was a fine artist who must in some way be saved from himself. He was appalled to hear of the affair with Mair Morgan and took it upon himself to visit her at Glanmor, without first talking to Caradock, in an attempt to persuade her to break off the relationship. He enlisted the aid of Diana Bradley in getting the young woman's husband out of the way, but he reckoned totally without Mair's own brand of resourcefulness. Whatever the affair had started as, it was something she had no intention of giving up, and the ensuing confusion made matters a great deal worse, precipitating an intense crisis which was only partially resolved by the tact and goodwill of Michael Beauchamp-Beck.

Extract from David Hayward's official biography.

And my pure fool was well and truly hanged. The enchanting perfumes of the rose of hell. Poor Idris, weeping. 'It was not my fault. I didn't know. The woman is a devil....' Weakness and foolishness and hypocrisy. I knew. I saw what she was and she excited me. She excited me as no other woman. Not Helen, not Brenda, none of them. They were all substitutes, nothing more. The long, long kiss…

I have played over the sad little scene and it is now a bedroom farce. Idris with his solemn curate's face making his earnest point and that stirring of mischief and malice in her eyes, the irresistible challenge. What could she have done? Better leave it… there were no limits for her…. It still excites and sickens me. A sensual abandon that was absolute. The impulse of Circe to make bestial and subjugate. And then to weep in front of my cold anger, the icy dart of knowledge: the burning of the Fool's wound, the cure that left an exhausted spent body, a withered soul. And I fashioned her for my own destruction.

So leave me now. All of you. We do not share suffering and I have been sick for a long time. Shared pleasures and not sufferings make for friendship. No. I will not bend the bow again. I will burn the last papers: there is nothing more to say. Landgrave and his Helen shall burn together. I do not wish to see Troy or Greece again.

> *The cave and the rotting wound,*
> *Where the singing wheel of the seasons became the cycle*
> *Of an endless repeated ritual of sickness and pain.*

And the savour of blood as she smiled and her lips stretched back in triumph and there was a hideous and sublime climax in her passivity, the beautiful eyes veiled, the silk black hair trailing, the white, white skin….

I have lived too long on…

472

The noise of the shutter. What was that? The creaking of boards. Conjured demons returning once more. I will see none of you.

'I do not understand it,' Ganuret said. 'The rage was terrible. It was terrifying. And worse for being contained.'

Major Ganz looked troubled.

'You did right to tell me. It might well bring on an attack and we are at least forewarned. Wait.'

He went over to a telephone and pressed the buttons to call an internal number, speaking quickly and softly in German. Ganuret, bewildered and still frightened, caught little of what was said but assumed that Ganz was talking to one of the doctors. He came back, sitting heavily at his desk. Ganz made a profession of calm, but his eyes were bright with anger.

'Now then,' he said. 'Explain.'

'I don't know that I can explain anything. I was alone. She came into the room, wearing the black dress that she had been wearing at dinner. She stood there, looking at me. Her face was completely empty, very pale. She reached behind her back and then lifted her arms so that the dress fell away. She was naked and very beautiful. She demanded that I make love to her. She told me...'

Ganz lifted his hand. The frozen skin over the scar on his face seemed to be stretched tighter, so that his face was almost distorted.

'I have heard enough,' he said. 'Why did you tell the General?'

'I don't know. It was a compulsion that I couldn't shake

473

off. She told me, when she went away, to tell no one, that it was a betrayal of trust....'

'And so you felt an immediate need to confess.'

'Is she mad?'

'Possibly deranged. I sometimes feel that we are all a little deranged. It was inevitable, I suppose. A pity that you could not work off your somewhat pathetic guilt by choosing some other confessor.'

'But the General has talked to me so often about weakness and understanding. And you yourself have told me about his own struggles. It seemed obvious....'

'Oh, indeed! Do you suppose it was not obvious to Angela?'

'But why?'

'A betrayal. As she said. Waldeck clings to old and, for many, outmoded notions of loyalty and innocence. It is absurd. To a realist like myself it seems obvious that if a beautiful girl strips off her clothes before an ingenuous fool he will fuck her and be joyfully initiated into whatever else she has in mind.'

Ganuret winced.

'Oh spare me your exquisite sensibilities,' Ganz snapped. 'You've caused enough harm, however unwittingly. At least, learn to live with your stupidity. The General holds to his own views of chastity which are bound up with a kind of vague compassion that he fails to achieve. He wishes to do good. He is benevolent. But he is unable to feel love for those he would serve. Compassion without love, if it can exist, is sterile. Occasionally, the General is possessed with an overpowering sense of guilt. He has no one to whom *he* can confess. He suffers one of his terrible attacks. When you came along, he took a great liking for you and it seemed to some of us that you might help him. As soon as we were convinced you were what you seemed to be, we invited you to stay.'

'You virtually compelled me to stay.'

'And it has been a failure. If it is Claudian's work, it is masterly.'

'What is?'

'It's obvious. Waldeck was able to find in you the kind of Platonic raw material that he could fashion into projections of himself. You lack his genius, his nobility, his splendid ambition; but you have innocence and generosity, the positive virtues of unwisdom. And the tired old man could pretend you were all the things he had not been and never could have been.'

'It's surely not so terrible,' Ganuret said, hearing himself blustering feebly. 'I was seduced by a beautiful girl. What is she, for God's sake? If she is his mistress, then I did not know. And if she is so sensitive a matter for him, why does he keep her and why does he allow her to behave as she does? I'm surely not to blame for that.'

'He tortures himself deliberately,' Ganz said. 'Others use the situation for their own ends. She is his daughter.'

Ganuret was surprised but no more: perhaps it was a shock to a father to hear from a man that he had possessed his daughter and that it was she who had seduced him. The General's rage still seemed to be disproportionate. For a betrayal, some kind of compact of faith was necessary and there had been none. Ganuret had been used in a tactical struggle and any affection or bond that existed between him and Waldeck was accidental, casual – there was no deep, quasi-mystical significance to it. And then he became aware of Ganz's stillness, the concentration in his eyes and on the gaunt, refined, mutilated face. He felt a chilling sensation inside akin to the fear of an already fleeting nightmare.

'His daughter,' Ganz repeated slowly.

'You mean...?'

The Major nodded his head.

'So perhaps you begin to understand,' he said. 'The General is assailed with many difficulties. He is physically strong, but his health sometimes gives cause for concern. Mentally, he is often tormented.'

'And you expect one day to regain power?' Ganuret said. 'Is he fit to govern any longer?'

Ganz laughed. It was a sudden, unaffected, rasping noise. He was genuinely amused.

'How little you understand!' he said. 'As you say, you are not to blame. We shall decide what is to become of you.'

Extract from Promethead. *Hazel & Sims, 1967.*

It's surely not unusual for a writer of fiction to cast himself in a variety of roles which have nothing to do with his fundamental reality. I would guess that Michael Caradock did this more with a view to exploring arguments and attitudes of mind than emotional states. I don't think he found it particularly difficult to imagine how people felt about something: he was an acute if dispassionate observer and listened very closely. It was much more difficult for him to construct arguments or formulate ideas which were alien to him. He read a great deal and argued with the books he read. He used to scribble on scraps of paper, which were subsequently always lost. But he was not a trained thinker.

Snow is right about this: though, as usual when he is right, for quite the wrong reasons. Caradock wanted to be Philoctetes – but with a difference, in that he didn't want to help win the war. If you remember, nor does Philoctetes, in the Sophocles play, until Heracles appears and puts his foot down. Well, Michael Caradock was his own Heracles as well and he wanted to opt out at a heroic as well as a human level.

We were always friends. I suppose along with Emlyn Savage and Simpson, I remained a friend, but this may have been accidental because I spent quite a lot of time out of the country. I certainly made no attempt (as Faber did) to draw him out of his isolation and perhaps I was trusted because of this. We were never in competition. I'm sure that Michael would have quoted Nietzsche at you. 'We often owe the fact that someone is a friend to the lucky chance that we give him no cause to be envious.'

Michael Beauchamp-Beck in BBC radio programme.

After a while, it's inevitable that anger and disappointment that have been turned inwards must change focus. With benefit of hindsight, it's now possible to see that there is an underlying resentment of his quite avoidable *enslavement* to Mair Morgan – and he described it by that very word, when I first asked him about her – which goes a long way back, certainly before anyone other than Diana Bradley had any suspicion about them.

The girl in *Promethead* is a sort of harpy and I should say physically a fairly accurate description of Mair. And she crops up in the *Coriolan* book in one or two guises, as also in the last novel: in distinct contrast to the very cool and extremely nice central woman. It's possible I suppose that Caradock had already cast the unfortunate girl in that way and thereafter merely played out a thoroughly unpleasant fantasy: but I doubt that he was devilish enough or energetic enough.

His affair with Mair started cynically, got out of control and became – with its various complications – an excuse for rancour. A great pity and still very difficult to see in perspective.

James Faber in BBC radio programme.

The only person who really understood him was Savage. He was able to take him as he was, without wanting to change or cure him. I think they became friends because they recognised and respected in each other a similar desire for isolation, which neither was ever likely to achieve. There are people like that. I asked Savage what he thought about what happened and he simply did not answer. He just walked off....

Dr Anthony Simpson in BBC radio programme.

| 164. Ext. Caradock islet. Day. Medium close shot Emlyn Savage with islet and house in background. | *Savage*: (Sync.) He took great pleasure in the countryside and if I am any judge he was at peace with himself then. I used to ask him if he missed |

the city and the life he'd been used to. And he used to smile. But at the same time he'd say that he had come to all this too late....

165. Ext. Estuary. Day.
Panoramic shot of estuary and headland

Savage (V/O): He was right. He understood himself and there was no chance of him being able to live a simple and uncomplicated life because he'd got into the habit of asking too many questions and never believing any of the answers. I sometimes think it was a mistake for him to come here in the first place, but that once he had come he would have been better left alone. I don't know what it is that makes a man want to write books or anything about the gift: I just think things would have been better for him if he'd lost it.

Extract from television programme, 'Landscape of a Prophet'.

Marcus Conrad looked up and watched the swallows: a rapid flutter of wings and then the easy skimming through the air, the wheeling and assured flight. He took a couple of deep breaths. The air was fresh. It was the first time that he had noticed it was spring. But spring it was, sure enough. The trees were that lovely pale green that each year he forgot and the sky was a clean blue and the wind was fresh.

He went on watching the swallows. They must be the first ones of the year – it was only the second week in May. He found himself delighting in the elegance of the birds, the dull blue sheen of their backs and wings in the soft sunlight as they swooped and swerved. And quite suddenly he remembered himself as a child, which was strange: because he seldom thought about his childhood and had no clear recollection of what he had thought and felt. For no reason, now, he knew again what it had been like standing alone on a patch of grass, looking up at swallows above a cluster of apple trees, just coming into leaf. He remembered the greyish-green twisted old trees very clearly and saw them as they would be a week or so later in blossom. He had enjoyed that too: the swallows and the apple blossom. He had been ill and it was the first time he had been allowed out, muffled up. Someone called to him not to stand on the damp grass. Automatically he obeyed, not thinking.

It was not the precise moment that mattered, though, it was the generalised memory of being completely alone. On his own. When he was allowed on sufferance into the games of other children, he was still on his own. He knew that they did not like him though he did not know why; he knew that they despised him because he was easily frightened. And where their games were practical, involving bold physical acts, his were all in the imagination, complex and detailed. They swung from trees, lit fires, climbed steep rocks: Marcus saw himself achieving far more difficult feats, rooted despairingly to the ground. As he had got older he had retreated more and more into the imagination, creating a whole thickly populated sequence of interrelating worlds of footballers and cricketers and newspapermen and entertainers. It had been a daytime isolation that he had never minded: at night he was afraid of being alone. And out of that sense of being alone and the exercise of his imagination had come the ceaseless dreams of a different life away from the valley: a montage of landmarks from films or magazines all containing the confident, smiling, successful man he would grow into – not one a hero or a man of action.

And out of this child, of whom he could remember little more, had somehow emerged the young Marcus that he remembered all too well, contemptuously intelligent, aggressively well informed: eventually, triumphantly sophisticated. Yet even he had cherished isolation, something beyond privacy, the capacity to retreat into an inner confidence when faced with new experience or the inescapable superiority of others. A trick learned in childhood. Not even learned. Something that had happened and had brought comfort and that he had managed to imitate, until he could make it happen at will.

Marcus had set about making sure that he was right. He had played up his differences where they applied. He had watched and annotated the lives, conduct and manners of others. He had astutely applied the lessons of art to life, sometimes making the kind of empirical blunder that still caused him to sweat with embarrassment, but on the whole managing the bluff until it was bluff no longer.

The swallows had flown off. He wondered what had

happened to that sickly child, when and how the meta-morphosis had occurred. Somehow that child's mind had been a blank; there had been no future at that moment of watching the swallows above the apple trees: just an immediate and total sense of being alone.

He saw a kestrel across the thick tussocky moorland that swept down into a shallow glen, bleak and brown even in the sunlight with the somehow inevitable grimy track, half grown over, leading to some spent shaft. He watched the delicate, flickering balance of the bird as it tilted on the light spring breeze. And then it swooped.

Marcus turned away. He could not see the killing, but he could imagine it. Perhaps oblivion was better achieved at a sudden painful stroke: better than a long, conscious, futile growing towards nothing. The village was still there. On the other side of the hill. Young Marcus Conrad, in his bright college blazer, smiling: so sure of what was ahead, so certain of what mattered, so absolute that he was right.

Extract from A Coriolan Overture. *Hazel & Sims, 1969.*

The theme of isolation in Caradock's work seems to be usually associated with the notion of suffering. The symbolic heroes that he chooses as a basic framework for his extremely complex structures are all to a lesser or greater degree characters who suffer extremes of physical anguish as well as spiritual pain. The most notable must be Prometheus, but Laocoön and Coriolanus also undergo considerable trials as a result of their intemperate or reckless behaviour. Other important figures from myth behind Caradock's imaginative processes are Philoctetes,

Amfortas, and indeed Heracles, whose apotheosis was agonising. Even the central characters in earlier novels – Baldwin and Fleming, who have no immediate analogous models in myth – are characters who suffer physically as well as emotionally.

Caradock used certain images over and over again to link the matter of individual isolation with the idea of pain, vulnerability, and deliberately inflicted suffering. The most obvious sequence occurs in the *Laocoön* novel in the 'Tortured Beast' passage where he describes the events at a poor, ill-managed bullfight. There is no doubt about where his sympathies are: the heroic figure is that of the tormented animal and he spares little pity for the dangerous and not entirely unmettlesome activities of the tormentors. In the discursive and intricately allusive manner of the novel, Landgrave uses the basic imagery of the *corrida* to attack the affectations of artists, especially novelists, in making patterns of ritual heroism, extending this beyond bullfighting to other situations of trial where there is a heroic victim, *who has a choice*. In this section, Landgrave devotes himself to the whole problem of endurance – especially in battle, attempting to define the nature of courage, sacrifice and responsibility. The philosopher's own experience is comparatively trivial – but the range of his inquiry and points of reference is enormous: always returning to the two conflicting philosophic arguments relating to man outside Nature, and man as part of a 'whole' with Nature.

In the same novel, there is further imagery associated with the hunting of boars. As Landgrave lies dying he hears the noise of the hunt and in the delirious train of his thought, the spectacle recurs, the imagery of the savage, courageous, though not particularly noble, beast cornered and ultimately torn to pieces. Landgrave's contempt for human bloodlust is all the more intense for the fact that in certain places beasts are especially bred for 'sport' and subsequently 'hunted' from fast motor vehicles. This imagery again occurs thematically throughout the novel, often in metaphor or allusion, the false rusticity of the rich 'sportsmen', safely getting away from it all. At another point in the novel, this scorn is levelled at weekend cowboys on an American ranch, one of several extended images which attack false pastoral games played by megalopolitans: but the essential anger is directed at those who designate unnecessary victims. Caradock obviously holds that the essential cruelty of existence is enough. If he is reluctant to admit any generalised impulse for love, he is resolutely against gratuitous manifestations of hate: he does not believe that universal charity is possible, but he thinks that acts of savagery, vandalism and spite are at any level to be met with absolute resistance. What he is less certain about is the form that this resistance should take.

This imagery of isolation and torment grows in scale whether it concerns humans or animals in the later books, but it is abundantly present in the earlier work: in the small boy's horror at the hare being run down by two dogs in the early story 'The Quarry', in the stoning of the bird in 'Kingfisher'; in Baldwin's anger with louts teasing an old alcoholic vagrant in *The Low Key of Hope*, and even in the cool, self-contained Fleming's brutally contrived attack upon the little officer who shoots things for pleasure and who in a typically nasty scene describes how once he killed with a catapult a chaffinch that was perched on some wires, 'singing its bloody heart out'. Whenever Caradock wants to underline a point about human cruelty and mindless evil, the eye of his central character falls upon some concrete act of torment, sometimes involving people but invariably a gratuitous cruelty to a helpless animal.

H.-J. Kastner: Patterns of Despair. *Hazel & Sims, 1973.*

Spectacles of suffering in the mind are easy. The artist in love with corruption of matter, the processes of decay and its colours, the distortions of shape, great carcases of rotting flesh stinking, the twist of limb, shriek of muscle: all in the name of art, the safe, cringing imagination performing monstrous acts of torture and probing into the gluey ooze of degeneration. How different from the camp and the stockade. The atrocious laughter of freedom fighters, ingenious for barbarism, the orderlies in the psychiatric hospitals with syringes of fire at the ready to madden with pain and degradation, the sex-crazy torturers in the gangster republics. The artist, the writer clasps his sweating, noble forehead in pain and horror and strikes a new attitude: the most feigning, the most noble – the safety of the survivor, the self-preservation that is necessary to record an atrocity. I am sickened of it. How do I know how I would respond to daily torture, and lice, and disease, shit, the sight of blood fresh on the walls and floor. Badly I do not doubt. I would break. I would cringe. I would break apart. Never mind, I shall take another drink, and then another. Finish the bottle and then I shall burn the book.

Shriek of the nightbirds. The lapping of the waters of Hades.

Sad Acheron of sorrow, black and deep;
Cocytus named of lamentation loud
Heard on the rueful stream; fierce Phlegethon
Whose waves of torrent fire inflame with rage....

It must be late. I had better lie down. The lake of Avernus had no birds. A dark and mournful place without birds...

I waited always for the swallows, the light greens of springtime trees, the washed sunlight. The spring will not be long: I wonder if I can still find it in my heart to feel that lift, that little lift, of happiness with the arrival of the swallows over Lethe's lake, making my way to the shrine and cut my heel upon a flint weapon lying in the fresh new grass. It does not matter who fashioned the edge. The wound is my own.

Disgust is self-activating, noisome, the distortion of the line, corruption of the cells and from the heele (as say the best Phisitions) to the preuie partes there passe certaine veines and slender synnewes that yf those veynes there be cut a sonder, the partie straighte becommeth cold and unfruiteful. The flint is sharp. The dart: the missile. And caves of lamentation become the deepest silos of pain.

'I don't think that I *care* enough,' Baldwin said.

Natasha laughed lightly. He looked across at her suspiciously, but the laughter was sympathetic. She was not laughing *at* him.

'Don't you know?' she asked.

'It's very difficult,' he said. 'In the abstract, of course I care a great deal about what happens to people. I know

486

there are terrible injustices and wrongs and I know that unless something is done there is going to be an awful disaster eventually, but I can't feel it.'

'At least, it's honest of you to admit it,' Natasha said. 'Most of the people that I meet of your age on the paper are full of passionate intensity that is almost one hundred per cent fake.'

'Some of them are all right,' Baldwin said.

Natasha made a wry face and crossed her legs so that one pointed shoe touched Baldwin on the shin. He did not move and nor did she: perhaps she thought it was the leg of the table.

'So,' she said. 'You want to be a great journalist and you believe that you have to *care*. Well, I suppose it's true. The very best do care. There are a handful of them. And then there are all the good, honest pros, like my dedicated husband.'

She glanced at her watch. Baldwin looked at the clock. It was already past ten.

'But there are an awful lot of fashion-chasing idiots who want to see their name at the end of a column so that they can air their trivial opinions.'

'I'm not sure that I want to be a great journalist. I'd like to do the job well but...'

'Ah!' said Natasha. 'You want to be a novelist. Not a poet. If you wanted to be a poet you'd work in advertising or publishing or faff around in the BBC. Am I right? You want to write profound novels and you think that this is going to provide the rich raw material of experience.'

Baldwin flushed. What she was saying was fairly harsh in tone but somehow did not sound unkind.

'I'm ambitious,' he said. 'I know I can write.'

'Good for you. And if you're serious about it, you go on believing in yourself and don't be put off by the sort of semi-literate ass you'll meet on the paper. I don't mean Jim: Jim is interested in novelists if they're kidnapped, murdered, juicily divorced or trapped in some hellhole behind Communist lines. I mean all the clever little chatter-boxes who'll dismiss it by telling you that everyone's written a novel at some time or other.'

'It's still a question of sincerity, though,' Baldwin said.

'No. It's not. It's nothing to do with sincerity. Honesty, perhaps. But fiction is a dissembling art. Let's have another drink. I don't suppose Jim will turn up much before eleven. Perhaps some dramatic story has broken that only he can handle.'

'What can I get you?'

'I'm paying. You can fetch them. A large gin and tonic and whatever you want yourself.'

The pub was relatively empty. The remaining drinkers had all had a little or a lot too much: some were mourning privately through cigarette smoke or over doubled-up newspapers and unstarted crosswords, others arguing with loud bar-room jocularity that meant nothing, one or two listening blearily to fluent woes from fast-talking, pale companions, murmuring insistently. There were not many women – a couple of young girls laughing in a corner with the only perceptibly merry group; and two separate ladies boozily accepting compliments, the one from a white-moustached dandy and the other from a fat, sly character in an overcoat pudgily but irresolutely clutching at her thigh: both women looked to Baldwin indistinguishable. He moved around the curve of the bar to try to attract the attention of the landlord and so that he could still see Natasha. She was an attractive woman. The black coat with the high collar set off her fair hair nicely. She sat with her hands deep in the pockets, watching the other people in the bar, her face expressionless. He went back with the drinks and sat a little further away from her so that he could look discreetly at her knees from time to time. Jim treated her much too casually. Baldwin could not understand it: she was intelligent, feminine, warm...

'It's bad luck missing the theatre,' he said.

'Oh, I'm used to it. Anyway, I've enjoyed talking to you. It hasn't been so bad, has it?'

'No, no. I didn't mean that. Of course not. I've had a marvellous evening. It's just I thought you must be a bit disappointed....'

'I haven't been disappointed for years. My children are sometimes disappointed. I am merely bored. Sorry, I'm not being disloyal.... Do you know, I don't even know your name? Someone must have said it at the party the other night, but...'

'It's Baldwin. Hugh Baldwin.'

'Hugh. That's a nice name. It suits you. I'm not being disloyal – but Jim's whole life is the paper and I suppose it's quite a lot of mine and then there are the children: but one does get bored. It's rather a luxury being able to confess it. Cheers.'

'Cheers.'

'It's very nice of you keeping me company. I'd have thought there was metal more attractive about.'

'That would be very difficult to imagine,' said Baldwin, in what he judged to be the nick of time.

Natasha gave him a slow, definitely provocative smile.

'That's extremely charming of you,' she said. 'Tell me more about yourself. Where did you say you come from?'

'A place called Shotover.'

She asked him questions which he answered as briefly as was possible, while still remaining polite, until he found himself talking freely about his parents and himself and how different he was from them and how he had hated the place.

Natasha had moved nearer to him, so that she was now quite close.

'And is this what it's all about? Not caring enough?' she said. 'You're not the first one to feel guilty about making a break, you know.'

'Well, not exactly,' Baldwin said. 'We were talking generally then – about overpopulation and famine. It's not quite the same thing. In fact, it's the opposite. I care a bloody sight too much about me is what I mean.'

'You think too much,' said Natasha.

She tilted back her head and did something with her lips that could not have been deliberate, but which was very stirring. Baldwin was frightened and excited at the same time. He heard her stockings rub against each other as she moved slightly. Then, fortunately, before he could even think of making a fool of himself, Jim MacLean came into the pub, rugged and busy and pipe-smoking.

'Hullo, darling,' he said. 'Hullo, Sid. You still here? Nice of you to keep an eye on her. Sorry about this, love. Hell of a fracas at the last minute. Story from Berlin. Russians being bloody awkward again. Trouble is as soon as anything of that sort happens, everyone expects another bloody airlift. I had to get things organised. Now then, Sid, what are you having? Least I can do after you've been so gallant. Have a short. Large Scotch. I insist. Anything with it? Gin, Tash? Right. My God, I could do with a shot myself.'

*

It is true, Baldwin thought. What I said to her was true all along. I am so completely self-absorbed that I never give a thought to anyone else and it is shameful. It is bloody shameful when the world is full of people suffering that bloody Sid Baldwin – Hugh Baldwin, Hugh, Sid, what does it matter anyway – is only interested in his own festering *amour propre*. He was revolted with himself. Not with the act but with his motives. It was not like the time with the whore when he had been physically disgusted: this had been, in its way, beautiful and passionate, but it had been wrong. And he had gone to her purely because – impurely because – June had led him on and then turned off, laughing, with his hand under her knickers scrabbling away frantically. All right! Hugh Sidney Baldwin had thought, I know where I can get it and a much classier woman than you will be ever, you stupid fluttery deb. I can make it with a real, mature woman who has as good as told me she will and there is something genuine between us. There is understanding.... And June had given him a peck on his sullen, burning face and said, laughing, that he was extra sexy when he was sulking.

491

So with the children out of the way and MacLean in America, he had gone to her flat and she had known why he had come there and after all the civilised preliminaries and the drinks and the chat and the bloody cashew nuts, he had moved over to her and she had opened her mouth and her blouse and her legs and he had taken her on the sofa, without a clue about what he was doing other than that it worked and it seemed to work for her because she made a hell of a lot of noise. And then she had taken him to bed for the rest of the night. At least, it had been, he found later, one of the spare bedrooms. He was glad about that....

But the shame was terrible. What he had done was wrong. Wrong. He had gone after another man's wife, a gentle and lovely woman, to appease his own pathetic pride, and it was symptomatic of the way he was. Only what *he* wanted mattered; only the way his paranoid and arrogant personality reacted could count for anything. And to hell with everyone else. Let them all rot, burn, starve, tear each other to bits, as long as Sid Baldwin's vanity was unscarred and his self-esteem intact.

Extracts from The Low Key of Hope. *Alvin & Brandt, 1954.*

Caradock deals over and over again with the private moral dilemmas of characters who put their own immediate self-interest first and who are, in one way or another, ashamed of themselves for doing so. Tudor, in *Angry Sunset*, does not actually suffer for his ambitious disregard of other people's feelings – but he is made aware by his elderly friend, Mr Jones, and by one of his sympathetic teachers, of his own ethical and political immaturity. Because he is a thoughtful and basically well-intentioned boy, this worries him for a while: until he soars away again on some flight of aesthetic fancy in which he dreams of dedication that is matched by achievement. All the time in the novel, Jones stands for compassionate humanity that sees the happiness or tribulations of a single life in the perspective of history past and present.

Tudor, however, fares a great deal better than Baldwin, Fleming and even Laertes Jones, in that we are not shown palpable retribution for his attitudes in the form of some kind of physical or emotional nemesis. This may be because Tudor is at least faithful to his artistic standards and will not compromise them. It may, of course, be that Caradock wrote the novel while still a young man and had not yet discovered how easy such compromises are and how quickly youthful ideals are modified for sound pragmatic reasons. Baldwin suffers for his indifference, not only in paroxysms of guilt and remorse, but in the physical blow dealt to him by a very cruel fate. The barren detachment of Fleming, in a way echoed in the cocooned ingenuousness of Laertes Jones, is rewarded by severely damaging repercussions upon the vanity of the one and the sanctimonious hypocrisy of the other – although Laertes Jones' self-mockingly innocent commentary is at least a token of saving grace.

Self-interest and true-self-importance in Caradock are always aspects of intense vulnerability and his heroes inevitably become victims of their own near-sighted pursuit of some personal vindication of their image of themselves.

It is not plainly or coherently enough stated to be a 'message': but Caradock seems to assert with increasing force the need for an individual to care and to see himself in an ethical perspective for his own moral welfare. The ideas are expanded in the two collections of essays in a more abstract way, as we shall see in a later chapter; but, as theories, lack something of the immediacy and impact that may be found in the earlier works of fiction.

Extract from Douglas Rome: Michael Caradock *in Writers of Today series, 1969.*

While I stand in awe and admiration of Wallace Stevens' claims for Poetry as the Supreme Fiction and see that, even in the age of television, it offers the more demanding an intricate and desired form of diversion – 'the reality of sensation and fancy beneath the surface of conventional ideas' – I find it necessary all the same to say a word on behalf of the not so supreme fiction as practised by most serious novelists, some biographers, and a few minor poets at a more personal level. As I understand it this does not involve the interpretation of a *mundo* which 'almost successfully resists the intelligence', but the observation of the world as it is in as many versions as possible for a single artist.

It has still to be proved that television is potentially one of the most powerful anti-democratic forces at work in modern society – with its lulling spells of entertainment and simple storytelling punctuated by punditry and political cant, least dangerous when emanating from recognisable politicians. Nevertheless, a little reflection will indicate how this facile medium which has been allowed to develop so trivially might be used, and perhaps is already being used,

494

by determined and subtle subversives. Its influence cannot feasibly be balanced, but it can be checked.

The serious theatre reaches a small and regrettably fashionable audience interested more in the phantasmas of ideas than in ideas themselves: the serious cinema tackles its opportunities admirably within its limits (in spite of the absurd telegraphese invented by the savants who write about it) and is at its best when at its least solemn. Even so, it lacks the protean versatility of prose fiction which can embrace so many ideas, circumstances, events, characters from so many different perspectives, in so many different forms and using such variety of structure and style. A very great novel such as *War and Peace* or *Crime and Punishment* or *Our Mutual Friend* or *Tom Jones*, let alone *Ulysses* or *Finnegans Wake* or *À la recherche du temps perdu*, cannot be presented in some other artistic shape, because its very greatness depends upon the fact that it was conceived, fashioned and accomplished in *literary* terms as an extraordinary amalgam of observation, analysis, projection and imagination, tempered by old wisdom and given a bright sheen by new interpretations – sometimes even by new ideas.

We live in an age where art is thought by many to be dismissable and is increasingly dismissed by the new breed of performing *fantoccini* of supposedly high intelligence who twitch and flicker before us and then are heard all too frequently. In an age of egalitarianism run riot, the opinions of noisy amateurs are eagerly canvassed and the judgements of the ignorant valued. (The new mages of science and medicine, who hitherto needed only protection from one another, are finding – somewhat to their discomfort – that even they are vulnerable to vociferous and often ill-informed criticism on allegedly ethical grounds.)

As long ago as 1924, in *Principles of Literary Criticism*, I. A. Richards warned:

The common avoidance of all discussion of the wider social and moral aspects of the arts by people of steady judgement and strong heads is a misfortune, for it leaves the field free for folly, and cramps the scope of good critics unduly. If the competent are to refrain because of the antics of the unqualified, an evil and a loss which are neither temporary nor trivial increase continually. It is as though medical men were all to retire because of the impudence of quacks. For the critic is as closely occupied with the health of the mind as the doctor with the health of the body.... What is needed is a defensible position for those who believe that the arts are of value.... With the increase of population the problem presented by the gulf between what is preferred by the majority and what is accepted as excellent has become infinitely more serious and appears to become threatening in the near future. For many reasons standards are much more in need of defence than they used to be. It is perhaps premature to envisage a collapse of values, a transvaluation by which popular taste replaces trained imaginings. Yet commercialism has done stranger things....

It is hardly necessary to note that the situation forty years later is very much worse. The quacks are everywhere and the noise they make is beginning to be deafening.

It is my most sincere belief that the not so supreme

fiction has an even more important part to play in the defence of excellence than the Supreme Fiction which is Excellence and, as such, virtually indestructible but of necessity difficult to approach and understand: and I hope in the rest of this essay to examine the ways in which the novelist can – through his choice and treatment of subject matter, through his manipulation of structure, through his experiments with form and style and through his receptive application of certain metaphysical hypotheses – work towards this vital task of preventing the threatened collapse of values.

Extract from 'Not So Supreme', essay in An Elemental Wound. *Hazel & Sims, 1963.*

In preceding chapters I have tried to look systematically at Caradock's work from the point of view of his content, that is to say his choice of subject matter; his characterisation – with particular reference to recurring figures who share similar strengths or weaknesses; his use of metaphor and imagery and what they imply about his way of looking at the world. I have also tried to examine Caradock's stylistic peculiarities, notably his approach to different units of prose composition, and have extended the ideas suggested by this study to his approach to structure. Two central conclusions have emerged: the first, an impression of a man of restless intellect who had deliberately, when young, severed all connections with his recognisable and identifiable past in order to recreate himself in some composite image of his own idealisation and who, having failed, spent the rest of a fecund but unhappy creative life trying to rediscover the truth about himself; the second, a clear picture of a dedicated stylist, lacking confidence in his own skill and originality, who was passionately concerned with standards and consistently disappointed by his own achievement.

Trying now to assess the impact of Caradock's work, I think it is necessary to take immediate note of two significant aspects of his thought as expressed in the epigraphs to his last completed major work, *Promethead*. The novel entitled *Laocoön* is of inestimable value and interest in arriving at some overall critical survey of Caradock's intentions: but it is not absolutely finished, even if it is complete, and we do not know what changes (perhaps what drastic changes) Caradock might have made to the typescript had he not died so suddenly. We have a great deal of evidence from his friends that he was less and less pleased with his work and, according to habit, destroyed much of what he wrote soon after it was written. It is an appetising work of scholarship to speculate on what the ultimate shape of *Laocoön* might have been, but Caradock's distressing secrecy means that there are no notes, sketches or early drafts to offer clues about his intentions.

Promethead, however, is unquestionably finished and it is probable that the two epigraphs, both taken from Nietzsche, offer not only a key to the purpose of this, Caradock's most significant mature novel, but to his work as a whole.

As the novel itself has been, sometimes wilfully, misunderstood, so have the epigraphs and much has been made of their source. Nietzsche's volatile and impatient mind, often self-contradictory, finds little sympathy among the committed critics of the present generation for whom the tablets have already been handed down and there is no question of arguing with thunder, enveloped in a high mountain cloud.

The first of the epigraphs is: 'The soul must have its chosen sewers to carry away its ordure.' It is, I suggest, a clue to the intense personal anguish of Waldeck especially, but also in some degree of Claudian, Ganz and even Ganuret, all of whom are in different ways aware of their impurity, that the soul is no sweet natural meadow, but a swamp in need of draining and keen attention. This is a familiar idea in Caradock's non-fiction, where he frequently suggests that human character is neutrally disposed to good and evil and it is only the rigorous discipline of the intellect that makes an individual opt for good – which is the capacity to subdue self-interest and savage egoism for the benefit of others.

Part of Caradock's much-advertised despair is the difficulty of reconciling this moral certainty with the ethical and political impracticabilities of achieving the ideal in a world where power matters more than goodness and where abstract goodness, untainted by religious power systems or ideology or humanist power vacuums, is unattainable. Furthermore he sees no hope of achieving such a world and this leads him to the point of view set out in the second epigraph from Nietzsche: 'The philosopher has to be the bad conscience of his age.' He can only (the philosopher) offer the hypothetical ideal of perfection and in so doing must inevitably castigate the obviously inadequate state of his own age and of the world in which he lives.

Promethead involves an interplay between personal standards of morality and critical standards of ethical comment on an existing system. In detail, it is an examination of the way in which ideal behaviour is compromised by self-interest, desire for power and political manoeuvring, in order to establish a state of disequilibrium that will favour one man or one faction at the expense of most others. With Dr Kastner, I find it inconceivable that these ideas should be thought, as they are by so many commentators hostile to Caradock, to be extreme right wing.

Stephen Lewis: The Novels of Michael Caradock. *Molyneux, 1971.*

Isolation is achieved then. Nothing. Neutrality. The state of being open to the flux of good or evil. The state of nothingness.

Yes. I shall burn the book. It is all nonsense. There is nothing. There never was anything. Goodness is neutral and passive and only evil has force and energy. The equation is amiably falling into place, now that the assumption that the intellect works towards good is no longer valid. We'll come to the proof later. The mind, at last, of the barbarian – Gothes, of whom it is written that, having in the spoile of a famous Citie taken a fayre librairie, one hangman (bee like, fitte to execute the fruites of their wits), who had murthered a great number of bodies, would have set fire on it. 'No,' sayde another very gravely, 'take heed what you doe, for whyle they are busie about these toyes, wee shall with more leysure conquer their contries.'

And the gates are already breached. The Goths are in the arcades of the West End and filtering through the conduits of civilisation. I will take no responsibility for fayre librairies: only for my own small act of defiance. Good night wise barbarian.

Snow was for landscapes and maturity, the reasonable perspective from warm libraries which gave onto the barren beauty of winter mountains – now shining in bright clear light, now opaque in the dense tumbling of litter from the sky. The hissing of crabs roasting in the bowl, tu-wit, tu-whoo, a merry note; the woodcutter, sharpened by the keen air, vigorous at his task; old gossips around the woodsmoke; pure voices managing worship from the freezing chapel. Sentimental, of course: winter is not what it used to be. It used to be, he remembered, another kind of disappointment: a transformed world of muted outlines and glistening beauty that was cold, wet and numbing. The exhilaration of the slide ended in the sickening lurch of the fall, the thump, the jeering laughter; there were ambushes and snowballs cored with stones. Like so much of childhood, it was an index of the malice of which children are capable.

Snow in Venice for a man who had learned that he was dying and would surely not see another February seemed appropriate: in contrast to high summer, shining, gold-laced water, gleaming buildings, a clear glaring sky. Now looking from the Riva degli Schiavoni there was a bleakness in the air, a dankness from the water, a blurring of weather where snow and greyness commingled over brownish canal so that it was only just possible to make out the white-fringed outline of San Giorgio Maggiore through the thickened air. It was possible though to forget that snow was a more hostile and insidious form of rain.

501

He turned back and walked along the quay where the snow was still printed but fresh and crisp; the gondolas were staked out by strange, bare limbs of bent, distorted wood. The lights in the stern iron triform street lamps were already switched on and beginning to throb in the murk. One or two people ventured out onto the trellised jetties to gaze, quite pointlessly, at a patch of oily water. In the distance someone was running comically through the snow with big, silly strides to amuse some children. And on a spit of land the great edifice of San Salute pushed forward, magnificently and foolishly evident of great purpose, a grand design, a famous republic, a marvellous jumble of art and failure sinking into a polluted lagoon. The sick thoughts of a diseased and incurable body. This now was the problem: how much the vitriol of his imagination was generated and refined by a disease that he had only days ago heard about, which was killing him. He had always despised the critical fudge that clung to the sides of any literary stockpot, a nasty froth and sediment that made the broth seem less pure. Now he *had* to wonder whether the physiological course of a disease had affected his thought, his ideas, his affections, his responses. He heard it said that sufferers from this or that illness were inclined to this or that pattern of behaviour. And Landgrave was not literary. He was an academic who had, as occasion demanded, tried his hand at other things to be of service. It did not matter, except to him. He found, or thought he found, walking along the tracked snow in the direction of San Marco, past small dark-clothed groups of gesturing people in woollen scarves and hats, that he did not want to be intellectually poisoned by a physical disease that he could not control. How could he help it if vicious fluids were changing him chemically? How could he resist? How could he protest? What was a vicious fluid? Or substance? Or molecular event? Landgrave's hatred and resentment was ineffable. It was not a matter of accepting finitude: it was the debasement of being and decaying, having been allowed to dream of something grander.

Dogs before the fire dreamed. As the men came in from the cold and splayed themselves besides the kitchen women, the dogs twitched and whimpered. The old ladies laughed, one of the farmhands threw something at the stupid beast. A girl smoothed down her side. A man struggled with the choke in his phlegmy breath. Very cold. Frost thick on the windows. Icicles on the rims of low buildings to break and clink. And the poor dogs dreaming in the warmth: twitching and whimpering...

A dry and withering cold, which congealeth the crudled blood and frieseth the wetherbeaten flesh, with stormes of Fortune, and hoare frosts of Care.

He remembered though the placidly ancient priest who had long since abandoned priestliness but not the habit of goodness, who (in very enviable health) had always held that age was a comfort, that it was not cold or dry or withering: that it brought relief, that it gave more than it could take away. The curiously tough old face, nothing saintly in it: red and pugnacious. Warning him. He was never going to find out:

> Such was the end of this Ambitious brere
> For scorning Eld.

How had he scorned? The snow was beginning to seep through his good leather shoes and he felt cold, shivering, and quickening his pace to reach his hotel, alcohol and dry socks. He could review his sins of omission in the bar.

Extract from 'February' episode of Laocoön. *Hazel &
Sims, posthumous.*

What... what do you want?
  What are you doing? No. Do not...
  Wait. Think what you're doing. What is it you want?
  See, where the Kingfisher dives.... There.
  No. No. I...

10

The body of Michael Caradock was discovered on the morning of 27 January 1970. He had been killed by several brutal blows from a billhook, six in all, but the body had not been mutilated or hacked about as was later reported in the less responsible sections of the Press. The wounds were to the head, shoulders and arms and either of the blows to the head would have caused his death. The weapon had been discarded alongside the body, which was found lying in one of the large rooms, on the ground floor of the house overlooking the estuary, which Caradock used as a sitting room. There was a small amount of damage but not consistent with any great or protracted struggle.

Caradock's corpse was found by county police accompanied by his friends Dr Anthony Simpson and Emlyn Savage who became immediately fearful for his safety after the earlier discovery of the murder of Mair Morgan. She had been strangled. There was an immediate search for Mrs Morgan's husband, Hugh Morgan, who, it appeared, had not been home the previous night. He was quickly found: staying with relatives in the cathedral town of St Davids, some thirty miles along the coast. Mr Morgan was naturally profoundly shocked by the murders and was at no time under suspicion of having committed either.

The identity of the man who killed Caradock and Mair Morgan was not difficult to establish and prove, because he made no attempt to cover his tracks and, after arrest, immediately confessed to Police Constable Ivor Garrett and Dr Simpson, both of whom he knew well, what he had done.

Robert Griffiths, nicknamed Bob Y Pant (Bob of the Dale), lived alone in a small and shabby cottage which belonged to one of the neighbourhood farms. The farmer, who had no use for the building, allowed Griffiths to live there free, and in return the mentally subnormal but extremely powerful young man did odd jobs for him. Sometimes he was asked to help in some specific work (for example, sheep-dipping or harvesting), to do a particular task requiring unusual strength, which was a source of much pride to the poor fellow. But usually he came and went as he pleased – turning up to see whether there was anything for him to do on most days and wandering off when the job was done. He was fed when he was around, given a little spending money which he supplemented by doing other casual work around the village. His mother, who had died some years earlier, had been herself a little simple-minded and had worked as a maid in the farmhouse. His father was thought to have been a tinker, who had stayed in the locality for a short time and then disappeared.

Griffiths had no history of violence. Occasionally he was persuaded to perform some harmless act which proved his considerable physical power and he was very much aware of his strength. For the most part, however, he had a friendly, cheerful temperament, grinned a lot, and wore a habitually bemused expression – but he was given to sudden, abrupt movements and shouting, behaviour of no particular interest or significance to those who had always known him, though alarming to strangers. He spent much of his time in the local pubs but was not an immoderate drinker, perhaps taking two or three pints of mild beer in an evening. He liked company and enjoyed being among the local men, even though he participated very little in their conversations or games of cards. He was treated to glasses of beer, given the occasional hot meal by someone for whom he did an odd job and for the rest of the time lived on bread and cheese and pies.

Only on two occasions were there stories of his breaking out. Griffiths was very fond of animals, especially dogs, and was surprisingly gentle in handling them. Once he had badly beaten another man in the village who had been ill-treating a dog. The action had been calculated and mean, it appears, in that the man had waylaid the animal which had caused him some nuisance and was hitting it mercilessly with a horsewhip. The matter was, by popular agreement and feeling, forgotten when the other man, whose jaw had been broken, was persuaded not to press charges. In a small community, such persuasion, entirely passive, can be powerful. The other time some loutish young bravos (after drinking too much) had challenged Griffiths to a fight: there were five of them but Griffiths had been holding his own quite well, egged on rather shamefully by older men who should have known better. It was all very good humoured to begin with, rough horseplay and no more: but inevitably tempers began to fray. The fight was stopped by Hugh Morgan who happened to be passing and who gave all concerned, except Robert Griffiths, a severe lashing with his tongue. Hugh Morgan was strong and confident enough to intervene in what was undoubtedly an ugly scene.

The intervention served to increase hugely Robert Griffiths' affection and admiration for Hugh Morgan. They were of a similar age. Morgan's parents had always been kind to his mother. The young Hugh had always been encouraged to see that Griffiths should never be made a butt of the cruel games of other children. Hugh was clever, handsome and physically well coordinated: not as strong as Robert Griffiths but much more adroit. This hero-worship was entirely harmless and rather touching: but when Hugh Morgan was insulted and harmed by the behaviour of a stranger, the gossip and rumour festered and turned poisonous in Griffiths' slow mind so that he decided on his own form of vengeance.

This terrible impulse, however, was further complicated by a devotion and desire for Mair Morgan that no one had suspected in Robert Griffiths. During the hours immediately following his arrest, Griffiths wept a great deal and talked with moderate coherency about his feelings for Mair. He had been found by the police, accompanied by Dr Simpson and some local men, sitting under some trees, at a spot which he particularly liked, not far from his cottage. Although Dr Simpson was suffering from the grief and shock of his friend's death, he and the police shared a feeling of intense pity for the bewildered and pathetic man who seemed only too aware of what he had done.

Griffiths' adoration (a word used by Dr Simpson and Diana Bradley, both of whom talked to him often in succeeding weeks) for Mair Morgan was partly because he thought she was beautiful and partly because she was married to Hugh. At the same time his sexual desire for her made him feel deeply ashamed: Hugh was his friend and it was wrong to think in that way about the wife of a friend. In his eyes, Mair's conduct with the stranger was not a matter of deception: it was a wicked betrayal. He had always had a pleasant relationship with Diana Bradley and it was to her that he talked most openly about his feelings. From her discreet account, and Dr Simpson's equally restrained description, of conversations with Robert Griffiths, it has been possible to piece together a version of his motives and movements.

On the previous evening, Griffiths had gone (for no definite purpose) to the White House, where Hugh Morgan lived. They had been talking about Hugh in the pub and Griffiths had wanted to see his friend and sympathise with his misery. Then, at the house, he had not known what to say, so he had stayed in the grounds and watched the house from some bushes. Eventually, a light had come on and he saw Mair Morgan looking at herself in a mirror. He saw her turn and there was shouting. He recognised Hugh

Morgan's voice. The shouting had continued for a while and he had heard Mair laughing and a door slammed. He stayed in the garden for some time and then went away.

The next morning he had tried to stop Hugh Morgan who was driving out of the village. Hugh waved at him but 'looked nasty' and did not stop. Griffiths went to the White House on the pretext of asking if there were any jobs that needed doing but really to talk to Mair and to ask her to 'be good to her husband'. There were some logs that were to be moved and one or two other minor tasks. When Griffiths finished the work, he went into the house, where he was usually given tea and something to eat after completing whatever task it was he had been told to do.

He could not find Mair downstairs, so he had – greatly daring – ventured upstairs. She was lying fully dressed on a bed and was frightened when he appeared. This upset him and made him 'full of nerves'. He had started to talk to her about Hugh, finding it very difficult: then he had told her how bad it was for her to go with the stranger and how wrong to Hugh. She began to laugh. It was the same sound as he had heard the previous evening. Mair was sitting on the edge of the bed, looking (Robert Griffiths said) 'terrible', by which Diana Bradley understood him to mean intolerably desirable. He had gone to her to stop her laughing. She had become frightened again. He had killed her, but had no recollection of details.

Then, realising what he had done, he went at the flood tide over to the islet where Caradock lived, intending to beat him. Caradock was not only responsible for hurting Hugh, but now for the death at *his* hands of Mair. He saw

510

Savage in the village, and Dr Simpson was in his surgery, so the stranger would be alone.

Nevertheless, he waited for the rest of the afternoon to make sure that there was no one else in the house. It was cold so he went into an outhouse and must have fallen asleep. When he woke up it was dark. He found a billhook in the shed along with other tools and picked it up 'in case he might want it'. Then he went around the house several times before going in.

Griffiths insisted that he had not intended to kill Caradock – but to beat him. Then when he had seen him, he had felt a terrible rage. There had been (he said) a fight and he had used the billhook. It was decided that Robert Griffiths was obviously unfit to plead and he was committed to an institution for the criminally insane.

Numbed as they were by the suddenness and savagery of events, Anthony Simpson and Diana Bradley both did everything in their limited power to understand and help Griffiths. Hugh Morgan, for whom the shock was enormous, suffered a severe nervous collapse and some time after went to live in another country. He never went back to Glanmor.

Emlyn Savage, who maintained throughout these events a grim and unforgiving silence, has since told me that he had himself approached Caradock about his affair with Mair Morgan. He had pointed out that it could do a lot of harm and that the woman (in Savage's opinion) was not worth it, although he had not subsequently told Caradock about any of the village gossip about her. Caradock had been evasive but not hostile: he was apprehensive about possible village reaction and about Hugh Morgan, whom he hinted he thought, potentially, a violent man. 'When he was not in the same room in the pub' (Mr Savage concluded) 'I don't think he knew Bob Y Pant existed.'

Extract from David Hayward's official biography.

At first, I thought it was quite a good thing for him to try to settle down in Wales and to get over his carefully nurtured dislike of the place and of his early years at Cwmfelyn. Then I became less sure. I'm afraid that if we were friends, then it was on my side. I regarded Michael as a friend, but I'm not sure that he ever trusted me. I'm not sure that he ever became reconciled to English public-school urbanity – which he accused me of on many occasions. I did not see him in the last year of his life: which is to say he refused to see me.

So I find myself having to ask two questions: how real was his desire for isolation and how much was it a consequence of multifarious resentments; and was the pain, the spiritual pain, which he writes about so often and which has been emphasised by certain responsible critics, such as Kastner, really genuine?

I think that the isolation was something he imposed upon himself because of his restless, impatient and intolerant character. He had a very low threshold for boredom when it came to himself, and for disappointment when it came to others. Like a number of writers and artists (not to mention the vast majority of scientists) he was egomaniac and saw things in relation to his work. He didn't much care whether people liked him but he wanted to be taken very seriously. At the same time, he would not risk himself to other opinions and for this reason he disliked most people he met in his London years, because he felt patronised and underrated. In fact quite a lot of people who were prepared to like him found themselves rebuffed or snubbed, for no apparent reason. In due course this disappointment included many more people and Michael dramatised it all into his grandiose isolation. Perhaps 'grandiose' isn't quite fair, but it went beyond the artist-as-outcast idea and I think it was, shall we say, exaggerated at least.

The spiritual pain I think was real and unfathomable. There were times when Caradock really hated himself, when he thought that all his work was meaningless and that he was a failure. I believe, though I have no evidence to support my opinion, that he wished very much that he had no urge to write whatsoever. Beyond this, he took a profoundly pessimistic view of human character, of any possible future for mankind, and saw very little hope for even the most temporal alleviation of our misery. Ultimately, the two psychological forces – the one induced, the other real – sapped his creative energy. I'm told by those people who remained in contact with him that he no longer thought there was any point in his work – and this is borne out by some of the passages in the *Laocoön* book.

His death was, of course, a severe shock, but I cannot honestly admit any sense of loss. Great sorrow at the time – but no overwhelming feeling of waste, because I had the sad impression that he was already spent.

James Faber in BBC radio programme.

An immediate and terrible sense of shock and of waste, because I was sure that there was so much there of real

513

value – once he had reconciled himself to himself. Far beyond this was, of course, my own personal sorrow. We had known each other for very many years and had been close friends, especially as young men. Like all friends, we had our differences, but the sort of bond struck in early manhood is very durable. It is impossible, really, to analyse what one feels. It is still very close and I happened to know, though not as well, the other people involved – so it was deeply upsetting.

I should say that Michael was in a very desperate state of mind when I last saw him. He was listless and apathetic. He had always been (except when he was an undergraduate) extremely secretive about his work: but now he claimed to be doing none and to have nothing left that he wanted to do. We were all surprised when the *Laocoön* manuscript was found, though his publishers knew of its existence, it seems. One could not help feeling that he had lost all enthusiasm for living – because his work was the most vital thing in his life and his work had ceased to matter, indeed ceased to mean anything. He was comparatively young still – only in his early forties. I think he was frightened by all the empty, barren years ahead.

Idris Lewis in BBC radio programme.

What we must conclude is that in his denial of the *Se*, the withdrawal pattern from life instincts, Caradock was attempting a systematised escape from stimulation which led inevitably to a psychostasis in which the sex impulse was used proto-consciously as a means to achieve, not a release of the *Se* thereby admitting a kinetic pleasure principle, but guilt. This, as has been already indicated, was a theopsychotic state and Caradock's sexual energisation was a form of repetition compulsion aimed at a positive abnegation of personality through the devitalising effects of guilt fictions. Once again the methodology involves psychodramatics, one of Caradock's favourite devices. In this way, using an elaborate autonomic fictomorphosis in which melancholia became misanthropism, he was able to act out the conceptualisation which he used to justify his will to be nothing, as put forward in a sequence of essays written between the nihilistic satire *Broods of Folly* and the centrally revelatory *Promethead*.

The paradox is recurrent and consistent in that it reflects the only committed resolution of a life-denying obsession in the distortion of a basic life principle, the sex drive. Far more effective than the early libido damming, learned from socio-repressive cultural trends in his childhood envirography, this libido-diluvial behaviour brought an overpowering and morbid guilt connection that was itself an automatic *and* autotelic renunciation of life principles.

The origins of this in the counteractive vectors at work on Caradock, causing the vitanegatory scale which brought about his final psychoform, are obvious. Desiring to probe beyond the restricts of revivalist puritanism to the primal animism of a pagan and druidical culture, Caradock found himself yet frustrated by another psycho-antithesis particularly destructive to his mythopoeic consciousness – his acceptance of the Apollonian cerebro-central modifier force that seemed to offer solutions. It took many years for this struggle to work itself out in Caradock's psychodramatic systematisation, but when the climactic conflict arrived, it produced a repetitive cycle in which the death principle became dominant.

Irving Haller: The Centaur and the Druids. *Heseltine, 1972.*

The idea of Michael Caradock's death being the culmination of some intricately contrived 'death wish' is patently absurd. He was always liable to fits of depression, which became more serious and lasted longer the older he grew. At the University, it was always possible to get him to snap out of them, but obviously in the last year or so of his life there were fewer and fewer people to encourage that. I was in Rome, Brussels and Strasbourg from late 1968 and I saw Michael only three times, once after something of an emotional storm involving various others, between October of that year and the time of his death in January 1970. On the first two occasions he was quite normal – according to his particular lights. Entertaining and amusing in conversation and full of the most alarming prognoses; in private a little melancholy, bored with himself and his work but determined enough to try to achieve something better. On the third, he was seriously upset but *not suicidal*. And surely if this 'death wish' thing means anything, there must be the possibility of some definite act of self-destruction. There was absolutely no question of it. Perhaps I don't understand the Freudian theory and it is all a question of fantasies and substitutes – I certainly can't follow that American who wrote a remarkably silly and obscure book about Caradock – but Michael Caradock was simply going through a bad patch and in due course he'd work it all off in another book. I'm one of his executors, that is one of the literary executors of his estate, and we know that he intended several ambitious projects after the *Laocoön*, but no one has been able to find any notes or sketches. This isn't surprising because he tended to chuck them away, once he'd got an idea straight and fixed in his head.

What I find outrageous and offensive is that people have tried to make a completely fortuitous murder, committed by a man who was obviously not responsible for his actions, even more dramatic than it was with all this rubbish about a 'death instinct'. It was the most appalling accident. I met Mair Morgan once and she too was obviously profoundly bored – in much the same way that Michael was: with herself as well as with the circumstances of her life. It was an accident that they met, that they subsequently discovered some kind of diversionary excitement in one another, that it affected their respective natures in the way it did and that there was on hand a mental defective who acted with unforeseeable violence.

I feel, please do not mistake me, a sense of loss and of grief, because I liked Michael Caradock and I never quarrelled with him. I also admired his work and agreed with his own estimation of it: that it was good without being excellent. I do not know whether he would have ever achieved anything great. Speculation is a waste of time. At the same time, I am struck by the horrible irony of the manner of his death.

He always feared violence that was sudden. The concept or image of the barbarian was a very real one for him and one of the things he disliked about the early Greeks was their capacity for instant violence. Politically, it made historical figures such as Domitian and the Renaissance Italians and Hitler fascinating and terrifying: although he recognised how much more dangerous the Stalins and Maos and Bismarks are. (That's rather unfair to Bismark.) What I mean is that irrational violence troubled and at the same time interested him more than planned and organised violence though I suppose the worst nightmare (for Michael Caradock) was a state prison staffed by criminals. He believed that there was no lower depth to human malice and that the intelligent were always victims of resentment in such a situation. I think it was clearly for this reason that he feared crowds, especially when they were almost mobs. I remember going back to college with him one November the Fifth, which used to be – I don't know whether it still is – an occasion for unsurpassing idiocy in post-war Oxford, and there was a great yelling crowd approaching the Randolph Hotel which was one of the places they used to attack. I thought it was all extremely stupid, but Michael was shivering with anger – that people should make a sport out of mob violence.

But that is incidental. He was always very nervous of mad people – you know the kind of unfortunate character you sometimes see yelling obscenities in the street or behaving in a generally uncontrolled way. And also of drunks whom he was sure would get violent. And so it is the sudden violence of his death, coincidental with his own worst fears, that I find so appalling, rather than any nonsense about a death wish.

Michael Beauchamp-Beck in BBC radio programme.

It is, as no doubt many readers who have bothered to persist this far have already remarked to themselves, a piece of colossal impudence to borrow from Aristotle's extremely difficult metaphysical concept in an essay about responsibility and detachment as it affects the artist, the thinker, or the thinking individual. Aristotle was after all talking about an eternally active thought which he calls 'God' whose activity is prompted by love and is the summit of excellence – untainted knowledge of the highest knowledge which is 'God' himself. 'It must be that the divine thought thinks of itself (since it is what is most excellent) and its thinking is a thinking about thinking.' It follows (as Russell has pointed out) that if God is concerned with thought about himself, it may well be possible for men to love Him, but it is not possible for Him to love men.

What I find so appealing in the ideas of Aristotle is the dispassion and equilibrium which allows him to presuppose the indifference of a God that he postulates without even bothering to put it into words. The wisdom of Aristotle surpasses for me the knowledge of all the scientists who would be able to put him straight on substances: the idea of God's indifferent impulse as prime mover implies a perfect benevolence which has nothing to do with sentimental charity and as such is the absolute of goodness. And, returning to Aristotle's classification of substances, it is pleasing and even exhilarating to find that, among the third and highest class, equated with 'God' we have, unsensible but imperishable, the rational soul of man. I take courage from the notion, whether or not it has been proved, that the rational soul of man can at least aspire to absolute goodness, the impersonal and indifferent benevolence of God.

Aristotle, however, had his own ideas about the 'good' and it would be dishonest to ignore them, which are quite distinct from though, of course, coherent with his idea of 'God' – who is by His every nature not interested in the 'good life' of men. Goodness for Aristotle is first a matter of function and appropriateness. As such, human goodness – the effective functions of a man for 'good' – involves thought, which is what distinguishes man from animals; but thought itself is not enough and it is man's capacity to control instinct and urge by thought that is significant, making ethical standards and moral virtue possible. In this context we may very well recall Santayana's remark in his essay *Egotism in German Philosophy* that 'The barbarian is the man who regards his passions as their own excuse for being' and who does not, as he puts it, 'domesticate' them.

Aristotle's view of moral virtue is that it is a sort of skill of the spirit, something achieved by application and practice and seems to aim at a state of equilibrium that makes a man benevolent: he does things without consideration of advantage to himself and does them gladly, whereby Aristotle suggests that a virtuous life is a pleasant one. (This surely is far from generally so: a virtuous life may be more endurable, but it is by no means happier than any other.) He goes on to a more dubious argument about virtue being the mean between opposing vices and to a discussion of responsibility and choice: then he offers his excellent commentary of wisdom and the difference between practical and theoretical wisdom both of which are components of the intellectual virtue that he ultimately suggests is the highest. Practical wisdom presupposes moral virtue and means that a man does the right things – not necessarily in order to achieve some goal but in order to live life well: cleverness is incidental and it is experience that matters in settling a practical problem; deliberation before action is by no means always necessary (or practicable) but an action may subsequently always be justified on reflection, if it is a good action. (Aristotle does not pay much attention to the favourite human vice of self-justification or rationalisation.) This leads to the highest form of virtue – theoretical wisdom, which concerns unprovable premises (concepts and truths) leading to demonstrable evidence of what follows from them. This virtue, which is an imitation of God, makes for the happiest life and is available only to the very few. Not surprisingly.

What impresses me about the Aristotelian attitude in respect of his metaphysics and ethics is his insistence upon individual virtue and what I understand to be the selflessness implicit in such virtue – so that benevolence has nothing to do with advantage or fear or love. It is not an insurance policy. Nor is it as in so many political ideologies, particularly on the left and what is known as the radical right, a matter for social compulsion. If I seem here to ignore Aristotle's *Politics*, I would point out that this is very much an aspect of his 'practical wisdom' and as such not the highest state of virtue to which men may aspire. For my part, in this essay, I am trying to investigate a state of selfless benevolence which seems to me to be desirable in men and impossible because of practicalities: the fact that many men opt for evil, for profit, for advantage, for lust, for power and that many more are too stupid or too lazy to avoid manipulation by such opportunists. Politics are necessary to curb these men and to organise what is practical and least harmful for the many – allowing, as happens in liberal democracy, the criticism of theoreticians (who may very well be wrong) that is sometimes strident because the theoreticians themselves are frustrated by their intellectual limitations, their spiritual weaknesses and their suspicion that what they are trying to do is an absolute waste of time since they will be thwarted by ideologists or founders of religions.

I am not suggesting that such theoreticians should regard themselves as extra-special, certainly not as supermen. In fact, compared to the ideologists, as they are all well aware, their impact is negligible – because they offer suggestions about good and ideologists offer suggestions about power and its attainment. It is from the unlikely (to many minds) source of Nietzsche that the warning comes: 'A hatred of mediocrity ill becomes a philosopher.... Exactly because he is the exception, he must protect the rule.' Given Nietzsche's own disposition to consider himself as very exceptional indeed, this is sound opinion and for the word 'philosopher' we might substitute 'artist', 'statesman' (*not* politician), 'physicist' or 'theoretician'. The protection of the rule is the service of others and such service should be rendered impersonally and selflessly. None of us know how brave or resilient we should be in the worst circumstances, particularly if these were to extend over any length of time: immediate suffering is a quick and effective destroyer of high moral intention. But, at the last, mercifully spared such experience so far as many of us have been, we are thrown back upon ourselves and our reserves of theoretical wisdom. Why be good? Why serve? Why live? Why attempt to contribute infinitesimally to the perpetuation of what is, in the conviction that eternal activity is excellence, and that what is should be.

Spinoza, the most accessible and attractive personality among thinkers of the past, acknowledges, with Aristotle, that while man should love God (the idea of excellence), God cannot love in return and does not love in the beginning. And Santayana in his introduction to the *Ethics* of Spinoza writes:

> Let a man once overcome his selfish terror at his own finitude, and his finitude itself is, in one sense, overcome. A part of his soul, in sympathy with the infinite, has accepted the natural status of all the rest of his being. Perhaps the only true dignity of man is his capacity to despise himself.

This 'capacity to despise' I identify not so much as commonplace disgust at myself when I indulge some base urge or act in an ungenerous way to the detriment of another person, nor even with my fear that in a police state I would act in a cowardly or ignoble fashion: it is my certainty that I am incapable of achieving selfless benevolence.

It is this selflessness of purpose that makes the sacrificial hero morally and intellectually so powerful and pervasive a force long after the ritual significance of his sacrifice (usually some form of appeasement or animistic prophylaxis) has been forgotten. Originally human awe of the universe and our understandable craving to feel loved by an omnipotent creative entity suggested the correlation of sacrifice with divine love and the necessity of human charity to satisfy an emotional need. (It is hardly necessary here to go into detail about the ways in which the sacrificial impulse or event has been corrupted and defiled by the requirements of ideologies.) Now, whether we are in awe of the universe (about which we know more) or not, I suggest that we must come to terms with an intellectual need: an understanding of the Promethean hero as a figure who dares impossibly in the face of immense odds knowing that he cannot succeed: but not in order to be heroic. By such understanding, it might be possible to estimate the conceivable excellence of individual responsibility even if it is no help at all in offering a glimpse of inconceivable excellence.

Extract from 'The Unmoved Mover', essay in The Philosopher's Stone. *Hazel & Sims, 1965.*

They came up to the car grimacing and gesticulating, their faces seeming huge as they pressed against the glass peering inside, their eyes fevered and sulphurous, their mouths cracked open. There was all the time the dull, deep roar of sound. Ganuret saw that in the half-track troop carrier just ahead Ganz was standing towards the back below the gun, easily balanced, keeping an eye on them. He looked as though he was completely without fear, one hand resting on the side of the vehicle within reach of a firmly buttoned holster. Ganuret thought that if anyone opened fire, there was no question of Ganz drawing his revolver quickly. The soldier manning the gun, slightly above Ganz, leaned against the bucket seat, also entirely relaxed. He was a young lean man in a bush jacket and a light blue beret, one of the parachute batallion. The muzzle of the gun pointed skywards, threatening no one.

As they approached the old outer wall of the city, the St Julien gate, the broad autoroute narrowed from twelve to eight to four to two tracks. The crowd which had been straggling diffusely all over the road was now denser and more concentrated. The dull roar was broken by sharp, sometimes shrill, voices, all angry. There were more women about, and terrier-like children with quick, knowing faces darting like parasite fish.

Claudian sat very still as though holding himself together. He was not wearing uniform. His face was very white and he looked straight ahead, yet Ganuret did not think he was afraid.

'All right,' Waldeck said to the driver. 'Signal Ganz. Enough of this.'

The driver flashed his headlights several times. Ganz stopped the troop carrier. Waldeck shifted himself laboriously.

'Open the door,' he said to the driver.

Claudian stared at him, but said nothing. The General put on his heavily braided kepi and stepped out of the car. The people stood off a little. Ganuret noticed that Ganz and the soldiers in the troop carrier had made no move. All were watching intently, as was Claudian. At a sign from the General, the driver slammed the car door. Waldeck stood facing the crowd, a square, curiously squat, and yet impressive figure in his officer's greatcoat. He held up his hand and spoke. There was a faltering of sound in the immediate vicinity of the car and then an incredible rising murmur that grew in intensity and which Ganuret realised was the General's name repeated in a score, a hundred, a thousand disjointed voices that somehow gradually coalesced until there was a chant of the name. The General had thrust forward his hand to a man in the crowd who had clasped it and now everyone wanted to do the same. Waldeck set off through the crowd, which opened up in front of him. The original circle of people to whom he had announced himself were sticking close to Waldeck, grinning excitedly, as though it was their special prerogative. Ganuret saw that Ganz and one of the soldiers – a hard-looking sergeant in the same camouflaged bush jacket and blue beret as the soldier on the gun – had jumped down from the troop carrier and had closed in on either side of Waldeck, who took no notice of them. The sergeant was carrying an automatic rifle, but casually – more as a badge of office than as a weapon.

They walked on at a steady pace, a wider and wider lane opening in front of them and the chant of Waldeck's name now thundering from the mob. Waldeck passed under the old city gate. Claudian ordered the driver to follow and the army vehicles in turn followed them. They drove slowly through the gate in time to see Waldeck pause, breathe deeply and look around as though possessed with an almost mystical wonder. Then he drew himself up, squared his shoulders and saluted the city. Ganz, very quickly, snapped to attention and did the same. The sergeant followed suit. Then the General held out his arms.

Claudian made a sort of choking noise in his throat. Another mob spilt out of a square, filling the entire road leading to the St Julien gate. They stopped. So did the crowd behind the General. Waldeck himself, accompanied only by Ganz and the paratroop sergeant, continued across the open space under the old wall, the wide hemicircle of cobbled ground. Suddenly the firing started, apparently coming from one of the tall buildings at the mouth of the square. Claudian hissed. The crowd began to yell and scatter. So did the other one nearest the shooting. Waldeck did not hesitate for a single moment. Ganz very rapidly regained composure and stayed with him. So, greatly to his credit, did the sergeant whose instinct had been, correctly, to split for cover and return the fire. The mob's noise dipped in volume and then rose again in wild cheering. After a moment or two, the shooting stopped....

*

Ganuret looked down from the balcony, astonished at the shift in mood that seemed to have changed a mob into a people. There was all the enthusiasm in the upturned faces and in the happy noise that might have been expected from a liberated people – but a people who had been liberated from occupation and not merely overturned in a domestic coup. Furthermore, a coup without much bloodshed or suffering: a great deal of shouting in the streets, a great deal of authentic danger – but nothing much to disturb the ordinary prosperity of the nation, no real threat to the ordinary course of civilised politics. Merely a more dramatic change of government than might have been expected at a normal election. Ganuret was not accustomed to such reflection and realised that his stay, whatever it had really

527

been, on the General's staff had educated him a little in the chicanery of professional politics. There was expectation in the crowd below: it was of all sorts, all classes, all ages. National flags were being waved. The soldiers around the square were smiling and off-duty servicemen were in among the people, swigging from bottles, and embracing girls with laughing faces and bright clothes. There was a sort of pause in the noise and a kind of collective gasp and then the gathering of breath in several thousand throats for a roaring cheer which broke. A few seconds later, the General, with Ganz and another soldier a pace or two behind, appeared from the steps of the building and strode out into the square. Ganz and the other soldier, perhaps the same sergeant who would by now be an important symbol, stopped simultaneously and smartly after about fifteen metres. The General moved on to clasp hands, receive the tears and kisses of people who had some forty-eight hours earlier expected to be torn apart, had expected perhaps to be tearing each other apart.

'Waldeck triumphans,' said the voice of Claudian behind him.

Ganuret turned around. Claudian looked tired, but he was smiling with the enigmatic amusement of an ambassador at a reception that was too diplomatically significant to miss and yet not very important. He crossed to the parapet and looked down at Waldeck burrowing into crowd where small circles of enthusiasm and space appeared like raindrops on the surface of a large puddle.

> 'Blood and destruction shall be so in use
> And dreadful objects so familiar,

528

That mothers shall but smile when they behold
Their infants quartered with the hands of war;
All pity chok'd with custom of fell deeds,'

Claudian said.

He turned leaning on the balustrade to look at Ganuret, still smiling.

'That's what they think he has saved them from. That's what he thinks he has done. Unless we consolidate, it is merely postponed. Do you think this euphoria would last through the next economic crisis, or whatever it might be? We are giving in too readily. All over the world. I suppose you think this is the end.'

'I suppose,' said Ganuret, with a new composure in the presence of Claudian, 'that you are about to tell me it is the beginning.'

Claudian bowed with exact irony: the right kind of condescension to a rather silly young man.

'I believe in certain things,' he said. 'I am sure that I am not a great man, as Waldeck seems to be. He has, at least, proved his strength. To himself as well as to others.'

'What is it that you believe?' Ganuret said.

Claudian turned his back on the scene in the square – on the noise and the lights and the unexpected colour. Somewhere there was a succession of explosions that frightened no one, obviously fireworks. And a moment or so later rockets began bursting in the clear night. Claudian leaned his back on the stonework, smiling steadily.

'Moderation,' he said. 'The defeat of any faction that seeks control over the whole. I do not wish to control, I wish only to guide. I am a lawyer by training and I want law to prevail: I do not want to see government by the military, by the police, by the industrialists, the bankers and least of all by the tribunes – always self-elected – of the people, who are much too bored with politics to concern themselves with those who would be commissars. I believe in justice and I believe that justice is a guiding not a ruling principle. It is also beyond the scope of one man. So I do not believe in paternalism except as a means to a sane end.'

'You are using the General.'

'Yes. As he has used me. And as we have all, in an uneasy coalition of interests, used one another. Well, I will make a confession to you. I too am tired. This should be a triumphant moment. It is not. It is an interval during which half the cast cannot rest because the other half will stab them in the wings before they can reappear on stage. In all these years the only one of us who has been able to indulge in the luxury of weariness and isolation has been the General. The thing that I desire most is isolation: but I am too intricately involved in all this.'

He gestured behind him. Ganuret had moved away from the balustrade and could now only hear the enthusiastic noise from the square.

'I don't mean what the General is involved in. I do not have his charismatic qualities. I believe that is how they are construed. But I am wearisomely involved in making sure that a good and sometimes inspired leader is used to lead. May I suggest to you that exile and isolation can be less exhausting than a quiet waiting game in which one tries to achieve change without violence from the inside? And I am exhausted. Tonight, I am exhausted.'

'Is there anything preventing you... just giving it all up?' Ganuret asked.

'It would be a bitter thing to give up now, after so many years. After struggling patiently and discreetly to maintain balances, to keep the General's purpose alive, to counteract certain influences in his entourage. Besides, I believe in what I am doing. I believe in my own cause.'

There was a great shout from the square.

'I expect that Ganz is offering him a kingly crown,' said Claudian smiling, but not bothering to look. 'Which he will, of course, thrice refuse. No. I am weary, Ganuret, because I do not like the fickleness of those people. I'm not pretending that they are the Roman mob. As things go in the world, they are a reasonably stable electorate anxious only about their prosperity; but in the last five years they have thrown out seven administrations and this time we were really near insurrection. And they are liable to turn again under the influence of subversives. I wouldn't really care if the subversion meant a just and orderly society: it does not. It means the routine of forms and officials backed by a secret police. It is conscience through the proper channels in triplicate, signed and countersigned. I am not a patriot like Waldeck, or (for that matter) like Ganz. I am simply devoted to order. As such, civil war has always seemed to me the last and worst resolution of differences and I have spent twelve years of my life, either training myself for the work of averting it, or actually working to prevent it. It is why I threw in my lot with Waldeck.'

531

Claudian stepped away from the balcony and moved towards the windows. There was still shouting and fire-works. Ganuret followed the neat, immaculate former ambassador into the huge empty salon with its chandeliers and gilt and towering walls.

'Why should I tell you all this?' Claudian said. 'First, because it doesn't matter. Waldeck is not interested and Ganz would not hear anything that he did not already know that might be used against me. Second, you are here: and even *I* sometimes need someone to talk to and complain at. It is because I am succumbing a little to the anticlimax after winning. The coup worked. There was no bloodshed. Or very little. And the triumph seems almost complete. So tonight I can indulge my daydreams of isolation and privacy and see myself alone with my books and music on a high mountain where the air is very clean and cold and I have little to do but ponder the greatness of others.'

'I find it difficult to believe,' said Ganuret.

Claudian shrugged.

'Of course,' he said. 'Sophistry becomes a habit. I have rehearsed deception so well that I have become a virtuoso. I have still a great deal to do. After the jubilation tonight and tomorrow and the day after, will come the new awakening, the questions and promises, the declaration of interests, the thrusts and counter-thrusts for power and I must be there along with a few like-minded people to serve our ideal of order and justice – and, indirectly, the General and the people.'

He glanced around the room.

'Very grand,' he said. 'I think I shall get some sleep.

There is food and drink downstairs in one of the reception rooms, if you want something. Everyone will be much too exhilarated to dine normally tonight.'

There was another roar from the square and the sound of the General's voice, echoing and metallic, over some amplified system, beginning a sonorous speech.

Extract from Promethead. *Hazel & Sims, 1967.*

It was Caradock's habit when using a myth as source material to adapt and work in most of its aspects at some point or other of his treatment. In the *Promethead*, as well as the original classical story of Prometheus through which he explores the motivation of his central figure Waldeck and his predicament of serving without indulging vain-glorious ambitions of cosmic defiance, Caradock used the Germanic myth of *Parzival* taking some important aspects from Wolfram von Eschenbach but also working a great deal from Wagner's adaptation in the nineteenth-century music drama, *Parsifal.*

It is not surprising that Ganuret, an obvious trans-mutation of the original name, Caradock's pure fool, enters a besieged city, though at the end rather than at the beginning of his Quest – we note his part in its relief is entirely passive: nor is it unusual that he should contract a relationship with the temptress Angela, now much reformed, after the coup and during the ensuing political drama. (Caradock has introduced two ideas of his own, linking the temptress with the spiritually wounded General: she is his daughter and their relationship is, or has been, incestuous. The reasons for this appear to be

533

that Caradock thought that, in a modern context, the sin had to be emphatic for the General's guilt to assume such proportions; and the innovation adds much tension to the situation.) So he uses certain aspects of the original in a different place in order to tie up loose ends. Although in the original, there are certain obvious parallels, with the Oedipus story – in that Parsifal helps the besieged city and marries its queen, while in search of his own dead mother – it is perhaps overimaginative of Professor Haller in his most interesting study of Caradock (from the standpoint of the professor's own psychological theories) to suggest that this small technical elaboration is the key to an Oedipal predicament in Caradock.

Certain other commentators too have been eager to relate a certain restlessness in the author to that of his heroes, but it must be obvious that this restlessness, where it occurs, is spiritual rather than physical. In the same way, many of these critics have ignored Caradock's own remarks on the making of fiction and have insisted on seeing parallels for certain characters in acquaintances and friends from Caradock's actual life. This is an unwise guessing game, although it may be superficially entertaining. It is most unlikely that the wild Angela, for example, is modelled on the unfortunate young woman with whom Caradock was involved and who so tragically died in the same violent sequence of events that culminated the relationship.

It is always foolish to oversimplify Caradock's meaning, especially in an attempt to reflect some event out of his life. Often in any one novel there is a drawing together of material from more than one myth (in an arbitrary but nevertheless effective manner) so that the basic and usually obvious source is supported by cross-ties of allusion and analogy. Even then the myth original is only a vehicle for Caradock's ideas and although his novels are full of emotions, spiritual conflict, incident and landscape, it is the ideas that ultimately matter, explored as they are thematically throughout his work as a whole.

In the two long novels, *Promethead* and *Laocoön*, these ideas are presented with some clarity: Caradock is obsessively concerned with the ambitious, striving character who lacks the ability to love, especially where he is most loved, but who wishes in some way to contribute to universal good. At the same time this character is flawed in various ways, is usually heterosexually promiscuous and vulnerable, while at the same time indicating a puritanical fear and guilt about his own sexuality. He is often arrogant, supremely selfish and craves for 'separateness' which leads to spiritual isolation. In spite of a long resentment, either justified by fact or imaginary, he sticks to what he conceives to be a moral purpose but is, especially in the later books, convinced of its futility in the face of cosmic meaninglessness and human weakness to face such a universal void.

In the *Promethead* and *Laocoön* novels, Caradock returns over and over again to themes of plague, battle and civil terror – which in Landgrave's feverish delusions invariably include the destruction of some great work of art, or institute of learning, or archaeological treasure. Terrible acts of madness occur in rational men driven beyond endurance – such as the soldier whom Waldeck describes jumping into a trench and bayoneting unarmed prisoners after one of them had killed his comrade with a last grenade. Many of these incidents, scattered throughout the two long novels in particular, are drawn from actual descriptions of war, from Xenophon to the present day. Together with similar accounts of devastation, they have historical parallels which it is possible Caradock intended to balance the mythical characters and deeds upon which he bases most of his main figures and their actions. It would seem also that in the final novel, which appears to have been completed, Caradock had arrived at a position of terrible, unrelieved pessimism: for there is none of the hint of energy and defiance that we may find in *Promethead* or in the two collections of essays. We cannot now know if Caradock would have maintained this outlook, quite without hope, or whether a new surge of spiritual energy might have somehow freed him from its fearful constrictions.

H.-J. Kastnér: Patterns of Despair. *Hazel & Sims, 1973.*

Dried brown landscape. Desert. In the ruins of the temple among the broken stones, he remembered seeing what he thought was a lizard dart out from a crack in the paving and into the shadow of an uneven, jagged slab of a crumbled, fallen pillar. He went over and poked under the stone with his stick, idly: he was not really interested, he could not tell one kind of lizard from another, he did not know why he was molesting and tormenting the creature. He drove it out of its shelter. It was jet black. A scorpion. The pliant, jointed tail arched over striking at his stick. It was intensely hot, near the middle of the day and the small creatures could not stand the heat. There was an old legend that, threatened by fire, they stung themselves to death; and there had been a game played by bored soldiers which was to put one of the creatures in unprotected sunlight and watch it strike at the heat, as though at an enemy. Sometimes it wounded itself: but it was the heat that killed it. He had chased the hideous little animal, as gently as he could, back under the large stone with the point of his stick – but it was very frightened and scurried about on the baking grit of the temple court for some time before he was able to guide it back into shadow. It could not have been more than a minute, but it was distressing (having settled for benevolence) to see the small creature's suffering prolonged. He did not remember the name of the temple, which had been somewhere in the Levant, and the arrangement of that particular ruin had now faded. He had spent so much time among broken splendour, sometimes moved, sometimes interested, sometimes merely because he was there and everyone visited the ruins – at Nîmes and Delos and Paestum, Baalbek, Aegina, Petra, Olympia and Epidaurus. Sometimes transported; sometimes more disturbed by a scuttling black scorpion than by all the secrecy and solemnity of the past.

And now here the landscape was dry and brown. The grass had lost its colour and the trees were turning from red to papery brown, though plentifully leaved and in the distance the hills and rises of ground were grey or bluish to bring relief to a deadening landscape. Occasionally a bush was bright with berries or some unusual autumnal colour. He was glad to be in his own country.

O trustlesse state of earthly things, and slipper hope
Of mortal men, that swincke and sweate for nought,
And shooting wide, doe misse the marked scope:
Now haue I learnd (a lesson derely bought)
That nys on earth assurance to be sought....

They drove in silence. Galen was quick to understand when he preferred to be quiet, after all these years. He had long ceased to think of himself as a servant and Landgrave had always looked on him as a friend: though there was no doubt much to report about what had happened in the year during which Landgrave had been travelling and though Galen always enjoyed listening to him describing what he had seen, he understood now that silence was necessary. Landgrave had noticed, had been watching for, the waver of concern in the kind, corrugated face when they first met at the port. From it, he had learned that he looked ill. Of course, Galen knew – but, whatever it was, clearly showed in Landgrave's face: the face he took note of, but no more, in the mirror each morning; not remarking any particular change. Yet change there must be.

But nowe sadde Winter welked hath the day,
And Phoebus weary of his yerely taske,
Ystabled hath his steedes in lowlye laye,
And taken vp his ynne in Fishes haske.

The sun emerged low and strong from a bank of towering cloud from a patched November sky in which the colours and shapes changed almost from moment to moment.

Landgrave pulled the shade down: it was too bright. Two, three, four magpies flashed low over a wayside field. O carefull verse. He wondered who the unfortunate lady had been, the Dido who must have killed herself for love....

And he thought once more about Catherine, how much he loved her and how vital it had been for them to separate. That too had been a selfish act and he understood her grief had been bitter: but she too had known why, after the happiness of their few months together, at the end he must be alone.

'I do not want to leave you. It will be worse because I shall not be able to help you and I can only imagine what you will be suffering.'

'Yes. But you understand.'

'I think so. Only because it is what I think I would wish for myself. I should not want you to be there. And yet it is not easy to accept. I feel I am doing what you want because of cowardice.'

'No. I am the coward. It is vanity, in part....'

Catherine had somehow managed to laugh and had taken his hand. She had never seemed more beautiful, her face was strained with sorrow and she was close to tears which escaped now as she laughed. Her hand was cool, almost cold, and he stroked the long fingers with his own, which were warm and sickly, until he became aware that it must be an unpleasant sensation. She did not take her hand away from his left hand.

'I love you, Catherine,' he said, 'more than I believed was possible.'

She said nothing, turning her head away so that he

could not see her face. Discreetly, he too looked away.

And she had gone quietly and early one morning, so that there was no occasion for weeping and grief, leaving only fresh flowers for him. From Cap Ferrat, she knew he would have no difficulty getting home and that he would not need her. But he had needed her: however courageous and splendid it had all seemed. From the moment she had left he had known that he needed her. And he needed her now – because he was frail of spirit and weakened in body and he could *not* after all face what was to come alone. He, Landgrave, sometime scholar, erstwhile philosopher, failed poet, witness to so much suffering as official traveller and inspector of human grief, had wept bitterly for himself as he could never recall weeping in childhood, when misery observed seems timeless. He tried very hard not to imagine Catherine: and then he had thought about her – knowing that she would live through her grief and he had tried to share the grief because he knew that she had loved him too. And he hoped that she might love again. It would not be the same as theirs.

The anger and the bitterness were draining away. Exposed to the intense heat in the bare temple yard, the scorpion had wounded itself – but it was not stinging itself to death. The wound was an accident and the creature was waving its poisoned barb, foolishly but bravely, against the empty, hostile air. And it would succumb to the heat. In a place to which its kind had fled from the cold.

Landgrave began to feel tired but peaceful. The lonely splendour of man outside Nature and the craving for 'wholeness' and the conflict of one notion with the other was a matter for fresh and youthful speculation, easily diverted by beauty, or what gave pleasure. Even the benevolence that Catherine had somehow translated into care was something for maturity. Solemnities and sonorities of man alone, helpless, but dignified, proud, responsible. He did not know how long this sense of peace would last, should the pain begin and he must find excuses for bearing it....

'*La mort ny mord*,' he said suddenly, aloud.

'Beg your pardon,' Galen said. 'We shan't be long now. I expect you recognise this. It's always lovely this time of year.'

Extract from 'November' episode of Laocoön. *Hazel & Sims, posthumous.*

A clue to the fundamental weakness of Caradock's approach to subjects which he is alleged to have treated seriously is to be found most obviously in *Promethead*, a novel set nowhere. All that action and agonising takes place in an unspecified country, presumably in Western Europe, which appears to be suffering a mixed bag of political, constitutional and economic ills which have occurred in the capitalist democracies since the thirties. There are one or two obvious historical parallels for Waldeck among leaders, or would-be leaders, who have sulked in their tents until the call has, or has not, come: but even so none of these real historical figures bears much kinship to the politically ridiculous, and personally monstrous, hero whom Caradock labels as Promethean.

How much more difficult to place the action in a real country where the ethics, politics, psychology of character and history would be related to the actual experience of readers: but how much more satisfying. The fact of the matter is that Caradock lacked the guts to attempt something in an area where he has been generally acclaimed as perfectionist. He refused the artistic challenge of relating his theories to reality in England, France, West Germany, the United States or any of the countries out of which he might have contrived a framework of events to express his ideas. The integrity, which has been so praised for its aesthetic dedication and tenacity, proves to be as barren as the spirit behind the ideas set out in the essays 'A Modern Ethic' and 'The Unmoved Mover', where Caradock's reluctant notion of charity is at last (with a touch more honesty) discarded in favour of a sterile 'benevolence' which has nothing to do with human warmth, contact or cordiality, and is the excuse for a mind reaping at last the harvest of its own scorched-earth policies....

*

Caradock's much-advertised treatment of sex, as I have already indicated, is the sex of voyeur magazines – the luxuriantly exposed female organs suitably befrilled and bestockinged in inviting, submissive or degraded poses – suggesting that there was no natural appetite compatible with healthy relations with a woman; so we find a social attitude that also goes for the dressed-up, the unnaturally titillating, in daily relationships. Without making too much of it, I am suggesting that Caradock's fetishism and snobbism are akin to each other and that both are symptoms of an etiolated, almost wilfully decadent, rejection of what is straightforward, natural and real.

542

I find it a rather bad joke against myself that what I feel about much of Caradock's work, especially the earlier books, is neatly expressed by Wagner (of all people) writing about Jewish music (of all subjects) in the nineteenth century. That unquenchable fount of Gothic wisdom says that Jewish music was 'bound to cultivate the surface qualities of attractiveness, technical skill, facility, fluency, charm, glitter, surprise, the striking effect'. But, he suggests, underneath all this is a terrible coldness. I am no judge of nineteenth-century Jewish music, but certainly all these attributes listed above can be justly applied to the work of Caradock and, underneath the superficial glitter, there is indeed an appalling coldness. There is no real 'heart' in any of the books – from the stories, which many otherwise stern critics are disposed to like, through the early novels to the huge pretensions of the essays and the last works of fiction. There are too many theories, some of them admittedly clever and even startling: but these theories are hardly ever related to life as it is lived and understood by ordinary people, who perform an essentially routine rather than a 'creative' task in society. There is also far too much technical elaboration, although Caradock was never able to achieve the kind of dazzling performance he admired and desired (quite regardless of its impact upon the untrained but thoughtful reader). He used a structural complexity and an intellectual pretension consistently to conceal a basic triviality of interest. The focus of his attention is invariably an effete and bored middle class spiced with a few curiosities. (All people with origins in the working class or foreign countries are for Caradock curiosities): and he never attempts to understand the aspirations and problems and joys and griefs of real, unaffected, decent people....

*

I began in the earlier sections of this book by damning Caradock as a mythomaniac, determined to bring about a self-apotheosis by casting himself as various heroes who may have, in their appropriate time, fulfilled some legitimate mythological function. The mythopoeia was on his part indiscriminate and he borrowed, if that is the apt word, from classical and non-classical sources with equal facility: Prometheus, Parsifal, Amfortas, Philoctetes, Heracles, as well as a host of lesser characters, have been identified by scholars favourable to Caradock's work as archetypes for his characters: but I believe that the disease (for it is unmistakably a literary disease) went much deeper and that Caradock was determined to live a myth, compounded perhaps of random facets from these gigantic figures.

I hope, in the course of this study, that I have systematically shown the course of this obsession, which became more degenerate in direct proportion to Caradock's social and philosophical pretensions; and I have tried to show how a natural gifted writer was perverted by attitudes which in the mid-twentieth century are not only undesirable but false and therefore untenable. Art for art's sake is no longer a concept with any credibility: art must be for people's sake and as such it must mirror their lives and aspirations and it must reach the widest possible audience.

What Caradock's mythopoeia conceals, as I have shown in

544

my examination of his non-fiction, is that he was capable of very little originality: almost all his philosophical notions are borrowings, though often distorted in a thoroughly contrived way, which is fairly clever, to give the impression of a new light thrown upon an accepted idea. The hard-headed reader comes away from the essays, as he does from the fiction, with an overpowering impression of self-pity run riot and masquerading as supermanic depression. At its most ridiculous this occurs in 'A Private Iceberg'; at its most sterile in 'The Unmoved Mover'; and at its most contemptible (in all that is implied by the epigraphs from Nietzsche) in *Promethead*, where the grandiose note struck by his glib aphorisms is intended to dignify a huge wail of discontent, from someone blind to political and economic facts of life without reference to which literature is an irrelevant confidence trick.

Richard Snow: The View from Lemnos. *Medusa Books, 1972.*

There is in Caradock a somewhat wistful admiration for writers who are either optimistic or affirmative. This suggests to me a degree of self-awareness that allows for the humour and irony that I have tried to show in Caradock's attitude to himself, as well as a seriousness of preoccupation with literary standards and with the kind of ideas that must be a part of literature.

Apart from the irrepressibly optimistic side of Nietzsche's extraordinary character, Caradock found much to like, indeed to revere, in Joyce, Eliot, Stevens, Sartre, Camus and Pound – all of whom are ambitious writers of tremendous seriousness and concentration. They indicate a breadth of political and philosophical interest that is not specially remarkable, but also a preference for writers who were all myth-makers and furthermore myth-makers who sought solutions: Eliot's Christian; Stevens' non-Christian but spiritual; Sartre's Marxist; Pound's some bizarre amalgam of right-wing theory subservient to unimpeachable standards of artistic excellence. Joyce and Camus were both writers who felt extremely pessimistic about the future and about man's destiny: but neither was able to restrain a kind of faith and enthusiasm in *man* (and indeed even more so in *woman*) that transcended any gloom that they were prey to. It is something beyond the merely cerebral and indicates the limitations as well as the depths in Caradock which some of his more austere essays have obscured. There is no doubt that the writer he most envied was Camus, who was able to reconcile serious thought with hedonism and who wrote with such ease and elegance; a writer, it is worth noting, who was quite sure of his roots – even in exile.

Caradock's close friends have told me that he read very widely and that he admired Proust, Mann, Hardy, Conrad and especially Dickens: I have restricted myself to comment about those authors he wrote about, though among these was Sartre whom James Faber, for many years a colleague and friend of Caradock – and himself a lecturer in Philosophy – discounts as an influence, on the grounds that Caradock was full of admiration for the novelist, without having understood the philosopher or the political polemicist. Richard Snow insists that all the authors who are the subjects of Caradock's essays are right wing, though he is eager to point out their myth-making appeal.

In this last chapter I should like to examine the effect of Caradock's reading upon his thought and work and say a few words about the pessimism of his last long novels, again bearing in mind a phrase from Nietzsche: 'All good things are powerful stimulants to life, even every good book which is written against life.'

Stephen Lewis: The Novels of Michael Caradock. *Molyneux, 1971.*

It's quite true that Michael was restless, but I think that he was trying to recapture a first intoxicating sense of being set free that he felt when he first left Wales for Oxford, moving through England on a sunny morning. He once told me that the journey always affected him in the same way: he felt foolishly elated with a high anonymous pleasure that had nothing to do with anyone but himself.

But there were also many other pleasures that he shared with other people, Fay Mackail, Brenda Thackeray, Diana Bradley. He dropped the comic xenophobia after a while and he really loved many places in Italy, especially Rome, where there was also some sense of freedom. Read the bits in *Laocoön* about Rome. And think of the lyrics about London and even the prose poems about Cwmfelyn in his very first book. It's so easy to ignore the simple and straightforward things.

Michael Beauchamp-Beck in BBC radio programme.

He was very harsh about his own work on the last few occasions when we met and I quoted to him something he had used by Santayana in an essay, about the only true dignity of a man being that he could despise himself. And for a moment there was a brief spark and he was back as quick as a flash with Nietzsche and, 'The man who despises himself nevertheless esteems himself as self-despised'. It made me think he had far from given up. I was wrong.

James Faber in BBC radio programme.

166. Ext. Glanmor. Day. Diana Bradley, with her back to the sea, looking directly at camera. Caradock's house and island in background

Bradley: (Sync.) There are some people who have said that Michael Caradock chose to be at odds with whatever community he was living in and that he needed to feel antipathy before he could work – as though the creative juices in his body could not be released unless he could indulge this form of paranoid independence. I know quite well that he came here to Glanmor to cut himself off from people working in London and to think about his future work. *Promethead* was virtually written, and merely in need of revision. He wrote the short novel *A Coriolan Overture*, quickly, to amuse himself, when he was feeling contented. And he was always

Move in on Diana Bradley

experimenting with forms, ideas – for essays and so on.

For some reason in the course of these experiments, he began to have very grave doubts about his work. He thought he was losing something. Always brutally critical of himself, this depressed him at first and then brought on an attack of the restlessness which friends, who had known him much longer than I, were able to recognise.

167. Ext. Caradock house. Day. Cut to islet and house, zoom in on high empty staring windows

(v/o) *Bradley* : He admitted that here at Glanmor he had been at peace, even happy for a while – but he claimed that it was making his mind soft and flabby. Various friends, rightly or wrongly, seemed to encourage this view and tried to persuade him to move. He would not – because he liked the place. He genuinely loved the wildlife and his walks with his friend, Emlyn Savage. And he talked, a little incoherently, about *another* defeat. (Sync.) I think, and perhaps I am wrong to say so – but I would claim the authority, that he deliberately set out to make his life difficult again in order to

Diana Bradley in close shot. To camera

goad himself into writing. The outcome was the book published as *Laocoön* and a great deal of unhappiness for himself and for others. Mair Morgan has often been misrepresented. She was a beautiful, fairly inexperienced, conventional girl. Michael charmed and then captivated and then obsessed her: but he also released something in her which was (quite apart from the murders) self-destructive. The affair had been going on for some time before it became known. Mair Morgan, in turn, was now exerting power over Michael Caradock. There was scandal. He withdrew into a state of listless despair. His violent death was an accident, of course; but it is difficult not to feel that the despair was engineered.

168. Ext. Estuary. Day. Long tracking shot of house and islet, over open waters of estuary to Glanwydden headland	MUSIC: Richard Strauss: *Tod und Verklärung.* (7) Fade music and hold under (V/O) *Trevelyan Lloyd*:

Tranquillity did not come easily to this difficult and dark visionary. The peace which he had sought in his retreat to Glanmor became deafening in its echoes but enervating in its unhurried ease. There was too much time for memory, there were too many things to be remembered. Caradock's delight in the natural world could not compensate for artistic lethargy that could only brood but could no longer create....

Lose MUSIC.

169. Ext. Glanmor village. Day. Stop camera, looking inland along cleft of the valley over the village of Glanmor

(v/o) *Lloyd*: Perhaps after a walk in these woods and fields, with the cries of birds, the proliferate flowers, the animals running free, Caradock returned to his grim island and wondered on the different course that his life might have taken, if his youthful pride and ambition had not taken hold of and ultimately strangled a rare lyric gift, if he had not exchanged his singing voice for the hollow despairing intonations of an oracle....

Fade in gently MUSIC: Wagner: *Siegfried Idyll* (8b). Hold under...

170. Ext. Cwmfelyn scene. Day. Mix to view of Cwmfelyn from Careg Hywel down valley, with James Maple as 'Tudor' in medium long shot with his back to camera

(V/O) *Lloyd*: And if he had not lost that ability to sing and with it perhaps something of the ability to care, how much richer and happier his own life might have been, and how much delight he might have brought to so many who are untouched by his complex despair.

171. Ext. Glanmor estuary. Day. Mix to view of Glanmor estuary with islet and house, with James Maple standing in exactly the same posture but now older, more weary, still in medium long shot with back to camera

Peak MUSIC slightly and take down....

(V/O) *Lloyd*: As it was, this gifted writer turned his back upon a beautiful landscape which he could read and interpret with unusual wonder in favour of the desert and the snow-plain, the grim tundra and scorched rock of his cerebrations. The lyric imagination turned inward and turned sour.

Lose MUSIC. *Pause*

Take Maple abruptly out of shot, leaving empty landscape	(v/o) *Lloyd*: The irony is terrible and tragic.

Sequence from television programme, 'Landscape of a Prophet', written, compiled and narrated by Trevelyan Lloyd.

There is a heavy frost and all along the valley the dipping lines of the terraced houses are gleaming silver in bright moonlight. The roofs of clustered houses huddling into the opposite hill are white and shadowed. I have never seen so many stars: I do not know their names but I recognise the patterns they make. This is my first cigar, a Wills Whiff, and I am alone and happy.

Where there are trees the frost and moonlight together are working magically – in the gardens, along the river bank, around the school and on the hill below the park; even brightening and whitening the edges of darkness along the Church Wood. The air is calm and clean: no noise, no smoke, or fumes, or sulphur or flare of fire. It is all beautiful. It is Christmas Eve and very cold....

Passage from 'Frost over the Valley', prose poem in Metaphors of Twenty Years. *Vortex Press, 1950.*

Rhys loved so many places in what was really a very ugly and spoiled patch of earth. He could not help wondering what it must have been like in the old days, the ancient days of the Mabinogion, which Rhys read not for the stories or myths but because they stirred in him endlessly marvellous images of what the land must have been in all the changing splendours of the different seasons. He made the best of it as it was and there were enough glimpses of beauty to suggest what it once must have been: willows in early spring, beside a pond across the hill reflecting the pale blue sky; wild flowers in the bank on the turn of the road towards the Gilfach colliery where he worked; snow hiding all the scars of the mountain; even the sweep of the rain as it came up the valley. Rhys often thought what it would be like to stand on a hill, unafraid of getting wet, enjoying the rain as something natural: rather than trudging through it damply to work.

He had seen other places only in books – places outside Wales. Rhys did not like cities and had no desire to see London or Paris or Rome or Athens. He would like to have seen the Alps and parts of Scandinavia, especially Norway and Finland; he would also like to have seen Vermont and the Rocky Mountains and certain parts of Canada – northern, temperate places where there was a change of season, a migration of birds and animals as well as those who stayed, where things were never the same but did not change from year to year. But he was not dissatisfied with what he had because it gave him so much to work on in his imagination. Rhys had admired other parts of Wales that he had visited – Snowdonia, the Black Mountains, the gentle countryside of Carmarthenshire, the coast where it was still unspoilt west of Gower and in mid Wales; he loved Breconshire and spent most of his holidays walking alone there. For all that he got more satisfaction from glimpses of natural beauty and evidence of wildlife in his own village: it proved to Rhys, after he came above ground at the end of the shift, that whatever industrialisation had done and however much the way of life had changed for the worse there was still much to love, much that would always survive, much that could not be spoiled, or polluted, or tamed.

Extract from 'Kingfisher', story in Metaphors of Twenty Years. *Vortex Press, 1950.*

Richard stood at the edge of the pond and threw stones into it. He had seen some boys once, with Grandfather Watkins, making the stones skip and skim across the water. This had looked splendid. They made the stones bounce four or five times and Grandfather Watkins had laughed his big blue-eyed, white-moustached laugh and called the game 'ducks and drakes'. Richard did not know how to make the stones skip, but Grandfather Watkins said it was all a trick of the wrist and he would show him when his back was better, or his father would. For the moment Richard was throwing stones as hard as he could at the water, almost as though he wanted to hurt it.

Grandfather Watkins and his father were standing some distance away talking. They both carried walking sticks although Richard's father did not need one: Grandfather Watkins was leaning on his heavily, Richard's father was playing cricket strokes with his, though still talking very seriously all the time. Richard knew they were talking about him and what they called his sulkiness. They did not know why: when after going for walks every Saturday and Sunday with Grandfather Watkins as well as sometimes in the evenings in the summer, he had suddenly refused. He would not tell them: because he knew they would laugh. Grandfather Watkins laughed a great deal. He had laughed

when the dogs had killed the hare. For three weeks Richard
had refused to go on walks and now his father had come and
insisted that he should. Richard had kept away from them.

'Hey!' his father shouted. 'Come on. It's time for tea.'

Richard flung the last stone into the pond and kicked
along, yards behind them. Unexpectedly, he saw his father
lift his arm and put it over Grandfather Watkins' shoulder
and pat him. Grandfather Watkins had his head down.
Ahead of them, Richard saw a skylark rise steeply out of
the grass and climb, singing, into the fresh sky.

Extract from 'The Quarry', in Metaphors of Twenty
Years. *Vortex Press, 1950.*

As a historian by profession, I am aware how easy it is to be
prejudiced or predisposed and I am relieved to learn from
my scientific friends that they too have to guard against
'willing' desirable results that will fortify brilliant theories. I
have, therefore, tried to concern myself with Caradock's life
as it was. *Not* as it might have been. At the same time, I
have included, where it seemed relevant, opinions of people
who knew him intimately on where it might have been
different, where it might have altered course. I have often
wished that I could have introduced the forty-year-old man
(incidentally the man that I knew myself) to Miss Westlake,
Howard Paul and others; also that some of the people who
knew the older Caradock could have commented on the
adolescent. I suppose most people who work on a biography
do cherish such nonsensical reveries.

Two notions, which I wish clearly to disassociate myself
from, have gained a certain amount of currency in the

popular scandal that followed Caradock's murder: one is that he was deliberately capable of creating a disturbed situation involving the unhappiness of others in order to stimulate his own artistic glands; the other is that he was a simple man who had somehow been led astray. In answer to the first nonsense I am prepared to offer incontrovertible evidence that Caradock was a compulsive and self-critical writer who was too busy observing, and making fictions out of what he observed, to need direct stimulation. He could be alarmingly indifferent to others: but he did not intend hurt or harm. He was obviously capable of infatuation – but he was reluctant to love. And whereas this was partly because he did not want to be hurt, it was also because he did not want the responsibility of hurting others. My answer to the second notion is linked to this fundamental attitude of mind – Caradock decided in his early teens that he was not happy and that he must make a separate life for himself away from the Caradock house and the Jenkyn influence; away from the Cwmfelyn valley, his associations with it, and its impression of him. He must start afresh. As with many others, he found escape to an English university the means of breaking free. (It is for a great many Englishmen!) And because he was an able and hard-working student, though by no means an academic marvel, he became interested in ideas. It is ridiculous to suppose that his abandonment of lyrical stories and prose poems was a matter of conscious and histrionic choice: it was the way one individual artist developed.

At the last Caradock was concerned with literary and artistic standards which he was sure were daily sinking. He thought, even in the sixties, that language was steadily debased by the half-witted locutions of broadcasters, who substituted formula and cliché for thought and to whom the public were (willy-nilly) exposed every day of their lives. He detested the commercial confidence trick which supposed a 'pop' *Culture*; and the trendy intellectuals who sought popular fame (and money) by packaging it in quite meaningless jargon. He loathed above all else the cheapening of what was truly great – in the arts or in the world of ideas. He was fond of quoting I. A. Richards and describing his own stance as embattled. He was fighting *against* cheapness and debasement. He believed that all art and especially literature *must* survive. James Faber recounts a bitter argument in which he asked Caradock: 'But for whom?' Caradock was not able to answer. Gradually, he withdrew from the fight. He no longer wanted to help win the battle for a decent liberal society, in which the artist was free, serious and questing for something new. Ghastly as its circumstances were, his physical destruction was nothing compared to the corrosion of his spirit which was bringing about a terrible disintegration.

Extract from David Hayward's official biography.

The door was opened by Claudian, wearing a discreet blue uniform with unobtrusive stars on the epaulettes.

'Thank you for coming,' he said. 'He is ill and he asked for you.'

'Angela wants to be admitted.'

'He will not want to see Angela. This is no time for family sentimentality, Ganuret. We shall see that she is comfortable. It would in any case discompose her and we cannot have that.'

'What happened?'

'How much do you know?'

'I know that the General is said to be dying, that you are in a uniform, and that the police have taken over from the army.'

'The civilian authority has reasserted itself with full confidence of military support. This uniform is merely so that I can, in the next few days, move about rapidly without unnecessary delays.'

'Ganz is dead....'

'Yes.'

'So this is what you mean by "justice and order"?'

'It is. Ganz waited too long. A month after that triumphal entry. And think of all that has passed since: all the lost opportunities, all the missed alliances – with the workers' organisations and the civil pressure groups. It was a time when Ganz and his allies could have forced the General's hand, without any loss of prestige to him. But they hesitated. Waldeck believed he was again in absolute control. His terrifying strength started to return. Meanwhile, my own allies were in charge of the civil arm, communications and telecommunications, the executive; we had forged alliances beyond our own. The General wanted to address the people. Ganz temporised. *We* agreed. And then it was too late. Ganz had to act: a direct armed challenge. Loyal to him: the parachutists, the marines, one armoured column. Indifferent: the rest of the army. Hostile: the Air Force. Irrelevant: the Navy. Against any more disruption of their lives: the People.'

'I should like to see General Waldeck now.'

Claudian made one of his familiar gestures, which, in diplomatic, civilian dress, had seemed at worst ironic; but which was now sinister: the dark-eyed smile, the little apologetic spread of the forearms, the little tilt of the suave head.

'Of course. He is in that room. But you must be prepared. The General shot himself. It was our fault because we should have checked that his ornamental revolver was not loaded. When he learned what had happened to the soldiery, he made certain demands which we were not able to meet. We explained that they intended to use him. He accused us of the same thing which we, rationally, admitted. He said that he must think. He retired to his office and some time later called for me. When I went in, he drew his revolver. In the subsequent struggle, in which two guards, from the General's own regiment, came to my aid, the General shot himself in the abdomen.'

'Justice and order,' said Ganuret.

'Of course. Ganz represented the brute force of military dictatorship: the refulgence of privilege. Waldeck was an archaism: such huge, superhuman leaders can no longer exist. Government, what is just and what is orderly, must occur by consensus. Greatness is out of date: feasibility is what makes life, such as it is, go on. You may see the General now.'

The solid powerful body, heavily bandaged, lay in a ridiculously ornate bed. There was some kind of transfusion drip fitted to the left arm and an array of machinery with wavering dials and flickering electronic bleeps disposed nearby. The General looked very old, his

560

head very white and his skin very leathery and yellow. The medical staff – two or three nurses and at least one doctor – stood by. A soldier sat at the door. Ganuret went up to the bed.

The General opened his eyes, recognised Ganuret after an obvious effort of will, and smiled. His mouth fell open to reveal gums without teeth: it was slack and pink and moist, helpless and hopeless. No doubt the old man was drugged and not able to control his features. Yet the eyes were still expressive, glowing feverishly and strained, but still aggressively conscious. The General stretched out his right hand. Several medical persons reacted. Ganuret took the thick fingers, expecting them to be limp. Waldeck gripped his flaccid palm fiercely and powerfully. The mouth was shut and firm again. The old man slowly and deliberately shook his head from side to side. He did not try to speak and Ganuret could not certainly interpret the dark ironic message in his eyes.

Extract from Promethead. *Hazel & Sims, 1967.*

It was a comparatively small figure and curiously good looking, well preserved, where he had expected something ravaged, time pocked, and huge. Somehow the imagined composition from frontispiece illustrations in torn school-books had seemed more impressive, more expressive of the agony of the big, old, muscular man. The suffering of the other figures had always seemed real enough but incidental. The quarrel was with the prophet: the pain and poison inflicted by the serpents were his. It was even disappointing; until he looked at it closely, walked a few steps to the right,

561

compared it with the fastidious reconstruction, and returned. Gradually the feeling of awe happened to him, tracing the missing fragments of the original around the ancient remnant. He thought of Lessing inspired by the same group. And then of Nietzsche. And of all those who had, since the miracle of the Renaissance, found inspiration in antiquity, hoping that on the other side of the next Dark Age some debris would remain to bring warmth and true passion to men who were experienced enough to understand their own painful insignificance. The continuity of endeavour. To understand. To fail.

Here was the doom-laden figure who had insulted the blank, wooden fetish, even in the moment of his destruction piously misconstrued by a sanctimonious feeble ruler; the blasphemer in the temple of Apollo; the unhonoured prophet. Landgrave stood a long time before the group in the nearest he had ever known to a trance – with images and allusions, ideas and metaphors, memories and revelations, hopes and resentments washing against and over him.

He was not sure how long he had stayed there. It was cold and it was even getting dark. There were not many others in the courtyard. He shivered. A dry and withering cold, which congealeth the crudled blood and frieseth the wetherbeaten flesh, with stormes of Fortune, and hoare frosts of Care.

He made his way out of the Vatican Museum and picked up a taxi without difficulty, in a curious state that might have been nervous excitement or straightforward fever: he could not stop shivering, he was sweating and he felt cold – as though he could feel the wet coils of the sea-serpents about his own limbs and body. Landgrave was frightened and alone, as he had chosen to be. There was nothing left for an ailing mind in a diseased body but the reinterpretation of old nightmares. Dreaming and dying were the things that could be accomplished alone. He paid off the driver in front of his gleaming hotel. Doors opened. People called him by name. Smiles, keys, letters, willing service. For a price. Dreaming and dying.... He stared at himself in the looking glass but failed to see Laocoön. He heard himself muttering:

> 'Wisdom and goodness to the vile seem vile
> Filths savour but themselves.'

From opening chapter of the Laocoön *novel. Hazel & Sims, posthumous.*

APPENDIX:

DETAILED SYNOPSIS OF CARADOCK'S WORK

Metaphors of Twenty Years. **Vortex Press. 1950.**
Caradock was introduced by Jeremy Philbrick to Reginald Webber, owner and operator of the Vortex Press, subsequently bankrupt. Webber was eccentric and enthusiastic, but disposed to be dictatorial; very helpful to young writers.

Six Stories: 'The Quarry'; 'Blackberries'; 'Paradise Terrace'; 'Lending Library'; 'Kingfisher'; 'Flower Clock'.

Prose Poems: 'Evening Walk'; 'The First Time I Saw Paris'; 'View of the Bay'; 'Palais-de-Danse'; 'Diary of a Fortunate Young Man'; 'Magic Lantern'; 'Frost over the Valley'; 'Night Passage'; 'Oxford and the Weather'; 'West End Camera'.

Essays: 'The Foundling Generation'; 'Subtopia'; 'Hubris Revisited'.

Sketches: 'Portrait of the Artist as a Young Turk'; 'The Cloister and the Cadena'; 'Mastermen Unready'.

Stories

'The Quarry': A small boy, Richard, goes for regular walks with his Grandfather. They live in an industrial village but it is still possible to get into unspoilt countryside and one of their favourite routes is through a disused quarry. The Grandfather knows a great deal about country lore which delights the boy. One day, however, they see a hare chased by two fierce dogs. The old man laughs about it; the boy is frightened and horrified as the hare is caught and killed. He no longer wants to go for walks with the old man, who is upset. The boy is ashamed and will not explain his reasons because he fears he will be laughed at.

'Blackberries': A group of friends know a spot on a stretch of common where there are particularly good blackberries. The place is sunny and full of pleasant associations for them – they are all rather gentle children – until one day they find the body of a young woman who has been shot. They have to talk to the police and are sensitive to the horror of the situation. Later, two of the boys have to cross the common at dusk on an errand: they are very frightened and feel, although they cannot define it, in some way defiled.

'Paradise Terrace': A man called Garnett, who has become successful in his chosen career, returns to the Welsh village where he spent his childhood. His family were middle class and he was sequestered and bored: one memory stands out for him – when he was allowed to visit the grandparents of a schoolfriend who lived in a terrace on the edge of the village. The story describes a rapturous day – playing football in a park, making dams and canals of a stream, exploring a ruined works, eating fish and chips from a shop. It was the best day in Garnett's childhood; but when he returns to the village, by chance, he finds that the terrace has been torn down and replaced by a housing estate.

'Lending Library': A gently funny story about a pretty romantic young girl who works in a lending library and is assiduously courted by a young RAF corporal. It is 1944 and the twelve-year-old boy who is infatuated by her knows it is all hopeless, as he watches masochistically, from the concealment of appropriate books, the innocent and amorous love play.

'Kingfisher': Rhys is a miner, a shy and solitary man who takes great pleasure in Nature. He puts up with his job underground but finds much comfort even in the ugly, spoiled village in which he lives. He reads a great deal and looks around him for evidence of the beautiful, virgin land that he imagines in the past. He has several walks which he particularly enjoys. On one of these, along an old canal bank, he sees a kingfisher. He is delighted. Then some boys appear with a catapult and kill the beautiful bird. Rhys is enraged. He chases the boys along a disused railway, but they are too quick for him. He falls heavily and lies sobbing on the ground, while the children jeer from a safe distance.

'Flower Clock': A seventeen-year-old boy has arranged to meet a pretty, feckless girl with whom he is infatuated near a flower clock in a town park. The girl does not come. He waits, gradually becoming more and more miserable. Nearby on another bench, is a considerably older woman – in her mid-thirties. She has been watching the boy and they fall into conversation. They spend the rest of the evening together. Nothing much happens. He kisses her. She is kind to him and finds in his gentleness something that is different from her dreary marriage, her children and her in-laws. At the end of the evening, he takes her to the bus station and they both go home.

Prose poems

'Evening Walk': Unsympathetic description of a mining valley from a young man about to leave it.

'The First Time I Saw Paris': Imagined description of Paris, with much Romantic reference to Baudelaire and Rimbaud.

'View of the Bay': Summer Saturday in a seaside town.

'Palais-de-Danse': A young man's first experience of being drunk and an unsuccessful love affair at a Christmas party.

'Diary of a Fortunate Young Man': Five very lyrical but enigmatic passages about a love affair, perhaps with an older woman.

'Magic Lantern': The cinema of childhood.

'Frost over the Valley': Sympathetic description of winter night.

'Night Passage': Autumn evening, a nightingale singing, vague discontent.

'Oxford and the Weather': Four lyrical, wildly euphoric sketches.

'West End Camera': Baudelairian sketches of first London impressions.

Essays

'The Foundling Generation': Articulate account of the confusions felt by children who grew up during the

1939–45 war and who found themselves as adolescents among ex-servicemen in a nuclear age with the threat of the Cold War. A mild flirtation with existentialism. The 'foundling' metaphor is developed from the notion of a child who wishes to disown its parents (and who hopes it is a foundling) to a young man who wishes to disown the world he lives in.

'Subtopia': An unsuccessful satire, loosely based upon Sir Thomas More.

'Hubris Revisited': A more determined and vivid affair with existentialism and a reasonably well-argued examination of the possibility of tragedy in an age without gods.

Sketches

'Portrait of the Artist as a Young Turk': Self-portrait. Rather self-conscious but agreeably self-mocking. Arrogant, but indicating that the young Caradock had very definite ideas about where he was going.

'The Cloister and the Cadena': Satirical account of Oxford and its literary and artistic fashions and foibles while Caradock was an undergraduate.

'Mastermen Unready': The general unpreparedness of young graduates for mature adult life and for careers. A sense of purpose as opposed to the educational conveyor belt which turns out technologists or executives for the most part. Funny metaphor based on the Captain Marryat novel.

Angry Sunset. Vortex Press. 1952.

Published once more by Reginald Webber, who was

568

enthusiastic about Caradock as a lyrical writer. Webber's fortunes were in decline and he used literary disagreements to pick quarrels with Caradock, accusing him of pretentiousness and bitterness. Nevertheless, the novel is essentially lyrical and is technically moderately ambitious in that it alternates the third-personal narrative focused upon the young man, Tudor, with a first-personal modified interior monologue from his elderly friend, Mr Jones. Caradock's impatience of his Welsh village was becoming more obvious.

Tudor is an ambitious young man, eager to leave his home for University. He is studious and serious, desperately keen to get to Oxford (though Cambridge or London or anywhere else will do as long as he can get away), but not absolutely sure what he wants to do with his life. He spends a lot of his free time walking on the hills above the ugly industrial valley in which he has been brought up and has struck up a friendship with a local-government official, Jones, who is on the point of retirement. Jones is a lyrical almost rhetorical character who sees from the mountain, where they walk every so often, a field full of folk. He has a rich and imaginative sense of the past – mythological as well as historical – and identifies passionately with the village and the valley. He has also, however, read very widely and talks penetratingly about the authors whom Tudor has so far discovered, as well as about others that he has not yet read. Tudor wonders why such an intelligent and eager man should be trapped in such a humble job: first, there were family problems which obliged him to get a job when he might otherwise have gone to a university; second, he married a sickly wife whose demands upon him were considerable and who would not leave her home. Jones, sardonically, suggests that it is easy to find excuses for thwarted enterprise that was never there. Tudor conceives this to be bitterness and a sense of failure. Throughout the book the boy's impressions are set against what the man really thinks as they talk about his past, the valley's past and Tudor's future – as the boy gets his scholarship and prepares himself for what he sees as escape, pitying Jones for his lost opportunities and stoical regret. The novel ends on the eve of Tudor's departure for Oxford, as the two men watch one of the many impressive autumnal sunsets above the industrial landscape that they had, in the past months and years, admired together.

The Low Key of Hope. Alvin & Brandt. 1954.

The quarrel with Vortex Press, deliberately inflamed for what he considered to be Caradock's good by Reginald Webber, sent Caradock to a new publisher. Webber was subsequently bankrupted but helped by a number of successful writers and public figures whom he had coaxed or goaded into print and confidence, including Michael Caradock. Webber died in 1966, professing little admiration in public for Caradock's later work though said to take a more favourable view of it privately. Caradock had wanted to attempt something more technically daring with this new novel, but was dissuaded by his publishers who favoured a more orthodox structure than he had originally planned. The novel was published during Caradock's National

Service in the Royal Navy, after he had abandoned his post-graduate work at Oxford.

Baldwin, who has very consciously modelled himself on the Joyce/Stephen Dedalus model, is a very clever young man who has done extremely well academically. His parents wish him to go into the family grocery business and Baldwin is appalled by their narrow insensitivity. He is ambitious and hopes to become a writer. Showing remarkable coldness to his parents and to other people, notably an older woman librarian with whom he has had a mild affair, Baldwin leaves Shotover, the northern industrial town where he was born, for a job in London on a newspaper.

He is delighted by London and wanders euphorically around the streets, eagerly taking everything in. His happiness, however, is partly spoiled by his awareness that many of his new acquaintances and colleagues find him comical: he is gauche, naïve, much too enthusiastic. Baldwin's massive self-confidence, largely borrowed from the young Joyce, helps him come to terms with this minor discomfort.

He makes fairly uneasy friendships with other journalists and reporters – some of them very clever, others cynical and pedestrian. Caradock includes a wide variety of newspaper characters, presumably, since he had not at this time had any contact with journalism, based upon people he had known and met while at Oxford. They are nevertheless quite accurate. Baldwin cultivates the literary world, goes to poetry readings, sees *avant-garde* plays in theatre clubs and so on. He resists coldly all attempts at reconciliation from his parents. Meanwhile he falls in love with one of the secretaries on the newspaper, an upper-class girl called June Farquar. She finds him 'amusing', but has several other far more important people in mind. Baldwin takes to long walks at night, sometimes with a friend – Cummings or Smolenski – but often alone.

He decides he needs sexual experience and so goes to a prostitute. She is a lively and pretty girl who misunderstands his requirements. Baldwin is physically sick at her ready acceptance of what he considers gross deviation and then indulges various neurotic ideas about himself. He is doing well enough, but not outstandingly, at his work and begins to think that this is because people are laughing at him. Further advances from his parents crystallise his paranoid hatred of his origins, which he blames for his sexual innocence and his social ineptitude.

By chance he meets Natasha, the wife of his deputy editor, first at a party and subsequently when her husband is unexpectedly busy and she is at a loose end. She is a beautiful woman, very bored with her life, and much desired (as he learns later) by several of his colleagues. She takes to Baldwin and makes it fairly clear that she is available. Out of loyalty to her husband, whom he likes, and his conception of respect for her, Baldwin does nothing. Through Natasha he meets many more influential people. He is doubtful about his motives.

Baldwin talks to Natasha, to Cummings and Smolenski, but most of all to himself. He begins to do quite well on the newspaper and has one or two pieces published in literary magazines. June Farquar seems to show interest in him, encourages him up to a point and then switches off. He finds out that she is regularly sleeping with Instone, a drama critic whom he particularly detests. This does not help his paranoia.

After a visit from his father, begging him at least to visit his home, Baldwin goes to Natasha, knowing that her husband is in America. She understands why he has come and allows him to take her. They spend the night together and begin a steady, very erotic affair. She is instrumental in getting his first poems published. Baldwin now has guilt to spice his ordinary spiritual discomforts and continues his lonely walks late at night. Secure in his relationship with Natasha, he begins to see himself as a naturally solitary character who is beginning to feel at home.

Then, one evening, he sees some louts ill-treating a vagrant and tackles them. Later, on one of his midnight walks alone, he is savagely attacked and crippled. He wakes up in a hospital bed, to find his parents at his side, tearful and assuring him that they will look after him. He learns that he is paralysed from the waist down.

Carcases of Tall Ships. Alvin & Brandt. 1956.

Published immediately after Caradock finished his National Service and had returned again to Oxford to complete his D.Phil. work. Caradock had been able to accept the routine, tedium and discipline of his time as a rating, but had, without being in any way obtrusive, despised the wardroom. Fleming, the icily detached young man, unlike Caradock, is an authentic Dartmouth officer at once confident and vulnerable: he nevertheless embodies many of the faults and defence reflexes that Caradock recognised in himself. Once again an upper-class, unsympathetic girl occurs who treats Fleming, Caradock's central character, contemptuously. She is portrayed with some savagery and some commentators have looked for an original, without success. Caradock was once again advised by his publishers against a projected scheme for using different narrative techniques in this novel for the three separate strands of the plot, but profited from their opinion to develop the character of Fleming and to involve him (originally an outsider) in the bitter sequence of incidents that serve as a focus for the whole novel.

Fleming is an efficient officer of studied elegance and detachment from the traditional naval family. He was educated at a famous school and at the Royal Naval College, Dartmouth, but his attitude to service life is cynical and a little supercilious. He fits in easily enough although he views his brother officers with cool amusement and takes his duties seriously, but only up to a point. Fleming's relationships with women are pleasant, discreet and strictly to his own convenience.

Attached to a shore establishment in a small town, he watches the life around him with his practised irony: notably a bitter feud carried on between a brilliant young Commander and a passed-over Lieutenant-Commander, much less showy but more reliable; the intense and comical territorial rivalry between a First Officer in the WRNS and the First Lieutenant of the establishment which involves a sequence of outrageous and elaborate ruses and practical jokes; and finally, the jealousy and resentment of a pretty young woman, married to a philanderer who once pursued her very ardently, who is planning some kind of humiliating revenge on her husband. This last woman suggests to Fleming that they have an affair, but he is much too wary. Then, a new Third Officer joins the establishment. At first, Fleming is impressed by the girl's physical attributes but remains at his usual tactful distance. Gradually, however, he becomes infatuated by her and at an intensely sexual level. She uses this to her own advantage. He suspects her of unusual promiscuity and is not far wrong. In an unpleasant climax, he loses control of himself and causes a public scene. As all the other events that he was able to remain aloof from resolve themselves, his own life and equilibrium undergo serious disturbance. At the same time, the novel is an acutely satirical account of the peacetime Navy.

Broods of Folly. Alvin & Brandt. 1960.

A satirical novel and the last of Caradock's books to be published by Alvin & Brandt, who refused both of Caradock's next books (two volumes of essays) on the grounds that they were only interested in his fiction. Nevertheless, the agreement between author and publishers was terminated amicably. The title of the novel, adapted from Milton's *Il Penseroso* ('Hence vain deluding joys/The brood of Folly without Father bred...'), is used to describe Caradock's impression of literary and artistic London. The technical execution is marginally more ambitious, but once again Caradock was prevented from trying a variety of forms by his publishers. (Wisely, it would appear, from the coherence of a fairly complicated picaresque novel.)

Laertes Jones is a Welsh schoolmaster and poet in his late twenties, a pious and dutiful young man from a God-fearing family. He arrives in London to look for his sister, Amelia, from whom no word has been heard for several weeks. His parents fear that she has disappeared and so Laertes' summer holiday is to be (if necessary) consigned to her retrieval. Their fears prove to be accurate. Amelia, last heard of as a secretary at the BBC, has vanished. Seeking her at Portland Place, Laertes Jones is befriended by a producer called Leydon Wells. Together (very much in the manner of the two brothers in *Comus*, pausing to moralise and review the action) they search for her along the length and breadth of intellectual London. Although Laertes, a thoroughgoing innocent, is unaware of it, Leydon Wells has his own plans for the eventual seduction of the young man. In the course of his searches, Laertes meets all the monstrous forms of contemporary high and low culture from critics to scientists and is involved steadily in a sequence of adventures, some of which are dramatic, others amorous and many utterly farcical. Once again the basic stance of the central character is isolationist and the comedy conceals perhaps a savage and destructive anger. The novel ends, when Laertes finds his sister, with her reaction to being found. Leydon Wells' perfidious intentions are discovered in time to preserve Laertes' normality: his chastity has long since been discarded in the course of his perilous odyssey.

An Elemental Wound. Hazel & Sims. 1963.

A collection of critical and philosophical essays, refused by Alvin & Brandt, who were then offered Caradock's ideas for his next book, also a collection of essays. It was agreed that, since Caradock did not foresee writing another novel for some time and certainly did not want to write the kind of book that Alvin & Brandt had published, his contract should lapse. The essays were accepted by Sean Moran on behalf of Hazel & Sims, who subsequently published all of Caradock's work.

Critical essays

'Silence, Exile and Cunning': An essay on James Joyce, incorporating Caradock's own assessment of the artist's weaponry.

'The Singer not the Song': Essay on Ezra Pound, with ideas on the relationship of political opinions and art.

'Servitude and Grandeur': Essay on Wallace Stevens, with ideas on the relationship of stoicism, hedonism and art.

'The Elder Statesman': Essay on T. S. Eliot, remarks on the artist as a private man and on reconciliation.

'Je suis que...': Essay on Jean-Paul Sartre, with further reflections on politics and art, in the light of the artist's and the philosopher's function.

'Sum! Sum! Sum!': Essay on Albert Camus, with reflections on affirmation and despair and further remarks on stoicism and hedonism.

'Labyrinth to Let': Essay on the contemporary novel and attitudes to fiction.

'Sterner Stuff': Ambition in literature and what it means.

'Formal Identity': Questions of style and technique and their relationship to the personality of an author, as distinct from his ideas.

'Not So Supreme': A comment on the purpose of prose fiction and an inquiry into its range and scope.

Philosophical or social essays

'An Elemental Wound': The artist's impulse and what causes it.

'Santayana in Paddington': Aesthetics and the facts.

'A Private Iceberg': Isolation of the artist in normal society.

'Facts of Life': The problems of communication.

'Hope and Charity': The problems of living in a world without God and religious faith.

'A Modern Ethic': An attempt to live decently and responsibly without sentimental charity.

'Going Back': An investigation of nostalgia, with remarks on the nostalgia of hatred.

The Philosopher's Stone. Hazel & Sims. 1965.

A second collection of essays subtitled 'lyrical' and 'philosophic'. In fact, the lyrical essays are, apart from the moving 'An Idea of Remembered Love', all sequences of prose poems, more controlled and mature than their equivalents in Caradock's very first book, but essentially seeking to capture and recreate a particular moment and (usually) a specific scene. The philosophic essays are long and challenging and mainly concerned with the place of fiction alongside history, myth and event. The final third of the book is taken up by the long essay 'The Unmoved Mover', in which Caradock, starting from Aristotle, tries to define the position of the 'artist, the thinker and the thinking individual' as a force for good in the contemporary world.

Lyrical essays

'Landscapes': Largely rural scenes, usually in France or Italy: for the most part straightforward word pictures – but usually attempting to relate a mood to a place.

'An Idea of Remembered Love': A lyrical attempt to define intense happiness and deep affection as experienced by a young man.

'Urban Lyrics' (often referred to as 'London Lyrics'): Prose poems about London – morning in St James's Park, Covent Garden at Christmas, Seven Dials, St Mary Woolnoth, Ludgate Hill, The Temple of Mithras, Spaniards Corner, Charing Cross, London Pubs, etc.

'Promises': The most untypical of Caradock's published writings. Short epiphanies of optimism, generally regarded as sentimental.

Philosophic essays

'Fiction and Truth': An attempt to define Fiction and to relate it to what laymen and philosophers call Truth.

'The Philosopher's Stone': The function and labour of the Philosopher, amateur as well as professional. The distinction between moral philosophy and metaphysics, on the one hand; and the kind of philosophy that embraces both and systematic analysis, on the other. Philosophy and Ideology.

'Ruins in Sunlight': Fiction and History. The response of the individual to History, a sense of exaltation and despair.

'Parallax': The relationship of fact, memory and fiction as

they occur to one man in his lifetime.

'The Unmoved Mover': A long essay in which Caradock tries to make his own point of view clear. Although he often writes about the greatness of Plato, he is much more a disciple of Aristotle. He relates his argument to Aristotle's idea of causes and then to his description of 'good' and 'virtue' in the *Ethics*. From this point Caradock tries to make clear and to justify his own conception of a dispassionately noble purpose, outside religion or ideology and untainted (as he would have it) by sentimental notions of brotherly love or charity. He investigates the requirements for this kind of selfless 'goodness', always related to an absolutely purposeless universe (in spite of Aristotle) which is irrespective of the fate of man, itself finite.

Promethead. Hazel & Sims. 1967.

A long novel in which Caradock tried to gather together in fictional form many of the ideas and theories expressed in the two collections of essays. Originally he intended to try something structurally and technically diverse, which his publishers encouraged, but in due course he decided that he wanted to express certain ideas very forcibly and that technical complexities might detract from their impact.

Caradock had been reading Nietzsche extensively and had subsequently referred to Wagner, Schopenhauer and various Greek texts relevant to Nietzsche's thought. There is some evidence that Caradock was worried about his own increasing pessimism and misanthropy. Personal events in his life had led him to opt for a quiet, rural isolation, although all the early drafts of *Promethead*, the first two allegedly very different in form and (according to the author's habit) destroyed on completion of the next, were written in London. As the character of Laertes Jones testifies, Caradock had always viewed the innocent with some suspicion if not distaste and Ganuret in *Promethead* is always a little untrustworthy. Caradock was able to accept purity and tolerate stupidity: but not both in the same individual when freely advertised. His attitude was always unashamedly elitist. He believed in excellence – particularly in the determination of culture – and tried to reconcile this passion with liberal politics and the detached concept of social benevolence or service which he strives to define in more than one essay.

Because of his admiration for Camus, Caradock's Promethean hero was necessarily a considerably modified version of any Nietzschean *übermensch* and Axel Waldeck is in part a spiritually bereft man struggling to find a substitute for the departed God; in part a guilt-ridden sensualist who would like nothing more than the irrevocable divorce of his refined 'soul' from his rotten body; in part a power-fantasist who is inspired by images of wars, strife and intense suffering, upon which he dwells with impartial and macabre intensity. Most of all, however, Waldeck is a leader and a great leader who has already proved himself, militarily and politically. He is a sort of 'magnificent servant' who sincerely and absolutely believes that he can and *must* work again for his nation and its people. The trouble is that he believes in the ideal of service but has lost all confidence in a good and happy future.

In Caradock's view, twentieth-century history had vindicated most of Nietzsche's opinions and theories – at least as he interpreted them. At the same time he believed that the aloof thinker was detested and reviled, particularly when he offered pessimistic ideas about the human condition: that is, ideas that were in the short term unpalatable and uncomfortable. There is some suggestion in the novel that it was easier for the philosopher-artist of atheistic bent to function in an age when God (whether or not he had deserted them) was still accepted by the majority than as a member of a blandly irreligious society obsessed by materialism and foolishly ignorant of the implications of political ideologies. Caradock was obsessed by the shabbiness of contemporary life, the cheapness of standards, notably as portrayed on and set by television – on which shallow fictional characters were allowed to seem more real to an undiscriminating audience than the events and people in their own lives. This obsession was extended to a loathing of cultural trendiness – in the arts, education and daily life. At the same time, he was concerned about the corrosion of spirit in his own hero.

The antipathy to women of Waldeck is a part of Caradock's periodic retreat from ordinary, uninhibited sexuality into a gloomy puritanism, that is often histrionic. Nevertheless, the real torment of Waldeck in this respect is too vividly described to be a mere pose. It is also important to note that Waldeck has been wounded and suffers considerable pain from a physical disease. He is, in the vein of the true Nietzschean hero, resistant to torture, even when it is self-inflicted.

Axel Waldeck is a patrician who by accident, destined for an easy, distinguished career, is involved in the horrors of a war of attrition. (At no time does Caradock specify a country or a war, though historical parallels are obvious and his characters are clearly living in the period between 1911 and 1966. While it is profitless to look for paradigms among the characters, it is reasonable to identify both major wars and attendant political strategies with background events in the novel.) He pursues a military career from which he emerges briefly into politics before returning to the army at a time of emergency. His country suffers a bitter defeat, but Waldeck becomes its leader in exile. Through the humiliations and tribulations of this period, he maintains a fierce dignity and sense of honourable purpose. After many barren years he returns to a position of potentially absolute power which he relinquishes. In an election he is rejected and subsequently, more or less, edged into voluntary exile. The wound to his pride and to what he thinks he deserves is exacerbated by his private guilt, the result of intense sensuality, as well as a growing depression. Waldeck is surrounded by a faithful entourage of politicians and soldiers who believe in him and his standards. They are backed by considerable resources and Waldeck himself is a very rich man. Søren Claudian and other politicians, on the periphery of power in their native land, acquire a foothold and then a dominant influence in the ex-General's household. They are opposed by Major Xavier Ganz, Waldeck's Chief of Staff, an implacably patrician soldier. Although Claudian and his associates are employed by the succession of weak governments that have followed the demise of Waldeck, they remain in close touch with him and are seen as useful by the Ganz faction who re-establish ascendancy.

Into this situation comes Piers Ganuret, a young poet and librarian who is on holiday. He is drugged by small-time criminals in a bar, but manages to drive away. He crashes his car badly outside Waldeck's mansion. At first, he is looked after for simple humanitarian reasons, then Ganz and others become suspicious that he might be an assassin. At last he witnesses one of Waldeck's bouts of manic insanity and is prevailed upon to stay, on account of the General's affection for him. This, as it happens, is entirely real – established in an early meeting between the distracted Waldeck and the young man. Ganuret is interviewed by Major Ganz, meets Claudian, and is prevailed upon to stay in the retreat. In subsequent conversations and during the flarings of Waldeck's instability, he begins to understand not only the political circumstances but the spiritual despair of the old leader. Waldeck harps upon themes of plague and war, ambition and bitterness, voluptuary weakness, but hints, somewhat feebly, at his own malaise. Ganuret remains discreetly silent.

He watches, with academic interest, the struggle between Ganz and Claudian and their factions for supremacy. Both need the General and yet Ganz is more devoted to the man: Claudian appears to be an opportunist, prepared to use a symbol. Elitism, Service, Individual Weakness, Charity and Chastity are all themes pursued in the intricate game played at Waldeck's court, during which Waldeck is often in a state of withdrawal.

As Ganuret is accepted, as Waldeck's personal secretary and librarian, he is introduced in the social life. He meets a girl called Angela, who is unusually wayward among rather stupid and typical young people. While undergoing a sequence of lectures from Waldeck on his favourite themes and the thin line between sanity and oblivious savagery, Ganuret is also made aware of the political manoeuvring of Ganz and Claudian. The General expresses great affection for his clean and innocent mind.

He is seduced expeditely by Angela, who subsequently compels him to taste and enjoy extremes of voluptuous pleasure. He feels a remote and indefinable remorse which he confides to Waldeck and is astonished by the old man's obvious frenzy, which he manages to contain. Ganz explains the situation. He prepares for Ganuret's departure (however it is to be effected), but Waldeck offers reprieve.

They set about an uneasy reconciliation as excitement in the entourage grows about the political and constitutional disquiet in their native land. Rebellions and demonstrations, backed by branches of the armed forces, lead to Waldeck's reinstatement as leader. There is a short period of triumph: then a conflict between Claudian and Ganz. During this time Ganuret finds an enormous change in Angela and in himself, while also becoming aware of some of the aspirations of Claudian. In a showdown, Ganz and his associates are put down ruthlessly. The General makes his gesture and is mortally wounded by accident. Claudian must accept the wrong role for the wrong reasons, having thwarted the right leader for the right reasons. Ganuret and Angela do not matter any more – until it is Claudian's turn.

585

(Various sources in myth are traced by commentators, notably H.-J. Kastner in *Patterns of Despair*. Hazel & Sims, 1973.)

A Coriolan Overture. Hazel & Sims. 1969.

A surprise novel, described by Caradock as an 'essay in autobiographical fiction' and finished in a relatively short time after Caradock has moved to Glanmor. Interesting in comparison to the earliest of Caradock's books, *Metaphors of Twenty Years*, in which he described the same painful process of growing up. There are arguments about this later book, notably about how much is fiction and how much is autobiography, but there is a genuine quality of mockery in it. At the point where Caradock's unstinted irony becomes self-derision, he is at his least and most tolerable.

Marcus Conrad, a middle-aged, successful politician, finds himself in South Wales on a speaking engagement. It is a very long time since he visited the area, having established himself in a Surrey constituency reasonably early in his career. Things are not going too well for him: there is a Liberal revival which threatens his seat and he has profound doubts about the *people* he represents, while convinced about the *policies*. He stops his car and is moved on an impulse to revisit the village where he was brought up.

He thinks about the young, confident Marcus Conrad – who detested his origins and was full of so many ambitions and scorns. The short narrative describes the young man's foolishness and gullibility in gentle, carefully aligned prose, which does not detract from the brash young hero but emphasises the sadness of the older man. Once again a temptation for some commentators to look for parallels between Caradock's life and fiction. A part of the book is devoted to the young Marcus' love affair with an older woman, which is significant: but much is concerned with his own discovery of himself as an individual. The narrative ends with the forty-five-year-old man retreading several paths and driving off without anger or haste or sorrow. Consigning the follies of the past to the past and dedicating those of the future to the future: for the moment hoping not to crash the car.

Laocoön. Hazel & Sims. 1971 (posthumous).
A provisional title given to the only papers found in Caradock's house in Glanmor. His executors (Michael Beauchamp-Beck, Fay Mackail and Sean Moran) agreed on the title without challenging subsequent theoretical alternatives. Since the typescript was found intact, without corrections, it was assumed that Caradock intended to offer it for publication. His usual practice was to destroy all drafts of a work except the most recent. Whatever Caradock's final intentions were for this novel, they were obviously precluded by his very sudden death. The existence of the book surprised most people still in contact with Caradock, although Sean Moran of Hazel & Sims knew that he had been working on a long novel of some kind.

Laocoön is a dense and rather difficult novel which describes the last year in the life of a philosopher, Landgrave, once an academic, and an unsuccessful creative writer. He has spent much of his life thinking about the problem of mortality, about the future of civilisation and about the function of individuals in an inscrutable universe. Now he has to come to terms with the fact of his own imminent death as well as with what he considers to be his own failure. This failure is partly spiritual, associated with Landgrave's sense of despair and his pessimistic view of existence and the future; but it is also in part the middle-aged man's feeling that his life has been largely pointless and irrelevant and is now shortly to end. This leads him to ask what is relevant and to consider questions of pleasure and pain and to review some of his own actions.

There is a certain loose symbolism associated with the zodiac and the changing months of the year, where Landgrave draws on Spenser's *The Shepheardes Calender* and the *Très riches heures du Duc de Berry*, both of which are obviously loved works of art. There are vividly recalled moments from Landgrave's personal life, along with reconstructions of significant events that seem coherent with his ideas of the moment, anecdotes along the lines of medieval and Renaissance 'sets' of tales usually told by or to Landgrave, and strikingly unusual moments when he is absurdly delighted or frightened by some banal occurrence. The book is an attempt to gather together Caradock's ideas, memories and phobias.

At a serious philosophic level, although Caradock would have been the first to disclaim any credentials as a philosopher, his invention, Landgrave, is trying to reconcile an idea of man outside Nature, who cannot therefore be judged as though he is a natural object (derived from the later philosophy of Wittgenstein), with an idea of man achieving a 'wholeness' with Nature even when 'Nature' is pointless, relentless and absolutely indifferent. Against this absurdly grand reconciliation, History happens and historians and philosophers occur. Poets, painters, sculptors, musicians and mathematicians make their patterns. Fictionalists try vainly and *vainly* to create substitutes that will make the original comprehensible, credible or endurable.

The figure of Laocoön is variously symbolic. He is a genuine prophet who is not believed. He actually challenges the huge idol by hurling a spear at it (causing the arms of the men concealed inside the Wooden Horse to clash – an event misinterpreted by the superstitious). Laocoön had incurred the displeasure of Apollo by making love to his wife before his altar. Finally, the prophet is destroyed by serpents emerging from the sea. Once again his death is misinterpreted by Priam. Caradock's use of these symbols is arbitrary and complex: he seems to see Apollo as a destructive as well as a creative force generating energy that must eventually be exhausted, to whom the human act of *love* is insulting because it is defiant as well as impulsive; and Poseidon as an immense and haphazardly destructive force of destiny. Where Apollo's destruction is a long-term, intellectual process of using up all the energy that there is until there is nothing, Poseidon's destruction is immediate and reasonless.

The novel begins with Landgrave on a winter holiday in Rome. He has been troubled by various symptoms of ill health and is rich enough to travel at leisure. He visits places and works of art that he already knows, including the Laocoön group at the Vatican. This group moves him particularly and he begins to piece together its symbolic meanings for him. While in Rome he learns that his illness is a fatal one and that he has little more than a year to live. He resolves to spend the year visiting other places which he remembers with pleasure or where he experienced some kind of profound change.

Travelling from Rome to Venice he arrives there in the snow and is first of all overwhelmed by the beauty of it all. He goes about the city, revisiting churches, palaces, and art galleries, meditating as he does on Venetian history. At last he admits to himself that what he is trying to do by all this intensive concentration on the past is to avoid facing his own death. He breaks down, but privately: bitterly reluctant to leave so much beauty, so much that he has loved and enjoyed for Nothing. He begins to wonder what it would be like to be old, looking for consolation. Then, by sheer chance, he meets an old acquaintance who is staying in Venice. This man is a scholar, an historian and an amateur astronomer. He is also very old. Landgrave confides in him. They talk and the old man brings him some relief. The section ends with a beautiful description by Landgrave of a comet he once saw when a young man.

He goes on to France, stopping at towns he knows. Eventually at Angoulême he meets a divorced woman, Catherine, some years younger than himself. She notices that he is unwell when they are both visiting a church and offers to help. They become friends and perhaps (though it is never explicitly stated) lovers. Certainly, they love one another as their relationship develops. Landgrave tells her about his past life: he is the only surviving member of a fairly rich family whose fortunes he describes, while talking about his own career as soldier, academic and writer. He has a house in England to which he intends to return which is looked after by an old friend and servant who has been with him for many years. Catherine, who has read some of his books, understands that he is ill and soon realises that he knows he is soon to die. She suggests that they travel together, which in succeeding sections of the book they do. Catherine talks about herself, and her own past. Landgrave is very much at peace with her, but subject to severe reversals of mood – depression, despair, remorse, fear, anger. These he keeps from Catherine and his bad moments are punctuated by their gentle and lyrical times together as they visit the isles of Greece, Italy, Spain and France – moving all the time as though in search of something. History, works of art and myth are all interwoven with factual events and occasions.

The year progresses and eventually Landgrave and Catherine make their way back to Rome. Here Landgrave achieves the philosophic reconciliation that he thinks is important and believes himself to be intellectually ready to face death. His illness has progressed and he is now in more pain. In a very moving passage he persuades Catherine that they must now separate. She is, of course, very reluctant and deeply upset. At last she agrees. She leaves him quietly, and obviously with great sadness, in a town on the Côte d'Azur.

Only when she has gone does Landgrave fully realise what she has meant to him. He returns to England by sea and goes back to his secluded house in Sussex, where he is looked after in what remains of his life by Galen, his man-servant. In this time he is at first peaceful, calm: delighting in the rural autumn of England; but in due course he suffers more, including frequent bouts of delirium, and it is in these that an underlying fury and a terrible despair, that is almost hatred of the life that will survive his own, shows itself in images of destruction, horror and carnage. In lucid inter-vals, Landgrave's courage and moral virtue reassert control. He dies in mid December, emerging from a vision of desolation into a final calm.

The sections of the book are titled separately:

'Capriccio'; 'The Bringer of Relief'; 'Unruffled Lakes'; 'The Fleece of Colchis'; 'The Tortured Beast'; 'Children of Leda'; 'The Crab's Claws'; 'An Illusory Nobility'; 'Virgo'; 'Questions of Balance'; 'The Scorpion'; 'The Hunter and the Hunted'.

Appendix taken from David Hayward's official biography of Michael Caradock, giving details of his published work.

With thanks for original permission to quote these extracts. Faber and Faber and the executors of the TS Eliot Estate for extracts from 'The Elder Statesman', *Collected Poems 1909–1962* (p298 and 301) and *Selected Essays;* Faber and Faber for an extract from *The Letters of Wallace Stevens*, edited by Holly Stevens; Jonathan Cape, extracts from Henry Reed's *A Map of Verona* and James Joyce's *Portrait of the Artist as Young Man;* Routledge and Kegan Paul for extract from I. A. Richards *Principles of Literary Criticism;* Rutgers University Press extract from Germain Bree's *Camus;* Calder and Boyars for extract from *Albert Camus or the Invincible Summer* by Albert Macquet; Oxford University Press for extracts from *Albert Camus and the Literature of Revolt* by John Cruickshank; Hamish Hamilton for extracts from Philip Thody's translation of *Lyrical and Critical Essays* by Albert Camus.

Foreword by Duncan Bush

Duncan Bush is a novelist, poet and translator. He was born in Cardiff in 1946, and educated at Whitchurch Grammar School, then at Warwick University, Duke University (USA) and Wadham College, Oxford.

His work includes *Aquarium* and *Salt* both of which won Arts Council of Wales Awards for poetry and were republished later in a single volume *The Hook*. His collection *Masks* won the Welsh Book of the Year award. His most recent collection of poetry is *Midway*. He has also published two novels, *The Genre of Silence* and *Glass Shot*. He is currently working on a new collection of poetry, and preparing his translations of the complete poems of Cesare Pavese.

His most recent novel is *Now All The Rage*, which was published in 2008.

Cover image by John Piper

John Piper, the son of a solicitor, was born in Epsom in 1903 and educated at the Richmond School of Art and the Royal College of Art, London. His work reveals a particular interest in landscape and architecture, turning from abstraction early in his career to a more naturalistic approach.

Piper exhibited regularly in London and set up the contemporary art journal *Axis* with his wife, Myfanwy. In 1944 he was made an official war artist. He also collaborated with his friend, the poet John Betjeman, on the *Shell Guides to the British Isles*.

He died at his home in Oxfordshire in 1992.

LIBRARY OF WALES

The Library of Wales is a Welsh Assembly Government project designed to ensure that all of the rich and extensive literature of Wales which has been written in English will now be made available to readers in and beyond Wales. Sustaining this wider literary heritage is understood by the Welsh Assembly Government to be a key component in creating and disseminating an ongoing sense of modern Welsh culture and history for the future Wales which is now emerging from contemporary society. Through these texts, until now unavailable, out-of-print or merely forgotten, the Library of Wales brings back into play the voices and actions of the human experience that has made us, in all our complexity, a Welsh people.

The Library of Wales includes prose as well as poetry, essays as well as fiction, anthologies as well as memoirs, drama as well as journalism. It will complement the names and texts that are already in the public domain and seek to include the best of Welsh writing in English, as well as to showcase what has been unjustly neglected. No boundaries will limit the ambition of the Library of Wales to open up the borders that have denied some of our best writers a presence in a future Wales. The Library of Wales has been created with that Wales in mind: a young country not afraid to remember what it might yet become.

Dai Smith
Raymond Williams Chair in the Cultural History of Wales,
Swansea University

LIBRARY OF WALES
FUNDED BY

Llywodraeth Cynulliad Cymru
Welsh Assembly Government

CYNGOR LLYFRAU CYMRU
WELSH BOOKS COUNCIL

'This landmark series is testimony to the resurgence of the English-language literature of Wales. After years of neglect, the future for Welsh writing in English – both classics and new writing – looks very promising indeed.'

M. Wynn Thomas

WWW.LIBRARYOFWALES.ORG

LIBRARY OF WALES titles are available to buy online at: